PRAISE FOR
CHARLES D. TAYLOR'S
SHADOW WARS

"A page-turner . . . the pacing is fast and the action furious and detailed."

—*Publishers Weekly*

Commander Matthew Stone: A member of the U.S. Navy's elite SEALs unit, he served in Vietnam with valor and distinction. But two decades after the American withdrawal, he has one last mission to complete . . . not in the jungles of Southeast Asia, but in the citadels of wealth and power in Hong Kong.

Leila Potter: She came to the Wall in Washington to remember her brother, and instead saw a man who had served alongside him—a man she thought was MIA. The chance encounter has already made her a target for a hit man; now, to draw out the truth, she is prepared to offer herself up as bait.

PRAISE FOR *BOOMER*

"Tom Clancy, move over . . . one of the best naval thrillers since *Red October* . . . gripping reading from the first intriguing page to the edge-of-your-chair finale."

—Nelson DeMille

MORE PRAISE FOR *BOOMER*

"Taylor ratchets the suspense well past the breaking point . . . *Boomer* is a hell of a fine sea story."
—Stephen Coonts

Hugh Young: A former CIA spook in Laos, he walked away from the Vietnam War with a lucrative heroin trade—and now heads a legitimate corporate enterprise. A man of wit and charm, but most of all a man of ruthless power; if crossed, he can become as hard as the diamonds on his fingers.

Jerry Santucci: A Bravo Company private, he signed on with Hugh Young and traded in his khakis for tailor-made silk suits. For twenty-five years he has indulged his every fantasy, but now he's made a careless mistake: He went to the Wall in Washington to see his name etched in stone, and is about to discover that no amount of blood or money can erase the past.

PRAISE FOR *DEEP STING*

"Powerful and compelling . . . Naval suspense at its best."
—W.E.B. Griffin

MORE PRAISE FOR *DEEP STING*

Lt. Col. Randolph Wallace: A Pentagon bureaucrat overseeing the POW/MIA section, Wallace has been on the take from Hugh Young for years. His tainted wealth brought a pledge of absolute loyalty, and when long-buried names begin to surface, the ultimate debt may finally come due.

Captain E. P. (Penny) Carson: Assigned to the POW/MIA desk at the Pentagon when Leila Potter came to her with the story of an impossible MIA sighting, she started rooting around in some long-buried Pentagon files. But in digging into the dirty history of Bravo Company, she may also be digging her own grave.

Books by Charles D. Taylor

Show of Force
The Sunset Patriots
First Salvo
Choke Point
Silent Hunter
Shadows of Vengeance
  (pen name: David Charles)
Counterstrike
Warship
Boomer*
Deep Sting*
Shadow Wars*
Sightings*

*Published by POCKET BOOKS

SIGHTINGS

CHARLES D.TAYLOR

POCKET STAR BOOKS

New York   London   Toronto   Sydney   Tokyo   Singapore

This book is a work of fiction. Names, characters, places and
incidents are either products of the author's imagination or are used
fictitiously. Any resemblance to actual events or locales or persons,
living or dead, is entirely coincidental.

An *Original* Publication of POCKET BOOKS

A Pocket Star Book published by
POCKET BOOKS, a division of Simon & Schuster Inc.
1230 Avenue of the Americas, New York, NY 10020

Copyright © 1993 by Charles D. Taylor

ISBN: 0-671-73632-9

First Pocket Books printing December 1993

10 9 8 7 6 5 4 3 2

POCKET STAR BOOKS and colophon are registered
trademarks of Simon & Schuster Inc.

Cover art by Broeck Steadman

Printed in the U.S.A.

To all of the members of the crews of:

USS *Glennon* November 1961–June 1962
(DD-840)   February 1963–September 1964

USS *Cony*   August 1962–February 1963
(DDE-508)

They were men I was honored to serve with, and I came away with much more than I had an opportunity to give.

ACKNOWLEDGMENTS

There has been nothing easy about the Vietnamese POW-MIA situation since the day the first American was captured there. Almost thirty years later there is still nothing easy, or acceptable. Among those who assisted me in researching background material for this book, I was fortunate enough to talk with the following individuals who represent diverse positions: Ann Mills Griffiths, Sue Scott, and Mary Currall-Backley of the National League of Families of American Prisoners and Missing in Southeast Asia; Captain Eugene "Red" McDaniel, U.S. Navy (Ret.) of the American Defense Foundation; Ken Bailes of the Department of Public Affairs for East Asia and Pacific, U.S. State Department; Commander Ed Lundquist, U.S. Navy, former public information officer for the MIA desk in the Pentagon. These people were forthright in expressing their personal opinions, and I thank them for educating me; their willingness to discuss the POW-MIA situation from their unique perspectives allowed me to understand the complexities of the subject more fully. Since this is a work of fiction, however, there is nothing in these pages that represents their position. Gary Comerford, Naval Investigative Service (NIS) was helpful with my questions.

I would also like to thank former Congressman Nicholas Mavroules and his Washington office personnel, and Bill McDonald, Larry Bailey, and Jake Jaquith for assisting me in establishing these and other contacts. Dan Mundy and Phil Craig provided incisive comments on the manuscript. Paul McCarthy's detailed editorial suggestions made a tremendous difference to me and this novel, and my agent, Dominick Abel, continues to pour oil on the waters at the

ACKNOWLEDGMENTS

right time. My friends whose names inhabit these pages are certainly characters, but the characters in this book are entirely fictional. Thanks to Computer Solutions in Gallows Bay, Saint Croix, for being my office away from home.

Of course, none of this could have been done without my favorite critic, my wife, Georgie.

"For that I was not with you, in my time, at Khe Sanh, and Danang, and Hue, and all the other places, is for me now, looking back, a great surprise, and even greater disappointment, and a regret that I will carry to my grave. . . .

". . . the truth is that each and every one of the Vietnam memorials in that cemetery [sic] and every other—those that are full, those that are empty, and those that are still waiting—belongs to a man who may have died in my place."

From the *Wall Street Journal* excerpt of Mark Helprin's address to the Corps of Cadets, West Point, 15 October 1992

SIGHTINGS

PROLOGUE

THE MAJOR COUGHED, HIS TONGUE FIGHTING A LOSING BATTLE with the dust on his teeth as he peered up at the burning Laotian sun through a yellow-brown cloud of grit. He grew more bitter with each mile, because he was sure that the ancient jeep would become his coffin. It was a pity that he could remember none of the simple prayers for the salvation of his soul that had been forced upon him during his youth.

The most disconcerting fact wasn't that he was a passenger in an old jeep that had seen better days. It was that the vehicle, an antiquated, decrepit rattletrap sure to kill him, would have been condemned by any rational human being. But Han, the driver, was far from rational. The springs had ceased functioning long ago. A persistent screeching sound from under the hood certified the maturity of the engine and probably the number of years since the last oil change. Gauges were a thing of the past; the dashboard had rotted out long ago. The ignition switch hung by a wire just above the accelerator. Dust swirled into the cab where floorboards once existed. Wooden benches had replaced the seats, and each bump on this narrow dirt road cut into the jungle added another bruise to the major's rump. He was sure the

1

long-departed French had been the first to classify this jeep as junk.

"When was the last time you drove this cow path?" U.S. Army Major Joslin growled, mopping a dirty handkerchief at the sweat flowing down his neck. It was the third time he'd asked.

"Fi' day 'go, Major, when I las' see white man." The same answer each time. "My driving bad?" Han asked with a wide toothless grin. Then, without waiting, he answered himself. "'Mericans candy ass." He glanced at the major with sparkling eyes as the jeep left the ground briefly before returning to earth with a shattering crash of loose parts.

This was the first jungle trip for the major, one he hadn't looked forward to, and he promised himself that it would be his last. Whenever he was forced to leave the air-conditioned comfort of the Pentagon, his next and only stop was usually the U.S. embassy in Bangkok, also air-conditioned for a bureaucrat's pleasure. Lieutenants were the ones who were supposed to go into the puckerbrush and sweat their asses off. They were perfect for chasing down sightings when the Defense Intelligence Agency said there was enough validity to a sighting to send a live body to check it out.

The photo had been too good to dispute. "Not only is this photo an original, the cameraman was pretty damn good, for some rice farmer who doesn't know shit about high-speed shutters." The photo intelligence expert had been impressed. There was no evidence that anyone had screwed with the black-and-white that had come by courier from Bangkok. "You have to realize that the subject of this photo"—a Caucasian who was talking with two Laotians in Western dress in what appeared to be a native village—"had no idea someone was snapping his picture. Our cameraman must have been hiding, because we can tell the camera was in shadow. What we ought to find out after you ID the white guy is who was taking the picture and why."

That was why Major Joslin had been unable to convince

his superiors that one of the lieutenants could handle it. The photo was too clear; the subject was obviously Caucasian. "Full Accounting," as in Joint Task Force–Full Accounting, meant exactly that—a full accounting of every American who had ever been sent to the Vietnam War, and every single sighting of every possible POW-MIA would be investigated. The photo was so good—no retouching, nothing cut into the negative—that there was no doubt that the individual was a Caucasian.

The problem was that the powers that be at the U.S. embassy in Bangkok had been informed by the photographer, who hoped to make some finder's money as a reward, that the white man was a former POW. That started the wheels turning in the Pentagon to avoid the media getting involved.

DIA had come up with half a dozen names that might fit the general description of a man who hadn't been seen for twenty-five years. Since the media had yet to be alerted, there'd been no reason to contact families. Copies of the photo were purposely kept to a minimum. No need to get the media or the special interest groups excited if this was one more in a long list of hoaxes.

The major turned to the interpreter in the back of the jeep, a lieutenant who looked as if he might have taken a couple of laps around his rosary beads if he'd carried them. "Talk to him again. I can't understand what he's saying. Find out how much farther we have to go to get to this godforsaken place. And try to find out what he knows about cameras. I can't believe that he actually took that picture." Then he looked more closely at the stricken countenance of the lieutenant. "You're not going to barf, are you?"

The answer was a shake of the head. The lieutenant leaned forward, grasping the wooden back of Han's seat, and began shouting his questions in the driver's dialect above the raucous noise of the jeep.

Both hands came off the steering wheel as the Laotian turned to respond each time, gesticulating as he spoke.

Twice he grabbed the wheel just as the vehicle seemed ready to leave the road.

"Almost there, sir. Less than a mile, I think." The lieutenant touched the major's arm. "He still insists that he was the one who took the picture."

"Well, for Christ's sake, if he can handle a camera like that, why can't he drive a jeep? All I've heard is that no one could take a photo like that without understanding cameras. What the hell did he think I was asking him before we left his village?"

"He didn't know, sir, and he— Oh, shit!" the lieutenant exclaimed as his body became airborne for an instant before returning to the rear wooden bench with a bone-jarring crunch. "He said your English was so poor he couldn't understand you. But he'll understand if this provides us with a solid lead and he makes some money. He's terrified of the men with the Caucasian in the photo. Says they kill people for no reason at all."

"Isn't that just great?" Major Joslin shouted. "I suppose he just plain forgot to mention that to us." He reached down to the .38 holstered on his right hip as if to make sure it was still there.

During the briefing at the embassy, there'd been a casual mention that they were heading into heroin country. After the flight to Vientiane, they'd take a smaller plane to Luang Prabang; then it was into the country. That was the reason for the side arms. Normally the growers were peaceable types who left the authorities alone as long as they, too, were left alone. But you could never be sure, according to the briefing officer.

"Ask him if—"

The jeep lurched sideways as the driver frantically jammed his foot on the brakes. It skidded to one side of the road before fishtailing in the opposite direction. The driver's face was twisted in fear as he fought the steering wheel.

They came to a stop no more than ten yards from a dust-covered black vehicle that blocked their way. The sudden silence was magnified by the natural hum of the jungle life around them.

"Shoot, Major! Shoot dem," the driver screamed in an unnatural, high-pitched howl. One hand extended toward four armed figures who had appeared from behind the car and were advancing toward them.

The major noted in his last seconds alive, as he dug frantically at the still-holstered .38, that three of them appeared to be natives, though their dress was Western. The last one was Caucasian, and the major was trying to remember why his features seemed familiar when an AK-47 opened fire. Then all four were firing at one time.

When the shooting ceased, the Caucasian gave an order in the local dialect. "Search them."

The torn bodies of the major, the lieutenant, and the driver were laid out in the dirt. Their pockets were emptied, the contents of the major's briefcase dumped in the pile.

The Caucasian sorted through the materials until he found what he wanted—a photograph. He held it out at arm's length. The message to him that had originated from Washington had been correct. "Nice likeness," he muttered to himself in English. *Like looking into a mirror, you stupid son of a bitch.* Then he turned to one of the others and pointed at the driver's corpse. "Is that the one who took the picture?" he asked.

"Yes. We found out where he had the film developed."

"Good. Strip the bodies. Leave them in the jungle. The animals will finish the job tonight." He turned away and walked over to the car, slipping into the back seat. He preferred to suffer the heat of the vehicle rather than to endure the burning midday sun. As he watched the corpses disappear into the undergrowth at the edge of the dirt road, he felt a brief pang of remorse. It was too bad they'd had to dispose of the Americans that way, but there'd really been no choice. Those persistent bastards just weren't going to learn to leave well enough alone until it was too late for them to back off.

"Before morning take care of the place where the film was developed," the white man said.

"The owner, too?" the oldest one asked. "He's a relative of my sister's husband."

"Yes, I'm afraid you'll have to. I understand that the American military has become very efficient about tracing such things."

CHAPTER 1

THE *WALL*—A TRAGIC SLASH IN THE GREEN EARTH, A SYMBOL of . . .

Leila held her breath until her chest ached.

. . . of Vietnam . . .

Leila, transfixed by the desire to turn away, even to run from that symbol she understood too well, gazed across Constitution Avenue through the gray drizzle. Umbrellas seemingly rose out of the ground, moving ever so slowly, pausing, floating effortlessly as if defying gravity, the heads they shielded still invisible.

Shivering against the raw breeze sweeping down the Potomac, she squeezed her eyes shut. But no matter how tight they were, the umbrellas continued their awkward tarantella across her eyelids.

Leila opened her eyes and looked over her shoulder to the little grove where Albert Einstein sat behind the bare trees, head down, his great stone mind moving at warp speed. If his statue came to life and the shaggy head rose to stare across Constitution Avenue toward the Wall, would his genius brain rebel when those umbrellas floated into focus and when those people appeared to rise ghoulishly out of the earth?

The roar of jet engines lifting another aircraft into the low-hanging clouds jarred her out of her reverie. Once again she forced herself to focus on that distant slow dance of the umbrellas. *You have no choice, Leila. It's your duty. You are the only family he had.* It wasn't a strange, distant voice that urged Leila Potter to cross Constitution Avenue. It was her own. The voice was distinctly hers, and it had always been there. *This is the way you assuage your guilt . . . this is the way you assuage . . .*

She stopped halfway down the path leading to the eastern end of the Wall, her attention directed at the black flag pinned across the front of a booth. In the center was a man's profile, black against a white background, head hanging slightly down, barbed wire and a guard tower in the background. The few words inscribed on the flag were all that were needed: POW*MIA—YOU ARE NOT FORGOTTEN. She fingered the inscribed silver bracelet on her left wrist, her lips forming the man's name inscribed on its surface—Jerry . . . Jerry Santucci. One more warrior who'd never returned. *No, not forgotten, at least not by some of us.*

The cobbled walkway leading into the slash in the earth widened into a flat slate, its wetness slippery against the leather soles of her shoes. Leila stopped even before the slate widened, mesmerized by an older couple kneeling before Fifty-eight East, the fifty-eighth granite slab to the east of the center of the Wall. The man leaned a small framed photograph of a young sailor in dress uniform against the base of the slab. Then he extracted a small American flag from the inside pocket of his jacket, removed a flat chunk of plastic from an outer pocket, inserted the thin wooden mast of the flag into a hole in the pedestal, and set it beside the photo.

The woman had been clutching a small bouquet of flowers to her chest, and now she removed one, a long-stemmed red rose, and laid it in front of the sailor's photo. Then she turned her head to the man, tears streaming down her cheeks, and whispered a few words. He nodded without

8

raising his head. Then, one by one, she carefully placed the remaining eleven roses with the first.

Leila had observed countless private ceremonies during earlier visits and now she forced herself to look away from the couple. Others had also stopped, some out of respect, some out of curiosity, a few to share those few short, cleansing moments of grief. Some of the gifts left at the Wall were harder to understand—the bag of M&M's probably represented the candies administered to some wounded as placebos when the medics ran out of morphine—but this was as simple as life itself, or the loss of life. The man was the first to move. He rose to one knee, paused to place both hands on that knee, then used them with great effort as a lever to push himself erect, gradually rising until he tottered onto both feet.

He waited patiently, hands folded, occasionally dabbing at his eyes. The woman remained huddled before the great granite slab, shoulders racked by silent sobs, her form reflected in the polished stone. Finally he reached down and very gently took one of her elbows as if to help her stand up. But first she reached out and ran her fingers across the name engraved on the twelfth line from the bottom. Leila remembered how one of the veterans had once explained that simple cleansing gesture: "The power of touch, to feel, to sense the name of a loved one is a part of the healing process." Then the old lady allowed him to lift until, still kneeling, her back was straight. But when he bent down with the other hand to raise her to her feet, the man stumbled.

Instinctively Leila moved toward them. But another individual was quicker, a bearded middle-aged man with longish hair hanging out from under a floppy jungle hat. His hair was matted against his neck by the steady drizzle. He was dressed in worn fatigues, yet they were starched. Four rows of faded combat ribbons covered the left side of his chest. He bent down and lifted the woman to her feet as if she weighed nothing. Then he hugged her tightly, whispering into her ear. When he released her, he also hugged the man.

Leila stepped back as the old couple trudged slowly up the grade and past her. When they rounded the end of the Wall, she walked over to the man in fatigues who was staring down at the photo of the sailor. "That was very kind of you," she offered, knowing as she spoke that her words weren't nearly enough.

He turned to look at her, tears streaming into his beard, the tragedy of a lost world etched in his face. "My parents were both dead by the time I came back," he whispered as he turned and walked away.

We all did some dying, she thought. *Some of us over there, forever, the rest of us back here. I was . . . no, not really a kid, but still young enough not to understand why . . . too old not to hurt. . . .*

His words took her back to the day Danny's letter arrived at her grandparents' house. Somehow he had managed to send a letter that arrived on her sixteenth birthday:

Dear kid or I guess it has to be Leila now—no more kid,

I'm near a place called the Iron Triangle and they don't sell birthday cards here so you're going to have to settle for a letter from your ole brother. It's messy because I'm writing this in a hole I just dug and I'm sitting in three inches of water. I don't think the army has figured out how to get letters like this on time to girls who are having a sixteenth birthday. I want you to know your brother is going to be thinking about you on that special day. I have a calendar I carry around with me and I mark off each day I'm over here so I'll know how many days I have left. But there's one special day I marked before I left home and that was my little sister's birthday. So now your sixteen years old!!!! I can't believe I've got a sister whose grown up into a young lady!!!! I showed ole Jerry Santucci your picture this morning and he didn't even believe me when I told him you were going to be sixteen. He said you looked at least twenty-one and he wanted me to get him a date with you when we get back. I said I would but told him he'd better be careful because you were special, and he just laughed and said that was up to you. But you know Jerry. He was the one who had dinner with us before we shipped out and I guess he really did think you were twenty-one. Hey, I'm so proud of you. . . .

And that was when the doorbell had rung to interrupt Danny's birthday letter to her. *"Hey, I'm so proud of you. . . ."* In retrospect, it was eerie. First the letter, then moments later the doorbell . . . As the years passed, somehow it seemed more than fate. Of course, Leila had been the only one home so she didn't know what to think when she opened the door. An army officer was standing there, a captain with his hat in his hand, and their parish priest, his face set in a mournful expression.

She'd vaguely remembered some of the words after her grandfather arrived, having been called from the nursing home where her grandmother lived—"Tay Ninh," the "Iron Triangle," followed by hastily prepared detail such as "a company-size battle," "exceptional bravery"—but none of that meant anything to a teenage girl on her sixteenth birthday who'd just been told her brother was dead.

Sweet Sixteen! How bitter the memory remained.

A couple of weeks later a letter had arrived from Danny's commanding officer, Captain Ledbetter. The captain had explained how everyone in Bravo Company seemed to know her because Danny had been so proud to show her picture to them. Her brother told his buddies how he and his little sister had been alone since their parents were killed in an auto accident and how his sister had run the house even though their grandparents had helped to look after them. Leila should know how brave Danny had been in their firefights in the Iron Triangle. A heavy weapons company had slipped down the Ho Chi Minh Trail from the north and crossed the Cambodian border near Tay Ninh to reinforce communist units already in the Iron Triangle. Danny had died during a major battle maintaining his position against tremendous odds. As a result, Bravo Company had been able to accomplish their mission, holding their perimeter until sunrise when the enemy slipped into the jungle and eventually escaped back across the border into Cambodia. Captain Ledbetter had put Danny's name in for some very important medals, which he hoped would be awarded soon, and the captain also added how proud he would be to shake her hand when he returned home if the opportunity presented itself.

The opportunity never had come. She assumed the captain had forgotten about her after he sealed the letter, and Leila Potter was just as glad, because from that day forward she wanted nothing more to do with Vietnam or any other war. She was sixteen years old, alone except for sickly grandparents she rarely saw, and she had her life ahead of her.

Once again now, gazing sightlessly at the people staring at the Wall, she sensed the inner struggle beginning, one side of her brain trying to force those overwhelming memories into the open, the other side pushing them back into the recesses of her mind. It required all of her willpower to send that initial message of movement to her muscles.

Leila's feet seemed to sense when they arrived at Forty-two East, for they shuffled to a halt and gradually turned without any recognizable orders from her mind until she found herself facing the huge dark slab. Her reflection was marred by neat lines of names engraved into the stone, five names to a line, sometimes six. Unconsciously her eyes came to rest on the third name on line forty-four: Daniel Jeffrey Potter. Although the names were more difficult to read when the granite was wet, Danny's name flashed on and off like a theater marquee until she forced her eyes shut.

When she sensed her body swaying as if she might fall—it seemed to happen each time she visited the Wall—she allowed her eyes to open. As always, her gaze dropped to other lines, to the next slab. Her memory had been engraved by the same sculptor, each letter chiseled into the gray matter of her brain. She was unable, as always, to avoid locating the other names: Paul James Ledbetter, Alfred William Arison, Felix Gonzalez, Franklin Roosevelt Wil-

liams, Edwin Antonio Kelley, Geraldo Vincente Santucci
. . . and so many other names from his platoon that he'd
mentioned in his letters—not as close as those in his squad,
but Danny seemed to know everybody.

A letter from Danny's platoon commander, Lieutenant
Kelley, had followed two weeks after the captain's, because
the lieutenant was afraid Ledbetter had never written Leila.
She hadn't known about Kelley's death until she saw his
name a dozen lines below Danny's. The others followed
soon after Arison, Gonzalez, Williams, and Santucci—
especially Jerry Santucci—had all been in Danny's squad.
All . . . gone. Why? What had happened that they were all
killed, separately, yet over such a short period of time?

Leila ran her fingertips over the ID bracelet. How could
she ever forget Jerry Santucci? There was a cross beside
Jerry's name, indicating he was still listed as missing in
action. Strangely enough, there was also one by Lieutenant
Kelley's name. What did that really mean after all these
years? Jerry was the one Danny had brought home for
dinner. She'd been only fifteen, but she'd cooked dinner for
the three of them, and she remembered Jerry saying he
wished he had an older sister who could take care of him like
she took care of Danny. *Older!* Leila had never said a word
about her age that night, and apparently Danny hadn't
either, until that day in the Iron Triangle when he showed
his buddy, Santucci, her picture and told an unbelieving
Jerry that his sister, Leila, was going to be sweet sixteen.

Leila remembered her dreams that first year after Danny
was gone, because she had somehow always imagined that
Jerry Santucci would come home from Vietnam in his
uniform and ask her for a date and . . .

But Jerry had never appeared, and gradually that dream
had vanished. She graduated from high school and was
given a full college scholarship by the local American Legion
post, mostly because Danny had been awarded the Silver
Star and become their local hero. Jerry Santucci receded
into the back of her mind until that day early in 1986 when
she had forced herself to visit the Wall for the first time.

There were so many people that first time that it was almost impossible to get close to Danny. She remembered how a vet in a wheelchair, when he saw her little bouquet, had bulled a hole through the crowd for her in front of Forty-two East. He'd had the book of names in his lap, and when he saw her staring blankly at the shiny stone surface, he'd said, "Please, let me help you. What was his name?"

"Potter . . . Danny Potter."

"Potter, Daniel Jeffrey, Forty-two East." He'd pushed forward in the wheelchair, nudging gently. "Make a hole. Make a hole." He looked up brightly and beckoned to her. "Right here. Line forty-four. He's just a bit below the middle."

Leila saw the name and reached out. She ran her fingers over Danny's name, back and forth . . . back and forth. . . .

"He'll appreciate the flowers," the man in the wheelchair offered. "They all do."

Her eyes dropped down toward the base of the slab, and that was when she saw the name Ledbetter. Paul James Ledbetter. "That's why he never came!" she exclaimed, turning to look down at the man.

"Who? Who never came?" he asked in surprise.

"Danny's captain. He said in his letter that he'd visit. But he couldn't. He was killed too." Her gaze drifted a couple of lines above Ledbetter, and she saw another name: Franklin Roosevelt Williams. How could she ever forget that one? Danny said they all called Williams "Mr. President." She reached out and let her fingertips pass over Williams's name as if to let him know he wasn't forgotten.

"Do you remember any others?"

"Jerry Santucci," she blurted.

"Santucci . . . Santucci . . ."

She turned when there was silence.

"I'm so sorry, ma'am. He's here. Geraldo Vincente Santucci, Forty-three East, line thirty-nine." He was the one who explained that the cross meant Jerry'd been MIA.

"Arison."

They found him.

14

"Gonzalez."

"Felix?"

"Yes."

"Next slab over. He outlived his buddies for a while." He looked at her sadly. "Those were tough days, ma'am, some of the deadliest in the Nam. And that was a real killing zone your brother was in."

"Edwin Kelley?" she had asked hesitantly, afraid that the man who had written the second letter might be there, too.

"Strange! Another MIA."

There were others whose names she remembered, but she wasn't going to put herself through that, not that day, nor could she do it to this man in the wheelchair whose pain-racked eyes studied her own compassionately. She'd go through Danny's letters for those names and come back some other time. "Thank you. I appreciate your kindness. I . . ."

"I do it for them." He waved his hand to encompass the entire wall. "For every one of them." And he was gone, directing the chair through the separating crowd—"Make a hole . . . make a hole"—down to the base, up by the west side, and then he stopped to pay homage to the statue of the three soldiers who appeared awestruck by all the civilians in their jungle.

That had been her first time.

How many times? Leila asked herself now, remembering that day in 1986. *How many times have I visited the ghosts of Forty-two East, Forty-three East, Forty-four East?* The names on the Wall started with the death of the first adviser on the top line of One East. One East began in the middle, where the east and west walls joined. The names, beginning with that first adviser, proceeded in order, normally five or six names to a line. The lines ran from top to bottom on each slab, according to date of death, down to Seventy East. They started again on Seventy West, at the opposite end, and continued, again from top to bottom, to the last name on the bottom line of One West at the apex where the two walls met at the base of the gash in the earth. One hundred forty slabs,

58,188 names now, 2,273 unaccounted for, 1,124 KIA but no bodies. She'd never had to look past Forty-four East because the remainder of Danny's friends were apparently dead three-quarters of the way down that section. *Why so many of them? Why over such a short period of time?*

The names danced across her mind's eye as they had since that first day, and it was a moment before she became aware of an individual making a rubbing of a name on Forty-three East. The name was high enough that the person doing it had to to stand on tiptoe, stretching as his pencil moved back and forth across the white paper. Gradually the gray-black image emerged from the stone onto the paper, the stark whiteness of the name bringing a dead man back to life: Geraldo Vincente Santucci.

Jerry! He'd copied Jerry Santucci's name! There was a shock of recognition, a person she'd grown to know more in death than life. Leila held her breath, wondering who . . .

A relative maybe? Perhaps a close friend who would take Jerry's name back to a Santucci unable to visit Washington?

He finished and stepped back a few paces to her right to appraise his handiwork, holding the sheet of paper at arm's length. Then he glanced over, aware that she was staring at him.

Oh, God, no!

The features had changed so little in twenty-five years. Jerry'd been Italian-handsome, aquiline nose, dark eyes, dark eyebrows, square jaw, low hairline, curly black hair. Even the tiny scar on his right cheekbone, evidence of his first automobile accident, remained—"My first stolen car," he'd claimed proudly.

When Leila was fifteen, Jerry Santucci was considered cute by teenage girls, and mysterious in a way because of his pronounced southern European features. One of her first thoughts now was why she'd thought he was so good looking. Age had fleshed out the face a little, added lines, and there was gray in the still thick curly hair. Only the eyes had changed, so much so that the young male good looks, with that devil-may-care James Dean glint that teenage girls loved, had been transformed into something sinister. The eyes scared you.

Jerry Santucci had copied his own name. Jerry Santucci had just brought himself back to life.

He was turning back toward the Wall when she said, "You haven't changed that much, Jerry. Have I?" How had she been able to speak? *How can I be so calm?*

For no more than a split second, as his head whipped around in her direction, his eyes registered total, unguarded shock. The shock of recognition. Leila had expected that. Yet well before he responded, a protective switch snapped on. His expression became totally blank. "Are you speaking to me, ma'am?" The voice was as she remembered, perhaps with the addition of the deep scratchiness of a smoker. The New York accent was gone, replaced by an odd lilt she couldn't identify, almost as if he were a foreigner speaking perfect English.

"I've never forgotten anyone I had a crush on, Jerry. You must remember me—Leila Potter, Danny's sister. I made you your last home-cooked dinner before you and Danny went to Vietnam." She marveled at how calm she felt greeting a dead man as if they'd just met for the first time at a cocktail party. "The scar on your cheek"—she reached out to point with her index finger—"from your first stolen car is still there."

"I beg your pardon." A look of irritation appeared. "I've never met you in my life. My name isn't Jerry. And I can assure you I've never stolen a car," he finished with a scowl.

What was it, that accent? His intonation, distinctive and distinctly odd, was strange, foreign, more polished than the raw New York sound that she remembered. She might even have apologized for a mistake if the day before she hadn't studied the picture of Danny and his four buddies taken in Saigon. They'd had the sun at their backs, and Williams's black face was hard to distinguish. Gonzalez was easier to identify because he was the only one with a mustache. Arison was middle-of-the-road, nondescript. Jerry Santucci had been beside Danny, turned to the side, facing the sun, his features prominent. There wasn't the least doubt in Leila's mind that it was the same man who now scowled at her.

"The stolen car was your story, Jerry." She closed her eyes and took a deep breath. *How can I be so calm?* "But I'd know you anywhere. I was looking at your picture last night, the one taken during Danny's last liberty in Saigon." Was that a flicker of recognition at Danny's name?

"I realize any loss of a loved one is regrettable, ma'am. I'm sorry I can't be someone you hoped I was." He was carefully folding the paper displaying the rubbing of his name.

Leila had no idea why she uttered the next sentence. She'd never considered herself brave. "Curiosity got the best of you, didn't it, Jerry?" Then, before he could react: "I'm sorry I said that. I don't mean to upset you. I won't ask you any more questions about yourself. All I want to know now is how Danny died, if it was the way Captain Ledbetter wrote me." There was the flicker of recognition again, just a flash through the blankness. "Please, I don't care what's happened. I just know you must have been there when Danny died. He mentioned you in every letter because you were his best friend, and I've got to know what happened. Please."

He slipped the rubbing into the inside pocket of his suit jacket. That was another thing that had seemed odd about seeing Jerry Santucci again. It wasn't the face that surprised her so much—that was unmistakable—it was the dark, very expensive-looking, custom-fitted suit. She'd seen pictures of Jerry in uniform, and when he came to dinner that final night he was wearing a Janice Joplin T-shirt. Now he was dressed like the chairman of an international corporation.

"I won't tell a soul, Jerry. I've never forgotten you. See, I still carry your name on my bracelet, almost eight years now . . . right after I learned you were missing." She extended her wrist to show him the ID bracelet.

He straightened his coat, buttoning the middle button, silent.

Then she added with a touch of desperation because he

appeared to be leaving, "I've tried so many times to get access to the records, but for some reason nothing is really clear, nothing about that exact moment. You must know. You—"

"You've mistaken me for someone else." He turned abruptly in the direction of the west end of the Wall, beginning to work his way through the crowd toward the Lincoln Memorial.

Leila hesitated, even took a few tentative steps to follow. "I'm staying at the Crystal City Marriott in Arlington if you want to . . ."

But Jerry Santucci was moving rapidly. He bumped into a lady in a Japanese tour group preparing to take a photo of the Wall. Her camera slipped from her hands. He reached out, snatching it from the air, and handed it back. Then Leila heard him say something to the woman in what must have been Japanese, for she laughed and responded in the same language. Was that what she'd recognized in his few brief responses to her? Was that singsong intonation more common to him than English?

What had Jerry Santucci become?

Leila didn't remember passing any of the Metro stops on the way back to Arlington. It was habit that made her look up and recognize the Crystal City station signs as the train came to a halt. Familiarity, more than anything else, took her through the underground pathway to the Marriott where she was staying. When she snapped on the light in the bathroom of her room, the face that was reflected back from the mirror frightened her.

"You really do look as if you've seen a ghost!" Leila said out loud, surprising herself. She wanted the real world to know. Then, silently, eyes squeezed shut, knowing the real world wasn't ready for that: *How do I tell someone that I just saw a man who I thought had been dead for twenty-five years?* She didn't once doubt her own judgment. She knew she'd seen and talked to Jerry Santucci. But now what should she do? Who would believe her? Whom could she trust enough to tell her story to? The military? The Pentagon was a ten-minute walk from the hotel. But would they be any more cooperative than in the past?

Jerry Santucci's flight across the Pacific from San Francisco was fourteen hours. It was dark when he landed in Hong Kong and the short cab ride from Kai Tak Airport to Kowloon, impossible during the day, still wasted another hour. This particular trip was always exhausting, and the evening traffic infuriated him. All he really wanted was to go home and sleep, but he'd wired ahead that he needed to talk. Sleep could come later.

Jerry decided against the harbor tunnel and had the cab drop him at the pier where he took the Star Ferry across Victoria Harbor to the main island. The ferry at night was refreshing. It brought him back into contact with *his* world, the one he'd escaped to so many years before. He walked the few short blocks from the ferry terminal, allowing the sea air to clear his mind.

Their building, Inchar House, just blocks from the elegant Mandarin Hotel, was one of those new chrome and glass structures that reared into the sky as if the designer intended to outshine Victoria Peak's grandeur. The main entrance was exquisite, a gleaming patio with small, dancing fountains before a two-story glass front, then a massive waterfall in the lobby illuminated by colored spotlights. It was an elegant address, the immense bronze plate on one column identifying it as the International Charities Center. They regularly brought visitors to their thirtieth-floor office, which looked out over the world's most beautiful harbor. The view alone was enough to impress anyone, if the structure didn't. Not a soul in the world could be immune to the splendor that was Hong Kong.

But Jerry bypassed the main entrance, turning instead up the alley at the side of the building. He walked another forty feet to a doorway lit only by a single overhead bulb and punched a code into the entry mechanism. After the one-second buzzer sounded, he added three more numbers to the code and pushed through the door.

A stairway curled down two flights to a dimly lit hallway

that stretched fifty feet to a single doorway. There was no handle on the door. Once again he punched in a code on the button panel to one side of the door, then pressed his palm against a mirror just above the panel. The door slid to one side, and he stepped into the elegant secondary office of International Charities, Ltd.

"Hi, Connie," he said to the lovely Chinese woman at the reception desk.

"Jerry, welcome back. Hugh's been waiting for you. He has an engagement soon," she added.

Santucci nodded, murmuring, "I'll keep that in mind," and strode to a door behind her. He knocked and, without waiting for a response, pushed through into a large, ornate office. "Hugh, sorry to make you stay so late. Connie told me you've got something going on shortly, so I won't keep you long."

Hugh Young came around from behind the desk and shook Santucci's hand. "Nothing that can't wait, Jerry. Come on." He gestured to a sofa against the wall. "I want you to sit down, and I'm going to mix you a good stiff drink."

"Hugh . . ."

"Now, listen, Sergeant," Young said, leading him by the elbow to the sofa, "I'm going to make that an order if you don't sit down and relax, and I haven't issued an order for well over twenty years. Now, sit." When Santucci, who'd never been a sergeant, sat, Hugh, who'd never been in the army, put up a hand and added with a smile, "Good. Now, stay. You sounded like a wreck when you called from San Francisco." Young filled two glasses with ice, then poured Jack Daniel's to the rim in both of them. "I'm not going to have an old friend burn himself out on my behalf." He handed one to Santucci, raised his own, and said, "Cheers, old pal."

"Thanks, Hugh," Santucci said, taking a long pull. He savored the sour mash and licked his lips. "I didn't know how much I needed one of these."

"Here's to the first, but not necessarily the last." Young sat down comfortably at the other end of the sofa and crossed his legs. "I almost can't remember the last time I rubbed elbows with the military. How long has it really been? Has to be more than twenty years," he mused. "Shit, more than twenty-five. Getting up on thirty. Sort of forgot how long we've been hanging out together. But you're a buddy, you sounded worried on the phone, and you're not going to hold anything inside until it's convenient for me. Understand? You look like shit, too. Now, what's got you working on an evening?"

Santucci stared at him for a moment before saying, almost in a whisper, "I think I fucked up, Hugh." Then he shook off that sentence. "No, I don't think. I know I did. I really fucked up." He reached into his jacket pocket and extracted a folded sheet of paper. "Open it," he said, handing it over.

Hugh Young unfolded the paper and stared at the name— Geraldo Vincente Santucci—stark white against the pencil background. To the left of the name was a small cross. Young handed it back. "You always wanted to see your name in lights, Jerry. So now you have. Granite's just about the same. You've been to the Wall. What's the big deal?"

"I was recognized," Santucci answered with a hiss.

"Can't be. You're dead."

"Past tense. This broad took one look at me and called me Jerry."

Young frowned. Then, after studying Santucci's face, he rose from the sofa and moved over to open the door to the outer office. "Connie, would you be good enough to cancel my dinner engagement? Just say I've come down with the flu."

"No need—" Santucci began.

"Hey, Jerry, it could have been me not so long ago. I visited the Wall myself once. Had to," he added, nodding to himself. "I almost cried because my name wasn't up there like yours. Honest to God, I said to myself, 'I could have been one more good guy who gave his life for America,' and I almost got choked up thinking about being dead. No shit." He took a long drink. "I had but one life to give to my country, and I didn't. Think about that."

Santucci managed a grin. "I can't remember what I was

thinking at the time. That broad completely took me by surprise."

"Do you know her?"

"Didn't at first. Do now. You don't know her, Hugh, but you know about her brother—Danny Potter." He looked for recognition on Young's face. "When our unit was operating near Tay Ninh, the Iron Triangle . . . all that good shit. Remember?"

"Yeah, okay, the Iron Triangle. I do remember. You and Eddie still talk about it sometimes. Jesus! Danny Potter. That's a name I haven't thought about in a while. Wasn't he one of the first kids who found out?"

"You got it. He was the one who threatened to blow the whistle. If you also remember, it was arranged for Mr. Charlie to take care of the problem."

"How'd this girl know you?"

"I thought about that on the flight back. Danny took me home for dinner one time. That's the only time she ever saw me. Maybe she saw some photos, too. More than likely. Shit, I don't know. But I figured on the flight back here that it's been at least twenty-five years since that one time, and I'll be goddamned if she doesn't take one look at me and say my name like we were out on a date." He shook his head in wonder. "The other thing she said is she wanted to find out how Danny died, because the military records people wouldn't help her. Can you feature that? After all that time, she's still wondering about her brother's death."

"Would you have recognized her?"

"Not in a crowd of one. Not until she mentioned her brother's name. Then I knew her like it was yesterday. Cute kid then."

Young glanced at him with a grin. "Still good-looking?"

Santucci wrinkled his forehead. "Yeah, I suppose so . . . for an American broad." He sipped his drink. "As a matter of fact, considering she's got another twenty-five years on her, she looked damn good, the type I'd ask out if I was still messing with round-eyes." He put down the glass. "You know, she must be at least forty by now, but she looked better than the picture I have in my mind of her as a kid. Her hair was sort of a dirty blond then. Now it's golden. Looks natural."

"Blue eyes to go along with it?"

"Nope. Brown. I remember that from the day I visited with Danny. They were very soft."

"You've got a good memory, Jerry."

"Hey, Hugh, when someone scares the shit out of you like that, it's just like taking a picture. You don't forget a wrinkle." He winked knowingly at Young. "You know me, I love women."

"Too bad."

"Huh?"

"Too bad she has to be disposed of."

CHAPTER 2

LEILA POTTER DIDN'T CARE FOR THE REFLECTION SHE PERceived in the hotel room mirror. "You can use a good boot in the ass," she said out loud, glaring back at herself. She pondered her choices. She could cry. *Go ahead. Be an asshole and cry.* That was an unappealing option. She could call the police, but it took only a moment to imagine her own reaction if she were the desk officer answering the telephone: "Got another psychotic here who claims she's just seen a man who's been dead for twenty-five years." She could call any number of people and obtain any number of reactions, but now wasn't the time. Think it out, she told herself. You're supposed to be the most organized person in the world, and you've spent your entire life trying to avoid situations like this.

Leila did possess another exceptional talent, one she'd developed to perfection since she was a child, and one she often avoided as she matured because it provided much too easy a way out of her troubles. It was pure escapism; no matter how bad things seemed to be, no matter how high her stress level, she could stretch out on her bed or on a couch and turn her mind off. In just moments she could be sound asleep, her soul at peace with the world, her problems mercifully avoided. Was this—should this be—one of those times?

She sat down on the bed in an attempt to sort out her experience at the Wall. But it was like swimming against a swift current. It seemed impossible to accomplish what she was so capable of doing, separating each incident that she remembered, putting each in its proper order, and analyzing it as a part of the whole experience. When she was engaged in this process, her mind functioned at breakneck speed, which was one of the reasons she'd been selected by her employer to visit Washington half a dozen times a year to lobby their local elected officials and critical bureaucrats.

It's not working, Leila. You lost control. Your shield's breaking down. Don't talk to anyone yet. So she slipped off her shoes, stretched out on the king-size bed, and was asleep in less than a minute.

There were no dreams. Her mind was in neutral. Leila was both intelligent enough and stubborn enough to acknowledge that taking such an easy way out could be a mistake, so she rarely employed sleep. But she needed time.

It was dark out when she awakened two hours later.

Why in hell did I turn off like that? The blackness of the room was frightening. Where was she? She turned her head toward the window, and the lights of the Crystal City office buildings were instantly familiar. She was at the Marriott, on a business trip, and she'd been to the Wall to see Danny . . . and instead she saw . . .

Jerry! Her breath caught in her throat. Jerry Santucci.

She could feel the same sensations returning—surprise, fear—so many that she could also feel that same confusion returning. That was why she'd slept—hidden. *Don't let yourself come apart like that again.* It was a command issued instantly from her ordered brain to her troubled heart. It was also instinctive. She'd let the afternoon's events gain control of her mind, but she wasn't about to allow that to happen again.

Leila Potter wasn't the kind of woman who allowed

intrusions from the outside to influence her life like that. She was organized, she controlled her own fate, and she was an expert at turning away those aspects of the outer world that troubled her. Nothing was going to change.

But it already had.

She'd come face to face with a dead man. Never for a moment did she doubt that she'd seen Jerry Santucci. And she was ready to admit now, as she moved over to the window and drew the blinds, that he was one outside influence that hadn't the slightest chance of disappearing. He couldn't be shut out like a bad dream. There was absolutely no possibility that she would be able to exercise that superb mind control and erase him as she had erased Vietnam so many other times. She turned on her heel. The digital clock on the bedside table blinked—6:00 P.M. *Do something intelligent, something conducive to thinking.*

She undressed quickly and took a long, hot shower. Then she wrapped a spare towel around her wet hair and pulled on the terry-cloth robe hanging in the bathroom. She dug through the desk for the room service menu, perused it briefly, and was about to call for dinner. *No, wait a second. Don't touch that phone.* Sitting alone in this room would be one more way to escape . . . or to hide.

She went back into the bathroom, blew her hair dry, then put on a fresh outfit that she'd packed in case she went out to dinner. Somehow—she wasn't sure exactly how yet—she'd be damned if this afternoon's experience was going to control her. She looked in the mirror. *Ready, Leila?* The woman in the mirror smiled slightly. *Yes. Ready.*

Leila was already in the elevator, her thoughts turning to dining alone, when she convinced herself she needed more than dinner. Once again she'd succeeded in blanking emotion from her mind. She was in full control and had begun planning as she dressed how she would think this out. When you've been on your own since the age of sixteen, you learn how to control those weaknesses of the mind that so many others accept. Anything would be possible if you could just shut out what you didn't want. *And you are going to handle this Jerry Santucci thing.*

The bar was dimly lit, a whorehouse plush like so many of the Marriotts, but it was decent enough that a woman could have a drink without being bothered by men. She ordered a dry amontillado and knew after a couple of sips that that wasn't the answer.

It required one scotch and soda to determine exactly how she wanted to approach Harry Jensen, and a second to clarify her purpose in her own mind. Jensen was the top aide to her congressman, Chuck Goodrich, and Harry'd become a friend. The advantage to returning Harry's friendship was that he was gay, and to Leila that meant nonthreatening. She could ask him out for a meal or a few drinks and he was as charming as could be and provided the support her company needed.

On a whim, she asked the bartender for a telephone and called Jensen, who lived in an apartment near Crystal City. Harry wasn't drinking, but he thought dinner with an attractive lady a wonderful idea and he was sitting across the table from her in the Marriott's dining room within twenty minutes. "But I haven't given up wine, dear, and I'm going to order us a good bottle so we can relax while you tell me this story I won't believe."

They were well into dinner and a second bottle before Leila finished telling Jensen about running into Jerry Santucci at the Wall. She had covered everything from the day Danny brought Jerry home for dinner before they shipped out to Vietnam to his brief moment of recognition that afternoon. "It was Jerry Santucci," she affirmed, "right down to the scar on his right cheekbone from his first stolen car. And he knew I knew." She looked across at Harry and squeezed his hand. "I made a promise to myself long ago not to let my personal problems interfere with business. But this time I have to back down on that promise."

Harry Jensen was handsome, not effeminately so like so many of his kind, she thought, and he understood women better than most men. He reached across the table and covered her hand, the one that had maintained a nervous pattering as she related her story. "You poor thing. No one needs a shock like that." He poured some wine into her glass. "I know you said you'd had enough, but you need something after all that, and I don't want you too hung over tomorrow when we get you someone to help out."

Leila looked up hopefully from the glass. "You know what I should do?"

"Oh, goodness, yes, that's my job, my dear. Constituent relations. Remember, my boss was a POW in Vietnam, he testified before Kerry's Senate committee, and I'm sure I've told you before how sympathetic he is to anyone who had a relative there. Plus, why do you think Chuck Goodrich keeps getting reelected? Certainly not on his personal charm, not with those big cigars always sticking out of his face. He gets those votes because Harry Jensen keeps his constituents happy." He sat back in his chair with a smug grin. "After all these years inside the Beltway, I know everybody who needs to be known, or I know where to find them."

Harry woke her with a phone call at seven-thirty the next morning. "Hey, sleepyhead, you've got to get yourself on Pentagon time."

The curtains were drawn, the hotel room still dark. Leila glanced over at the digital clock. "Too much wine, Harry." She cleared her throat. "What do you mean Pentagon time?"

"Why, I thought you would have learned after all your lobbying in the District that it's a contest over there to see who can get to work the earliest. You've been there before, dear. You know the military has its own timetable. If someone arrived on time, he'd be considered a shirker, duly noted in the official records. I had Captain Carson on the pipe by seven-fifteen this morning."

"You didn't mention names last night. Just who is Captain Carson?"

"POW-MIA desk. Carson, first initial E., middle initial P., Captain, U.S. Army. Captain Carson is assigned to the office of the deputy assistant secretary of defense for POW-MIA affairs, who is established under the assistant secretary of defense for international security affairs. That office was set up in late 1991 as part of the new Full Accounting task force. But forget all the bureaucracy bullshit. Carson is one sharp cookie and has agreed to meet you by Security at the south entrance of the Pentagon at exactly eight-thirty— zero-eight-thirty, in military terms."

"How the hell will I know Captain Carson?"

"The same way everyone is identified at Security. They shout out your name, and you jump."

Carson, E. P., Captain, U.S. Army, was petite and attractive. "Call me Penny," she said with a pleasant smile as she led the way down the wide, endless Pentagon corridors. That came after Leila referred to her as "captain" and mentioned that she hadn't been informed that E. P. Carson was female. "The initials are a terrific way to control the macho men in the military who worry about competition."

"I think Harry Jensen was just playing with my mind. That's why all the women get along with him."

"I don't know Harry Jensen well, but my boss says the man can do no wrong, not to mention that he's the front man for Congressman Goodrich, who fronts for us on the Hill. Since Harry also told me you come as a friend rather than an enemy, I'm looking forward to starting out on a friendly basis."

"Enemies?" Leila asked curiously as they rounded a corner and started down another of the interminable waxed corridors. "Who? What kind of enemies?"

"That depends. Some days they're from the Hill, if their constituents have a beef and think we're trying to put them off. Other times they might be special interest groups who are convinced we're trying to conceal information. They're paranoid about that. Oh, damn," she said, half turning toward Leila, "you're not with some group, are you?"

"Nobody but me. I'm a loner."

"Wow, my boss keeps telling me I've got to be more diplomatic if I'm going to survive in this place. Well, who haven't I covered? Relatives, I guess. Even relatives—whom we really care about, by the way—are convinced we're burying the last chance they might ever have of seeing a loved one alive if we locate proof that an MIA should be changed to officially dead. Criticism comes from all directions; a lot of it seems kind of crackpot from my side of the desk. But I suppose most of it's well-meaning because they all hate the bureaucracy just like you and me."

Leila studied the woman walking beside her. Captain Carson was easy to like, but she was also definitely military in her freshly pressed army green uniform, her back straight, her arms swinging as if she were marching unconsciously. It was also obvious from the guarded stares of the men they passed that she was very feminine from a male vantage point, even though she used a minimum of makeup. Penny Carson had short brown hair, brown eyes, a well-pronounced figure that couldn't be hidden beneath the army green, and a pleasant, sincere smile that forced others to smile back. She was a woman very much in control of herself.

"I hope Harry didn't say I hated the Pentagon," Leila remarked. "Honestly, I really don't. I've been here before for my company. We consult for defense industries sometimes, mostly aircraft, and that's a downer these days. Most of the officers in those procurement programs are pilots, and they're very male and very macho. That's why I was surprised to meet a female here." She was happy to find a woman in an area she assumed would be all male. "I've usually found the military more cooperative than the civilian sector."

"Thanks. The compliments don't come too often around here." Penny Carson smiled as she indicated a doorway to their right. "My office is right in there. Not a big space, but we make the most of it."

They stopped by a coffee urn long enough to draw two paper cups of coffee before entering the captain's small office. There was enough room for a well-traveled metal desk, a worn visitor's chair, and a computer to one side of the desk on a small typist's table. A large map of Southeast Asia, decorated by pins with heads of various colors, covered much of the back wall.

Penny Carson picked up a pen and poised it above a

yellow notepad. "I'd normally start out by saying that we record all personal interviews concerning sightings and that would be for your benefit as much as our own. That's Department of Defense policy," she added, rapping the pencil on the pad. "However, those sightings are always on foreign soil, and the interviews are done by our people in the field. See, you've already made my day interesting. All I know, Miss Potter, is that your situation is unique. Even my boss doesn't know anything except that Harry Jensen's promised you'd blow my socks off." She stopped for a moment as if she expected Leila to begin talking.

"I'm not sure how to—"

"I should clarify DOD's position also by stating that we don't start out with preconceived ideas. That's why I don't know anything about your situation, Miss . . ." She stopped and said, "You know, you're already on a first-name basis with me, but it's not working in the other direction. If you prefer to keep it that way . . ."

"Please, I'm Leila, and I prefer it that way. It's just that this whole thing is so difficult for me to understand. I've been thinking ever since I got out of bed about how to explain myself."

"If you don't mind, it might be easier if you let me start out by asking the basic questions we need answers to. Like—is it your brother you're concerned with?" She studied Leila more closely. "I did look up your last name in the computer, and I know you had a brother killed in Vietnam."

Leila shook her head, then sipped her coffee before answering. For years she'd pushed that lost, lonely segment of her life into the far corners of her mind, and she'd been reluctant to bring it forward again—until the shock of seeing Jerry Santucci. "No, it's not Danny, although I wish it were. Danny's dead. It was a crying shame because he was such a beautiful kid, but he's been dead for twenty-five years. I accept that," she added softly. "The man I saw yesterday was very much alive." Then she allowed everything she'd repressed to come to the surface. She told of her first visit to the Wall, the unusual number of men lost from Danny's platoon, her attempts after that to learn more about Danny's death, and ended with the encounter with Jerry Santucci. It was such a relief, a catharsis, to put everything she'd suppressed into words.

Penny Carson took occasional notes, interrupting politely to ask questions a few times, the last time asking incredulously, "This man was actually making a rubbing of his own name?"

Leila closed her eyes. "Yes." She took a deep breath. "It is rather macabre, isn't it? I mean he's been dead, at least to me—hell, to the world—for twenty-five years."

"You don't have any doubts about his identity, do you?" Captain Carson had turned to the computer and was inserting some data as she asked the question.

"Not at all. Why do you ask? Is this the kind of thing you were talking about—some crackpot looking for attention?"

"As I mentioned earlier, I've run into some pretty strange people in this assignment. Believe me, they come in all shapes and sizes, and they rely on some unique forms of communication—dreams, séances, ghosts, voices in the dark. But I don't want you to get me wrong. I'm not trying to back away from my good ole girl approach. I understand why people don't want to let go of their loved ones, especially those who have someone still unaccounted for. Ah, here he is: Santucci, Geraldo Vincente."

She raised an index finger. "The Iron Triangle. I've read about that place," she said, turning toward Leila. "You see, I was only three years old at the time, but I know exactly where it is." She stood up and turned around to point at a spot on the map. "Right here, northwest of Ho Chi Minh City, near where Cambodia bulges into Vietnam, the place called the Parrot's Beak."

"Ho Chi Minh City. It used to be Saigon," Leila said wistfully. "We're all probably better off because they changed the name."

"I hadn't thought about that," Carson said, looking carefully across the desk at Leila. "We're not so different in

33

age, but there really is a generation separating us, isn't there?" Without waiting for an answer, she pointed at Leila's left wrist. "That bracelet is also from another generation. Is that someone specific or did you just send in your check and get that back with someone's name engraved on it?"

Leila slipped off the silver bracelet and handed it across the desk without a word.

Captain Carson turned it in her fingers until the name stood out. "Geraldo Vincente Santucci," she read aloud, pronouncing each part of the name with a separate breath. Her eyes held Leila's. "I see . . . I see. We're getting pretty close to the gut, aren't we? How long have you worn this?"

"Since 1986 when I saw the cross beside Jerry's name. After it all sank in, I went over to one of those booths the vets have set up by the Wall and asked what I had to do to get a bracelet. That's how I got the phone number for the League of Families—"

"They're good people," Penny Carson interrupted.

". . . and they took care of it for me."

"I know it's crude of me to ask, but I have to. Do you have some sort of thing for this Jerry Santucci? Maybe you've had a crush on him since you were sixteen?"

"Perhaps I did when I was a kid. But, no, I'm not still carrying a torch. The bracelet was symbolic to me more than anything else. I guess my original thought was that I was wearing it in Danny's memory. Jerry was his best friend, if you know what I mean." She looked at the captain with a puzzled expression. "Why?"

Carson smiled wistfully. "I think that's one of the reasons I was given this MIA account. Most of the family members who are still searching for MIAs are women, naturally. They're the ones who waited and lost. People like me are supposed to separate emotion from reality when we talk with the families. And it's a fact of life that all the senior officers from that era are male, and they figure women can discuss emotions more comfortably than men. Most men are embarrassed to ask women questions about their feelings, especially grieving women. You're not grieving, Leila, but every man in this building would have been scared you were and wouldn't have known how to talk to you."

"I never would have considered human emotions were a problem."

"That's why I'm sitting at this desk running this account. Okay, let's get down to business again. What did you talk about with this man at the Wall?" She held up her hand when Leila's forehead wrinkled. "Please. I understand your emotions are a little raw today, but it's my job to avoid identifying personally with what you've told me. The army wants me to keep an open mind, even if I do believe you, and I do. But I'm going to try not to call him Santucci just yet. Now tell me what was said to the best of your recollection."

Leila repeated the brief conversation as clearly as she could, amazed that each word they had both spoken seemed committed to her memory. "I wanted to know how Danny died. Was it just as the letter said? Or was there something else? The Pentagon was very polite, but they didn't have much to say, except to support what Captain Ledbetter wrote me."

"You mean you don't know how your brother died? The army never told you?" Carson asked in surprise. The sincere smile that seemed to be a part of her uniform disappeared and was replaced by a frown. Her eyes narrowed perceptibly.

"The letter I got from Captain Ledbetter, Danny's company commander, was the type of thing I guess every CO wrote to the next of kin: Danny was a credit to the army, to his company, a hero who held his position all night against great odds, recommended for medals." She stared bitterly at a spot on the wall above Carson's head and added, "In a way, it was the type of bullshit you see on television, but I'm sure he meant it all."

Carson nodded knowingly. "Created by the same men who wanted a woman sitting here today."

"There was another letter, written a few weeks later by Danny's platoon leader. He said he was writing because there was no record that Captain Ledbetter had written me.

Lieutenant Kelley's letter had the same bullshit, but it also mentioned a different situation—a perimeter defense. When I was sixteen, I didn't think about details like that. It wasn't until years later that I began to think about it."

"Do you have those letters with you?"

"No. They're home, buried in a dresser drawer. I didn't think I'd ever want to look at them again."

"Will you please send me copies?" Carson asked, making a note on her pad of paper.

"Of course. There's another odd thing. Lieutenant Kelley is also missing. There's a cross by his name on the Wall."

Carson typed Kelley's name into her computer. "Santucci and Kelley ended up MIA on the same day!" Her left eyebrow arched curiously. "It's going to be difficult to track them down. For some reason, the normal data is missing. It's almost—damn it—almost as if someone tried to delete the file. The two of them just disappeared while on patrol near the perimeter of the company's position. There was apparently an ambush. No bodies were found except that of the radioman. Kelley and Santucci just never reappeared.

"There's a notation here that the local Vietcong were being paid by Hanoi to turn over American prisoners to the North Vietnamese regulars and that's what we'd normally assume was the final disposition of the case." She jotted something down on her yellow pad. "A lot of the data in our computer came from the old hand-typed files. They weren't using computers in the field then. I'll see if I can check out the original files and learn anything else. Now back to yesterday."

Leila licked her lips thoughtfully. "When I saw Jerry, so many memories came back at one time in a rush. But the most important thing was that Jerry ought to know the entire story about Danny. Since the military has never really answered all of my questions, I was sure Jerry would know. And when I asked, I don't think I've ever seen such a look in a man's eyes before." She stared across the desk at Penny Carson, shaking her head in wonder. "Horror, fear, anger . . . I'm not sure what that look was. Jerry Santucci's never going to tell me what he knows about Danny." She leaned back in her chair. "Does your computer have the answers, Penny? Can it tell me how Danny died?"

"It should. And that's also why I'm here," Captain Carson added firmly. She typed the necessary information into her computer and waited expectantly. Then she struck a couple of more keys. Wrinkling her forehead, she chewed on her upper lip before typing in additional instructions. "Strange," she murmured to herself.

"What's strange?"

"Your brother's records don't look right. Same sort of garbage the Kelley and Santucci files had," Carson muttered without looking up. Again she went back to the keyboard. This time she stroked her chin slowly as she read what appeared on the screen. "Was the body returned, Leila?"

"Yes."

"Closed-casket funeral?"

"Yes."

"Did the local funeral home do any preparation?"

"Not that I know of, Penny. I was only sixteen at the time."

Captain Carson glanced briefly at Leila, then went back to her computer. "I forgot. That wouldn't occur to a teenager." She punched another key and the printer came alive as she called to the clerk in the outer office to come in. "Here," she said to the private first class. "Take this print out down to Colonel Wallace and tell him I can't go any further in an investigation until I get his initials on this. Then go down to the vault and pull this file. No one should give you any crap with the colonel's initials on this."

While Carson's clerk was gone, she explained to Leila that the data on the cause of death for most KIAs could normally be called up on the computer. In Danny's case, there had been an odd notation that the cause had been inconclusive. "I've seen a few others like that," Carson said. "Usually the explanation is in the old files that just never got fed into the computer properly because of clerical errors."

It was half an hour before the clerk returned with the file. Leila fidgeted in her chair as Captain Carson thumbed through sheets of paper yellowed with age until she found what she was looking for. After scanning the page quickly, she smoothed it out on her desk and reread it, then explained it to Leila.

"The cause of death is much the same as most of the others I see—multiple wounds. That seems plausible. The date's right. Place of death—Ben Suc, near Tay Ninh—is right. Everything just as it should be, especially if a family gets nosy and wants to know everything. The army doesn't want civilians exposed to anything too gory.

"However, there's a handwritten note that looks like it might have been made at Ton Son Hut. That was the mortuary at the air base in Saigon where bodies were prepared for shipment home."

She pushed the paper across to Leila and pointed at the notation. "Some technician made a note that the only apparent wound was a single bullet hole at the base of the skull—nothing about multiple wounds. There're a couple of exclamation points after that, which makes sense since that kind of a wound would indicate the bullet came from behind. Kind of odd during a firefight, wouldn't you say? And it looks as if the technician made an attempt to cross the notation out, but not enough that it couldn't be read."

"Almost as if he meant this to be seen by someone."

Carson nodded. "It slipped by, or perhaps no one had time to care. Maybe a busy day. I've read reports that there were days when the flow of corpses was so heavy the technicians had a hell of a time keeping up. Whoever wrote that note thought the cause of Danny's death was strange . . . but he didn't have enough time to investigate it."

"Why wasn't the technician's note recorded on your computer?"

Captain Carson shook her head. "Beats me. But I think it gives us a reason to look into your brother's death a little deeper, doesn't it? I'll keep a copy of this." She called out to the clerk, who made a copy of the page with the note and a couple of other pages before she was told to return the file to the vault.

"Would you write down the names of the other men in your brother's platoon who were also killed? All the names you recognized on the Wall. I want to bring them up on the computer so I can print some hard copy on each one."

"I guess maybe you don't think I'm one of those crackpots you mentioned earlier," Leila commented as she wrote down the names etched in her memory just as they had been on the Wall.

"No. I think you have as much right as any other relative to know how Danny died, and I also think that you've been given a runaround because you weren't difficult enough. You've got to be a pushy broad in this world, Leila. I also believe you saw someone who was a dead ringer for Jerry Santucci. And because you watched him take that rubbing of Santucci's name, I'm going to go against my professional judgment and say that maybe you've helped me with one of my own crackpot theories."

"What's that?"

"It's not a complex theory, Leila. But some people don't like to hear it. There are live Americans over there in Southeast Asia, and not all the sightings have been made by raving maniacs. I just happen to believe those men stayed there by choice, and you can't imagine how that pisses off the special interest groups. Maybe, just maybe, you sighted one who's gotten a little too curious."

Ed Kelley heard the telephone chirp just once in the outer office before it was answered.

"International Charities, how may I help you?" Song's English contained just the slightest hint of an accent. Her voice was high and lilting and friendly, the kind that made a caller feel that she really cared.

The photo of Kelley and the two Laotians, the picture that had been removed from Major Joslin's corpse after the ambush in Laos, stared up at him from the wide gold-embossed blotter on his desk. Beside it lay a photo that had remained in the recesses of his wall safe since they'd moved to the Silom Road office in Bangkok four years earlier. It was a picture of him when he was still a lieutenant in Vietnam.

"Oh, good morning, Mr. Young," Song replied happily in the outer office. "Of course I recognize your voice."

Memories of that old photo had kept Kelley awake a good part of the previous night. He removed it from the safe as soon as he'd entered the office that morning. After Song had brought him his coffee, he closed the door and taped both pictures on the wall behind his desk to catch the full light from the window facing out onto Silom Road. He'd studied them close up, then moved back one step at a time until the faces were no longer distinguishable. Then he did the same thing from either side, increasing the angle until the reflection from the window became a mirror on the glossy surfaces.

"He's on the private line, Mr. Young," Song lied perfectly. "But let me tell him you're calling."

Kelley stared at the two photos, now lying on his desk. More than twenty years had gone by. His thick, curly hair had receded slightly in the front, but he still combed it in the Ivy League style with a part on the right. It was longer now, but he still had it trimmed once a week at the barbershop in the Dusit Thani Hotel around the corner on Rama 4 Road where the barber was most discreet about disguising gray hairs. Kelley had put on weight during his early years in Hong Kong, but that had disappeared in the hot, humid Thai weather, and now he was no more than ten pounds over his Vietnam days.

There was little of his Irish name in his features; his Italian mother had seen to that. His face was long and angular, nose straight and pronounced, cheekbones prominent, jaw wide and hard. American women had once thought he was cute. Asian women excused his sharp looks because they were fascinated by his curly hair. If the photos had been in color, the blue eyes from his Irish father would have been striking. Except for some added lines in the face, there wasn't a doubt in the world that it was the same man.

"Ed," Song said, stepping into his office, "Hugh Young is calling from Hong Kong. Do you want to talk with him?" She'd sensed he was troubled when he excused himself after dinner the night before and went home by himself. He was even more preoccupied this morning.

"Yes," he answered without looking up. He lifted the

telephone and punched the blinking button. "Good morning, Hugh. I'd been planning to call you."

"Amazing prescience, Eddie." Young was the only man who ever called him Eddie, a habit he'd acquired when they'd met in that rooftop bar in Saigon during Kelley's early days in-country. "And are you planning to brighten an otherwise distressing day for me?"

"Hugh, we need to call in some debts."

Young responded after a few seconds of silence. "Oh, shit," he commented. "Not you, too, Eddie."

That made Kelley feel better. "I guess if you were here we could flip to see who goes first. Hugh, let's avoid the small talk. Someone got a photo of me when I was north of Vientiane a few weeks ago."

"Wait a minute. You weren't—"

"No, no more poppies. No, I have no interest in playing with the flowers again, Hugh. I just went to my daughter's wedding. Don't you remember from the days of our carefree youth that her mother's a good Catholic? The old broad insisted that I show myself rather than embarrass her in front of the boy's family. So I agreed. Whether you want to believe it or not, I have a warm spot in my heart for my firstborn, even if she is close to her mother. The wedding was celebrated in the village where her mother was born, an open-air ceremony even though it was Catholic, and everyone was in local dress. They even put on the reception in the old way. I thought I'd told you about going up there."

"You did. So go on."

"It seems that some of the boy's family is in the flower business," he continued, employing their old term for the profitable poppy industry. "Next thing you know, a couple of our old acquaintances recognize me and insist I have a few shots of the local firewater with them. And that's when some clown got a picture. I don't know who took it. I don't know when. There were so goddamn many flashbulbs going off, you'd have thought we were in New York."

"So some guy made himself a little money selling the picture," Young concluded. "Some smart son of a bitch." An underground business was flourishing in Southeast Asia

41

because certain Americans believed that some American POWs were still being held against their will. It was the business of ghouls, but there was money to be made by selling any photo of a Caucasian, or someone purported to be a Caucasian, with the claim that he was a POW.

"Correction. Some now-deceased son of a bitch sold the picture and I don't think there was enough time for him to spend all the money. But that's not the real problem. The photo got back to Washington, Hugh. That's how I found out about it. That little prick, Wallace, called me as soon as he got wind of it. For once, Randy's earning his keep.

"He told me the photo intrepreters did everything they could to discredit it, which they're supposed to do. When they couldn't find anything technically wrong and finally had to admit it was authentic, they called Hawaii where that new Joint Task Force–Full Accounting is headquartered, the one that replaced the Joint Casualty Resolution Center a few years ago. Those people insisted that a full major from their group in Bangkok run up to investigate. It's a good photo, Hugh, a very good photo. Wallace reported that the Pentagon kept it quiet because they didn't have an ID, but there have to be some equally good copies, and they have to be on some high-powered desks in Arlington. We need them back. I wanted you to know I'm going to be in touch with Randy Wallace until he gets his dirty little paws on every copy of that photo."

"Recognition of people who don't want to be recognized appears to be a problem today, Eddie," Young said with an exasperated sigh. "I think you make a good point—we're going to make Randy earn his keep after all these years."

Lieutenant Colonel Randolph Wallace was a bureaucrat, a career man who'd long ago reached his peak but hung in beyond his twenty years because of contacts and old debts, and the fact that his Vietnam Purple Heart was an honorable one. Once a soldier, he was now comfortable behind a desk doing the kind of work that men who wanted to remain in the field avoided. That was how he'd been assigned to the POW-MIA section, a billet Hugh Young had insisted he aim for years ago.

"I guess we shouldn't knock Randy, Hugh. He was on the pipe the minute he found out about that photo of me."

"Randy's a puss," Young said with a laugh. "A big, fat, lazy, deskbound puss." Wallace wasn't really fat, but Hugh loved to antagonize him.

"Randy may be a puss, but he's doing his job," Kelley responded irritably. It had seemed reasonable to knock Wallace a few moments before, but he'd done what he was paid to do. Kelley hadn't slept well the night before and he had little interest in playful conversation. "You were going to tell me about a problem on your end."

"Jerry was back in the District on business this week, making sure of a few crucial votes on the Hill concerning that Indonesian trade pact." He paused to make his point. "However, he decided to stop by the Wall."

"I've done that, too."

"Not quite like Jerry. He was so proud to see his name up there, he decided to take a rubbing for posterity's sake."

"I've seen lots of people do that—take rubbings, I mean."

"Sure, Eddie, but usually of a dear departed relative, not your own name, for Christ's sake." Young's voice rose. "And if that isn't weird enough, the crazy son of a bitch was recognized."

"You're shitting me," Kelley exploded. "By whom? Who could recognize a dead man after all those years?"

"Do you remember a kid in your platoon named Danny Potter?"

"Sure. But he's dead. Really dead. I made sure I identified his corpse. I even wrote one of those hero letters to his next of kin."

"Danny Potter's next of kin was the one who saw Jerry do the rubbing of his name. Apparently Potter was an orphan, but he had a kid sister. He even took Santucci home to have dinner and meet her before they shipped out. Looks like she never forgot him."

Kelley whistled unconsciously.

"That says it all, Eddie. We have no intention of letting her go around telling people that she saw him." Over the past twenty-five years, Kelley, Young, and Santucci created fortunes, new lives, new everything. They couldn't take a chance on letting it all collapse because of a haphazard sighting. The army was as tenacious as a mongoose when it came to deserters. Just one hint that a deserter could be found and they hung on until they had their man in the stockade.

"I mean, it's all going to blow over," Young said. "It was a chance in a million, and nothing's going to come of it."

Kelley nodded. "I suppose not. But I'd sure hate to see an army investigation over something like this."

Young knit his eyebrows. An army investigation could go so deep—too deep—and everything could come crashing in on them, like dominoes. "We have to eliminate the source of the problem."

"But you shouldn't use Randy. That's not his game," Kelley warned. "Get him involved in something like that and he'll fuck it up. He likes the money on the side, but he doesn't like it dirty. If you're planning to take out the woman, hire a pro. Save Randy for the clean stuff."

"That's exactly what I did," Young answered. "Jerry was so shaken, the first thought that came to him was Randy. 'Get Randy humping,' he kept saying. 'Get that broad before she starts talking.' So I explained to him again that Wallace was definitely not the type for anything wet. I've already hired someone else to solve Jerry's problem. For all I know, the job's done. I just hope she was shaken enough that she didn't think to tell anyone who might take it seriously. With his flight and everything, that was more than a day ago."

"It's already night back there, Hugh. If she's still alive, scratch another twelve hours, maybe twenty-four, before someone's ready to get the job done. They got to find out where she's living first. No one with any smarts lives in D.C. Then they have to set the hit up right. Then—"

"Maybe she's still in Washington," Young said hopefully.

Kelley wasn't happy with the conversation. His own predicament was bad enough. Christ, what a coincidence. Two of them at the same time was more troubling. And both were what the Pentagon, as Hugh Young explained, could call sightings if they were allowed to go too far. "Maybe she is. Hey, thanks for calling, Hugh. But I don't have time to be polite now. You handle your thing, and I'm going to call Randy at home and tell him to take care of mine. And after the shit's out of the way, we're all going to sit down with some Mr. Jack and make sure these things don't ever happen again."

"It's a done deal, Eddie. Right after I get back from my Singapore-Jakarta swing."

"You're off tomorrow?"

"Right. When he wasn't diddling his ego, Jerry did twist enough arms in D.C. to get the votes we need for the Indonesian thing. I just have to tie up some loose ends. Short trip, I hope. Hey, Eddie, a week or so from now we'll all be laughing about this shit. We're not going to let anyone fuck with us."

CHAPTER 3

PENNY CARSON SENSED THAT SOMEONE HAD JUST ENTERED HER office even before she heard the doorknob bump gently against the wall. She lifted her hands from the keyboard of her computer and leaned back in her chair, using just her index finger to clear the screen. She had always felt uncomfortable when people peered over her shoulder, no matter what she was working on, and right now she didn't want anyone to know what she was doing on her own time. She checked her watch—almost seventeen-thirty, definitely her own time—before turning around.

"You ought to be more careful, Penny," Randolph Wallace scolded playfully, displaying a warm, friendly smile. He was leaning against the door, his arms folded. "Never can tell what kind of weirdos hang out in the Pentagon after hours." Wallace certainly wasn't weird looking. He was in his mid-forties, slightly thinning brown hair, slightly overweight, his round face a bit jowly, his features nondescript, average enough for a deskbound lifer. The uniform was a definite asset.

She grinned back. "You've told me that before, Colonel."

"Randy. Always Randy after sixteen hundred." He liked that smile because he could forget her uniform and imagine her in something sexy. "Save that colonel crap for meetings."

"Right. Randy," she agreed, pronouncing his name carefully. "It takes time to remember those things after a hard day at the office."

"You said it, Penny, not me. Too many hard days at the office aren't good for a lovely lady like you. How about a drink? Not an invitation from your boss, though, but one from Randolph Wallace, who'd enjoy the company of an attractive lady before he heads to home and hearth alone."

Randolph Wallace was a new bachelor—a happy, aggressive one, according to the other women she'd talked with since coming to the Pentagon two months before. When he was going through the separation, they said he was horny but couldn't afford to do anything about it as long as lawyers were involved. But once his divorce was final, he apparently became a new man, setting his sights on any single woman who looked at him.

She smiled politely and cocked her head to one side. "You are persistent. I'll give you that." Every other day he seemed to invite her somewhere, and it never appeared to bother him when she turned him down. "If I didn't need to keep on at this machine now that I've got up a head of steam, I'd sail out the door with you right now." She'd been thinking all day about accepting one of his invitations, simply because she was sure there was something special about the Potter case and she would need some favors, but then she always hated herself for considering that approach.

"How about a rain check?" she said. "Tomorrow night? I'd love a drink now, and thinking about it for twenty-four hours will make it even better tomorrow evening. How about that?" She wasn't sure she wanted to date a man his age who probably had kids who weren't much younger than she was, nor was she especially interested in a man who was her superior officer, but her rank didn't seem to bother Lieutenant Colonel Wallace. So screw it. Take advantage of the horny bastard and hope he wasn't the type to get into rough stuff. It would be twice as hard to get the old files out of the vault if he dug in his heels and pressured her for sex.

His mouth turned down at the corners in a sad clown face. "I am so sad. I must drink alone tonight." Then he grinned. "But I am also so happy because tomorrow at this time I will have a lovely lady by my side. It's a done deal, Penny." He ambled over beside her chair and glanced at the blank computer screen. "What's got you so interested?"

"Just some ideas I've been playing with. Nothing to do with normal office routine. That's why I'm on Penny Carson's time now rather than the army's."

His eyes skimmed the papers on her desk. "Then it's none of my business. I don't pay much attention to what my people are doing unless they ask. I'm a trusting guy. I didn't even look at that chit your clerk brought down today—just signed it and assumed you were doing good for the army." He turned toward the door, then looked back over his shoulder. "Hey, I hope you're not just trying to be nice, that you're not going out with another guy after I leave." He nodded at her computer. "Screen's blank, as if you were closing up shop."

"Honest. I was just about to call something else up when you came in. All work, no play. Believe me."

Wallace glanced at his watch. "Seventeen-thirty tomorrow."

"It's a date. Want me to go home and change into civvies first?"

"Negative on that. We'll go to the officers' club at the fort." Maybe he could talk her into dinner, then take her back to her place to change. "Don't work too late, now," he called back as he went out the door.

"Cheap," Penny murmured to herself. Randy Wallace was eager to relive his bachelor days, but he wanted to do it on happy-hour prices.

She turned back to the computer to call up the dates of death for the other men from Danny Potter's company who had been killed in action. She knew Leila's brother had died on July 2, 1969, somewhere near the Iron Triangle. She studied the names on the screen.

McTavish, Michael, Private First Class, USA: 6/30/69. He had died a few days before Danny Potter.

Ledbetter, Paul James, Captain, USA: 7/7/69. That was only five days after Danny Potter.

Williams, Franklin Roosevelt, Corporal, USA: 7/15/69. Three days after.

Arison, Alfred William, Private, USA: 7/21/69. Almost three weeks later.

Gonzalez, Felix, Private, USA: 9/2/69. Exactly nine weeks later.

Santucci, Geraldo Vincente, Corporal, USA: 9/21/69 was the date he was listed as MIA.

Kelley, Edwin Antonio, Lieutenant, USA: 9/21/69. Odd! No matter how she considered it, that was strange. Two men from the same platoon—Kelley and Santucci were both listed as missing in action on the same date. The same firefight? Maybe it was just an error. She'd have to research that later.

Walters, Hastings, and Burns—all three victims of accidents?

Corey and Burris were all listed as KIA within a month after Santucci and Kelley were MIA.

Perhaps it would be worthwhile to do a little digging. Most such cases led nowhere. But who could tell? She had liked Leila from the first moment and wanted to help her if she could. She started to make notes on a yellow legal pad:

1. Bring up data on other units of Army's II Field Force in that region and representative units involved in combat operations in other regions at that time.

2. Compare number of combat deaths in region during period to similar situations. Note—especially so many from same platoon over such a short period of time. Check history of unit firefight. Note—probably need to research causes of death if I'm going to be accurate.

3. Dig up other unit histories broken down to the platoon level, if possible. Those histories are supposed to cover every hour of operations during the units' existence in-country.

4. Decide how you're going to con Wallace into giving you access to the vault without answering too many questions, if that ends up being the best source.

5. Santucci and Kelley—don't forget to verify MIA dates. Important!

6. While you're thinking, Carson, why don't you learn why Captain Ledbetter's company—or perhaps more important, Lieutenant Kelley's platoon— took such a beating in such a short time. Maybe there's a logical reason. Who knows?

Leila searched through her purse for the key card to get into her hotel room. Why the hell didn't they provide the nice jangly keys that you couldn't miss when you were going down to the lobby for a drink or dinner? She hated to admit her stupidity, but she was sure exactly where the card was—in the small bag of items she'd picked up earlier at the drugstore in the Crystal City Mall below the Marriott. Her arms had been full when she pushed open the door, and she'd dropped the card into the bag because she didn't have a third hand to open her purse. And that was where that goddamn card still was, in that bag sitting on the vanity by the sink. Damn!

She took the elevator back down to the lobby and explained her predicament to the desk clerk. In moments, she was on her way back up in the elevator with the bell captain, who explained in painful detail how it was now his responsibility to assure the night manager that the missing key card had been located and that it had not been stolen. He hoped that it was exactly where she claimed.

The bell captain held the door open for Leila as he flipped the light switch. "The night manager's pretty new, ma'am, and he's touchy about those cards. He really wants us to account for each one. Where'd you say you left it?"

"In the bathroom, in a paper bag of things I picked up at

the pharmacy when I came back at the end of the day. I'll get it."

Leila saw the shadow move just as she reached for the light switch in the bathroom. Her first scream came at the same time her knees buckled. Perhaps her reaction was a combination of fear and instinct. Whatever, she remembered later that her eye had caught a flash in the darkness as she was falling. At the same instant she heard a sharp ripping sound in the wall behind her, and this was followed instantaneously by a second flash. There was no loud noise, no explosion, she would explain later, although she did hear sounds, strange ones, like the splat of an egg landing on a hard surface. She was showered with plaster splinters from the wall behind her before she hit the floor.

Leila was aware of someone charging out of the bathroom, tripping over her legs.

"Miss . . ." she heard the bell captain call out. Then there was a terrified shout—"No!"—followed by an agonized cry.

She heard footsteps running down the hallway.

"Who . . ." Oh, God, she thought. . . .

She rolled over and looked up at the wall. Two distinct jagged holes, one slightly lower than the other, had torn through the imitation grass wallpaper and shattered the plaster. Oh, God . . .

"Are you still there?" she called to the bell captain.

There was no answer.

Leila's whole body began to shake uncontrollably as she rose to her feet. She put out a steadying hand as she moved back into the main room hoping against hope that the bell captain was still there. She glanced about tentatively. Then the screams began to roll from deep inside her chest.

The bell captain was sprawled on his back across her bed, arms spread wide. The top of his head just above his eyes was torn away, and the explosive force of the bullet had splattered a gory mess across the bedspread.

Doors opened in the hallway as people reacted to Leila's screams, but no one came into the room.

It was almost a full minute before a hotel security guard

arrived. He searched the room with a drawn gun, assuring himself there was no further danger, before putting his arm around the woman who was still standing in the middle of the room, eyes now tightly shut, too exhausted to scream or cry.

Edwin Antonio Kelley had long ago successfully shaken his roots, a personal goal secretly set on his sixteenth birthday.

His father had survived the Irish-rough streets of South Boston with a persistence that went well beyond his mental abilities. Eddie's mother, on the other hand, had lived the sheltered life of a treasured daughter protected by an Italian society that had been transported without change from the old country to Boston's North End. When they married, to the displeasure of both families, they found no welcome in either culture, so they sought a home on neutral ground.

Mattapan was becoming a melting pot as their only son, Edwin, grew up, changing from Jewish to Kelley-like blends and eventually to mostly black. A bright kid like Ed Kelley realized at an early age that the area offered him nothing. It was the type of place to leave behind.

Ed was smart enough to get into Boston College, aided by a combination of his parish priest's contacts and his rough and sometimes brutal hockey ability. He was no genius, but he worked hard to stay in college for one good reason: blacks, city kids, and those who flunked out of college were being drafted for cannon fodder for the war in Vietnam. It didn't take an excess of intelligence for Kelley to join the ROTC unit in college. If the war persisted until he graduated, he wanted some influence on just how he was going.

When Ed arrived in Vietnam in early 1969, he discovered that he had two advantages. One of them was a latent talent—an ability to learn languages and an especially good ear for the tonal nuances of Asiatic speech. He found that by watching Asian people speak he could use their physical presence, their hands, their body language, but especially their expressions to help him understand what they were saying. While dialects were more complex, he simply adapted as best he could and was pleased that people appreciated the fact that he was speaking their language at all. He never bothered to learn the written language, knowing that one day he could hire someone to do the writing for him.

The second advantage was of more immediate value to him: Ed Kelley had always been lucky—lucky because he was a better-than-average athlete, was bright enough to know at an early age that he wanted to get out of Mattapan, and had the ability to consistently surround himself with people who would help him get ahead. And he never doubted that his luckiest day was his first day in Vietnam before he was sent out to his unit. He was in the rooftop bar of a Saigon hotel when he met the man who would make him rich.

The conversation was casual, friendly, two lonely strangers drinking at a bar. It was dark out, and Kelley had commented on the bright flashes in the distance toward the Cambodian border as he spoke to the man on the stool beside him without really thinking about what he was saying.

"Our B-52s. Softening up something for an attack at first light. If the bombings are in support of U.S. troops, our guys won't find anything out there but huge craters. The VC'll disappear. But if it's for an ARVN operation, those guys'll surer 'n hell be ambushed. The VC can smell the difference between U.S. and ARVN."

"No kidding," Kelley responded with a note of surprise.

"No kidding," was the answer. The man turned on his stool and said good-naturedly, "I was trying to figure if you were lucky enough to be completing your tour or dumb enough to be starting it. You've already told me. You just arrived, didn't you?"

"You got it. What's so dumb about that?"

"That depends. You going to be in a support activity or a target?"

"Target."

"Five hundred bucks a month and all the bullets you can eat," the other man commented with a short laugh. "You need another beer, kid. As a matter of fact, if you're going to spend the next twelve months being a target, you need as many beers as you can swallow, and they're all on me tonight."

Ed Kelley had been able to spot the smart guys since he was a kid on the Mattapan streets. This was a smart guy. He could feel it. It was just a matter of feeling him out, and if this guy was willing to buy him beers Kelley was going to find out what his deal was. There was always a deal with these guys.

"Edwin Kelley." He stuck out his hand. "Soon to be a first lieutenant and hopefully not a target."

His slender hand was shaken by a much larger one. "Hugh Young. I hope you're not a target either, Eddie." He studied the young man who looked like an Ivy Leaguer except for the old-country Italian features, and Italian except for his startlingly blue eyes. "Somehow you look too wise to be one."

Young was a burly man, a little under six feet, like Kelley, but much heavier. He looked like a football player, thick neck, broad shoulders that seemed ready to pop the seams on his short-sleeved white shirt. He had a slight belly that covered his belt, but he wasn't really fat, just big all over. His tanned arms were well muscled, and he moved like an athlete whenever he left his stool for the toilet that night. He had close-cropped blond hair, blue eyes, and a steady grin that attracted a regular flow of appealing Vietnamese women, all of whom called him by his first name. More important to Ed Kelley were the gold rings set with huge diamonds on Young's little fingers and the cascade of gold chains around his neck. The man reeked of money. He obviously enjoyed displaying it as much as he did spending it.

First beer. "You in the military?" Eddie asked, knowing that would be the last place for a man like this.

"Civilian. Came over with the Company."

"Oh, a hot-shit spook." Eddie knew that was a term for the CIA. People never mentioned the agency's name.

"I was, until I decided who was going to win the war." Hugh Young explained that he'd been recruited out of college by the Agency, even before there was an American presence in Vietnam. It was exciting to be involved with the CIA when you weren't interested in graduate school or a job wearing a dull tie and a gray suit. He'd gone to Europe first, then volunteered for Asiatic duty when Kennedy authorized additional advisers for the Saigon government.

Second beer. "I didn't know you could write your own ticket in that business," Ed said.

"Only if you know the right people. It's no different from any other job. It's not what you know, Eddie. It's who you know."

"What place did you like best?"

"That's easy. Vientiane."

"Never heard of it."

"Great place. Gorgeous." Vientiane was the capital of Laos. The CIA called Laos "the other theater," Hugh Young explained. That was a war separate from Vietnam, a thousand-year war, but Hanoi had become involved. The U.S. objective was the same in both theaters, keep the communists from winning Southeast Asia, stop the domino effect at its source, keep the tide from rising.

Third beer. "I had no idea anything was going on up there," Kelley commented innocently. But he'd seen Young's jewelry and he'd heard that there was money to be made in the opium trade that flourished in Laos.

"You never heard of the Ravens either, did you?"

Kelley shook his head.

"They were part of my work up there. We were called the CAS, for Controlled American Source. The Ravens were U.S. pilots who got bored with the everyday shit down here. Those guys wanted action. They're a different breed . . . a different breed," he repeated wistfully.

"Being a target down here wasn't good enough for them. These guys disappeared from the world—what we called getting sheep-dipped. They gave up all military IDs, anything that would identify them as Americans, even signed resignation papers, although they'd still be eligible for promotions when they came back to the world. The only form I ever saw that meant anything was the form they signed to designate where the body should be sent in the event of . . ." Young shrugged. "We even had to set up our own insurance company to pay off the survivors' benefits so they couldn't be traced back to the air force. We had our own name for the operation—called it the Steve Canyon Program."

Young was enjoying his captive audience, chuckling to himself as he talked about the Ravens and watching the naive blue eyes widen in awe. The CIA operated the war against the communists in Laos, running it out of their station in Vientiane, he explained. The Ravens flew flimsy single-engine aircraft, spotting targets for air or artillery strikes, flying down the enemy's throat with little regard for their own safety. Young men like Hugh Young commuted between the capital and Long Tieng, the Ravens' secret base and the headquarters for General Vang Pao, the Laotian general who led the battle against the communist forces.

Fourth beer. Kelley shook his head in wonder. "I had no idea. Secret bases and everything. You only read about things like that in James Bond books."

"That's right. It was a great army that Vang Pao had. They were Meo tribesmen, right out of the mountains, so far removed from the real world that some of them would look under the planes to see what sex they were. They were also some of the fiercest soldiers I've ever seen. They were tough, disciplined, and mean as hell, and . . ."

Kelley had been watching Young and when the man dropped his eyes and hesitated, he prodded, "You were going to say something else."

"I was going to say they were an army that was well paid. But it really wasn't that so much. It was just that they never lacked for money. They were entirely financed by opium." Young looked up from the bar and caught Kelley's eyes to make sure his point had been made. It had. He'd been right when he'd seen Kelley walk into the bar. This kid was no dummy. It wasn't likely he'd accept becoming cannon fodder.

"Go on," Kelley said quietly.

Young stared down at the rings on his pinky fingers,

turning them so the diamonds caught the light, before he went on with his tale. The Laotians were sophisticated as hell when it came to growing the poppy and turning the by-product into high-grade opium. But the old-fashioned distribution system that had been aided by the French, especially the Corsicans, was deteriorating as revolution and bloodshed consumed Southeast Asia.

Fifth beer. "You know," Young began after he came back from a trip to the men's room, "I don't work for the Agency anymore. I think I told you that."

"You did."

"There was too much opportunity elsewhere. You know," he offered quietly, almost in a whisper, "the CIA had to set up systems to help Vang Pao. He had a war to fight. The product had to be moved to market." He shrugged almost apologetically. "We had no choice but to help for a while because we owned the aircraft. And it wouldn't have made sense to run the money through a regular bank. Someone would have wanted a bite out of it. It was really important to establish a reliable support system."

"Certainly," Kelley agreed, anxious not to interrupt the other man's story now that the alcohol was obviously taking effect.

There were people who'd once worked for the Company, Hugh Young explained, people on the periphery who'd worked on a contingency fee basis, and always those few who made a decent living by arranging introductions—all of them were anxious to help out. Hugh Young was certain after working in Vientiane for almost two years on a government salary that he would never be a good Company man, just as he knew before he graduated from college that the normal business world wasn't for him.

Sixth beer. "I was right, you know," Young said to Kelley. "My boss agreed with me and indicated his seniors did also. So we parted friends." He winked knowingly. "I believe we're even better friends today. I'm able to provide services which they desire, without their becoming involved."

"Sounds interesting," Kelley ventured, "like something I'd like to get involved with . . . when I get out."

"If you don't leave in a body bag, Eddie."

"I'll tell you two things about me that might interest you, Hugh. First, I'm willing to do almost anything—no, not almost . . . anything—to stay out of a body bag. Second, I'm not going home. I knew that before I came here." He was feeling the beer, the tiredness in his body after the flight halfway around the world, and the fear that came when a man's hopes for a long and happy life were on the line.

"Eddie, I've had a sense for some time now that my luck just wasn't going to quit. It hasn't, either," he stated with finality. "I don't know if you're aware of it, but I think you're one lucky son of a bitch, and I'm going to make sure of it. But all that comes later. Tonight you need a girl. Which one do you like?" Hugh Young's hand swept around to indicate any woman in the bar.

"All of them."

"Come on, Eddie." He punched Kelley in the shoulder playfully. "You should be more discriminating."

"I've never had an Asian girl, Hugh. I just came in today."

"Okay. I'll grant you that. You're new at the game, and you have to catch up." He pointed at two of the Vietnamese women and indicated that they should come over. "You're going to start with two tonight. By tomorrow morning you'll know why you'll never want to go back to Boston."

Ed Kelley couldn't believe his luck, but it wasn't the prospect of the two women that fascinated him. It was finding Hugh Young. The burly ex-CIA man was looking for someone, testing the waters just as Kelley was, and Ed Kelley had no intention of remaining a target for the next twelve months.

Colonel Randolph Wallace propped himself on an elbow and placed the telephone back on its cradle, then relaxed and fell onto his back, pulling the bedcovers up to his chest in the same motion. The light on the bedside table was still on. He steepled his fingers, staring at barely discernible wisps of cobwebs on the ceiling that seemed to float on drafts of air that he was unable to sense.

His former wife had been correct about one thing—the

bitch. His past would come back to haunt him, and now it had. In their early years of marriage, after he'd returned from Vietnam, she'd been more than willing to go along with him when they bought their first home. It had been elegant for a man on a captain's pay, and she never minded lying to people—telling them that they lived on Randy's salary and bought their goodies with money she had inherited from her aunt. It was easy for her to say that because for once in her life she was able to live the way she'd always dreamed. If Randy Wallace could give her the good life, she didn't give a damn where his money came from.

When they were stationed in Germany, they were able to travel extensively, but unlike other military personnel, the Wallaces stayed in first-class hotels and dined in four-star restaurants. Randy had a Mercedes shipped back when they received orders to return to the States. In San Antonio, which she at first assumed was the end of the world, their home was more elegant than the commanding general's. Back in Washington, they purchased a town house in Georgetown that had once been famous as the site of the ultimate society functions of the winter season. There was never a reason to have children; they would have interfered with a life that seemed to have emerged from the pages of a book.

But it wasn't his wife's rich aunt who had financed their comfortable life. It was Randy Wallace's past. His wife's teasing about that past eventually graduated to nagging and finally to outright taunting. She grew bored with him. She'd met too many other men who had even more money and lived a much more gracious life outside the military. At the end she and Randy couldn't stand each other. He had to remain in the army; he knew nothing else, and he was controlled by men who had bought his soul. His wife, hating the army a little more each day, had grown accustomed to another world. Randy Wallace had no alternative.

Even halfway around the world—night in Washington, but morning in Bangkok—the telephone connection had been so clear that Wallace imagined Ed Kelley's voice was what had made the cobwebs dance above him. "You saved the day when you called me about that picture, Randy. I can't tell you how close that fucking Major Joslin was to blowing the whistle. But I'm sure there have to be other copies. Your photo intelligence people in the Pentagon can do magic these days with their equipment, can't they?" It was a question that wasn't a question. Kelley knew what they could do.

Wallace nodded to himself. Of course they could. That was how they had determined that photo was no fake. That was why a major rather than a lieutenant had been sent out to that village. The word had already come back from the embassy in Bangkok that the major was missing along with his interpreter and the man who'd first brought the photo to their attention. All three of them had disappeared.

No bodies had been found. No vehicle. Not a trace. And the local authorities had yet to come up with anything. They were ready to dismiss it as another unfortunate attack by local bandits or perhaps by thugs from the drug cartel in the highlands. But the embassy wasn't about to let them off that easily because this time certain individuals in the Pentagon were sure they had a lead on an American MIA. The Pentagon also had just what Kelley was sure they had— multiple copies of his photograph. Wallace also knew they'd called in the Defense Intelligence Agency, which served as the intelligence analysis section for all POW-MIA incidents.

Wallace tried to reason with Kelley. "You didn't think taking that major out was going to solve your problems, did you?"

"I hadn't seen the photo until I found it on that major. That's why I'm calling now."

"I did what I'm paid for, Ed. I've stayed right here. I've kept my eyes and ears open. This isn't the first time I've saved necks over there. I'm not sure what more I can do."

"You can make sure every one of those photos, every fucking copy, is destroyed, Randy." The connection was perfect. Kelley's voice increased in intensity. Wallace remembered Kelley's temper—"the wrath of a blue-eyed Italian," he called it. "Every last fucking copy." The cobwebs appeared to dance with each word, as if Kelley's breath came through the receiver and climbed to the ceiling for the specific purpose of unnerving Randy Wallace.

"I have no idea how many copies there are or who has them."

"Don't bullshit me, Randy. The army never changes. When copies were made, some photo technician kept a detailed record of who got each print. The army doesn't know how to circulate something like that without a distribution list. For Christ's sake, Randy, you know and I know that some asshole in the army can probably tell the Chairman of the Joint Chiefs how many rolls of toilet paper are in inventory. Hell, they probably know how many yards of the stuff are being crunched together right this minute to serve their purpose in life. So don't even think about telling me you can't find out how many copies there are."

"Right," Wallace answered with resignation.

"And the same goes for who has those copies. Every single, last one. I want an accounting. Get that distribution list. More than likely, if this is as important as you say, that list probably even requires a signature or initials or something like that. Why the fuck do you think we've been paying you so well the last twenty years?"

Randy Wallace stared at the ceiling and thought about Kelley's final words. Oh, how the cobwebs had danced.

And how right that bitch had been. Randy Wallace leaned over and turned out the bedside light so he wouldn't have to watch those cobwebs dance to Ed Kelley's tune.

Jerry Santucci would learn years later that his introduction to Vietnam was nothing like Ed Kelley's. The only similarity was that he arrived at Ton Son Hut in a jumbo jet. But he, like Danny Potter, was a buck-ass private. Their platoon sergeant, returning for his second tour, never let them forget it. If there was anything between their ears other than sawdust, and if they wanted to stay alive for the next twelve months, they had no choice but to listen to Sergeant Buckminster, do exactly as he ordered, don't volunteer for anything unless he volunteered for them, and move their muscles only when he directed.

Their plane landed on a hot, steamy morning. By the time they hiked over to an unair-conditioned hangar, they were all soaking wet, and they sweltered under that tin roof until their papers were processed and half a dozen trucks pulled up to transport them to their units.

It seemed at first like back home, but their truck was soon off the hard surface of the old meandering Route 1, and they were bouncing on the wooden benches in the rear of the vehicle. The trip to their destination northwest of Saigon was a mercifully short two hours.

They knew they had arrived when the truck halted briefly and they heard other American voices. Then they were moving again, and they saw from the back that they had just passed through a gate, or at least they saw GIs rolling back barbed wire that might have resembled a gate. From there they saw vast yards of concertinalike barbed wire stretched out on either side of the road, and they would soon learn that it surrounded the camp, along with an array of fighting trenches. They would also find out that there were mine-fields beyond the wire.

The remainder of the day involved issuing bedding, weapons, ammunition, and other necessities of life for a buck private arriving in-country. Then they were assigned to tents grouped near the center of the compound. The one thing that did appeal to Jerry Santucci that evening was the chow. The food in base camps, especially those situated in "Indian country," was transported in by helicopter whenever possible and the cooks made sure that it was hot, that it tasted good, and that there was plenty of it. He'd later learned that good chow was considered essential by headquarters for men who might be eating their last meal, and by cooks who were sure that the continual production of good food would keep them in the base camp rather than on patrol.

None of the new men were assigned to perimeter guard duty or patrol that first night. But by the time the first rays of sun appeared the next morning, Jerry Santucci knew he was not going to survive as a private for the next twelve months. A patrol of six men had been ambushed less than a mile outside the camp. The sounds had been clearly audible—automatic weapons and grenades. It was all over in less than half a minute, and it had been terrifying to fresh-caught buck-ass privates. There were no survivors.

Later that night a mortar attack included a direct hit on one of the tents containing new men. Four were dead, three badly wounded, and the medics said one would be a quadriplegic if he lived. Santucci, like everyone else, had spent the remainder of the night in a wet foxhole waiting for an attack that never came.

Even though Sergeant Buckminster pointed out the next morning at roll call that the medevac helicopters had airlifted the wounded to a full-service hospital less than thirty minutes after the attack, Jerry Santucci remained firm in his commitment to himself—twelve months was too long. Even twelve days would be more than he cared for, but he had yet to learn how to solve his dilemma.

CHAPTER 4

THE FLIGHT FROM HONG KONG TO SINGAPORE WAS ENTIRELY over water, the South China Sea, and with nothing to look at but an occasional freighter Hugh Young usually slept most of the way. His preference was the afternoon flight. That brought him into Changi Airport well rested.

His regular chauffeur, Suraban, was waiting for him as usual when the blond, burly American cleared customs. "Welcome to you, Mr. Young." Suraban, an unusually tall combination of the many races inhabiting the island nation, greeted him with a smile and tipped his chauffeur's cap. He wore a short-sleeved white shirt and light blue slacks to accommodate the hot tropical weather. "I so pleased to see you again," he said, carefully enunciating each word.

Suraban thought the world revolved around Hugh Young. Not only did his tips add up to half of Suraban's yearly salary but the big American insisted on sitting in the front seat with him. The result was exactly as Hugh expected. The chauffeur refused to say a word about his favorite customer's stops or the people he met for business purposes, even when a client of Young's once offered Suraban an enormous payoff. Suraban was also vitally aware of that particular client's unfortunate passing soon after Young learned of the indiscretion.

"What are we driving today, Suraban?" Young asked pleasantly as they emerged from the main building. He truly believed that the car made the man, especially a Caucasian man, in Asian eyes, and he carefully selected the vehicles in which Inchar employees, even the nonwhites, traveled on business.

"The Phaeton, Mr. Young, your favorite. I make sure it was put aside when I hear you're coming to Singapore." It was Suraban's favorite also because sometimes Young insisted on driving it and then his chauffeur rode proudly in the passenger seat.

The silver vehicle was parked directly outside in a No Resting, Official Vehicles Only zone, and it was jealously guarded by a police officer who tipped his cap to Young as Suraban held open his door. "Welcome to Singapore, Mr. Young," the policeman said with a slight inclination of his head.

The drive down East Coast Parkway was always a pleasant one. Young sometimes had Suraban stop at the park to watch the young girls come down the huge water slide in their bikinis. The two men had great fun commenting on the perilous flights down the slide, especially if there was a chance that a bikini top might come loose.

The first time Hugh Young ever saw Singapore was from the sea. That vision remained etched in his mind. It had been the final stop on a cruise he'd taken with a lovely young lady, and he'd risen early to watch the city as the ship entered the harbor. It was as impressive as Hong Kong, if not more.

Singapore radiated power. It could have been New York or Chicago he was seeing with all those modern buildings punctuated by a skyscaper displaying the giant blue IBM logo. Hundreds of ships lay at anchor waiting their turn to offload or pick up cargo.

Hugh Young remembered the rush of ideas that had flooded his mind that first day as he realized the limitless possibilities of Singapore. To think how impressed he and

Eddie and Jerry had been years before when drugs brought in such easy money. Today they were no longer limited by the needs of the user community. He smiled to himself now, realizing he'd been unconsciously nodding his head in agreement with that resolution of their board of directors soon after he offered his detailed expansion plans more than eight years before.

Singapore would be perfect. It had been agreed upon unanimously that even though the opium and high-grade heroin business continued to experience a tremendous growth spurt, hard drugs were not a business for Inchar to invest in over the long-term. International Charities, Ltd., should concentrate their total energies on isolating new international markets with long-term growth potential. The time had come to allow their initial seed business to die gracefully. There was no intention of instantly cutting off the attractive cash flow. That would be irrational. It was simply wise to plan for the future.

Even from the water, he'd known—Singapore! It would be his second city. And his board of directors agreed, as long as the cash rolled in and their retainers increased each year. They knew that they'd been selected by International Charities, Ltd., to establish contacts for the company, and they also understood that Hugh Young had been aware of their weaknesses long before he invited them to bring their expertise to the board.

The broad streets of Singapore welcomed any individual with a purpose—citizen, business traveler, or tourist: "Bring money. Any currency will do. Bring dollars, pounds, pesetas, kopeks, lire, marks, yen." Those streets radiated a vibrant personality unlike that of any other city he'd ever seen. "Bring money," they said, "for that's what our city thrives on." And Singapore did thrive.

The wide, clean, tree-lined sidewalks teemed with people of all races rushing about the business of enhancing Singapore's economy. Gleaming skyscrapers housed international corporations that had turned Singapore into the financial capital of Asia, second only to Hong Kong, and those moneymen waited for 1997 when Beijing would take over that British island. Singapore's deep natural harbor allowed it to aspire to become the trade and shipping center of the world before the end of the century. Elegant shopping centers around wealthy Orchard Street housed boutiques ranging from Benetton to Gucci, and shoppers could dine in sidewalk cafés and sleep the night away in the finest international hotels in the world. Singapore was synonymous with wealth.

If there was one aspect of the city Hugh Young appreciated more than any other, it was the universal respect for law and order. Even though most of the police were in civilian clothes, their presence was felt everywhere. There was no jaywalking. Traffic laws were stringently enforced and obeyed. No vehicles entered the downtown area without a special registration. Hardly anyone smoked in public because the government said it was bad for their health, and that declaration was reinforced by heavy fines for disposing of a cigarette in the street. And finally, drugs were almost unknown because the law was tough and swift—up to ten years in prison for possession, death for selling the more dangerous drugs.

What better example for the board of International Charities? Hugh had told them that someday even the United States might realize that tough laws were the solution to the drug problem. Singapore was a city where citizens respected each other's rights because the government ordained that they should. Young appreciated that. Fear was an excellent means of solving behavior problems.

The Phaeton carried a special registration, and Suraban drove Young to the front of the Dynasty, a hotel he considered as elegant as Hong Kong's Peninsula. As the doorman stood back for him to get out, the day manager appeared by the side of the car. "Mr. Young, welcome back to the Dynasty," he oozed, flashing a toothy smile." All of us are so pleased to have you visit with us again." The Dynasty catered to the wealthy, but no one tipped like Hugh Young, and no one's name was remembered so well by so many employees.

Young shook the proffered hand and made a mental note

to remind the Dynasty's managing director once again that he appreciated the intent but preferred not to be greeted so effusively in public. The years had changed his appearance as they had that of the others, but there was still the off chance that someday a hotel manager or headwaiter would be dripping all over him when an old acquaintance, maybe a case officer from the Company or even one of those crazy bastards from his days at Long Tien, would notice and say, "My God, Hugh Young! I thought you were dead all these years. Won't everyone be surprised?" As far as he was concerned, there was no "back home." There was Hong Kong, and there was the rest of Asia. His past no longer existed.

Young always took the suite on the top floor of the Dynasty because of the exquisite view of the harbor. It was said that a ship lifted or dropped anchor in Singapore every fifteen minutes throughout the year, and now some of those vessels actually belonged to Inchar Seaboard, one of many International Charities subsidiaries, and carried products from Inchar companies around the world. He never tired of seeing his original vision of Singapore take shape.

The bar was stocked with his favorite beer, Bangkok's Singha, and he drank an ice-cold bottle as he sat before his suite's expanse of windows in his shorts. No liquor tonight. No Mr. Jack with Yuan. No hard stuff. This wasn't Japan.

This evening was very special, the reason for stopping in Singapore before he went on to Jakarta. He'd invited the island nation's finance minister to join him for dinner. If he'd been dining with a friend, he would have gone out in a short-sleeved white shirt and slacks. But tonight called for a bit more formality. The sun was setting behind Jurong Park when he knotted his Thai silk tie before the floor-to-ceiling mirror and slipped on the jacket of his cream-colored suit.

As he stepped off the elevator into the lobby, Young recognized the same surge of pleasure he always experienced in the Orient when he dressed for dinner. It was in the stares of the people, mostly smaller Orientals, whose expressive eyes acknowledged that he appeared twice as big in the cream suit. It had been custom-fitted in Bangkok by Ed Kelley's personal tailor.

Over the years, Young had been able to hold his weight reasonably well because he could afford the private health clubs that helped to balance his love of good food and drink. He'd lost little of his still blond hair and few lines creased his tanned face. "You are a picture of health," he'd said aloud to his reflection in the mirror before leaving the suite.

The Dynasty is home to one of the most elegant lobbies in Southeast Asia, one that rises four stories from the polished marble floor. The subdued lighting is punctuated by immense chandeliers, themselves two stories high, suspended from the dark wooden ceiling. The walls are set off with polished teak panels carved with ancient stories that tell of another era. There is a lounge area to the left of the lobby as one enters the hotel. Plush chairs and sofas are set up around low glass tables where cocktails and refreshing tropical drinks are served by lovely Malay women in long native gowns.

Mr. Yuan was already sipping a glass of fruit punch when Hugh Young made his appearance. He greeted Yuan warmly, asked for the same thing the other gentleman was drinking, and spent the next half hour in small talk discussing the affairs of the world. It was impolite in that part of the world to launch into business immediately. That was a good deal of the reason they had essentially agreed on almost everything by phone before Young had left Hong Kong. It was a way of doing business that made both sides comfortable, especially when such a deal cut across differing cultures.

It was exactly eight o'clock when a maître d' in tuxedo approached, bowed respectfully to Mr. Yuan, shook Young's hand, and announced, "Your table is ready now. Would you care to order here or in the dining room?"

Young knew that Yuan had been waiting all day to savor the wines that he avoided in public. He thoroughly enjoyed the privacy of the Dynasty's exquisite French dining room. "We'll come with you, Jacques," he said, rising from his chair. "I hope you have a couple of bottles of my Cheval Blanc ready."

"Of course, Mr. Young. You're drinking the 'sixty-six now. You finished the last of the 'fifty-nine on your previous visit."

"Of course." It was exactly what he'd intended Mr. Yuan to hear.

Yuan was beaming as they were seated at a table in the far corner where few people would notice him dining with the big American, and he could enjoy some of the finest French wine in the world. Hugh Young felt that the Vendôme Restaurant in the Dynasty was the equal of Gaddi's in Hong Kong's Peninsula. But either French restaurant was perfect when you were solidifying a deal with an important government official. Young directed that the second bottle of Cheval Blanc be opened when they were seated to ensure that it would be ready for drinking when the main course was served.

Mr. Yuan was totally relaxed. "The other day when I attended a meeting in the prime minister's suite someone asked me if I thought there were indigenous companies better able to assist us with your project on Batam Island." He took a bite of rack of lamb, chewed thoughtfully for a moment before sipping his wine, then smiled as he inhaled deeply from the glass. "I told him that Inchar was as much a Singapore company as any other. You have incorporated here, constructed a number of buildings using local companies, even purchased the beginnings of your fleet through Singapore merchants."

Young nodded, indicating to the hovering waiter that he should refill Yuan's glass. "What has been accomplished on Batam Island to date is indicative of Singapore's financial strength. The combination of your offices and our entrepreneurial knowledge should create the greatest manufacturing center in this part of the world. I think you can tell your friend that we really do consider ourselves a Singapore company. I sincerely mean that. But our success can continue only through the strength of your government. Time is our only apparent enemy. That's why I plan to go on to

Jakarta tomorrow, with your permission, to explain the labor needs we anticipate."

The Batam Island Project was established by the government of Singapore in conjunction with the Indonesian government. That Malacca Strait island was chosen to become an example of how international cooperation on the Pacific Rim could establish new businesses, provide jobs, and create profits that would allow the poorer nations to compete with the Japanese and Koreans.

Singapore would provide the money and start-up management, and Indonesia would provide the labor. The cost of manufacturing was targeted at 25 percent below world scale, and there was room on the island for as many as three hundred industries. Hugh Young had recognized years before that Singapore needed corporations like Inchar to make Batam Island a financial success.

Mr. Yuan was an economist, not an industrialist, and he'd been easily convinced after his first meeting with Young four years earlier that the big blond man knew what he was talking about. After all, the financial statements of Inchar's parent company showed an extremely heavy cash position, and Inchar was anxious to invest. Yuan had committed his government's support to Young and Inchar, even to the point of inviting Young to his home often, once to meet with the prime minister. "You asked me to call Jakarta, and I already have. They're looking forward to your visit. However, I was unable to explain why you were so concerned about the time element. Everything will get done. The people in Jakarta know you well enough now."

Most of the important people in the Indonesian government either did know Hugh Young already or were aware of him, but he still did not have the entrée to the president's office that he desired. Now, without saying so directly, Yuan had just said that the deal was done, and personal contact was the means. If Yuan had made that call to Jakarta, the capital of the island nation, then the Singapore government had agreed, and that meant the Indonesian government was already involved.

There was no sensation quite like knowing that an entire

nation's government had acceded to your wishes. No, it wasn't quite that. The Indonesians hadn't acquiesced from their vantage point; they'd made a deal that benefited both parties. But now let them try to get rid of Inchar.

One more government, Indonesia. One more contact, which Yuan had apparently set up for him. And eventually Inchar would have access to a vital segment of Southeast Asia's capital base.

It was often difficult, even for a man of Hugh Young's vision, to comprehend the growth of Inchar from its inception in 1969. In those days, he'd been fascinated only with the possibility of unlimited amounts of cash. The actual idea of moving Vang Pao's product down to the battlefields had originated among other Americans with the Agency in Vientiane. These men were so loyal to the CIA that they were willing to work twenty-four hours a day to create a means of moving the drugs without involving the Agency directly. The importance of financing Vang Pao and his war against the communists became their sole objective. They preferred not to know who the end users were.

It was men like Hugh Young who made the decision to leave his friends, because he knew they would never hold it against him. In a way, their willingness to obstruct the Drug Enforcement Agency was almost like having the agents work for him, but no one on earth would ever be able to make the connection, and if they did, they'd never make it stick.

During those rough-and-tumble early years when he'd found men like Eddie Kelley and Jerry Santucci, the business had skyrocketed. Eddie and Jerry learned so quickly. They worked so hard. They offered ideas, expanded the market dramatically, recruited many others. They left no doubt in Hugh Young's mind that his chances of success had multiplied many times because of them.

Sometimes he tried to remember the names of those early men and women who had helped them grow, but there were too many. Some of them still remained, working in various cities in Asia, a few even in the headquarters in Hong Kong. But many others were dead—on the battlefields of Vietnam, in alleys and vacant buildings, on the floor of the South

China Sea, some even at their desks or in their elegant homes—for many reasons.

It was hard to imagine, as Hugh Young lay in bed that night in Jakarta, how it had all come together. If he'd been a religious man, he might have fallen to his knees and thanked some greater being for his benevolence. As it was, Hugh Young simply gave himself an imaginary pat on the back.

The detective in charge of the investigation by the Arlington Police Department told Leila she needed a friend. He explained firmly that she wouldn't sleep a second in any hotel room that night after the experience she'd just had. He intended to be that friend, he said, and would stay with her until someone came to relieve him. Because the District wasn't her home, the only person who came to mind was Harry Jensen. The detective called him immediately.

There couldn't have been a safer man than Harry Jensen for a woman who felt as vulnerable as Leila did. Half an hour later she was sitting before the fire in Harry's condominium sipping a scotch, and he was doing what he did so well, drawing the whole story out of her. She told him about her morning with Captain Penny Carson, and she said that the captain was searching for more information because she wasn't satisfied with the data in Danny's file. Knowing that Leila needed a good cry and a night's sleep, Harry poured her another stiff scotch and commiserated with her until she'd almost cried herself to sleep. Then he put her to bed in his own room.

Penny Carson wasn't as surprised as Harry'd expected when he called her.

"Have you found something unusual as a result of talking with Leila Potter?" he began without mentioning what had happened to Leila.

"There may be something unusual." She'd made a point of explaining to Leila that morning that she didn't really know Jensen, but that he had clout because his congressman was a former POW. She'd met Harry once or twice at briefings. Randy Wallace had told her that Harry was one of the few congressional aides who could be trusted, and she'd also heard that from other people. When your profession was the military and you wanted to make a career in a man's world, you watched your back whenever a bureaucrat showed a personal interest in you or your job. Colonel Wallace had reminded her more than once that you could get in trouble answering questions that you didn't have to. But Penny desperately wanted to talk to Jensen because he could be trusted. "Why, Harry?" she asked cautiously.

"I've had a long talk with Leila this evening. She's in my bed right now."

Penny knew all about Harry's preference for partners. "Go on, Harry. You've got my attention."

"There was a man in her room at the Marriott when she came back from dinner tonight. He took a couple of shots at her, and God only knows why he missed. But he did kill the bell captain who let her in. The detective investigating says only a pro can get into those rooms. He also says those few thieves who are good enough to operate in a place like the Marriott would never bother if they knew there was a chance of the occupant returning. He also said that there was no evidence that anything was even touched.

"He seems to think the guy was waiting for Leila and that the bell captain screwed up what would appear to be a professional hit, but the detective can't figure out why any pro would want to go after Leila. She's a nice, honest person, Penny. I like her. Things like this don't happen to people like her without a damn good reason. Now, don't you think we should talk?" Then he added quickly, "No politics involved with this one. Cross my heart."

"I like her too, Harry . . ." Penny's voice drifted off.

"I really mean it. This is between you and me. No politics. No bullshit. Help a nice person."

"Okay. You win, Harry. There's a lot that's odd. I don't quite know what it is yet, but I've been pulling up some data on the computer that looks strange when you have a mind like mine." She paused for a second. "Harry, the only other person I can talk with about this is my boss, Colonel Wallace, and sometimes I'm not sure he gives a shit other than to put in his time so he can get his fat retirement."

"There's something else on your mind, too, isn't there?"

"Do you remember that photo that surfaced last week in our office, the one that was supposed to be an MIA in Laos? And you don't have to act coy with me. I know it was supposed to be classified, but I'll bet you got wind of it."

"Go ahead."

"Well, there was nothing wrong with that picture. No touch-up. Nothing. Not a goddamn thing the experts could find. It was good enough to send an investigating team up from Bangkok to check it out. They even put a major in charge of the search. I just found out before I left my office that the major is officially missing, along with his interpreter, a lieutenant and the guy who took the picture, a Laotian. Not even a trace of the vehicle they were traveling in. They were up north of Vientiane."

"That's still indian country. How about drug dealers? Maybe he hit the wrong people."

"When I checked with a friend of mine who was involved with the investigation, he said they're thinking about that. But the big-time operators up there don't do that sort of thing to Americans, especially American military. Bad for business."

"What does this have to do with Leila?"

"Nothing yet. Just two sightings, two that we can't take apart. Since the fall of Saigon, there have been close to fourteen thousand reports associated with missing Americans. We've broken all of the information down on the computer. No more than eleven percent of those reports can be related to sightings of individuals believed to be Americans, and only three percent of these relate to people who were sighted in a captive environment.

"So figure in almost twenty years there's about four hundred reports of sightings that are at all substantial, and just about all of those have proven to be pure bullshit. Now we have two, literally the same day, that have us leaping off our bureaucratic asses. It's just odd that all this is happening right when Leila brings us this story and . . ." She corrected herself. "No, it's not just a story, Harry. You believe her, just like I do. Neither of these reports indicates that captivity is involved. These guys are loose, and right now it's just possible other people are dead because of them."

"You're getting out of your element, Penny, aren't you? You're not following the Pentagon line of thinking."

"Correction, Harry," she responded quickly. "I still have a career in the army. What you call the Pentagon line of thinking is based on the idea that all missing Americans are dead, they always were, but that every last MIA case will eventually be answered satisfactorily. And I do believe, Harry, I really do, that they will be resolved eventually, and I'll do my damnedest to make sure they are. That's my job.

"But right this instant you and I are talking about a couple of events that go beyond this office's everyday work. There's no law against my working on my own time, and the Pentagon will be very happy if I come up with something that enhances their standard operating procedures. I'm going to be at that computer at six tomorrow morning, Harry, and I'm going to be in that vault chasing down those original records. Why don't you bring Leila in with you? Tell your boss you're on to something that could make him look good."

"I'll tell Chuck Goodrich I'm on to something that will make him a senator, and he'll be willing to help." Harry had ambitions to work for a senator. Chuck Goodrich had the ambition that would make Harry a senator's aide.

Ed Kelley liked his company commander, Paul Ledbetter, from the first moment they met. Ledbetter was a West Point graduate, already halfway through his tour in Vietnam. As a first lieutenant and platoon leader in Germany, he'd made a name for himself during exercises designed to prevent the Red Army from streaming through the Fulda Gap into central Europe. His battalion commander had recommended that his request for transfer to Vietnam be approved, along with promotion to captain and a company command. Successful combat operations along with a few medals would give him the opportunity for early selection to major.

But Paul Ledbetter saw Vietnam from a slightly different

perspective. "I'm doing well here because the company's doing well, and so is the battalion," Ledbetter explained when Kelley reported to him for duty. "But the most important thing to me is my company. I would consider my tour here a complete success only if we make it without one casualty. Unfortunately that's next to impossible with the kind of operations we're involved in. But I'm telling you right now that our casualty rates are lower than those of any other company conducting operations of comparable intensity." He stopped talking and stared hard at Kelley to let that fact sink in. Ledbetter's perspective on Vietnam had no room for guts-and-glory types.

Ed Kelley couldn't have been happier. He'd heard enough about the area he was assigned to, through rumor and the few men he'd talked to in Saigon, to know that operations in that region had continued with such intensity that the nickname "Iron Triangle" had been earned. The battle for the hearts and minds of the population around Saigon would remain vicious.

"If there's one thing that will bring you and me together, Lieutenant, it will be your ability to bring your men back to this firebase alive and healthy after each patrol."

There were two types of patrol. At night one or two squads were sent around the perimeter to discourage the VC from getting close enough to launch attacks against base security. The battalion commander was concerned about making sure there would be no full-scale assault against his base as long as he was in command. Paul Ledbetter was even more concerned because there was no way to keep two men from creeping through the jungle, setting up a mortar, and launching half a dozen rounds into the compound, and those losses weren't acceptable to him. There could be no future for any career officer who experienced too many casualties. The two commanders' concerns were simply on different levels. Kelley supported both officers.

The second type of patrol was more complex. When intelligence determined there were larger VC units in the region, an operation plan was formulated to eradicate them before they neared the base. The goal was admirable, and the planners were always precise in their work. Either smaller units of the battalion would be moved into position along the Vam Co Dong River by the navy's riverboats, or helicopters would bring in larger units to trap and destroy the enemy. However, VC intelligence could be even more effective. Too often there was no enemy by the time the units had been dropped into position. When contact was made, short, intense firefights usually developed, and those could produce heavy casualties. The colonel and the captain often agonized over these losses. This was not to their liking.

Ledbetter stroked his chin thoughtfully as he spoke. "Our company has had its share of firefights, and we've lost men, Lieutenant. You see, I believe in ambush rather than direct confrontation. The colonel agrees with that. He generally accepts my theory. More often than not my company has been selected to cover a position to prevent the enemy's escape because I am a strong believer in that tactic. That also means our contact with the enemy has often been less than other companies'." He folded his arms and nodded to himself with satisfaction. "Perhaps that's why our casualties are more acceptable. Do you see what I mean?" The colonel had gone along with Ledbetter because he thought Ledbetter could cover his ass.

"I think so, Captain." While Kelley thought he understood, he wanted Ledbetter to make his point clearer. Had Ledbetter developed the fine art of volunteering to ensure that his company avoided more casualties? Kelley loved the concept if it was possible. Was there a way to keep out of those firefights? And if so, how? "But if you can explain why in a little more detail, I might be able to do my part right away to minimize our casualties."

Captain Ledbetter wasn't one to expand on his pet theories until he knew a lot more about his platoon commanders. "We'll get to know each other better, Lieutenant. I believe in leading by example. Stay close to me." He intended to survive his tour and get a job in the Pentagon where he could write his own ticket from then on. That was the smart way to get ahead in the army.

Ed Kelley did stay close to his company commander in

the following days, and he learned the subtle methods of this particular professional army officer. Ledbetter was the first one to make suggestions to the colonel when plans were being initiated, the one who volunteered to work closely with intelligence to coordinate the operations plan, the one who volunteered his company for what he would often call the critical position. The colonel usually agreed, and that meant Ledbetter's men cleaned up rather than initiated contact or cut off the enemy's line of retreat. Kelley was a quick learner, and he understood intuitively why Captain Ledbetter looked so good on paper.

At the same time Jerry Santucci was working equally hard to make himself one of Ed Kelley's favorites. That was the way a man stayed alive in Vietnam.

"Captain Carson," Randy Wallace began in mock seriousness, "I'm going to be upset with you. Last one to turn the lights out last night. First one in this morning. Too much work and no play makes the captain a very dull girl." The moment he noticed the lights already on in her office, he knew a few minutes with Penny Carson would make the previous night's phone call from Kelley easier to take.

She wheeled about in her chair, more surprised than frightened, to see him standing in the doorway in the exact location as last night. "Oh, my God, it's you!" she exclaimed. "Or I should say thank God it's you, Colonel Wallace. I was concentrating so hard I didn't hear a thing." The smirk on his face was especially unattractive to her.

Lieutenant Colonel Wallace was pleased with himself. Even at that hour of the day she looked good. He'd always preferred long hair, but Penny sure made the most of her short hair. "Hey, when I write your fitness report it's going to say, 'Captain Carson works too hard.'" He sauntered over behind her and glanced over her shoulder at the computer screen. "What has you working so hard this morning?" he asked bending down too close to her face.

She turned back to the computer to increase her distance from him. "I was going to ask for your help this morning, sir."

"Randy, please. Remember? You agreed last night. Hey," he added nonchalantly, "you don't want to make me feel like an old man."

No, he didn't look that old, but the puffy face seemed to predict that he never would reach old age if he kept drinking. "Sorry. I'll work at it. Too much of the army in me." She returned to his question. "You remember that special request you signed for me yesterday to get something out of the vault? Well, that's part of what I'm working on. I got a request for follow-up from Congressman Goodrich's office. This isn't really a sighting, in our sense of the term, but something like it." She wasn't about to explain what she was really doing until she reached a roadblock. Then she'd take advantage of his seniority and maybe even his ego.

Wallace perched on the corner of her desk. "You're not playing pattycake with the politicians, I hope. That never does us any good in the long run, you know."

"You've explained that before, but we both know how much Congressman Goodrich has helped us," she reminded him. "So I decided this was worth a bit of our valuable time," she went on. "You see, Colonel, this sighting was right here in town—at the Wall." She turned away from the screen and saw that for once she had Wallace's total attention. "It was reported by the sister of a boy who was killed in Vietnam. Her name's Leila Potter. She was visiting the Wall the day before yesterday and she saw a man taking a rubbing of a name." She pushed back in her chair. "Believe it or not, Colonel . . ."

Wallace started to raise his hand in protest.

"Okay, Randy. But only when it's just us. I don't like to call any officer by his first name in this building. Anyway, believe it or not, when this man turns around, she recognizes him. He was her brother's best friend. And he was taking a rubbing of his own name."

The colonel's forehead wrinkled curiously. His expression was one of a man who really wasn't concerned about what he was being told but wanted to remain polite.

"You don't get my point. A man whose name was on the

Wall was taking a rubbing of his own name," she repeated. "His own name! On the Wall! Leila Potter recognized him, spoke to him, and is sure he knew exactly who she was, too."

"What did he say to her?" Wallace asked politely.

"He said she was mistaken."

"I'd think so. Dead men don't come back to take rubbings—"

"Wait a minute, Randy," she broke in. "He's never been listed as dead. He's an MIA. That's why she was sent to us."

"There are no MIAs, Penny," Wallace stated emphatically. "They're all dead. I know it. You know it. Anyone with an ounce of common sense knows it."

"Damn it. Don't speak for me," she responded angrily. "I've spent enough time on this account to believe there are Americans who just plain didn't give a shit and deliberately never came back. This could be one of them."

Wallace was surprised at her reaction and, after last night's call from Kelley, anxious to dissuade her. But he also didn't want to be obvious. "Sorry. Apologies and all that good stuff," he said. "I'm not here to antagonize my hardworking people. I'm here to help, and if I can, I'll be more than happy to help you out." He patted her on the shoulder. "Hell, Penny, if you could come up with something on this, I suppose you could make your CO look pretty damn good to the boys who sport the stars on their shoulders."

She stood up, as much to get his hand off her shoulder as to reach for the papers on the other side of her desk. "You could start, then, by signing these requests for some records I need to get out of the vault. It would mean a lot to me, Randy," she added with a smile. "That would save everybody a lot of time."

Wallace stared with bewilderment at the requests Penny had already prepared. "Did you ever go home last night?"

"Sure. And I worked at home, too."

"You're dead serious about this, aren't you? I mean about a dead man coming back to—"

"MIA, Randy," she interrupted vehemently. "MIA."

"Okay. My apologies again. You are dead serious." He gave her a weak grin. "I'll sign everything for you. But if I do, you better not be planning to bust tail again tonight. We're still on for drinks after work. Right?"

"Wouldn't miss it. You've made my life so much easier today, Randy," she said, emphasizing his first name again. "You can't imagine what a lifesaver you are."

Wallace leaned over her desk and grabbed a pen. "These all for this one guy?"

"Some. I'm also doing some research into other men in the same platoon. There were a lot of combat deaths in that platoon over a short period, and another MIA from the same platoon on the same day as this guy Miss Potter saw at the Wall. I just thought I ought to check it out," she said apologetically. "That's what we're supposed to do. No stone unturned and all that. Right?"

"Okay. Here're all the John Hancocks you need," he said as he scrawled an illegible signature on each one. "I hope I'm not doing you a disservice here." He placed the requests on her desk, glanced quickly at his watch, and was turning to walk away.

She wasn't ready to tell him about Leila Potter's experience the night before. "I'll tell you this evening."

"Terrific." Randy Wallace waved as he left her office. He had a busy day ahead, too. He had to figure out a way to track down every copy of Eddie Kelley's photo.

Jerry Santucci had once dreamed of becoming an artist and that idea had been strengthened by a movie he'd watched on seven successive days when he was just thirteen years old. It was amusing to think back on it now, and he had no qualms about making fun of himself when he told his story to others. But he'd known even before the movie ended that first night that he wanted to draw, and he'd also known he would never be satisfied until he found his own Suzie Wong.

He went home to the tenement apartment in Queens that night and lay in bed picturing himself with sketchpad and pencil in hand crossing Victoria Harbor from Kowloon to Hong Kong on the Star Ferry. He never doubted that he'd have chosen to ride in ordinary class on the lower deck, because suddenly there she'd be—not Suzie Wong, but she would be just as lovely and just as mysterious and just as coquettish.

When she noticed him, she would know instinctively that he wasn't a tourist because he wouldn't be hanging over the rail, camera in hand, snapping pictures of every junk and sampan in the harbor like the average Caucasian on the first-class deck above them. He'd be cool, oh, so cool, just like William Holden, cigarette dangling jauntily from the corner of his mouth, confident grin. And just like the girl in the movie, she wouldn't know immediately that he was sketching her, just that he was admiring her as no man ever had before. Jerry knew that each time he looked up from the pad, her face would be just a little lovelier, she would be a bit taller, and her figure would be more rounded than that of the average Oriental woman. His Suzie would be a classic woman in every way.

No matter how many times he closed his eyes and conjured up that image in his mind's eye, she would turn and their eyes would meet a minute before they were to arrive at the Star Ferry terminal. But she wouldn't be mad and she wouldn't pout because he was drawing her picture, and she wouldn't disappear into the throng streaming off the ferry at the base of Connaught Road. Instead, she would come to him and ask to see his drawing. She'd be amazed at the likeness and ask if he'd draw some more pictures of her, and of course he would agree.

At that point his world would split from Suzie Wong's world. This girl would take him to her place, cook for him, make love to him constantly, teach him to speak her language. Oh, she would introduce him to a world he would never leave because he'd already come from a world he wanted no part of.

Jerry Santucci would have continued to go to that same movie on succeeding nights if he'd had the money. But kids like him who grew up on the poor streets of Queens and were forced to go to school by their parents could get money only by stealing it. So, after seeing the movie on seven successive days, Jerry took the subway to Manhattan, grabbed a lady's purse, went right back to Queens, and watched Suzie Wong fifteen more times in the next month and a half.

He also asked the art teacher in his high school to help him learn to draw better. That was his big mistake. He should have just gone on dreaming, because he was told after two months of frustration that he simply lacked the talent to draw anything. He considered killing the instructor but decided that might ruin his chances of getting to Hong Kong.

Though Jerry never went back to that movie again after his dream was shattered, he knew that once he escaped from the tenements of Queens he would never return. He would get to the Orient somehow, even if it wasn't as an artist, and he knew that once he got there he would stay forever. His only problem was that he didn't think he could steal enough purses to make the airfare.

Then came Vietnam while he was still in high school. Until Jerry located that tiny country on the map, he had no idea what part of the world it might be in. He was overjoyed when he found it was just a few hours by air from Hong Kong.

His first crucial decision in life was almost made then. If his family hadn't told him that he'd never get out of Queens if he didn't graduate from high school, Jerry might have quit school and enlisted.

But he waited. The recruiter told him he'd do better with a high school diploma. The idea that thousands of men were being killed each year in Vietnam meant little to him as long as the army would get him to Asia. He would make use of the army only until it got him what he wanted. He enlisted upon graduation, sure that he'd find a way to get to Hong Kong as soon as the government got him to that little country that was having a war. The war wasn't a special concern for Jerry Santucci, because he didn't really plan to take part in it. He only planned to stay around long enough to figure out how to get out of fighting.

The idea that the army would control him never really set in until he rode through that concertina wire into the firebase. It was his good fortune to be assigned to Bravo Company, Second Platoon, commanded by Lieutenant Edwin Antonio Kelley.

CHAPTER 5

Hugh Young considered himself a romantic, especially after his youthful days with the Agency in Long Tien supporting men like the Ravens and the fierce Meo tribesmen. His milieu had been the dark and deadly Laotian jungle; the previous generation's had been blue Asiatic waters bearing exotic names and deadly Japanese warships.

Now each time he looked down from a jet circling out over the ocean off Jakarta, he could envision the naval battles of more than fifty years before. He pictured the Java Sea and the Sunda Strait coming alive once again with big naval guns and torpedoes. The peaceful blue waters below the plane were transformed into flaming death and exploding ships. Those battles had been fought before he was born, but they were the beginning of the fascination and excitement of arriving in Indonesia's capital city.

Jakarta, teeming with nine million people—this was where businessmen created billion-dollar deals in modern skyscrapers that cast long shadows over stinking canals and shantytowns housing inconceivable throngs of ignorant, poverty-stricken people. Jakarta was where the contracts were signed. Jakarta was where the rake-offs were perpetrated and a man could make millions of dollars by signing his name. Jakarta was a fascinating, free-wheeling clash between East and West, and the excitement of conquering it sent chills down Young's spine.

Mr. Yuan had more than kept his promises of the previous day. Singapore's finance minister had made the vital arrangements between his government and Indonesia's that opened every door. The Indonesian finance minister was as pleased with Inchar's seemingly magical abilities as Yuan had been. Inchar appeared able to simplify the complex planning required in setting up new businesses in the Third World. The vast combination of smaller organizations integrated into Inchar could make these entrepreneurial concepts work.

Inchar's image had been promoted so well that the company was accepted as a totally Asian entity despite the Caucasians who managed it. Not once did the emerging Third World nations who consumed Inchar's expertise ever delve into its background. Everything was happening so fast in Southeast Asia that the past had no economic value. Only the wealth of the future was important.

It was no different in Jakarta than any other capital city on the Pacific Rim. The requirements of adapting a sprawling nation like Indonesia to a modern economy demanded a reassessment of the older prejudices toward Westerners and their sometimes grating methods.

Young had never stayed anywhere other than the Borobudur Intercontinental because that hotel had squash courts and a huge swimming pool. It was also only a couple of blocks from the ministry for whichever young official they had chosen to be his next squash victim. Unfortunately, on his first morning in Jakarta, Young had been forced to send the young man back to his office because of a dawn phone call from Jerry Santucci.

"Try that one on me again, Jerry," Young replied sleepily to Santucci's excited voice. "But slowly this time."

"He fucked up, Hugh. The guy you hired in D.C. fucked up. Is there any other way I can make it any clearer?" Santucci was excited and angry at the same time, and his shrill voice came amplified over the phone from Hong Kong.

Hugh Young opened his eyes again and rubbed them. He turned his head to look at the digital clock beside his bed as it flicked silently to 6:04 A.M. He reached over and pressed down on the button for the drapes. "Just a second, Jerry. Let me straighten out my head. It's an hour earlier here, you know." Floor-to-ceiling draperies on the opposite side of the immense bedroom whispered back to reveal a broad expanse of light pink sky to the northeast. Fluffy clouds hovered over the Java Sea. "Can you imagine how beautiful morning is in Indonesia, Jerry? I'm just a few degrees south of the equator, on the underside of the world. Imagine that." Although he didn't want to accept it at first, he understood what Santucci had just told him, but he needed to get his mind functioning properly before discussing it.

"Yes, I remember, Hugh. I was with you the last time. You loved the place. I even remember how you gave me a history lesson about W.W. II sea battles and all that shit. Personally, I don't care if I ever see Jakarta again. It was hot and dirty and it stunk . . . and I didn't like the women," he added with a snicker. "Now are you awake?"

"Yes, and I understand we have a problem in Washington. Please explain it to me without getting so excited, Jerry." Hugh Young had learned long ago that there was no more loyal individual in the organization than Santucci. What he lacked in native intelligence he more than made up for in dedication and perseverance. But he did have a penchant for speaking faster than he could think when he became excited.

"Well, if it was you who someone identified—" Santucci blurted.

"Believe me, I know how you feel about that. Now, what happened?"

"Your man was waiting in the woman's hotel room. From what I've been told, it was supposed to be a simple hit. But according to the morning *Washington Post* article, which incidentally was faxed to our office, she lost her key card to her room and the bell captain let her in. I guess he was waiting for a tip and probably talking to her when the hit man comes busting out of the crapper, misses her with two shots, and blows away the bell captain. Then he bolts without finishing the job." His voice peaked. "Front page of the *Post,* Hugh. Front page!"

Young looked at the bedside clock again. "Christ!" he exclaimed. "That paper must have been on the streets more than twelve hours ago. When the hell did all this happen?"

"Maybe eighteen, twenty hours ago."

"And you're just calling me now?"

"Hugh, I got the call about four hours ago, the fax two hours later. I decided, what the hell. No sense waking you up then. You know what a pain in the ass you are in the middle of the night. After all that time it took your people in D.C. to call here, what's four more hours?"

Young yawned silently. "I'm going to call that son of a bitch myself and . . . No, no, I'm not. Not from a hotel phone. Jerry, you make the call. I assume the asshole who screwed everything up is still on the street. Right?"

"As far as I know."

"I want his head. You tell them to let us know when that dumb son of a bitch is kissing the bottom of the Potomac."

"How about sending out a new man?"

"Jerry, Jerry, Jerry," Young replied. Santucci was so excited that he wasn't thinking straight. "I can tell you've been up most of the night. Not a second time. Not after the first one was screwed up. It would be absolutely insane of us to try again now. That would be like cutting off your pecker because it's been in the wrong places. No, you get the word to Randy Wallace to get in touch with me here. It's evening there. Perhaps that Potter woman's already told someone about seeing you at the Wall. If we tried again, someone might put two and two together. I want to know if there's a chance that her seeing you at the Wall might be associated with that screwed up hit. Just make sure you tell Randy I want to hear from him super quick."

After hanging up the phone, Young thought about going ahead with the squash game anyway. But that would be foolish, because Wallace might try to call him in the next hour or so. He called the duty officer at the finance ministry and canceled the match.

Hugh Young thrived on being a businessman, especially in the Far East. Here it was still romantic. When he was in college, the idea of traveling throughout Asia as he did now had seemed like something heroes in books did. Almost everyone he knew had minimal expectations on graduating from college—a job, a wife, a family, a dream that someday there might be enough money to travel a little. But his friends hadn't really believed that they could do the things they'd read about.

That was why Young had jumped at the chance to work with the CIA when the Agency recruited on campus during his senior year. That was the start of a new life. The job was exciting. Europe was exciting. Most of the men he worked with were exciting, because they were different from the guys he'd known in college. Generally, the CIA men hadn't been jocks. They weren't the type who got into student government or joined clubs either. But they were all bright and ambitious, eager to get away from a world they just didn't quite feel a part of.

When they talked after hours, it wasn't about wives or house repairs or sports teams. They talked about wars he'd never heard of, complex disinformation programs, smuggling weapons, setting up undercover businesses to finance secret operations, even establishing banks and companies called proprietaries to launder the money used to pay for covert operations. Hugh had read about such things in books, but he didn't think they went on in the real world. Yet there he was having a couple of friendly drinks with people who did exactly that for a living.

One could become moralistic about the situation, but it was a simple fact of life that opium and coca products were global commodities with unique politics and economics of their own. The money benefited everyone in the end, although none of them ever really considered the end users.

* * *

Fort Myers was up the hill from the Pentagon, situated on the northwest corner of Arlington National Cemetery. It was the home of the Third Infantry Regiment whose Caisson Platoon conducted the impressive and heartrending military funerals at Arlington; the platoon had been extremely busy the summer of 1969. The quarters for the chairman of the Joint Chiefs of Staff and the army chief of staff are just around the corner from Patton Hall, the fort's officers' club. Patton Hall faces the parade ground where retirement ceremonies are often conducted for distinguished senior officers. Fort Myers was the essence of military tradition. Hardly an individual could walk these streets without sensing the history and the power surrounding them.

"Damn," Randy Wallace exclaimed for Penny's benefit, pointing at the large clock in the lobby of Patton Hall, "I told Captain Carson that she worked much too hard." Wallace was not historically motivated at the moment. "My good friend Penny Carson," he continued with a wink, "just missed happy hour, which tolled at exactly eighteen hundred."

The hour and minute hands were indeed aligned at the bottom of the clock's face. "Sorry about that," Penny responded halfheartedly. "Remember I left a message with your office before fifteen hundred saying it would be eighteen hundred before I could get away."

Wallace had come to pick her up forty-five minutes ahead of that time and alternated between peering into her office to ask how much more time and pacing the corridor outside. She decided he was somewhat like a little boy who'd been told he was going to get a special treat and who was now impatient. But it was a bit unnerving to realize she was supposed to be that special treat.

"Well, at least we're not going to go dry," he commented sourly.

"Look on the bright side of things, Randy. After happy hour they don't pour billiards anymore."

"Billiards? What are billiards?"

Penny's brown eyes opened wide. "They do it at all the O clubs during happy hour. When you're paying a quarter a drink, or whatever they charge here, they're not pouring brand names. You want a martini, you're going to get old rotgut mixed three to one. And that is what has always been called a billiard."

His jowls seemed to bounce as he sat down heavily. "What do you know?" he said with a grin, as they slid into a booth in the far corner of the lounge, "A woman who knows martinis. I must be dating a heavy hitter."

Dating! Penny found that word difficult to swallow, but there was no reason to argue the point then. "Not really, Randy." She wondered how easy it would be to pry information out of Randy Wallace when he'd had a few. Drinking with him wasn't a method she approved of, but she'd known other army men like Wallace—"assholes" seemed the most appropriate term for them—and they'd give away the farm just on the hope that a woman might cooperate. "It's just that when I have a drink or two, you can be damn sure it's going to be a good one."

A waitress appeared and asked for their order.

"Martinis?" Wallace asked her with a know-it-all grin.

"Not tonight. I—"

"Oh, come on. I thought you were a martini fan."

"I'd prefer something else, thanks. Jack Daniel's on the rocks. Water on the side, please."

"Make that two," Wallace said. Not bad for a lady, he thought. Nothing sickly sweet for her. He hadn't drunk Mr. Jack since Hugh Young had last met him in Washington. Wallace knew that Young and Santucci drank a lot of that out in Hong Kong, and he'd decided a guy like Hugh Young might notice when he drank the same thing. It wasn't bad stuff. A little sweet for a scotch drinker, but why not impress the people paying the bill?

It became evident quickly that Randy Wallace could easily run out of things to say. Small talk wasn't his strong point. He also had an unpleasant habit of stirring his drink with his middle finger, then sucking it dry. After he ordered two more, Penny decided it was time to see how easy he was to manipulate.

"You haven't asked about what kept me at the office so long today," she said.

"Same thing as yesterday? Right? Same thing as this morning? Right? You're still trying to locate this dead guy someone saw at the memorial, the one taking a rubbing of his own name."

"You got it, my friend," she answered with an encouraging smile. "And I know a lot more now than I did this morning."

Wallace nodded, sucking the bourbon off his middle finger.

"Have you ever heard of a platoon experiencing more than fifty percent losses?"

"Hell," he interrupted, "one ambush and you've hit fifty percent. I was right in the thick of it, you know. Right in the Nam. Up to my butt in gooks. Lots of firefights. Even came back with some pretty fine medals including the Purple Heart, I might add."

She nodded, making sure that he saw her glance at the ribbons above his left breast pocket. Not a hell of a lot for a guy with more than twenty years, but he wasn't lying about the Heart. "I'm not talking about ambushes, Randy."

She explained the order of battle for the army units stationed in the Iron Triangle during June and July of 1969, especially the army's II Field Force, which worked with the Navy SEALs and the navy's Mobile Riverine Force. "I've been over some of the unit histories, although I'm going to have to get into them in more depth this weekend. Before June of 1969, Bravo Company's casualties were exceptionally light compared to the others. The commanding officer, a Captain Ledbetter, who was also a KIA, always seemed to have his company in the right place at the right time—cutting off escape routes, doing cleanup operations, never getting dropped into the middle of a firefight."

"Smart guy." Wallace hadn't been paying much attention until he heard Ledbetter's name. Ed Kelley had talked about a guy by that name. He didn't like where Penny was going, not after his mostly unsuccessful foraging expedition that day for copies of Kelley's photo.

Penny studied Wallace closely as they talked. It was increasingly irritating to see his finger in his drink, spinning the ice, licking the finger, spinning the ice again. Nerves, she decided. "Yes, smart guy," she agreed, "until June of that year. Then all of sudden his men began dropping like flies, especially his second platoon."

Wallace finished his drink in a gulp and waved in the direction of the cocktail waitress. "Another?" he asked Leila.

"No. I'll let you get one up on me. Now, pay attention, Randy," she chided and patted his hand until he looked up from the empty glass. For a guy who'd been so hot to get her out of her office, he sure seemed to have changed personalities with ease. "Bravo's platoon seemed to have more bad luck around this time. Whenever they were sent on perimeter patrol, they seemed to lose one or two men."

"That happened a lot in the jungle. I was there too, you know. I did my time in the Nam," he repeated. "Hell, the VC sometimes appeared out of nowhere and—*zap*—you're dead. Trip a wire on a booby trap, fall into a pit on a pungi stake covered with shit, sometimes just one shot from a sniper, one round hole in the middle of your forehead. A guy never knew," he added with the self-importance of a survivor.

"I've read all about it, believe me. But Leila Potter's brother was killed by a shot in the back of the head when the platoon was dug in on the perimeter. How do you explain that?"

"He was asleep, off watch, maybe even on watch. Perhaps he was more comfortable with the back of his head against the front of his fighting hole. Or it could have been a ricochet. I saw a lot of dead people, lots of them," he said with finality. "I can't even remember anymore all the strange ways they bought it."

"According to what I've read about Bravo Company, there was no firefight that night."

Wallace spun the ice in his fresh drink with his finger. "What's the purpose of all this, Penny? The army's paying you to chase down MIAs." And then he added irritably, "Not to do favors for some broad whose brother got himself killed almost twenty-five years ago."

Penny Carson sat back and folded her arms. It was time to dig a little deeper into Randy Wallace. "Somehow I don't think you like me, Randy."

Wallace's hands rose from beneath the table and formed a *T*. "Hey, time out. I don't want to get a lovely lady like you mad at me." His expression changed as if a curtain had been raised. "I'm sorry if I said something wrong about the poor woman. I know you're concerned. I just thought we might get to know each other better without talking business. How about it?"

"Sure." Randy Wallace clearly had just one thing in mind, but it wasn't going to happen. "It's just that this guy Leila saw at the Wall seems to have had some strange influence on everything that happened to that platoon."

"Penny, a lot of unexplainable things happened in Vietnam. We can spend a weekend together, drink martinis, and I'll tell you every one."

"What I've got to do is spend a lot more time looking into this Santucci—"

Randy Wallace sloshed part of his drink on his tie as the glass came away from his mouth. "Who?"

"Santucci. Jerry Santucci. Geraldo Vincente Santucci, to be specific." She noticed Wallace's head jerked visibly each time he heard the name, his jowls shaking like Jell-O. "He's the guy Leila Potter saw the other day at the Wall, the one who was her brother's best friend." She was surprised by Randy's reaction.

The ice rattled in Wallace's glass. His hands were shaking. "I'll be right back," he said, releasing the glass. "Head call," he added weakly.

"You look like you've seen a ghost," Penny said as he slid out of the booth. "Was it something I said?" What was it with Randy?

"No, not at all. Nothing like that. Just remembered a guy

in my own company who got killed. His name was something like that. Can't remember what," he said over his shoulder as he headed toward the men's room. "Be right back. Hold the fort, or at least this part of it," he added with a weak grin.

Out of the corner of her eye, Penny saw Randy Wallace stop by the bar for a shot before he went on to the men's room. When he came back to the table, he ordered two more for them. Later, when a considerably calmer and slightly drunk Wallace offered to give her a ride home, she thanked him and explained that she had some things to pick up in the Crystal City Mall on the way home. The walk was short, and anything would be better than fighting him off in the car.

The telephone began to ring as Wallace closed his apartment door. The hell with it, he thought. If someone wanted to talk, he could tell it to the machine. He glanced at the instrument and hesitated a moment before heading directly to the liquor cupboard. The ringing sounded louder. He checked a few labels before removing a bottle of bourbon. It was an angry, impatient ring. He half filled an old fashioned glass, still waiting for the answering machine to take over. When the telltale click came after the eighth ring and his own recorded voice began the spiel, he opened the freezer door, took out a couple of ice cubes, and dropped them into the glass.

Wallace stirred the cubes with his middle finger and took a deep swallow waiting until the long beep finally came. He listened expectantly.

"You son of a bitch, Randy. I know you're there and you've heard all my other messages. You chickenshit bastard. Stop playing with yourself and pick up the goddamn phone."

There wasn't the least doubt in Wallace's mind that the voice was Jerry Santucci's. Where the hell was he? Was he really in Washington after all these years? If he was, why hadn't he made contact before?

"Goddammit, Randy. This is prime calling time for me

from Hong Kong, but I'm not going to hang up this time. I'm just going to sit my ass down and wait until you pick up."

Hong Kong. Jerry was calling from Hong Kong. Thank God. He hadn't been in Washington. Penny's broad was confused. Wallace looked at his watch. It was the middle of the morning there. He took another gulp of bourbon. Should he pick up? It was usually Young or Kelley who contacted him.

"You're probably screwing some broad there, Randy, but I'm not going to get off the line. You get off her, Randy. Goddammit, you stop diddling her and pick up this phone. Go on, baby, let him go," he continued shrilly. "Make him pull out. I'm going to make both your lives miserable until you pick up, Randy. Come on, you son of a bitch."

Wallace actually smiled to himself. He knew he was drunk now and perhaps that was why Santucci sounded funny. What if Penny Carson had been here? Not the kind of girl to appreciate the Santucci humor. What the hell, he might as well pick up. If Jerry Santucci was in Hong Kong, how the hell could someone have seen him at the Wall the other day?

He popped another cube into the glass and added more bourbon before he picked up the phone. "Jerry, you little Italian prick," he started out, just to show he could be funny, too. "I was scared for a minute you'd been in Washington. What are you doing using up all the company money bothering me?" But even as he spoke, he felt that familiar chill run down his back, just like last night when Eddie Kelley had called. Christ, sometimes it was months between calls, and now it was two nights in a row.

"You been there all along?"

"No, Jerry. Believe me. I just walked in and heard you on the machine. And I wish you were right. I'd love to have the broad I was out with in bed right this minute. And I guarantee I would have put a pillow over the machine."

"Wait a minute." Santucci's voice rose an octave. "What did you mean you thought I might have been in Washington?" He'd hardly ever called Wallace because he couldn't stand the bastard. Randy Wallace belonged to Ed and Hugh.

"Nothing, Jerry. Just a similarity in names. I can't believe there's another Jerry Santucci in the world. Not a soul could compete with you," he added weakly. Christ, he thought, it had to have been Jerry who was seen at the Wall. But Wallace didn't dare to mention that. On the way home he'd been trying to decide whether or not to call Hugh. Wallace was scared of Jerry and hated to have anything to do with him.

There was dead silence on the Hong Kong end, which was even more unnerving than hearing Penny Carson mention Santucci's name. Wallace took another big pull on his bourbon. Shit, it couldn't be, not after this Kelley fiasco. His hands began to shake. Now he'd said too much. "Say something sweet, old buddy." *Oh, shit, they'll cut my nuts off if . . .*

"Now listen to me, Randy. You got a pencil and paper there?"

"Yeah."

"I'm going to give you a phone number in Jakarta, and you're going to dial it right after you hang up. Hugh's going to answer, and he'll take it from there. Okay? Don't do another goddamn thing. Don't talk to another human being before you talk to Hugh. He's been waiting to hear from you for two hours, and he is not—repeat: not—a happy camper. Okay?"

"Okay," Wallace answered with dread. Christ. It had been Santucci at the Wall!

Randy Wallace poured himself a full glass of bourbon before he put the call through to Hugh Young in Jakarta.

Leila Potter spent two nights at Harry Jensen's apartment.

The first one would forever appear to her as a series of vivid, terrifying images—a shadowy form, a gun, blood, death, horror—followed by strange faces, some kind, some bored, incessant questions, and the return of those images again and again. Only the understanding warmth of Harry Jensen relieved those few moments she was sure would remain in her memory forever and drive her insane. She had no idea of the passage of time as he fed her scotch and kindness and then tucked her into a cool, comfortable bed.

She spent the second night with Harry Jensen, amateur psychologist. Harry remained at home the next morning until she'd showered and dressed, and when she came into the kitchen she found that he'd fixed bacon and eggs and a big pot of coffee so there'd be plenty left after he went to work. Before going out the door, he explained that no one except the Arlington detective knew where she was. She should spend the day keeping herself occupied and he had just the job for her.

Since Penny Carson had agreed to research the case of Bravo Company's Second Platoon in depth, why didn't Leila spend the day writing down everything she could remember from the day Danny enlisted in the army until the day he was buried? Then she could recall her experiences since that first day she visited the Wall and learned how many of Danny's platoon had been lost. She could take the record right up to the day she saw Jerry Santucci. She should write down anything, anything at all that she recalled, no matter how insignificant it might seem. A detail might seem silly now but in the future, it could mean everything.

Harry called her four times that day to ask how she was doing.

Recall was indeed therapy. She'd written fifteen pages in longhand.

"I certainly didn't expect you to cook dinner for me," Harry said when he came in the door that evening. The smell of food cooking when he came home was foreign to a man who lived alone. "Did I have things in the kitchen that smell this good?"

"You had some chunks of beef in the freezer, odds and ends of vegetables, some above average spices, and half a jug of wine. Now we have beef stew, sometimes called boeuf bourguignon in expensive restaurants. What do you have in that bag under your arm?"

"Scotch. Now dinner's complete." He saw a stack of yellow lined paper covered with neat handwriting on the coffee table. "You had time to write all that down, too?"

The smile left Leila's face. "That, too. The stew was easy. Only a half hour to throw that together. I gave a couple of pints of blood to write those pages." She turned away. "I cried a couple of times, too, like I am right now. I thought I'd gotten all of the grief out of my system, Harry, but there's still so much that comes back that hurts, so many memories. No one should die young, no matter what the reasons. We ought to send smiling, back-slapping politicians out to fight the wars. The fighting wouldn't last more than a couple of days. But the memories are all there in those pages I wrote. I want you to read them, and maybe I'll remember some more if you ask the right questions."

Scotch, beef stew, and Harry's special brand of therapy. Leila knew she was a strong person and that nothing would come of dwelling on an incident that she'd had no control over. She'd never forget the shooting, but neither could she bring the poor bell captain back to life. She had her own unique problem, which Harry helped her to resolve. When she slept that second night, she dreamed that Harry Jensen was as straight as any man she'd ever met and that she fell in love with him.

When she awoke the next morning and found him again preparing breakfast, tears came to her eyes. That dream had been so real. When a concerned Harry asked if she needed another day, she held his gaze and said that wasn't her problem. "I don't know how to express myself. I just don't know . . ." Her voice drifted off, and she shrugged helplessly, but she still held his eyes with her own.

Harry had seen that look before. He understood. In an instant his arms were around her and he was squeezing her tightly. "It's no good, Leila. But if it'll make you feel better, I've elevated you to best friend, and that's the most I can do."

"You're right up there in my book, too, Harry." She pulled back slightly and smiled up at him through her tears. "I'd like to take another day, but that would be a cop-out."

He released her and turned back to the stove. "Going to stay in town?"

She nodded. "I'm going to call my boss right after

breakfast to explain that I need a vacation. Then I'll call Penny Carson. She and I have a lot of work to do."

"Great." He looked at his watch. "I'll call the manager at the Marriott right now. Your detective friend convinced him you deserved a room there for life. It'll be ready when you are. Any objections?"

"No. I already convinced myself I have to go back there if I'm going to see this through. But I hate to leave here . . . leave you."

"You're not leaving me. We're going to be working together on this." He smiled sadly. "It's just that you're not going to be a part of my intimate social life." He gave her a hug. "But friends stick together, Leila."

They left Harry Jensen's apartment together that morning, and Leila took the Metro to the Pentagon. Penny Carson met her at the security station at the top of the escalator. "Harry called me a few minutes ago," Penny said as she led the way down the wide corridors. "He said you set a new record for recovering from . . . from emotional trauma was the way I think he put it."

Hugh Young had liked Ed Kelley immediately, but he had wanted Kelley to spend some time in-country first. He saw it as a way of seasoning the youngster, making him appreciate the opportunity he was being groomed for.

Ed Kelley dreaded his days as a soldier. He never forgot his first patrol as a platoon leader on his own. Bravo Company had been lifted by helicopter to cover the escape route of a communist force near the Cambodian border. It hadn't been a dangerous patrol—no contact, no shooting. The only casualty was a man with a sprained ankle. But Ed was absolutely positive after it was over that his luck was going to run out if Hugh Young didn't get back to him quickly.

One incident the following day stuck in Kelley's mind like a wasp's stinger. Second Platoon's point man had discovered a carelessly prepared booby trap, which Sergeant Buckminster detonated harmlessly. However, the sergeant had also taken the trouble to relate some especially gory stories to Kelley about what happened to people who stumbled into those booby traps. It was his way of training a new lieutenant. Little did the sergeant realize that this particular lieutenant had no intention of facing such problems for the next twelve months.

Kelley had walked more patrols near the Cambodian border during the ensuing days. They seemed unending. Twenty-four hours seemed like forty-eight, even seventy-two hours, as far as Kelley was concerned. Day patrols. Night patrols. He never got enough sleep, but he had more than enough time to think about Hugh Young.

One night in the jungle, after inspecting the perimeter Buckminster had established, he thought back to the night he had met Hugh—his first night in Saigon. The guy'd gotten him screwed so well he thought he'd never walk again. And sometime in the early hours before his first full day in Saigon, he had come awake realizing he was overdue at the BOQ. He raced down the stairs of Young's villa, pulling on his clothes while imagining the court-martial that would certainly be his fate. But there was Hugh, sitting in his garden in his skivvies sipping a cognac with his coffee. He indicated that Ed should sit down opposite him and proceeded to calm the panicked Kelley.

Ed Kelley was driven back to the BOQ an hour later in a chauffeured car, and not a word was said about his tardiness. He immediately went to bed, just as Young had instructed. Later that morning he was awakened by a phone call from Hugh Young, who informed him that he now had two more days before he was to be shipped up to his unit.

"What do you mean, Hugh?"

"Just that. Two more days. I took care of it. Contacts, my boy, contacts. Catch up on your sleep or you won't be able to break last night's record with the women. See you at seven tonight. Same place."

That night Hugh had talked more about his business and explained he was interviewing for associates. "You impress me, Eddie. But I've got to get to know you better, got to make sure you want what I have to offer."

The night was a blur of booze, steaks, and new women, as was the next. Then he was sent off to his unit. But Hugh said he'd be in touch. He didn't say how, just that he would.

Those first nights in Saigon, a vacation rather than an introduction to a war zone, were forever fixed in Kelley's mind. He was sure that recalling them, as he often did on that expedition to the Cambodian border, had helped him maintain his sanity. Kelley arrived at the firebase unscathed, but worried that Hugh Young might not get in touch with him as he'd promised. Perhaps someone else had shown up in that hotel bar and appeared to be a more promising prospect to Hugh. But within a couple of days after his return, while another company was being mauled along the Cambodian border, the company clerk told Kelley to grab the next helicopter into Saigon for an interview with Army Intelligence. Kelley couldn't figure out why Army Intelligence wanted him until he saw the car waiting for him at Ton Son Hut—Hugh Young's car.

That day Young explained a lot more about the business he intended to build. The infusion of over half a million American troops into Vietnam had shifted a percentage of the demand for narcotics right into Vang Pao's backyard. While the general might not have realized it, Hugh Young did. Why ship product halfway around the world when you could simply hump it over the border into the adjacent country? The market had to expand, he reasoned, once the enlisted infantrymen realized that they had been assigned as moving targets for a dedicated and persistent foe for the next year of their lives. As Hugh told Kelley, once the GIs saw a few men in their squad slaughtered in any number of gruesome ways, the market had to expand.

Means of distribution had already been established in Vietnam, but they were clumsy and undependable. It was necessary to set up a system and run it like a Stateside business. Once an efficient means was established to deliver product to the end user, profit could be maximized without putting the system at hazard. Then, using that means as a model, the same method could be set up countrywide. He was looking for an enterprising individual to set an example for other equally ambitious men. The Iron Triangle would serve as a good test area because it was close to Saigon.

"Well, Eddie, what do you think? Interested?"

"I've always wanted to be an entrepreneur, Hugh. Yes, definitely." Then he became excited when he realized how businesslike that had sounded. "Yes, yes," he continued enthusiastically. "When are you going to make up your mind?"

Hugh Young and Ed Kelley hit it off so well this time that Young promised to communicate with the young lieutenant as soon as details were ironed out.

"I'll be talking with a few others. But it won't be too long before you hear from me, Eddie." This Kelley kid had more drive and intelligence than the others. Young would take him. But he'd let him sweat his way through a couple more patrols.

And after another weekend back at the firebase, Ed Kelley dreaded the idea of being left out of Young's plans more than ever. He'd led two more night patrols—without incident, fortunately—but between the two, another young lieutenant had walked into an ambush. Kelley hoped against hope that Hugh Young would not forget him.

And he didn't.

"Hey, Lieutenant," the company clerk called out as Kelley strolled past the headquarters tent on his way to the chow hall after he'd returned from the second patrol, "you got personal contacts at headquarters in Saigon?"

"Not that I know of. Somebody buying me a ticket out of here?"

The clerk was shuffling through the red dust now, waving a sheet of paper toward Kelley. "Nothing like that, sir, but there's classified material of some kind with Bravo's name on it out there in civilization, and this message says to send you. This is the second time. Your daddy a congressman?"

It had to be Hugh. But act dumb, he told himself. "You sure you got the right Kelley?" *It had to be!*

"You know of any others that spell their names with an *e* before the *y*, sir?"

This was it. This had to be it! "When do I go?"

"I guess you got time for chow, sir, if you gobble it down. There's a medevac airborne now for someone in Charlie Company who ain't got a chance unless they get him to Saigon super fast. But you'll have to make your own reservations back."

That was the easy part. Getting out was what was tough. Kelley already understood that most who left departed in a body bag. Thank God for Hugh Young.

Kelley never glanced out at the countryside on the flight to Saigon. He was that excited. *Hugh's going to save my ass. I'm the one he picked!*

The helicopter put down on a pad on the military hospital grounds. Hugh Young was waiting for him. He glanced up from his conversation with two nurses—one Caucasian, one Vietnamese—as the engines were cut and waved to Kelley who was peering out the side door.

Hugh came over and shook hands enthusiastically as Kelley jumped down from the helicopter. His first words were typical of Hugh Young. "Which one do you like best, Eddie?" he asked, indicating the two nurses. Kelley had always hated being called Eddie and had been in a few fights in his youth to discourage it. Hugh called him nothing else, but Hugh Young could call him anything as far as Kelley was concerned.

"The female," Kelley responded with a grin.

"Seriously, choose whichever one you want. I'll take the other. The four of us are going to have dinner at the best French restaurant in town tonight." Young was absolutely certain that all young men who were worth a shit must operate on exactly the same principle: the mind always worked at peak efficiency once the body was satisfied.

Ed looked at him curiously. "Hugh, that sounds great. But I just came out of a war zone. I'm supposed to be back by the end of the day."

Young ran a thick hand through his blond hair, and his blue eyes seemed to grin as much as his lips. "Come on over and meet them," he said, as if he hadn't heard Kelley's answer. "And don't worry about getting back. Who the hell do you think got you down here?" He gave Kelley a knowing wink. "Old Santa Claus Young here has already arranged for you to spend the night in Saigon. It's taken care of. The message has been sent. Lieutenant Kelley is required overnight at the request of higher authority, and that authority is a hell of a lot higher than anyone at that firebase you just came from."

"Captain Ledbetter isn't going to be happy."

Young's gold chains glittered in the sunlight as he half turned and dismissed Kelley's CO with a wave of his hand. "Captain Ledbetter may not like it, but Captain Ledbetter understands higher authority. So he'll just have to learn to like it. From now on, you're going to spend a lot of time traveling to Saigon."

Ed Kelley, who'd been afraid he'd been forgotten, decided to take the Vietnamese nurse. When in Saigon . . .

The product that most affected the GIs in Vietnam originated in the poppy fields of Laos, primarily the Plaine des Jarres, a five-hundred-square-mile plateau of grasslands and small hills situated at an altitude of three thousand feet. The name came from the many artifacts that had been found there—gray stone jars weighing anywhere from four to six thousand pounds that archaeologists decided might have been used as funeral urns by a culture that existed well before the birth of Christ. This beautiful and fertile plain had once been known for the expanses of eight-foot-tall sunflowers that grew as far as the eye could see and the great clouds of butterflies of every variety that hovered above them. Now it was known for something entirely different.

Long before there were Americans in Southeast Asia, even before the French colonized the region, there was a demand for opium. The opium was derived from poppies that grew as well as sunflowers. The natives considered opium an indigenous product for local use until they found they could export it to China and other neighboring countries. This encouraged them to enlarge their poppy fields. But it was the foreigners who came later who established the worldwide demand.

After the Second World War, the foreigners taught the

farmers and businessmen of Laos more efficient methods of processing the opium. And in the second half of the twentieth century, when the economics of war established the necessity of concentrating totally on the more valuable cash crop, the poppies, not the sunflowers, became predominant. Eventually the foreigners determined that the raw product could be turned into heroin locally rather than being transported around the world for manufacturing. Profit expanded exponentially when so many middlemen were cut out.

The Vietnam War altered forever the demand and the distribution methods. Generally, 1969 is the date given for the beginning of heroin use among GIs. The demand had begun before then, but there was no reliable highway or rail system along which to transport it efficiently. Hugh Young stared opportunity in the eye and grabbed for it.

Young had been so deeply involved in the CIA's unknown war in Laos that he, like his fellow agents, had come to believe in supporting its continuation through any means. Even before that fateful year of 1969, it became evident that the danger of Washington cutting off funding was about to become a reality. They all knew there had to be an alternative means developed to finance Vang Pao and his Meo warriors, the brave little mountain tribesmen who fought the communists so bravely. But the Agency couldn't assume the responsibility of delivering the product themselves.

So it was entrepreneurs like Hugh Young who resigned from the CIA and became members of the growing alumni organization which developed proprietary businesses that allowed the Agency the luxury of "plausible deniability." That meant that even though their covert operations around the world might be revealed by the overzealous, the unattractive methods of supporting them would remain in a gray world of ambiguity.

Young revealed the basis of the distribution system to Kelley. Transport planes flew into Laos with supplies to support the Meo. Too often they returned empty. It didn't make sense. Hugh Young sensed opportunity. He was the one who created the system that brought product into

Saigon aboard those empty aircraft. His military contacts were soon established, compliments of the various arms of the Agency in Vietnam. Eventually it was possible to move the end product by helicopter into the field to service his terrified consumers. The final element of the distribution system was the local salesmen who got it into the hands of the users.

That would be Ed Kelley's job—to recruit a "sales staff," as Hugh called it, and to coordinate receipt of shipments, arrange security, and provide a stable system of financial management in the field. His efforts would establish the ground rules for an eventual national distribution system to service a market that Hugh was certain had no limits.

Even before Ed Kelley jumped out of the helicopter that returned him to the firebase the following day, he knew that the perfect man to work with him was already in place— Private Santucci, a man he'd learned had a natural predilection for making money coupled with a strong desire to avoid the war.

CHAPTER 6

I'LL JUST BE A MINUTE," PENNY CARSON SAID. SHE TOSSED HER uniform cap toward a hook on the corner coat stand. "Ringer! What a shot," she exclaimed proudly, fluffing her short brown hair. "Why don't you sit down for a sec and take a look at these." She and Leila Potter had just entered her office. She handed Leila some of the printouts from her research the previous day and indicated one of the two easy chairs in the corner. They were separated by a small coffee table covered with magazines and old newspapers. "The rest of it's still in my safe. Give me a few moments to get my act together."

She'd barely been able to unlock her safe and remove the rest of the material she'd prepared when there was a knock on her office door. "Captain Carson, there's a gentleman here who'd like to see you," her clerk announced.

"Who is it?"

"Just a minute, Captain, and I'll—"

But Penny thought better of it. Time was too precious. "I'm busy this morning, Barker. See if he can make an appointment to come back after lunch. And find out what he wants."

A few seconds later Barker was back. "He don't want to go, Captain. He says he flew in from Norfolk this morning. He says somebody woke him in the middle of the night and told him he'd better get up here and see you. He's in no mood—"

"Excuse me, Captain Carson, I don't want to be absolutely rude, at least I don't want to pass my bad manners through a third party." A navy commander had pushed into the office past Barker. "I've been asked to assist in the investigation of the murder of Major Joslin, and I was told you were the first one I should talk with."

"Major Joslin?" Penny said. "I'm not sure I—"

"The one from the Full Accounting group, the one who was chasing down a reported MIA sighting north of Vientiane, the one who disappeared a couple of days ago," he said. "Your office is familiar with that incident."

Yes, Penny remembered, Joslin was the name. "You said murder?" She'd completely forgotten Leila's presence. Had it been confirmed? "Who made that determination?"

"We—I mean the Defense Intelligence Agency—had a team in Singapore doing a security review in preparation for home-porting a couple of our ships there. That team was ordered to Vientiane, and they located the site about eighteen hours ago. There weren't any bodies, but they came up with enough uniform pieces to identify the sources. DIA figures the bodies were left for the animals.

"I've been informed by a friend familiar with your work that you're researching an MIA sighting, and I . . ." He halted as he noticed Leila seated in the corner. "Captain Carson . . . ma'am." he nodded in Leila's direction. "I failed to notice you had a civilian in your office, and I apologize to you both." His last sentence was delivered formally, and he appeared to be embarrassed for having intruded. He backed toward the door.

"Don't go away, Commander," Penny said quickly. "Maybe we do have something to discuss. But first, you haven't introduced yourself. And I'd certainly like to know who is familiar enough with my work the past few days to pass the information on to you."

"That's easy. Your friend Chuck Goodrich."

That got under her skin. "Commander, I've never met Congressman Goodrich in my life, although I have received valuable assistance from his aide."

"Sure, everyone in the military knows Harry."

She was fascinated by what he'd just said about the dead major in Laos. "Harry's pretty much a stranger to me. For that matter you're a stranger, too, and I still have no idea who you are. Maybe you can—"

"Captain Carson, I owe you an apology again. My name's Stone—Matthew Stone." He pointed at the insignia on his chest. "I'm a Navy SEAL, Captain. I'm on temporary duty with DIA. It's sort of a special assignment in this MIA thing. I can explain everything after you're finished here," he said apologetically, indicating Leila. "And please don't get mad at Chuck Goodrich."

"Could you explain your relation to the congressman, Commander?"

For the first time, the serious expression on Stone's face softened. "Chuck was flying prop jobs when I first started jumping out of them, and we became good friends. He sure was a piece of work," he said with a good-natured grin. "He took one too many chances and finally ended up a POW. That's why he's interested in what you're doing, and that's why he recommended me for this assignment. Sort of twisted some brass arms, too, I guess."

He smiled self-consciously. "Damn, that's what happens when you get woken out of a sound sleep." He snapped his fingers as if he'd just remembered something. "The mind overlooks the little things, ma'am. You see, I did two tours of duty in the Iron Triangle—an early one as an enlisted SEAL; then I was XO of a SEAL platoon a year after I got my commission." His brows knit slightly. "I think you're familiar with the Iron Triangle, aren't you? Chuck told me you were." The expression on his face told them he already knew the answer.

Penny Carson nodded.

"Again, I'm sorry for interrupting. I'll call your office a little later." He was backing toward the door again, obviously hoping the mention of the Iron Triangle would mean an invitation to remain.

"Commander, would you like a cup of coffee?" Penny asked.

"Well, sure, that would be nice. But . . ." Of course he could use some coffee.

"Why don't you sit down and relax and stop worrying about interrupting us? You said the magic words—Iron Triangle. Right! You know that I know that. Miss Potter knows that," Penny said, nodding toward Leila. "Introduce yourself to Leila Potter and we'll have a cup of coffee. We're all essentially in the MIA business today. Leila's late brother is the other reason you're here." She stood up and moved toward the door. "Go ahead. Make yourself at home. The shy act doesn't work, Commander. I've met SEALs in this building before. Sit down there and say hi to Leila." She waved him toward the other comfortable chair by the coffee table and went into the outer office to ask for coffee.

Leila was sure Matthew Stone had to be in his mid-forties, close to her own age, but he looked younger. His uniform appeared custom-fitted around his broad shoulders and chest. Dark hair had receded somewhat in the front but remained thick enough to part on the left side and comb neatly, and there were tinges of gray around the temples.

High cheekbones often gave an individual the appearance of being thin, but Leila noted that Stone's neck was thick to complement his husky build. Small, dark eyes and a small-ish mouth gave his features a certain hardness. Yet that had disappeared with his obvious embarrassment and his courtesy when he'd first realized Leila was in the office. The rows of combat ribbons beneath the brightly polished SEAL insignia on his chest included the Silver Star, two Bronze Stars, and three Purple Hearts.

He extended his hand before sitting down. "Matthew Stone, ma'am. Matt, if you don't mind."

"I'm Leila Potter, Commander."

"Please, Matt really is okay."

She looked at him with a slight grin. "You're not used to

working with women, are you?" That was it. Penny had mentioned that most military men had trouble dealing with women on an equal basis.

"Not usually, ma'am, but there's never been a SEAL who didn't like women."

Having no idea what a SEAL was, she answered politely, "I don't doubt that." Then she smiled and nodded in the direction of the outer office where Penny had gone. "But I'll bet SEALs aren't used to women officers."

"There are none in the SEALs. But I get more used to them each time I come to the Pentagon."

"You said you were in the Iron Triangle. You must be familiar with names like Ben Cat, Ben Suc . . . Tay Ninh?"

"We had a base near there, ma'am. Did a lot of work from the Rung Sat Special Zone all the way up the Vam Co Dong River to the border, ma'am."

The military, she decided, still had a problem with women. "I'll tell you what. I'm a civilian. I'll remember to call you Matt if you call me Leila. People used to call my grandmother 'ma'am' when I was a little girl. I'm not that old."

"Sounds good to me." When he smiled, his face softened even more.

Penny Carson brought in a tray with mugs of hot coffee and cream and sugar and set it down on the table on top of the old magazines. "I sent someone to run down some doughnuts for us," she said as she pulled her own chair from behind the desk. When she was seated, she added, "I don't get many SEALs around here. You people tend to avoid the Pentagon."

"Correction, Captain, the Pentagon tends to avoid us. And I have to admit this place takes some getting used to. I'm still learning a hell of a lot since they decided I was getting a little old to play SEAL games. I guess my entrance here showed that," he said with another little-boy grin.

"My boss's nose would have been bent out of shape, but I'm used to senior officers barging in," she said, smiling. "However, none of them have put in time in the Iron Triangle. That's why you're really here, isn't it?"

"All I know so far is what Chuck Goodrich told me over the phone in the middle of the night," Stone began. "Something about someone—I assume now it was Leila—seeing a man at the Wall who was on the MIA list."

Leila nodded. "The man was taking a rubbing of his own name. That's what shocked the hell out of me. And believe me, it really was him. No hysterical reaction here."

"You can read over what I've dug up so far," Penny said. "The platoon Leila's brother was in suffered an extraordinary number of casualties. But from what we've been able to put together so far, they were all inflicted over a three- to four-month period, and the platoon's contact with the enemy doesn't appear to have justified it. Also, I was studying the entire company's KIAs last night, and it seems to me they experienced a higher than normal attrition rate among the officers and noncoms."

Stone glanced at the list of names and dates she handed him and frowned. "Three company commanders in eight months. That could be unusual, but they were all probably regular army captains bucking for a Pentagon assignment and trying to impress the guys who wrote the fitness reports. No, I think you've got to look at it another way. The VC were no different than we were. We all tried to take out the leadership whenever we got a chance. Whether it's a platoon or a company, especially with American units in the jungle in those days, you've stopped them for a while if the leader goes down."

"Leila's brother was supposedly killed in combat. She received letters to that effect, and he did receive some medals posthumously. But I dug up a handwritten notation that's been buried in our vault since 1969. It says Danny Potter was shot in the back of the head at close range. According to Bravo Company's daily report, his squad was out on the perimeter that night, but there was no confirmed contact. A few random shots were fired, apparently when the squad thought their position was being probed, but according to the information I've got, there was no contact. Yet the letters Leila received indicated a major battle, and Danny got some pretty impressive medals." Penny raised her eyebrows. "No contact? Commander, I want you to read this if you're going to—"

"I will," Stone answered. "But how about doing me a favor? We—you and I—aren't in the same command, and you know how uncomfortable I am here." His eyes brightened, and the small mouth spread into an engaging grin. "I promise I won't call you captain if you'll drop the commander. I'm Matt. Just Matt. How does that fit?"

"Fits fine as long as you don't use my first name in front of my boss. And if he shows up, I call him colonel, period." She thought for a moment. "You seem to know something I don't. You appear to be damn sure we're going to be working together."

Stone's expression hardened slightly for a moment. "That's because of one of the names you're researching. That name goes together with my dead Major Joslin in Laos. We could be reaching, but there may be a relationship here. There's a new computerized system that's been developed to analyze features from a photo—like the one of the supposed MIA Major Joslin was tracking down. What the computer came up with matches one of the names right there in your file—a guy named Kelley."

Penny Carson's mug came down with a crash, splashing coffee across the magazines on the table. She and Leila looked at each other. "He's the one who was reported missing the same day as Santucci." She looked back at Stone, her hand moving slowly, unconsciously up to her chin. Her next words were spoken between her fingers. "Santucci was the one Leila saw at the Wall. Someone's not coming clean with us."

Stone's small mouth seemed to recede into his jaw as he chewed on his lower lip thoughtfully. His eyes moved from Penny to the coffee table, and he nodded to himself before finally looking up at Leila.

Leila nodded. "It was Santucci."

"Both of them," Stone echoed, "on the same day."

Penny appeared to echo him as she added almost inaudibly, "Both MIA on the same day. Are you cleared to tell me what I want to know?"

"Just one thing," Stone began after a second's hesitation. "The computer could be wrong. It's not a totally refined system yet. It may never be. But it's the best they have up to now. We're told it works something like a police artist—you know, the one who listens to the victim's description, then tries to draw the bad guy's face. A couple of other names popped up, too. But it was Chuck Goodrich's call that got me in gear." He lifted his hands until his palms were opposite each other about four inches apart. "There's this much coincidence. We could be totally wrong. As of now, this all has to be under a high security classification."

"Why? If someone's been killed because of—" Leila said.

"You have to be careful—the families with MIAs . . . we have to be very sensitive. They've been supported. They've been victimized. And they haven't been left alone since the POWs came home twenty years ago."

Randy Wallace's day had begun poorly, mostly a result of the previous evening. *In as few words as possible, you're dragging ass,* he admitted to himself. Part of his problem stemmed from his call to Hugh Young in Jakarta, and he knew the other part resulted from the famous Loomis axiom: "Drunks don't sleep good." He hadn't.

There was no doubt that goddamn phone call would have the longer-term effect on him. "You have a mission, Randy. Two of them, actually," Hugh had stated coolly after Wallace had dutifully found him in Jakarta. Everything had deteriorated from that point. Hugh was afraid that someone might decide that seeing Jerry at the Wall had something to do with the attack in Leila's room. Worse yet, Hugh was concerned that "that Potter broad" might tell someone she'd seen Jerry, yet they couldn't take another chance of leaving a trail. But Hugh also made a point of trying to reassure Wallace. If there was no trail, the authorities would eventually add Leila Potter's story to a thousand others. "I'm sure all of this is coincidence, Randy. It won't happen to us again in a hundred years. No, make that a thousand. We should live that long," and Wallace could hear him chuckling from Jakarta.

Hugh's words were so reassuring that Randy carried the phone over to the kitchen counter and poured himself another stiff drink.

Then Young dropped his bomb. What he said next was really frightening. "That Potter woman walks as long as she doesn't talk. A second attempt now would be like waving a red flag. But if anyone believes her, if anyone gets wise, I need to know right away. We can't have anyone chasing around after Jerry. You knooooow," he said, dragging the word out for emphasis, "I'm especially worried about your people, Randy. They're too well trained in that investigation shit. If you even get a smell of something official going on, you either kill it right there or tell me who, what, why . . . everything. We'll make all necessary arrangements from Hong Kong."

Randy Wallace knew what the arrangements would be and closed his eyes when he thought about Penny Carson. He didn't dare mention their conversation a few hours before over drinks. He wished he'd never heard of Jerry Santucci, and now he found he didn't have the guts to admit that Jerry's name had surfaced. Nothing, no one, had ever come so close to learning the truth before. Randy Wallace was just plain scared.

"This is sort of like calling in a marker, Randy." Young pictured Wallace's chubby face growing tighter, the lips a little thinner. "This is what we've been paying for all these years. Maybe you gambled this would never happen. Inchar certainly hoped it never would. But our end of the gamble—all those greenbacks we've invested in you—paid off. Now, even though we're on opposite sides of the globe, even though we've rarely seen each other over the years, you and I are speaking on the phone like two gentlemen who know a debt has to be paid off."

Hugh Young emphasized that it was more important now than ever that every last copy of that photograph of Ed Kelley be accounted for. Hugh wanted Wallace to send a fax of the distribution list to Hong Kong. Then he wanted Wallace to call the Inchar office each time one of those copies was destroyed. "I don't give a shit how you do it,

Randy. And don't ever—and I really mean this—don't ever let anyone get even the slightest idea that you're the one doing it."

After finally hanging up the phone, Randy Wallace dropped some more ice in his glass and filled it to the top.

Now, this morning, he felt more like shit with each name he read on the distribution list. Why the hell did the secretary of defense need a copy of Kelley's photo? The man didn't know Ed Kelley and couldn't have cared less. He'd been given a copy just to cover his ass in case some reporter got wind of it and asked his mouthpiece at the weekly press conference about a mysterious photo. The media loved anything that smelled of a sighting. For that matter, how long before the press got wind of Major Joslin's getting zapped in Laos?

And how the hell was he going to get into General Vessey's office to steal his copy? That man was untouchable for Christ's sake. Why didn't Hugh just authorize him to hire a couple of heavyweights to break into some of these offices? That was the only way to get all of the prints. Might as well get another Watergate started. Shit! The army chief of staff? That was like knocking over SECDEF himself. Come on, Hugh. Get smart. Christ, his stomach felt like shit. He chewed two more antacids and knew he'd give himself the trots if he popped any more of them. That's what had happened when that touched-up photo of three Caucasians had turned up a couple of years before.

Where the hell to start? And for Christ's sake, don't think about Santucci.

He went out to his clerk's filing basket and fumbled through it until he found his own copy of Kelley's photo. Back at his desk, he very carefully tore the photo into small pieces and dropped them into the wastebasket. Then he glanced again at the distribution list. Fourteen to go.

That's one! But Santucci . . . Shit, how many others had Penny already told about Santucci?

Since he'd returned from his most recent Saigon meeting with Hugh Young, Lieutenant Ed Kelley's sixth sense about

Private Jerry Santucci had indeed been justified. Together they had an unusual ability to read other people, just as Young had spotted Kelley that first evening.

The system of transporting the product out of Laos had been set up using supposedly civilian aircraft. Once it got into Vietnam, the method of getting it to the firebases had been established by Hugh. That had meant dealing with more senior people, which was Hugh's specialty. The pilots on both ends knew nothing about the extra cargo. They didn't load the helicopters that went into the firebases and command posts. They just flew the birds and tried to avoid being shot down. In most cases, even the crewmen knew nothing about an additional package that might be included inside a box or crate.

Bravo Company was the initial test case and the beneficiary of some unusually low prices as a result. For the first week or so, Jerry was still feeling around for people he could trust. He would demand no less of a man than had been demanded in his own neighborhood back in New York. He insisted on absolute loyalty and absolute silence in exchange for a substantial commission base. He found his authority challenged early.

There had been two major deliveries before a private in Delta Company came to Santucci one day in the mess hall and asked to meet with him behind the latrines after chow. He wanted to set up business in Delta, and he readily agreed to Jerry's terms. At the same time, he was required to give the name of the individual who'd told him about Santucci. Jerry was furious. The rules of the game had been violated too soon. Jerry Santucci meant to set an example. The man who'd pointed out Jerry died the following night on the perimeter when one of his grenades mysteriously exploded—a freak accident. It was a lesson to anyone who was aware of the system that was developing. Even in the middle of a war, business rules had to be followed.

Ed Kelley was impressed with the rules practiced by his number one man. The lieutenant and the private were a natural team, the administrator and the operator. Santucci maintained security by keeping a tight rein on his people.

Kelley set up a unique bookkeeping method and devised a successful distribution system in a combat area. Purchasers were loyal because Santucci understood the enlisted man's values in Vietnam, and he knew the limitations of each individual's pocketbook.

He was a genius at arranging a free sample program, at enforcing a guarantee of silence from those who did not choose to become customers, and in introducing a point system whereby loyal customers could earn bonus deliveries. From the enlisted man's vantage point, narcotics were more than an escape from the realities of war and a grisly death. They were a means of getting even with their officers, getting even with the army, getting even with the people who had sent them to Vietnam to become targets.

In every organization there are dissenters who are unwilling to condone what they know is wrong. Danny Potter was one of those. But that wasn't because Danny was the original altar boy. He was just a normal kid who got along with everybody because he, too, liked beer and women, and he bragged even though he wasn't as familiar with them as he would have liked to be. Danny was normal. He bitched like everyone else about Vietnam, the firebase, patrols, firefights, officers, and his twelve months in-country.

Danny's violation of the vow of silence came unexpectedly. Like all the others, he had refused to blow the whistle on anyone until his squad and another from his platoon were selected for perimeter duty one moonlit night. Danny Potter had been close to Mikey McTavish when the little red-haired kid who didn't look more than fifteen freaked out on an overdose and danced away across the minefield.

Danny stared in horror as Mikey was hurled high into the air by a sudden blast. He'd been so close that Mikey's scream while he was still airborne and outlined against a setting moon would likely have haunted Danny throughout the night. Worse, when Mikey's body landed, it set off a second mine. Danny was showered with blood and brains and body parts. He was so terrified that he pulled his knees up to his chest, locked his hands around them, and buried his head between his legs for the remainder of the night.

When the first rays of the sun touched the perimeter, Danny's head began to move, ever so slowly, until his eyes settled on the remains of Mikey McTavish. And when they did, he was unable to stop staring until Sergeant Buckminster splashed what remained in his canteen on Danny's head. Then Danny realized for the first time that he'd lost control of his bodily functions and the god-awful stink in his fighting hole came from him.

Later that morning Jerry Santucci talked to his friend. "That could happen to anybody, Danny. It wasn't necessarily the shit Mikey was using. Something in his fighting hole, maybe one of those tiny snakes, could have bitten him. Maybe he just went off his rocker for a reason no one understands. Hell, it could even have been one of those things that blows in your brain. You know, the kind of weakness that's been with you all your life, and suddenly one day it's all over and *blam,* your brain's mush, and—"

"It was that shit you're selling, Jerry. How do you know how good or bad it is? You don't use it. Maybe it's going to kill everyone you sell it to."

"Now wait a minute, Danny. I'm not selling it myself anymore. I'm just involved in a business. I know the guys who do sell it, of course, but that's not the point. Nobody has to buy it."

Danny Potter heard Mikey's scream again, saw his crazed dance against the starry night sky. The explosion hadn't bothered him so much. He heard those every day. It was that small person hurtling through the air in the moonlight. It was that scream, the last sound Mikey McTavish ever made. And it was those grisly body parts. Christ, how he hated that term—"body parts." That's how the medics expressed it when they were mopping up after a firefight. It was really blood and gore and pieces of a human being, a friend who'd been alive just seconds before. And Mikey might still have been alive if he hadn't been putting that shit in his body.

Danny knew he was going to cry, but he didn't give a shit. "Jerry, you weren't there. You didn't see it." The tears streamed down his face. "You didn't get covered with . . ."

But he couldn't finish because he was on his knees in the fine red dust, retching.

Santucci waited patiently. He still liked the kid. Something about Danny Potter appealed to him. It was more than just the kid's sister, although Jerry'd promised himself he was going to get together with that girl when they all got back. "Attaboy, Danny. Chuck it up. Get it out of your system. We all have to do it differently." He leaned over and rubbed between Danny's shoulder blades. "There you go, kid. Feel better?"

Danny struggled to his feet, wiping his mouth with the back of his arm. "I mean it, Jerry. You're fucking people up. If you don't stop, I . . . Someone's going to have to . . ."

Jerry's hand was around the back of Danny's neck like a snake, thumb and fingers digging brutally into the muscles. "You'll what, Danny?"

Danny squirmed out of his grasp and whirled to face him. "Don't try any of that tough guy shit with me, Jerry. You're not like that, not the real you. Who do you—"

Santucci's hand whipped out. The impact of flat palm against cheek was sharp, and Danny staggered sideways. "Shut up, Danny. I don't want any of that crap."

Danny was caught off guard by the slap, more surprised than hurt. Through his own tears of anger he could see flashing black eyes, mean under heavy black eyebrows. "Does that make you a big-time hood, Jerry? Dealing drugs and being an enforcer, just like what you're trying to get away from back home?" Where was the laughing, carefree Jerry who had dragged the other men, drunk, through the whorehouses of Saigon?

"You don't have any idea, do you, kid?" Santucci's eyes had narrowed to a point where only the pupils were visible. His dark eyebrows appeared to join each other just above the bridge of his nose. "I don't plan to have my brains blown out by some hundred-pound slope in black pajamas. There's no way that'll ever happen, no chance Jerry Santucci's leaving this country in a body bag. No booby traps, no punji stakes, no claymores, no sniper, no nothing is going to off Jerry Santucci." He reached out and grabbed Danny by his fatigues and shook him. "Don't you care whether you live or die, Danny? Does it bother you whether you lose an arm or a leg, or maybe your sight?"

Danny struggled, pounding on Jerry's arms, but he couldn't shake him loose this time.

"How about your nuts, Danny? How'd you like them blown off? Do you want to go home a hero and announce to everybody, 'Well, here I am, but I left my nuts back in the jungle'?"

He pulled Danny closer until they were nose to nose. "I don't want to see that happen to you either, Danny, because you're a good kid. But you can bet your life that none of that's going to happen to me. This business, whether or not you approve, is what's going to save me and what's going to get my ass out of here before any little bastard in black pajamas greases me. And if anyone gets in my way, if anyone does anything that might screw things up for me, you included, I'll take them out. Do you hear me?" His final words were screamed into Danny's face. It wasn't until then that he glanced to either side and saw that they'd drawn a crowd. He released Danny and gave him a little shove backward. "Don't ever forget what I just said."

Danny gave him the finger. It was pure instinct. "Fuck you, Jerry." That was all that he could think of to say. He turned and walked back toward their tent. "Fuck you, Jerry," he repeated softly without turning around. "Fuck you . . . fuck you . . ." until he couldn't be heard.

Santucci took in everyone who had gathered around them with a sweep of his eyes. "That goes double for every one of you, because Danny's my best buddy."

Danny Potter lay back on his cot and thought about everything that Jerry had said. His mind drifted back to the conversation they'd had when he took Jerry home to meet Leila before they shipped out. Right after dinner, while his sister was washing the dishes, he and Jerry had made a pact. It was one of the few times he'd ever seen Jerry Santucci serious. They were both just as aware of the casualty lists as the mothers who checked them in the paper each morning to see if a friend's son might be included. Somehow, he and

Jerry promised each other, they would find a way to get home in one piece.

Well, Jerry was convinced now that he'd found his ticket home. He'd even sat down on Danny's cot one time when the tent was empty to explain what this new business could do for them both. Danny had said, "But it's a ticket that kills other people!" And even though he repeated that more than once, it had made no impression.

When Jerry finally came back to the tent after their confrontation and flopped wordlessly down on his own bunk, Danny got up and left. He was so confused he was literally sick to his stomach and Jerry's presence only made him feel worse. His best friend! He was in a quandary. But by the time Danny had covered the three steps from the wood floor of the tent to the red dust outside, he knew what he had to do. It would be futile to go through the chain of command, from Sergeant Buckminster to Lieutenant Kelley just to speak to Captain Ledbetter. Each would want to know why he wanted to see the captain, and they'd try to discourage him from making waves.

Instead, he simply wandered about near the command tent until Ledbetter appeared. Then he hustled over, saluted, and fell in step with the Bravo Company commander before Ledbetter could say a word. "Captain, sir," he began nervously, "are you aware that there is a severe drug problem in the company?"

The captain stopped dead in his tracks and, without looking around, said, "There are no drugs in Bravo Company. If you about-face right now and disappear, I won't even know who's trying to make trouble."

"A man died last night on the perimeter, sir. It wasn't the mines that killed him, sir. He overdosed. He went right out of his head. There were other men on perimeter duty last night who were so high that they probably couldn't have told you their names."

Captain Ledbetter turned to stare down at Danny. He was big—ten inches taller than the enlisted man he looked down at. With his short blond hair and deeply tanned face, he was the picture of what Americans envisioned as a leader.

Ledbetter pointed at the name patch on Danny's fatigues. "Now you've spoiled it for yourself, Private Potter, maybe for all of us. You are familiar with the Uniform Code of Military Justice. I had hoped this would be an absolutely clean tour of duty. You see, Private, I have spent all my waking hours twisting arms at battalion headquarters trying to keep every one of you alive. And it has worked. Bravo Company has had a lower casualty rate than any other in Three Corps.

"I did it for all of you, and now you're telling me that my men are throwing all my efforts back in my face." Ledbetter was struggling to control himself. His lips were drawn tightly back across his teeth as he spoke. "If you persist in what you are telling me, I will be forced as a result of the oath I took when I was commissioned to enforce the UCMJ. Drugs are a court-martial offense. If a court-martial is convened, that, in turn, will attract attention to Bravo Company. And, Private, all my efforts may then have been in vain. Now, Private Potter, taking into consideration that I will overlook the fact that you have already violated the chain of command, do you wish to pursue what you have just told me?"

Danny looked up at the captain. The man towered over him. His face was expressionless, but the threat was implicit. "Captain, we . . . we could lose a lot more people because of the drugs," he stammered. "They could end up doing something that might get the rest of us killed. I . . . I . . ." He was at a loss for words as Ledbetter glared down at him.

"An investigation. That's what's going to happen, Private, an investigation." He shook his head sadly. "And my first six months were so clean." He whirled and headed back toward the headquarters tent. As he marched away, he called over his shoulder, "I'm appointing Lieutenant Kelley, your platoon leader, as investigating officer, and I expect you to make a statement under oath as soon as he's prepared."

"Yes . . . sir." He'd been told by others that Captain Ledbetter was an unusual individual, but his reaction was totally unlike anything Danny'd ever expected.

That night, contrary to established practice, Second Platoon once again was selected for perimeter guard. Lieutenant Kelley called the chosen squads, one of which was Danny's, together before they moved into position. Sergeant Buckminster, who'd been suffering from dysentery, was being given the night off. Kelley would assume many of the sergeant's duties. There were reports of VC in the area, and there was a chance sappers might make an attempt on their position. Private Santucci would assign firing positions.

A little after midnight, Kelley reported seeing movement in the jungle through his night-vision glasses. There was a burst of automatic weapons fire from that position. A few grenades were tossed. Eventually Lieutenant Kelley reported by radio that the opposition had apparently withdrawn. There didn't appear to be any casualties.

At first light it was Jerry Santucci who called attention to Danny Potter's corpse in his firing hole. It was also Jerry, Danny's best friend, who wrapped Danny in his poncho and insisted on carrying the body back to camp over his shoulder. Kelley called in to headquarters for a medevac even before they left their position. An hour later Danny Potter's body was in the mortuary at Ton Son Hut being prepared for shipment back to the world.

Two days later, Franklin Roosevelt Williams, who'd liked the little white kid who made an effort to get along with the brothers, asked Sergeant Buckminster for permission to speak to Captain Ledbetter. He told the black sergeant that Lieutenant Kelley didn't like blacks, and that was why he preferred to speak to the company commander directly about the drug situation in Bravo Company and the confrontation between Santucci and Potter. Buckminster agreed that Kelley seemed to have an aversion to blacks and sent Williams to see Ledbetter. But Buckminster, being a career man, later had second thoughts and reported to Kelley that he'd made a mistake by going over his head.

Franklin Roosevelt Williams was point man the following day. He was just in front of Felix Gonzalez, when Felix spotted movement to his right and opened fire. In the brief firefight that followed, Williams was riddled with automatic weapons fire. Jerry Santucci was not on that patrol, but it was generally understood that his right-hand man, Gonzalez, did whatever Santucci asked of him.

Five days after Danny Potter's death and two days after Williams's, Captain Ledbetter, the officer who hated to open an investigation and who had attempted through any means possible to keep his company from encountering direct enemy contact, died in his sleep when a grenade detonated beneath his cot. The investigator sent to the firebase by the judge advocate general's corps to conduct an inquiry into the fragging incident reported the cause was probably due to racial problems. The investigator was an officer who benefitted often from Hugh Young's largesse. The sworn testimony of Lieutenant Edwin Antonio Kelley, who commanded Bravo Company's second platoon, was employed to substantiate the report.

With the loss of Captain Paul James Ledbetter, Bravo Company's fortunes changed. Their casualties also increased radically.

CHAPTER 7

BANGKOK WAS ED KELLEY'S CITY. HONG KONG HAD BEEN ALL right; Hugh Young and Jerry Santucci—especially Jerry—had adopted that city as their own, but Kelley knew after the first few days on his initial visit that he belonged in Bangkok.

It hadn't always been that way. During Kelley's short army tour in Vietnam, his only knowledge of Bangkok had been word of mouth. Whenever guys who'd survived the first half of their Vietnam tour returned from a week's leave in Bangkok, all they talked about was Patpong Road, three blocks of bars, massage parlors, sex shows, and lovely young women eager to relieve GIs of their money. As a result, he considered Thailand one big whorehouse, because he had no other reference.

Whorehouses held no appeal for him. So, as Inchar developed in the early days, he had bypassed Bangkok, leaving it to Hugh or one of the younger managers. But when the board of directors made the decision in the early 1980s to broaden their scope and ease out of the narcotics trade more quickly than planned, they suggested that Inchar should look into the Thai silk industry. The groundwork had been done by the legendary American, Jim Thompson, but the prices were still too high for most people. Why not analyze the potential for a profitable international business by streamlining manufacturing and refocusing the marketing?

Because Ed Kelley had been the instigator behind Inchar's highly successful Hong Kong tailoring business, he was selected to pioneer a new venture in a similar area. It was Hugh Young who persuaded him to give Bangkok a chance. "You're not like Jerry. That lovely little son of a bitch is an incurable Hong Kong romantic. He's going to spend his life searching for Suzie Wong."

Once settled in Bangkok, Kelley started out by learning everything he could about the mysterious Jim Thompson, the World War II intelligence officer who had remained in Indochina after the war and introduced the world to Thai silk. Thompson was Ed Kelley's kind of man, an inscrutable person who lived in a unique world and thrived on its charms. He created a market for an almost unknown product, amassed great personal wealth, generally preferred the company of Asians to that of Westerners, and left that world as he had come into it—under a shroud of mystery.

Jim Thompson had simply disappeared one sunny afternoon in 1968 while out for a stroll on Malaysia's Cameron Highlands. He vanished without a trace, leaving his fortune, a thriving silk business, an exotic home in central Bangkok, and any number of beautiful women who mourned him. To Ed Kelley, that was the kind of life real men aspired to.

Kelley went to the Jim Thompson house at 6 Soi Kasemsan six times before he was sure he understood the man. Thompson's home, just off bustling Rama I Road, was a monument to his own success and to the Thai culture and had become a museum. It was composed of several teak houses moved from the ancient capital of Ayutthaya and reassembled on the banks of a canal that meandered through the center of the city. A man's man had lived there!

He had created a retreat just blocks away from tall modern buildings and eight-lane city streets. This home was set in a beautiful Oriental garden. Thompson had filled the house with magnificent antiques from his private collection —jade statues, priceless wood carvings, laquerwork, and artifacts collected throughout Asia. Was it possible that someday people would flock to the Edwin Antonio Kelley home and pay the price of admission to see how another mysterious American expatriate had lived?

Once he understood the man, Kelley studied the silk industry. Before Jim Thompson, Thai silk had been a fine product in search of a market. In a few years Thompson had turned it into a major Thai industry and a fortune for himself.

But in the 1980s it was a tightly controlled business with many imitators. Kelley determined that his first priority was to remove the latter because they could make a travesty of the industry once he lowered the costs and expanded the markets. In less than a year there was no second-rate or imitation Thai silk. During this period of what he called "cleansing an industry," he'd gotten to know the high-quality producers and the intricacies of their business. They considered him a breath of fresh air, and some, in whispered asides, even compared his success to that of the late Jim Thompson.

During Kelley's second year in Bangkok, Inchar money modernized the production facilities of those people who developed faith in the expanded market that Kelley preached. By his fourth year Inchar had a major share in certain producers who would eventually control 75 percent of the worldwide market. The producers profited beyond anything they'd once hoped for. The comparisons to Jim Thompson were no longer whispered.

Bangkok was his! He would be the "Western" King of Siam! There was no need for Jerry Santucci's intervention, because this time Kelley had taken the business to the maximum.

Although Hugh Young had assumed Ed's time in Bangkok was temporary, Kelley had no intention of returning to Hong Kong. Anyway, he pointed out on the telephone, Beijing would control that country by 1997. And, unlike Jerry Santucci, he wasn't driven to find the ultimate Suzie

Wong. He had all the beautiful and exotic Bangkok women he would ever need. If he possessed a dream, it was to someday build a monument to himself, as Jim Thompson had done.

In the late 1980s, Kelley's analysis of the local gem industry provided similar results. Thailand mined its own rubies and sapphires and had become one of the world's leading cutters of colored gems. Kelley recommended to Inchar's board that they invest in the early stages of the process—mining, cutting, and bulk sales to the jewelry industry. The design, crafting, and customer sales, regardless of markup, were areas to avoid because some of the small family businesses and shopkeepers tended to short the gold content of the settings. That practice was difficult to control, and he felt that anything less than a quality product could draw unwanted attention to Inchar.

The Inchar board accepted his proposal. In less than two years much of the gemstone industry was under their thumb and jewelry manufacturers had no choice but to deal with them. The few who objected disappeared, literally, from the scene. It was another resounding success for Ed Kelley.

On the same day that Randy Wallace was mulling over the complexities of the distribution list of Kelley's unfortunate Laotian photo, Ed Kelley was to meet with the leading jade smuggler in Southeast Asia. He was from Myanmar, the country that had always been known as Burma and was still referred to by its previous name by most foreigners. "I will recognize you, Mr. Kelley, because friends of mine have described you," the Burmese had said over the phone. "I'm sure you are familiar with the two large carved elephants as you enter the Shangri-la's lobby. If you will be there at thirty minutes past noon, I will look forward to the honor of meeting you."

Kelley considered the Shangri-la an elegant addition to Bangkok. The hotel had been constructed alongside the Chao Phraya River, the city's main thoroughfare, five years earlier and was a model of luxury. The white-tiled lobby soared three stories high. Facing the river, one descended a few steps into a lounge with floor-to-ceiling glass that looked out upon the Chao Phraya on two sides. Beyond the windows, one looked down on beautifully kept gardens accentuated by a large pool with waterfalls and bridges. Swimmers and sunbathers could refresh themselves at a bar that looked out over the river.

The Burmese smuggler was sitting in an easy chair near one of the red elephants he'd mentioned to Kelley. Mr. Than lumped all Europeans and Americans under the general classification of "Caucasian." He'd always had a difficult time recognizing individual white people. Since his contacts had briefed him on Kelley's background, he was anxious to see for himself if the man really had become an Asian or if it was only an affectation.

Mr. Than knew Kelley the moment the doorman held the door for him. He didn't look like most other white men. His carefully cut Thai silk suit, his haircut, his mannerisms—all were those of an Asian businessman who was meeting another for the first time. The only oddity was the striking blue eyes, so penetrating they could almost have been sapphires, he thought. Than's initial impression was that this was the type of man he had been hoping for.

"You have gone out of your way to come to Bangkok, Mr. Than. I would have been delighted to visit you in Rangoon." These people expected a certain subservience from a round-eye.

"Not at all, Mr. Kelley. The flying time is little more than an hour. The effort involved in traveling to my airport and coming into your city from Don Muang Airport claimed most of my time. Your reputation was reason enough to make the trip."

Than already feels himself the one on top. "Is your room in the Shangri-la satisfactory? The manager is a close personal friend of mine and can have anything corrected."

"I will remember your offer if there is any difficulty."

It was a necessary dance choreographed years before, and Asian businessmen meeting for the first time adhered to it regardless of the purpose of their meeting. This allowed them to establish position, and in a case involving two different cultures, the ritual automatically gave the Asian the upper hand in most instances. Ed Kelley's participation in the dance established the fact in his own mind that he was starting out on an equal footing.

They moved down to the terrace for lunch after each was satisfied with how he would deal with the other. Their backgrounds were much the same. Both desired to bring an aura of respectability to their businesses. Mr. Than thought that dealing with too many wholesale buyers would increase the chances of attracting risky attention.

His government, during those rare moments when the politicians weren't feuding among themselves, had been assisted by UN trade representatives in concluding that perhaps Rangoon could benefit financially in the raw jade market. As a result, they'd approached Bangkok about curtailing the smuggling operations through joint efforts. Although Than enjoyed the formality of the dance, he already knew that Kelley's contacts in the Thai government reached into the palace. That was where such nonsense as curtailing smuggling would be eliminated.

Ed Kelley responded politely each time the Burmese made a point, while he allowed himself to enjoy the scene unfolding before him. The Chao Phraya River never lost its fascination to him. It was always brown, the color of rich milk chocolate, and much muddier during the heavy rains when the water hyacinth washed downstream in floes the size of small islands.

He never tired of watching the tailboats—long, slender water taxis powered by automobile engines—zip about the river, maneuvering gracefully through the congestion of water hyacinths, ferries, merchant ships, police patrol boats, barges, and literally anything that would float. Water was the means of commerce in this part of the world, a necessary, and to him romantic, part of the economy. As he agreed with each of Mr. Than's points, as he'd known he would, the Chao Phraya made the art of business even more exciting.

Kelley had researched Mr. Than just as completely as the

man had analyzed him. The Burmese smuggler was ruthless but an honest businessman. He was trusted by the people he employed to obtain the raw jade, from the newest miner to the senior managers, and he paid them well. His record in avoiding complications with Burmese officials was indicative of his own contacts in Rangoon. His deliveries were always exactly what he claimed. And Kelley's research had concluded that the demand for bright green cut jade would continue to expand among European buyers, thereby bringing much desired foreign currency to Thailand.

Mr. Than studied the Chao Phraya in imitation of Kelley. He was satisfied with their discussion. Time to resume the dance. "Your recommendation of this hotel was an excellent one, Mr. Kelley. I am indebted to you." Than had stayed at the Shangri-la a few times since its opening, but that had nothing to do with his comment.

Kelley nodded and smiled. "I must admit I've learned that you have exquisite tastes. Perhaps I should have booked a room at the Oriental for you." He'd been told by a former buyer that Than preferred the modern Shangri-la, but the Oriental was a status symbol that should always be included. "I look forward to the opportunity to meet you here in the future if we are to reach a business arrangement." He was sure they were both in agreement.

"I ask that you allow me to think about this for another day. Perhaps there are additional items we may want to consider." Mr. Than thought this was a deal made in heaven, but one never admitted that. One always forced the round-eyes to wait an extra day, to make them more patient. "Why don't we meet here tomorrow at exactly the same time, perhaps to conclude negotiations?"

"Thank you for your consideration. I was about to make that suggestion myself." There was no such animal as a one-day deal, no matter the advantages to both parties. This arrangement could have such long-range financial benefits to Inchar that Kelley had forgotten the photo of him in Laos in the excitement of the challenge.

As they rose to leave, a young lady at the adjoining table

studied both men admiringly. Her name was Marclay Davis; she was fresh out of Texas and fresh out of college, a starry-eyed Asian Studies major. Her job with the U.S. State Department included a six-month internship at the Bangkok embassy. It was the first time she'd observed an American—for she was naive enough to assume the use of English meant that Kelley was American—operating exactly like an Asian. There was something familiar about the tall, dark Caucasian man, and it occurred to her that perhaps she'd been dining next to someone famous. She mentioned it when she returned to work that afternoon, describing him to her boss at the American embassy.

It was a day later that her description and her story finally attracted more than passing attention. Her curiosity about the man's identity was shared equally by Colonel Nolan Benner, the new Full Accounting representative to Hanoi from the Pentagon. The colonel had stopped first at the Full Accounting liaison office at the U.S. embassy in Bangkok to assist in preparing the investigative report on the murder of Major Joslin in Laos. During lunch in the embassy cafeteria, he'd heard Marclay's boss mention her interest in the American who acted like an Asian; she'd also sensed a familiarity about the man's features, as if she'd seen him someplace before. She'd commented on how silly that sounded coming from a girl who'd just arrived in Thailand, but she'd mentioned it anyway.

Colonel Benner wondered if the man could possibly be . . . No, that was impossible. That man was believed to be in Laos. But what the hell! He said half jokingly that perhaps he was the man whose photo was on the cafeteria bulletin board, the one whose picture had been taken in Laos, the one whom Major Joslin had been sent to find. His comment was received with knowing grins. But he decided to find Marclay Davis after lunch anyway.

Unfortunately, the Burmese and the American concluded their business arrangements before Marclay Davis's sighting was taken seriously. Mr. Than had returned to Rangoon, and Ed Kelley was back in the Inchar office by the time the young lady decided that the mysterious American in the photo and the one she'd watched at the Shangri-la were the same person. But now Kelley been seen in Bangkok!

Colonel Benner called, and his orders were immediately altered to allow him to remain in Bangkok for an indeterminate period. After conferring with his people in the Pentagon, he was informed that a Commander Stone from the navy would be in touch with him by phone shortly.

Leila Potter had always referred to her job as public relations. Her boss, on the other hand, often noted for the benefit of directors at board meetings that her real value was as a tough and charming lobbyist. She was an expert at getting the attention of congressmen, and she knew that as well as her boss did. Leila's strength was that she was always the aggressor. She was an expert at getting elusive congressmen to speak to her, even to return her calls.

Therefore, she was pleasantly surprised to receive a call from Harry Jensen asking if she would please come to Chuck Goodrich's office. It had been a very busy day, starting with her early morning visit to Penny Carson's office, followed by Matt Stone's appearance. Stone's tentative correlation between Jerry Santucci and the other MIA, Edwin Kelley, had been emotionally draining. "But, Harry, I'm not prepared to speak to the congressman about anything right now. Really, I—"

"You misunderstand me, Leila. I'm not making this call for your benefit. I'm making it for Chuck's. You might say the worm has turned. He's doing the asking. He's asking you to come in here. It's very important to him." Jensen enjoyed playing word games. "Do you want him to say pretty please with sugar on top?"

"I don't know the man well enough to refuse, Harry. I've always been told never to bite the hand that votes for appropriations bills."

From the day he had set foot on U.S. soil in 1973 as a repatriated POW, Chuck Goodrich had established his personal priorities. By 1978 the political parties in his home district were both clamoring for him to run for office. With support of that magnitude, coupled with the fact that he never turned down a drink, a meal, or a speaking engagement, he selected his party, won easily, and had faced little opposition since then.

After being reelected nine times, he had considerable seniority in Congress and national name recognition. He also had his eye on exactly what Harry Jensen had predicted, the Senate seat that was to be vacated the coming year. The resurgence of the POW issue had tremendous political potential in his case. Because of his experiences, it was personal as well. Over four years as a prisoner had altered not only his priorities in life but his attitude toward his fellow man. He cared about people. Jensen had remained with Goodrich, even though better offers had been made, because the man proved to be more than just a politician.

Matt Stone was in Goodrich's office when Harry showed Leila Potter in.

"Leila," Goodrich said, standing up to shake her hand, "I've wanted to invite you here ever since Harry told me about your experience at the Wall." He studied the unlit cigar in his hand. "I wonder which one of us has visited there more often." He answered his own question by adding, "I guess I win because I live in the District." Over the years, Goodrich's life-style had helped to fill out the pilot who had been gaunt even before he was a POW. The congressman was of medium height and chunky, but a full head of thick, curly, slightly graying hair and a thick mustache made him look younger than he was. His glasses, which he used only for reading, hung from a strap around his neck. A cigar was as much a part of his face as his nose.

She smiled. "I go to the Wall to see my brother."

"I know. Harry mentioned that a few years back. I go to commune with old friends. I suppose it doesn't do much for them, but I need it," he concluded softly, staring at a picture on the far side of the room. "I like to go to see what others have left there. It's almost a religious experience sometimes, you see, maybe a little more sacred or holy because of those offerings. It sort of cleanses the spirit after too much time on the Hill." His eyes seemed to come back to the present as he changed the subject. "I guess Harry told you I was a pilot. But I suppose I wasn't so hot, because I got shot down." He gestured with the cigar. "Do you mind if I smoke? It doesn't smell bad; it's one of the best-made cigars in the business," he added hopefully.

"Go ahead, please. I don't mind." After all, she mused, it was his office and she was usually the customer.

Matt Stone spoke up as Goodrich lit his cigar. "What he's not telling you is that he wasn't a jet jockey. He flew all kinds of prop aircraft. That's when I first met him. When he got shot down, he'd just dropped a bunch of Vietnamese SEALs I'd trained, over the north country. He was on his way back and was flying too low when some peasant with a drainpipe got him."

"Old stories are an easy way to avoid the main subject, aren't they?" Goodrich dismissed Stone's comment with a wave of his hand and turned to Leila. "Leila, I need to explain where I'm coming from. A lot of it's in my mind, doesn't have a damn thing to do with being in Congress." He took a deep breath. "I owe people, some of whom I haven't seen since 1973. You've heard of the famous POWs, or at least they were famous to me. Ev Alvarez was the first American shot down, and he wrote some great books—honest books—about all those years. And I knew brave, wonderful guys like Jim Stockdale and Robbie Risner and Red McDaniel and Jerry Denton. You still read about them in the papers today. Great Americans.

"Each of them's gone their own way and done what they thought was right, whether or not everybody agreed with them. But there were hundreds of others you never heard of who were just as great and I wouldn't talk to you like this if I didn't include every single one. We were all stuck into prisons that were absolutely disgusting, inhuman, places with names like the Briar Patch, the Zoo, the Hanoi Hilton." He stuck the cigar back in his mouth. "None of us will ever forget a moment in any of those garden spots," he added softly, his voice cracking slightly.

There was absolute silence in Goodrich's office. His eyes expressed what he was struggling to put into words. The others sensed there was nothing they could say until he finished.

Goodrich blew a puff of smoke into the air. "I got there in early '69. By then, they weren't torturing us quite as bad as the first guys. Hell, those poor bastards before me went through mental torture that was as bad as the physical. The guards would beat them until they broke their bones, then deny medical attention until a man's body was so infected the others couldn't stand his stink. I didn't get tortured like that so much. But I heard about it, even in solitary, because there was a network, and Jim Stockdale had set up a military discipline system we all followed. And I learned a lot more that no one will talk about even now after all the books have been written."

Jensen was making signs with his hands when the congressman looked up from his desk, and when he was silent for a moment, Harry said, "Would anyone care for some coffee or ice water or—"

"If you're uncomfortable with this little monologue, I'm almost finished," Goodrich said.

None of them spoke up.

"Okay, I'll tell you why I'm relating this little story. I've been telling you about the live ones, the ones like me who were lucky enough to get back. It's a game of numbers and statistics. Of every two pilots who parachuted, one probably died in the jungle or was killed by angry civilians who didn't like the idea of getting bombed. That's what we assume." Another puff of smoke.

"Then there are a number who were either in contact after they reached the ground or were seen alive by prisoners who survived. They're in the group in limbo that we call discrepancy cases. You can't be alive because you're not here, but you aren't dead, either, because there's no proof you died. There are more assumptions than you can possibly imagine about what happened to our guys, and they're still coming up with more of them over in that big five-sided building across the river. Then there're special interest groups and certain individuals who have their own facts and figures—some real, some imagined." Two more thoughtful puffs of cigar smoke.

"But we all know," Goodrich continued, his voice softening perceptibly, "there are a lot of guys who weren't accounted for, and maybe fifty that General Vessey's group calls high priority discrepancies. I think that means there are more reasons for them to be alive than dead, even though logic says they're dead. There are fewer MIAs from this war than any other major one we've been involved with, but after twenty years, Americans can't let most of the realities, speak for themselves, not after what Vietnam did to us."

He rolled his chair back and put one foot up on his desk. He spoke around the cigar in the corner of his mouth. "They're dead. Regardless of whatever stories you hear, I firmly believe they're dead. No more POWs. Just MIAs. Except, I think, for a few . . ." His voice drifted off to a whisper. "I think . . ."

Leila stared at him, fascinated. It was almost like being privy to a confession. She managed a wan smile at his last words, which were spoken while looking directly at her.

"Talking about those men used to bring a few tears to my eyes," he said to her. "Probably more reflexive than anything else the past ten years, sort of like Pavlov's dogs. My heart's still with them, but the emotion's gone . . . most of the time. Now I've convinced myself each time I tell this story that it's no different than rehashing a championship football game that you lost. The game's over. No matter how many times you get back to it, the score's not going to change. It will never change. I can talk about Vietnam freely now. Some still can't.

"This POW-MIA thing is symbolic and, believe me, deeply emotional. Imagine if we dismissed them . . . if everyone like me dismissed them . . . and then one—just one—stumbled out of the jungle. What would that make us?

With what's happened the last few days, I've decided I've got to do something more for them."

He looked toward Leila. "And by *them* I mean the ones who fought, were captured, died." Another puff of smoke as he stared into space. "That's why I called Matt and asked him to come up here. And when Harry and I hashed over your situation this morning, we decided that you deserved to get into this if you want to."

He blew another thoughtful puff of smoke into the air. "I truly do think there're a few Americans still over there. But they're not the good guys everyone misses. They're bad guys. They wanted out. They deserted. It's as simple as that."

Harry looked over at Leila. He'd never heard his boss talk like this, and it made him uncomfortable. The tough guy had suddenly turned soft. "Congressmen will get down on their knees for votes," Harry said, "but they don't know how to ask for help when they really need it." He winked at Goodrich, who looked thoughtful for a second before he looked down at his desk.

Stone spoke for the first time, looking directly at Leila. "You deserve some answers, too."

"I probably should have told you before you came here, Leila," Jensen said. "A detective from the Arlington PD called me this morning. A body was fished out of the Potomac last night. They identified it as a local hood who's rumored to have done a couple of hits for the mob. He fit the description the police got of a guy who was in the Marriott the night of the shooting. He definitely wasn't a guest. The cops showed pictures of him this morning to a bellboy, a bartender, and a guest who apparently rode up in the elevator with the guy. There's no reason to think that you surprised a burglar. That man was a hired killer."

"I see." She nodded. Then she repeated herself. "I see." When she looked up, her eyes moved about the room, settling on each one for a moment. "I wondered about that, too, but I couldn't quite imagine why someone would want to kill me." A look of resolution spread over her face. "So where do we go from here?"

"There's more to it, Leila," Harry continued. "When Commander Stone met you today in Penny's office, that changed the whole picture. This Santucci and the other guy, whatever his name is, were MIA the same day, and then you consider that photo . . ." His voice drifted off. "There's just so much more here than we thought."

Stone spoke up. "We're coming from different directions, and maybe we're seeing something that isn't there. But, just maybe—and I mean maybe—you stepped in an anthill. With everything that Penny Carson is digging up with that computer of hers, I think perhaps we have two deserters listed on the Wall, rather than two MIAs."

Goodrich's sad eyes settled on Leila. "I'm concerned now that you saw one purely by mistake the other day."

"You mean Jerry . . . Jerry Santucci." Leila's eyes narrowed.

Stone nodded. "That may be why he, or somebody else close to him, wanted you dead. It would take too much time to put into words what a deserter really is. Civilians have a hard time understanding the contempt we have for people like that, but believe me 'contempt' may be too mild. There've been reports before about such men, but nothing firm. We've felt these people were out there, sort of like a bad smell. But now I think we have something solid. Let's say the man you saw really was Santucci. Who is he now?" Stone shrugged. "Then again, where does all this lead? Who knows?"

"I assume this little gathering is far more than just soul-searching," Leila said. She was growing irritated with their approach. She was the one who'd been shot at, and talking wasn't going to help anyone. "Bring me up to date. I deserve it."

"Before I came here today," Stone answered, "I requested a complete list of everyone who served in the Second Platoon of Bravo Company during 1969. It may be ready by the time we're finished here. Penny will break out the survivors during the heavy casualty period, and we'll see how many we can locate. Some of them will have died, and a few have probably just been swallowed up. But we'll interview the ones we can find over the next few days. Maybe we can dig up something that'll make more sense out of all this."

"Who's we?" Leila asked.

"Me . . . you, I hope. If it wasn't for you, someone might be getting away with a lot more than murder," he answered. "You've got a big personal stake in this. And just maybe the fact that you're Danny's sister might get someone to help us out. What do you say?"

"And then?" she asked.

Stone hesitated. "There's more than Jerry Santucci. There was the photo of that supposed American in Laos. I don't know how much Penny told you after I left this morning. But I'm still gambling that the two men are tied together. I'm going to be speaking shortly with Colonel Benner from the Full Accounting desk who's in Bangkok right now. There's a possibility that the man in the photo, Lieutenant Kelley—the one Major Joslin was chasing down in Laos—was seen in Bangkok by one of our embassy interns."

Stone leaned forward, his expression animated. "I like the tentative ID on this guy as Jerry Santucci's platoon leader, Lieutenant Kelley, because he was MIA on the same day as Jerry." He spread his hands. "I know this is still all speculation, Leila. But maybe there's a connection. Chuck has been kind enough to use his influence to get the FBI to do some favors for us."

Leila glanced around the room curiously. "You all act like there's some deep, dark plot."

"The whole MIA thing could open up again unless we do it this way," Goodrich cautioned. "You see, all we had to mention to the FBI was the possibility of attempted murder for hire and the fact that it might involve crossing international borders, and they were all ears."

"Just what is the FBI going to do?" Leila asked.

"If there's a relationship between Santucci and Kelley, and it really was Kelley in Bangkok, then we're working on the theory that Santucci may have headed for the Far East if you scared him enough. So the FBI's combing the airline computers for passengers who might have flown out of BWI, National, or Dulles the same day you saw Santucci, and connected with flights to the Far East.

"Once they have a list," Stone continued, "they'll break out the male passengers and their final destination, obtain their passport numbers, and check out each one through the State Department computer files. We should have a list of names of men who fit Santucci's age and physical description soon. Sounds complicated, but not really in the age of computers." He smiled and snapped his fingers.

"What if this man's not traveling under a U.S. passport?" Goodrich asked.

"I didn't know about that either," Stone responded, "but I did ask because DIA has verbal agreements with other countries. The FBI will request assistance from any Asian nation that has Caucasians traveling under its passports. It may take a little longer but fax machines make communication a lot easier these days. Leila can verify the passport photo."

"And if I identify this man as Jerry?" Leila asked tentatively.

"If Santucci did, in fact, fly back to the Far East, and if Colonel Benner in Bangkok tells me that the man in that Laotian photo is, or was, in Bangkok, then I'm going wherever Santucci's final destination was. There's no way we can tie Kelley and Santucci together yet. And Benner can't be two places at once. He just happened to be passing through Bangkok on his way to Hanoi when this tentative Kelley ID occurred. His regular assignment is to work with the people in Hanoi and track down remains. My people, DIA, are in charge of investigations of this sort. When we get DIA personnel to Bangkok, the colonel will go on to Hanoi."

Leila's eyes hardened. "Santucci's mine as much as he's yours."

Stone wet his lips and glanced at the other two before he

looked back at Leila. "We can arrange for you to go with me . . ."

"I hope you understand why I explained what I did," Goodrich interrupted softly. "I want someone from the families involved, not one of the professional MIA hunters. It would mean more . . ." His voice dropped off because he could already see her answer.

"I'm in, Commander. Like Mr. Goodrich says, I have an interest in this that goes way beyond the rules. I'll talk to anyone you can find who was in Danny's platoon. And I'll go to the ends of the earth if it will bring some answers. I don't want to be left out."

Ed Kelley and Jerry Santucci hadn't planned to leave their lucrative narcotics business in Vietnam quite as soon as they did. There were still problems with the distribution system on the user level, and too often the salesmen were also their own best customers. That was a simple fact of life for men who woke up each morning wondering if this day would be their last. Their own demand often ate up their profits, and that was when they pressed Santucci to let them charge more for their product. When the price went up, that resulted in disagreements that too often blossomed into fights and, in some cases, the necessity of removing certain individuals from the scene before they attracted attention to the source of the problem.

The event that directly contributed to their final decision was the death of Captain Ledbetter. That changed operations radically for Bravo Company. The men were no longer employed in mop-up operations or lifted in to cover escape routes. Bravo's new commander was looking for glory for his company. Ledbetter's fragging occurred on July 17. His replacement, Captain Hogan, was in place five days later.

By early August, Hogan had reviewed company records and detected his predecessor's penchant for obtaining the softest assignments. Battalion command also changed in mid-month, and Hogan's insistence that his company be immersed in the next operation was approved. He also requested that the investigation of Ledbetter's death be reopened. Hogan wasn't satisfied with the ease with which it had been dismissed. He was damned if he was going to be another fragging victim. HQ scheduled a hearing for the third week in September, when the battalion was scheduled for a week's stand-down.

Bravo was in the field for five days extending into early September. On the day they were lifted back to the firebase, Jerry Santucci approached Ed Kelley. "I've had it. Money or no money, it could have been my squad that got chewed up just as easily as the one that got their asses blown away." The second squad of Bravo's Third Platoon had been assigned a night recon around the position the company had dug into before sunset. Everyone heard the ambush, the familiar rattle of AK-47s favored by North Vietnamese troops who'd been rumored to be in the area, the ominous burst of grenades, and then absolute silence. They found ten bodies the following morning. Not one of the men had had a chance to fire his weapon. "It could have been me, and I'll be damned if I'm going to put up with that shit."

Kelley stared at Santucci. The exact same thing had been bugging him.

"For Christ's sake, it could've been you." Santucci was incensed, and the veins stood out on his forehead. "Are you crazy? Changed your fucking mind? You gonna be a dead hero so everyone back home can shed a couple of tears over that nice Ed Kelley? You never intended to hang around this long." His hands were shaking so much that he trapped them under his armpits. "Here we are with the chance to make a fortune. A fucking fortune! Don't you understand? For Christ's sake, don't you understand that you stop making money the instant you are dead? Dead is forever. Everything stops. You're zero. You're zilch. You don't take it with you and start spending it at the next stop." His eyes opened wide. "You're dead, Lieutenant Edwin Kelley. Dead, if we don't get the fuck out of here." He turned away, then turned back just as quickly. "And that fucking hearing over Ledbetter. What happens if Hugh can't fix that this time?"

"You're right." If they didn't get out, Captain Hogan was going to kill them, turn them into dead heroes. Or maybe his reopening that goddamned investigation would open a can of worms! The pipeline was firmly established; the demand for their product was steady, increasing actually. They didn't have to stay in the field to make money. Hugh Young had set up a number of distributors. He needed people like Santucci and Kelley to make sure the system stayed in place. "You're right."

The process of disappearing from a combat unit was not an easy one. No one ever managed to just walk away. That was called desertion, and the military police managed to corral almost all of the men who ran and then made the mistake of reappearing in a friendly village when they grew scared of the jungle. No firing squads had been used yet in Vietnam, although that was always a possibility. Instead there was usually a general court-martial, a stiff sentence in the stockade, dishonorable discharge, and loss of most of the rights that an American took for granted.

Ed Kelley and Jerry Santucci had never really intended to return to the United States. They had both understood for a long time that the Far East was their future. For them the uniform was only a means of getting there for someone who planned ahead. The army transported you to the battlefield. It fed you as long as you could fight. It almost always made sure you got home, alive or dead, after one year. It was time to take leave of the army.

Hugh Young once again arranged for Kelley to be sent to Saigon for a day. He was agreeable. "You guys have done everything you could to get this business set up. You've established a standard for the other corps areas. It is time," he admitted. "You're right. I need operational types like you to expand the business. I can't possibly keep up with it anymore." He didn't want to lose either one of them.

"I can get both of you out of there," he told Kelley. "That's the easy part. The tough part is getting it all set up and getting your asses safely out of there. I can arrange almost everything," he said with a deep laugh, "but I can't quite convince the VC to grab you and deliver you to my doorstep with a bottle of champagne."

"Go on," Kelley said.

"This will involve some big bonuses, Eddie, and I mean big. I'll make available whatever it takes. I mean it could take a sampan—shit, maybe a sampan and a helo, too. And when you're talking that kind of transportation, there aren't any freebies." Young stared at Kelley over his glass of Biere 75. "But getting your asses in the right place at the right time and doing it clean so there's no suspicion, that's the hardest part. You and Jerry will be officially MIA. This is what will make you real operators. If you can pull this off, you can do anything."

Kelley grinned. "No more army. No more patrols. No more bullshit." But his grin turned quickly to a frown. "You really are sure it can be done on your end, Hugh."

"Cross my heart. It's been done before. Not quite like we're talking because the others have been in places it was easier to disappear from. If we pull this off, we'll eventually be able to salvage some of the best guys in the other corps regions in the same way. I need guys in Rach Gia, Cam Ranh Bay, Qui Nhon, and Da Nang doing the same thing you'll be doing here. You guys will set the example if I can get you out."

"Don't say 'if.' It has a bad sound to it, Hugh."

"Eddie, do you think I'd let you go ahead and plan this if I had any doubts? Come on," he said, sitting back in his chair. "You know my background. How many pilots do you think we made disappear when I was still in the Agency? This is just a little more sophisticated sheep-dipping," he boasted. "Set up the proper scenario for me, whatever seems to fit in your ops this month. If it looks right, I'll approve it. I'll have the money to pay off the right guys. And eventually, before it comes time for them to rotate back to The World, any possible witnesses will disappear." Young spent the better part of the afternoon laying out the details.

There were three alternative dates, depending on when Kelley's platoon drew perimeter duty—September 19, 20, 21. The battalion would be on stand-down after that. On September 19, Ed Kelley contacted Hugh Young and confirmed the twenty-first. Ed was told about a slight change in the basic plans. Because VC gunners were so nervous about the choppers these days, no pilot would fly into that area of the Triangle. Santucci and Kelley would have to make their own way to a canal off the Vam Co Dong where a sampan would be waiting. "Providing the SEALs aren't planning an ambush that night," Young said with a laugh, "the sampan will deliver you to a safe pickup site and you'll be successfully MIA by the twenty-second."

On the night of September 21, 1969, the second platoon of Bravo Company moved out through the minefield to the perimeter of the firebase. Lieutenant Kelley selected eight men to set up an ambush with him near a jungle trail that had been used in the past by VC mortar squads. They moved into the jungle with Jerry Santucci taking the point for the first time in his short career. That would have been against the advice of Sergeant Buckminster, but the sergeant had been left in charge of the perimeter defense. Buckminster had argued with his lieutenant about the inexperience of the men selected, but Kelley insisted these were the men he wanted.

Santucci halted and gave the hand signals to seek cover. The jungle remained silent. Kelley and the radioman moved up with Santucci. The three of them eased forward. The rest remained to the rear, under cover. Then a flurry of automatic weapons fire ripped through the jungle ahead of them. The rest of the squad had been ordered to remain in position unless they were ordered forward. They stayed in place, terrified.

Kelley called the firebase. "My radioman and point man are down," he reported over the radio. Santucci had already killed the radioman. As Kelley spoke, Santucci was firing back into the undergrowth toward the other members of the squad. Kelley reported that he was unable to move, but that he was ordering the survivors to drop back and establish a defensive position.

"There's too many of them," Kelley reported moments later. Then his anguished voice rose perceptibly. "My weapon's jammed—" From that moment on, Sergeant Buckminster was unable to raise him again by radio.

Private Victor Ortiz coordinated the withdrawal of the survivors under what was later reported by the frantic soldiers as heavy incoming fire. Buckminster led the squad at first light to the contact area. The only body recovered was that of the radioman, who the sergeant noted had been shot in the forehead at close range. There was no trace of Kelley or Santucci. His strangest discovery in the contact area was the absence of quantities of blood and the ever-present hordes of flies that always appeared after a firefight. Buckminster also noted that there was little evidence along the trail of any enemy infiltration, and he reported this to the company commander.

Kelley and Santucci made it to the canal where the promised sampan was waiting. There was no SEAL ambush that night as the sampan moved through the complex of canals. Before dawn, a helicopter lifted them from a clearing that Hugh Young's intelligence network indicated was well away from any VC gunners. The hard part was over. The rest of their path to freedom was coordinated by Young.

The following day, before an official report could be filed, Sergeant Buckminster was killed by a grenade rolled under his cot in a fragging incident. The official investigation labeled his death a result of the increasing racial problems occurring in every corps area.

Hugh Young was concerned about the other members of the squad after hearing of Buckminster's oral report. Victor Ortiz's body was found behind a bar in Saigon. The cause of death was listed as a drunken knife fight. Three of the men who went into the jungle that fateful night—Walters, Hastings, and Burns—suffered accidental deaths. Two others, Corey and Burris, were listed as KIA in other Iron Triangle battles before Hugh Young's organization could seal their fate.

For Ed Kelley and Jerry Santucci, the war was over. And to those in their old neighborhoods who happened to remember them, they were heroes missing in action. A square in Mattapan was even named in Kelley's honor when he failed to return with the others in 1973.

CHAPTER 8

THE ONLY INDICATION THAT MATT STONE WAS IN THE MILITARY was his car's license plate. Other than that, he and Leila could have been an attractive couple out for a ride in the country as they passed through the hills of western Maryland. Both were dressed in civilian clothes—Leila in a skirt and blouse because Stone had been advised that the folks in that part of Maryland considered themselves southerners and that southern men had more respect for ladies in skirts.

He'd called Leila in her room at the Crystal City Marriott early that morning. "How can you sleep on a gorgeous day like this?"

The red numerals on the digital clock beside her bed read 6:30 A.M. "Is that you, Harry?" Leila asked sleepily, confused by the male voice.

"Negative on that, ma'am. This is your latest loyal friend, Matt Stone, assigned to protect you for the better part of the day, and I'm reporting for duty."

"What could possibly be happening at this hour?"

"We're going for a ride in the country."

"Let's do it during the day."

"This *is* the day, my friend. The sun is up. The birds have been busy for hours, and untold numbers of worms have gone to their reward. And there were a lot of people at the Pentagon, the FBI, and DIA who never slept last night."

Leila came wide awake. "Santucci?"

"No. I'm sorry. Not yet. But I think this is just as important. The computer search was done on the survivors of Danny's platoon. And the results are even stranger than some of the data Penny came up with on the casualties. These guys are hard to track down. The only officer left is Hogan, who was company commander after Ledbetter was killed."

"Where is he?"

"Don't know, exactly. He retired and disappeared into the Sierras. Collects his retirement checks from a post office box in Truckee, California. The FBI's San Francisco office hopes to track him down eventually. But we did have one bit of good luck. There's a man named William Corey who was in Santucci's squad. We've located him in western Maryland."

"Corey . . ." Leila mused. "Corey . . . Billy Corey! I'll bet that's a name Danny mentioned in his letters. Where'd you find him?"

"A little town outside of Cumberland called Midland. It's a good two hours from here. How about if I come by your hotel in twenty minutes and we'll have breakfast in the coffee shop before we go out there?"

"Twenty minutes? Where are you staying? You'll never get through the morning traffic."

"I've been at the Pentagon since the FBI came up with Corey's current address at four this morning. I rallied Penny because we had to get into the vault to find out about some of these names, and I wanted more on this Corey guy. How about it? I'm just around the corner. Twenty minutes?"

"Twenty-five, at least. Maybe thirty. Order me a couple over easy with hash browns and biscuits. I'll be off the elevator and sitting down with you about the time it hits the table."

Over breakfast, Stone explained that William Corey was a draftee who'd been critically wounded in a battalion-size operation in the Iron Triangle just before the Christmas truce. He'd been medevaced out more dead than alive and originally he'd been listed as KIA in Bravo Company records. It was one more oddity in the company's records. Apparently, Penny discovered, the medic who treated him figured he'd never survive the ride in the helicopter. Records showed that he'd gone from Ben Cat to Saigon to the Philippines to California and finally to a veterans' hospital outside of Philadelphia.

They found William Corey on a run-down farm outside the little town of Midland. The directions from the local gas station took them down a dirt road bordered by stone fences overrun by weeds and bramble. There was no name at the entrance to the Corey place but the blown-down silo made it easily recognizable. There was an unpainted barn with broken windows, long, vacant shadows once occupied by board siding, and a door that hung off its frame by a single bent hinge. The shabby, unpainted house was covered with torn, peeling tarpaper. What was once a broad front porch hung precariously down to a cement-block support on one end. Chickens, a mangy mongrel dog, and a filthy pig were loose in the yard. Junk—an ancient car, an old-fashioned tractor with no tires, a refrigerator, various pieces of furniture—littered the property. It was what most people would regard as the end of the road.

A fat, homely woman with straggly unwashed hair hanging over her eyes appeared on the porch as they got out of the car. She stared at them sullenly without speaking.

Stone climbed out of the car. "Mrs. Corey?" he inquired with a friendly smile.

The woman nodded and leaned forward to stare at him. Her face was pudgy and blotched, her age indeterminate.

"My name's Matthew Stone, Mrs. Corey, and this is Miss Potter. Is Mr. Corey available? We'd like very much to speak with him."

"Why?"

"I'm with the navy, ma'am, and we're doing some research that we felt Mr. Corey might help with."

"He was in the army."

"I'm aware of his service, Mrs. Corey, and I'm also aware that he distinguished himself overseas. That's what we'd like to talk with him about."

"He don't want to talk about it. Never has."

"I can understand that. I was in Vietnam myself, and I know a lot of people who don't want to remember their service there. But there's some people he might be able to help if we could ask him some questions. Is he inside?"

"Nope." She pointed a finger toward the barn. "Right there."

Leila had just climbed out of the car and almost cried aloud as she turned toward the apparition advancing toward them. William Corey had come out of the barn. Each step was anguished as he swung his stiffened left leg in an arc and placed it on the ground so that he could step with the right. His left hand was a three-fingered claw that swung out for balance with each step. He concentrated on them from a horribly disfigured face as he approached. The left side of his jaw was missing, his left ear was a gnarled chunk of flesh, and his left eye was a ghastly pure white.

"Mr. William Corey?" Stone asked to break the silence.

The man stopped a few feet in front of them. His lips, pursed into a misshapen bow, formed the words, "Who are you?" The voice was deep, but the remnant of his jaw barely moved. He wiped away the saliva that appeared from the effort.

"My name's Matthew Stone, U.S. Navy, and this is Miss Potter. I'm with the Defense Intelligence Agency, and I was just explaining to Mrs. Corey that you might be able to help us if we could ask you a few questions."

The good eye darted from one to the other, settling for a long moment on Leila, moving up and down her body before settling on her chest. "About what?"

"I know you probably don't care to discuss your service time in Vietnam, Mr. Corey, but there are some people you may have known, men you served with, that we'd like to talk about."

"Everybody I knew is dead," Corey said vehemently. "Forget it." He turned toward the house.

"But there is a possibility that some of those men may be alive after all, and that's what we'd like—"

"I'm the only one alive. Should have died," he growled. "That would have made those bastards happy."

"Made who happy, sir?"

Corey waved the claw at Logan. "How do I know who you are?"

Stone took out his wallet and removed his ID card. Corey grabbed it with the claw, taking great pleasure in shocking them with it. "Navy commander," Corey muttered, holding the card close to his good eye. "The only sailors I ever saw worth shit were SEALs working the canals. Crazy bastards. Saved our asses a couple of times."

Matt reached in his shirt pocket and took out his SEAL insignia, which he extended in the palm of his hand. The eagle, flintlock, and trident reflected brightly in the sun.

There was the possibility of a smile on Corey's face. "Where?"

"Iron Triangle. Nha Be. The Special Zone. Ben Cat. Tay Ninh."

Corey nodded. "Okay." He turned back toward Leila. "Who's she?"

"Miss Potter's one of my assistants. She's been working on our research."

Corey waved the claw at his wife. "Make some tea. Hot or iced?" he asked looking at Leila again.

"Iced . . . please," she answered haltingly. It wasn't much past ten in the morning, but the air was already thick and hot.

"That would be fine," Stone agreed as the woman headed inside.

"Sit there," Corey said, gesturing with his claw at a heavy board balanced on two stumps. "Inside's a shithole." He sat down on the edge of the porch, wiping away the trail of saliva that was inching down his scarred chin.

"Mr. Corey, the questions we'd like to ask you concern

the company you were assigned to in Vietnam, Bravo Company, particularly the Second Platoon."

The man stared back at him with the good eye. "Who's alive that's supposed to be dead?"

"We're not quite sure, sir. That's what we're trying to learn. There were extensive casualties in your unit, and an odd situation with MIAs. That's one of the reasons we're here today. As you may be aware, there's an ongoing investigation into the plight of our men still listed as missing in Vietnam. What we've found so far is that Bravo Company went from very limited casualties in the first half of 1969 to unusually heavy losses later that year. A lot of what we've come up with is very puzzling."

"There's nothing puzzling. They're all dead," Corey growled firmly.

"Did you know a man named Santucci? His full name was Geraldo Vincente Santucci."

There was a noticeable reaction to Santucci's name as Corey's good hand clenched tightly, but he quickly looked away. "Nope."

"Please, sir, if you could think back. Santucci was a member of the third squad in your platoon. I believe you were assigned to that platoon, Sergeant Buckminster's."

Corey studied Stone expressionlessly. Then he looked away toward the field on the opposite side of the dirt road. "They blew away Buckminster's black ass when he was sound asleep in his cot. Maybe this guy, Santucci, was killed—like all the others."

"One I'm sure you'll remember is your platoon leader, Lieutenant Kelley. Full name Edwin Antonio Kelley. He was—"

"Dead, too." Corey still stared across the road.

"Mr. Corey, they were both listed as missing in action before you were wounded, and it's possible that they're still alive. That's why we're—"

Corey stood up and glared at Stone. "Why?" Saliva ran down onto his dirty shirt. "Why them? What are you after? You one of those drug agents?"

157

"No, sir. You saw my ID card. I've been in the navy for about twenty-five years now."

The man pounded on his own chest with the claw. "Did you check to see how all this happened to me?"

"You were critically wounded in action according to the records in the Pentagon, sir. Originally you were listed as killed in action."

"I was in a dream world that day, mister. I didn't even know my own name. I was so high I probably hardly knew I was in Vietnam, and couldn't have given less of a shit anyway. The last thing I remember was all this shooting going on around me. I suppose I decided to quit that war because I remember I stood up and dropped my rifle and just up and took off down this path in the jungle. I don't know what direction I was going, but I guess I figured I was heading for heaven. I tripped a wire. The whole fucking world exploded. I wish it'd killed me. I'd be better off."

His wife pushed open the door from inside the house clutching three iced teas and handed a glass to Matt and to Leila. The third iced tea was in a cracked Mason jar, which she stuck in her husband's good hand. Then she placed a hand tentatively on his shoulder. "I heard what you said. You never told me that, about the drugs, I mean."

"A doc in the Philippines told me it was tougher weaning me off the drugs than it was putting me back together. The morphine and all just made the whole thing twice as tough." He was facing the dirt road again, but both eyes were shut tight. "I'd gotten to be a junkie just like all the rest."

"The rest? The squad, you mean?" Stone asked.

Corey's eyes opened, and he turned toward Stone. "Squad? You shittin' me? The whole goddamn company," he snarled. "Half the firebase, too. How do you think anybody was supposed to put up with twelve months of that miserable, no good, fucking war? You guys, you SEALs, you loved that shit. The rest of us were sent there to be cannon fodder, to get our asses blown off so's the rich people wouldn't. That's why," he finished with a whisper. "That's why."

"I wasn't aware that so many men were on drugs, Mr.

Corey. I'd heard but I had no idea of the extent. Why Bravo Company?"

"Get off it, mister. That's why you're here, isn't it? He doesn't fool me," he said to his wife, shaking his head in disbelief. "You going to try to send my ass up the river after all these years?" He took in the farm with the sweep of his claw. "Probably live better there than we do here."

"No, Mr. Corey, I don't want to send you anywhere. I'm just a sailor who wants to help some old friends. I know this is difficult for you." Stone sipped at the iced tea. It had a strong mint flavor. "This is good, Mrs. Corey," he remarked pleasantly, "very refreshing on a day like this."

"Get out of here!" Corey burst out. He hurled the Mason jar at the pig, which was rooting near the discarded refrigerator. He stood and whirled toward the two people. "Just get out. Leave me alone." His voice was a cry of pain.

Leila stood up and spoke for the first time. "Mr. Corey, we'll leave if you really want us to. But please, I need to talk to you, too. My brother was in your squad. He was killed in action, and we've found some strange notes in the army records." She was talking fast and the words seemed to run together, but she didn't want to leave because she was sure this man could help her. She was positive now that she'd read his name in Danny's letters. "My brother was killed on my sixteenth birthday, and he was the only person I had. All I want to find out is what really happened if it wasn't like the official records indicate . . ."

"What's your name again, girl?" Corey asked, his voice as soft now as it had been vicious a moment before.

"Leila Potter."

"Danny's sister?" he asked in wonder, his voice reduced to a whisper.

"Our parents were dead. Danny was all I had."

"Danny's sister," Corey repeated softly. He turned away and worked his way over to the Mason jar, extending his left leg to one side as he balanced on the good one, and picked it up. "Danny's sister," she heard him say again as he straightened. When he came back toward them, swinging the left leg in its wide arc, he stopped directly in front of

Leila. "Danny's little sister." Tears rolled from both eyes. His deformed face twisted into a mask of anguish. "He was a good kid . . . a real good kid, but they murdered Danny. The bastards . . . the rotten bastards murdered him." He slowly extended his clawed hand toward her, then jerked it back rapidly, reaching out instead with his good one. He squeezed her shoulder. "The dirty bastards murdered him because he was the only decent kid in the whole company."

Leila covered Corey's hand with her own. "Murdered, Mr. Corey?" She shook her head in disbelief. She knew about the bullet in the back of Danny's head, but she couldn't accept the claim that Danny had been murdered. It was as if the parish priest had issued a denial of the existence of the Holy Trinity. "Danny was killed in action. That's what the reports said. That's what Captain Ledbetter wrote in his letter . . . and . . . and Lieutenant Kelley also."

"Danny saw what the drugs were doing to us," Corey sobbed. "He and Jerry were like brothers . . . together since boot camp. That's why Danny tried to get him out of it before it got any worse. Danny told Ledbetter about the drugs, but Ledbetter refused to believe him." The words flowed out of his bowed mouth in a torrent, and the saliva ran down his chin as Billy Corey released what he'd been holding inside him for twenty-five years. "But they knew he ratted and they murdered him for it. Shot him in the back of the head. Then they fragged the captain because he was getting suspicious."

"How could they murder someone in the middle of a firefight?" Stone interrupted, knowing he was getting close.

Corey jerked his hand away from Leila's shoulder, suddenly aware by the touch of her hand of the intimacy of another person, an invasion of the privacy he'd erected around himself for so many years. He backed away until he halted against their car. Then, without looking, he gradually lowered himself until he was perched on the front bumper. "There was no firefight, mister. That was grand opera, a setup. All it took was someone to start firing out on that perimeter in the middle of the night. A second or two was all. And then the rest of us were so mind-blown that we were scared shitless, and we fired at nothing in particular. And before you know it, the imaginary enemy has been chased back into the jungle and"—he pointed a finger at Stone—"and the rat is dead."

He sniffed and wiped his nose and his chin with the claw. "That's how Danny was murdered. And others, too," he croaked. "Ledbetter might have suspected what was happening, but he didn't want to make waves. Then, when they got Danny, maybe he said something, maybe to Kelley, and that was his death warrant."

"Kelley was aware of everything?" Stone asked quietly.

Corey fixed his one eye on Matt Stone. "That bastard ran it all, mister. Took everything we earned."

It was after noontime when they left the Corey farm. They drove in complete silence down the dirt road with the overgrown stone walls, down the county road through the village, and neither said a word until they were finally back on the main highway.

"I'm sorry," Stone began softly. "That was a rough morning. I don't know you well enough to know quite what to say. It's so . . . ." He searched for the right words.

"This is the last chapter in Danny's story," she said for him. "Now I know what really happened. I didn't want to hear it . . . or believe it. I can't bring him back. It's over."

"No, it isn't."

Leila turned her head slightly and studied his face curiously without answering.

"You saw Jerry Santucci the other day at the Wall," Stone said. "He's alive. Danny's dead. And that arrogant, murdering son of a bitch was taking a rubbing of his own name." Stone's jaw was set, and his lips barely moved as he spoke. "I learned early on in the SEALs that you don't get mad. You get even. I want that son of a bitch. I want him for you. I want him for Danny. I want him for every kid in Bravo Company who suffered and died because of him. And if Kelley's alive, too, we'll get him."

When there was no response, he glanced over at her. Leila

was staring straight ahead. Tears were streaming down her cheeks, and she made no effort to keep them from running over her lips and down her chin.

Stone was at a loss for words again. He reached over and patted her hand where it lay on the armrest between them.

Leila answered by grasping his hand and squeezing it tightly. Her tears continued to flow silently. "Hold on for a while longer, Matt, please. Don't let go."

Hugh Young would have preferred to remain in Indonesia for another couple of days. Originally, his plans included a day each in the Indonesian port cities of Semarang and Surabaja. Both were undergoing rapid expansion, and if he saw an opportunity in either one, he would come back to Jakarta for another day. Anything that took place in that nation did so only with government approval.

After that, he'd hoped to go on to Kuala Lumpur. The Malaysians were into the fourth year of the Second Outline Perspective Plan, their new economic development program, which already encouraged outside investment in indigenous businesses. Prospects there appeared to be unlimited. He'd thought about going on to Rangoon, too, but that business could be handled by Kelley at a later date. Better to wait until it was evident that the Burmese government was going to allow the jade business to grow securely.

Instead, his phone call to Randy Wallace had changed his mind completely. Randy had said almost nothing, but his silence had been an alarm. After twenty-five years of common sense, and some tough personal security under Young's direction, Jerry had been recognized. That was dumb. The person who'd seen him hadn't been silenced as ordered. That was a mistake. Even Eddie Kelley had made a mistake, but that problem had apparently been solved.

These errors in judgment had occurred much too quickly for Hugh Young. Past security methods were suddenly irrelevant. Relying on Randy Wallace to erase a trail, even to warn them if ever there was a reason to worry, was one thing. But recent events served as warning enough. Randy was too dumb, or too chicken, to be relied on now.

Young called Kelley at his Bangkok office and told him that tickets would be waiting for him at Don Muang Airport on the next Cathay Pacific flight to Hong Kong, which would leave in exactly ninety minutes. Then he called Jerry and told him to be waiting for them at the airport. It was time to talk. The bad vibrations of the past few days were coming together for him and he didn't like what they presaged.

After twenty-five years—Christ, it really was that long—Ed Kelley and Jerry Santucci had both been recognized, or at least they had generated suspicion that they were very much alive. Coincidence? Yes, it had to be after so many years. Stupidity? Absolutely. After all those years, a man wouldn't expect someone to recognize him at the Wall. But why would Jerry take a rubbing of his own name when so many people were around? And . . . What the hell, Hugh might have done the same thing himself. But that photo of Ed Kelley. The silly son of a bitch should have known better than to let a stranger take photos of him. A setup maybe? No, unlikely.

Damn. They'd been so careful for so many years. They'd traveled under different names whenever they went to the States. All their papers, passports, anything that would identify them, had been prepared by experts within Inchar who were well paid. All Inchar associates, whether they were Caucasian or native, knew how severe punishment was for any individual who made the mistake of revealing anything about the company beyond the confines of the office. And the hourly employees knew nothing more about Inchar than their immediate responsibilities. It was a system that had worked perfectly for twenty-five years now, and there was no reason it should suddenly collapse.

Hugh Young knew he could survive without Kelley and Santucci, and sometime in the future that might be necessary. But right now he preferred to keep things just the way they were. If it ain't broke, don't fix it. He was sure these minor problems could be solved.

He always had a good feeling, a comfortable one, about coming home to Hong Kong. From the air, the island of Hong Kong was a perfect jewel. As they approached from the south side of the island, Young could pick out the open-air markets of Jardine's Bazaar and Jardine's Crescent on the trendy Stanley Peninsula, and the apartment towers of Aberdeen to the west. Then they were descending over the central hills, and the heart of the city lay off to the left sloping from Victoria Peak into the world's most beautiful harbor. They came in over Kowloon Bay while the Wanchai apartment towers glistened with the late afternoon sun. Home. Security. At least for the moment.

A reserved Jerry Santucci was waiting for him on the other side of Immigration. He ought to look subdued, Young thought. "Jerry, you know I wouldn't have asked you to pick me up if I didn't think it was important to all of us. Was Eddie able to make the flight I arranged for him?" Getting a flight out of Bangkok's airport wouldn't be Ed's problem. But it was sometimes a superhuman effort to get from the city to the airport. He'd only given Ed an hour and a half.

Santucci barely smiled. Something wasn't right when Hugh Young called from a place like Jakarta's airport and said that everyone's plans would change as of that moment. "Ed's plane will be here in about half an hour. Song called me right after he disappeared through Immigration. Said she watched him run for the gate and figured he had to be on the plane, because he didn't come back. That's pretty tight planning, Hugh."

"I decided after talking with Wallace this morning that it was foolish to wait for someone to come to us." And then he added with emphasis, "Because eventually somebody will, Jerry. We want to confront our problems and solve them before they get stuck up our ass."

"Whatever you say, Hugh. Why not fill me in on this sudden change of plans while we're waiting for Ed."

"No, not this time, Jerry. Let's just discuss business in general. We're doing a lot of good things, and we're making some damn good money. I don't want to talk about these new problems without the three of us facing each other. We've been doing it that way since 1969. You two have been head and shoulders above all the other people in Inchar. I want it to stay that way, and I don't ever want any of us to think the other two may be saying something behind our back. I'd say the same thing to Eddie."

For the next half hour they discussed various phases of the operations of Inchar's subsidiaries. And when Ed Kelley appeared, Young explained what he'd told Santucci and added, "I asked Jerry to reserve a room for us at the club. A lot has happened the past couple of days. So we're going to drive over to Aberdeen, have a swim in the pool, maybe a little steam, maybe a Jacuzzi. Then we're going to have a few drinks and a nice dinner while we talk things over."

Kelley seemed perplexed. "Has the bullshit that's happened scared you, Hugh?"

Young frowned at the question. "No, Eddie, none of it has." His eyes narrowed slightly. "But no one got a photo of me distributed around the Pentagon." And he turned to Santucci. "And no one saw me taking a rubbing of my own name at the Wall. As a matter of fact, no one really knows me or cares who I am. If that doesn't make my point," he continued acidly, "let's just say that I worry about my friends and leave it at that." He turned and walked ahead of them toward the outer arrival area.

A shiny black Mercedes with darkened windows waited just outside. As they came through the doors, a uniformed chauffeur who'd been standing by the vehicle talking with a policeman recognized them. He immediately tipped his hat, as did the policeman, and held open the rear door for them.

It was small talk once again—Young loquacious and outgoing, Kelley and Santucci guarded and answering in as few words as possible—as the driver maneuvered through the late day traffic around Kowloon and took the tunnel under Victoria Harbor to Wanchai. The setting sun seemed to magnify Victoria Peak while they climbed up the hills past the green of Happy Valley Race Track. As they came down the winding road on the other side, the islands to the west were outlined in a brilliant orange. Traffic was thick again as they wound their way through the narrow streets of Aberdeen, past the immense high-rises that teemed with tens of thousands of people. Many of them spent their lives in a single block, one family crammed into a small one-room apartment.

The Aberdeen Marine Club rose tall and white on the waterfront. As they alighted from the Mercedes, a playful evening breeze cooled them while it also bore the stench of the harbor to the elegant club. Thousands of boat people, extended families, spent their lives on junks lashed together in Aberdeen Harbor. The Marine Club had become a symbol of opulence amid poverty. This was where the wealthy Hong Kong Chinese played, a multi-storied club where they allowed an international membership to join them. There were two huge pools, health facilities, five floors of dining rooms, multiple bars, and special accommodations for the foreign businessman who knew his Hong Kong.

Hugh Young refused to discuss anything other than the success of the subsidiary operations until they had enjoyed one of the pools, then the Jacuzzi. He insisted on skipping the steam bath when he realized there was time for massages instead. And when he decided they were relaxed, they moved on to the private room Santucci had reserved after receiving Young's call from Jakarta.

The manager had placed comfortable easy chairs around a low, elegantly carved teak table that he remembered Hugh Young preferred. He'd also anticipated their requirements would be no different than in the past. The wealthiest members, especially the Westerners, were predictable. A bottle of Jack Daniel's, a silver bucket packed with ice cubes, a crystal water pitcher, and three squat, heavy-bottomed glasses sat on a lazy Susan in the middle of the table. A large bowl in the center contained a dozen floating gardenias.

Santucci filled each glass with cubes while Kelley cut the bottle's black seal with a penknife. Then Kelley poured a couple ounces of the dark brown sour mash into each one.

"To continued health, wealth, and a succession of beautiful women," Young said, raising his glass, the light dancing on the large diamond in his pinky ring as he waited for the other two to do the same. It was a toast the three of them had chosen for their own the year they opened the Hong Kong home office.

"All right, Hugh," Kelley said after they'd drunk. "You've had fun being mysterious. We've gone through the bathing ritual, the toast, and we'll finish the bottle. Let's talk." He leaned forward, forearms resting on his knees, piercing blue eyes fixed on Hugh Young.

"Please do," Santucci offered sarcastically. He wasn't used to this approach from Hugh, and it made him uncomfortable. The scar on his cheek seemed more pronounced.

"Okay. The bullshit's over." Hugh took another mouthful of the whiskey and swirled it around in his mouth before swallowing it. "We've done almost everything right since 1969. Inchar's about ready to celebrate its silver anniversary —twenty-five years, if you include the Vietnam days." He swirled the ice in his glass with a slight movement of his wrist. "But we're in a position to fuck up. Can't do that . . . can't do that," he repeated, shaking his head.

When he leaned forward toward them, his broad shoulders hunched into his thick neck, he seemed almost menacing. "We've come too far since then. We're all still healthy. We're rich. We still have beautiful women, even round-eyes if we want them." He was ticking each item off on the fingers of his left hand, the diamonds on both hands sparkling in the light. "We've got everything we want. We've stuck together. There's an understanding between us. I mean, this is so strange, so fucking unusual, for three guys from such different backgrounds who got together like we did."

Then Young sat back in his chair and slammed his fist into his hand. The steady grin had disappeared. "So I figured I'd better bring us together before we started screwing up that relationship. I love you guys. I really do. And I think we have to stick together and keep that love affair going or we're going to all go down the drain together." He looked to Kelley. "Agreed?" And then he turned to Santucci with raised eyebrows.

They both nodded.

"I've never felt any different," Santucci offered. His stubbornness had subsided.

"Same goes for me," Kelley agreed.

"Good. Because you both have got to keep a low profile for a while. And I mean really low. I'll take care of what needs to be done to protect what we've built for ourselves so you two can avoid personal appearances in the wrong places."

"How low?" Kelley inquired.

"Lower than whale shit on the bottom of the ocean, Eddie. When you get back to Bangkok, about the only place you show your nose is the office and your home. Same goes for Jerry here."

"For how long?" Santucci leaned forward.

"Until we have all the assholes off our backs."

"And how are we going to do that?" Santucci snapped. The defiance had returned the second he realized his freedom really was in jeopardy.

"I'm going to do that. I'm going to remove them," Young said matter-of-factly.

"We always solved our own problems before," Kelley offered uneasily. "That was how we agreed from the beginning. Create a problem, solve it yourself."

"And that's the way it was until I talked with Randy Wallace this morning."

"He's an asshole," Santucci commented.

"Yes, he is, a bigger one than we ever imagined. Anyone who'd spend his life being an army gofer has to be an asshole. And anyone who'd take someone else's money for all this time, like he has ours, is an even bigger asshole if he doesn't figure that sooner or later he's going to have to pay the piper. But he also happens to be the only asshole we have solidly ensconced in the Pentagon." Young glanced carefully at both of them as he sipped at the Jack Daniel's. "Without Randy Wallace, you two might already be dead meat."

"Okay, I'll take the blame for—" Santucci began acidly.

"There is no blame, Jerry," Young interrupted sharply. "Nor is there any blame for that unfortunate photograph of Eddie. Sometimes things just happen. They get out of control. It's not like it was intentional. What's done is done.

Partners who place blame on each other have serious fallings-out." He picked up the bottle and turned the lazy Susan slowly, pouring a couple of more ounces in each glass. Kelley placed ice in them as they passed in front of him.

"I don't intend to see Inchar destroyed for anything as foolish as personal condemnation. That's undignified and just plain selfish between people who've been through what we've been through. You both have made an effort to correct your mistakes. What I intend to do is resolve them once and for all—myself. I haven't been back to our nation's capital in quite a while. It is possible, perhaps even probable," he continued precisely, "that you both could be identified if I asked you to take this any further. So far, I can't imagine anyone has any absolute proof of your identities. No one knows me. This has become my responsibility, and I would expect both of you to act in the same way in the future for the others."

"This sounds interesting, Hugh. Care to tell us about it?" Kelley's mouth was a thin line setting off his angular face.

Young glanced at his watch. "Don't know if I can still wake up Randy, but it'll be fun to try." He rose from his chair and pressed a buzzer on the wall. A waiter appeared in the doorway, and Young asked him to bring in a telephone.

It was a little before seven in the morning at Randy Wallace's apartment, and both of the others could tell by the look on Hugh's face that he'd awakened Wallace. The conversation was short and one-sided. Near the end, Young's complexion darkened slightly when Wallace apparently disputed some of the instructions.

"Shut up, Randy." The muscles in Young's neck stood out as he spoke through clenched teeth. "Good. Now, you are out of choices. I expect to stay in your apartment because I have no intention of placing my name or any other on any hotel's register. And you are going to assist me in cleaning up this mess." He looked disgusted as he paused for a moment, listening. He tapped his glass and nodded to Kelley for a refill. "For what it's worth, Randy, I don't give a shit about that. We own you—heart and soul, head to toe—and don't you ever forget one cent of the bundle we've given you over the years. You've lived better than any other colonel in the army."

There was another pause as Wallace obviously protested. Young sucked on an ice cube, then spit it back in the glass. Santucci extended his middle finger toward the phone.

"Let me explain in as few words as possible, Randy," Young growled into the phone. "If you aren't there when I arrive and if you fail to cooperate, there will be no place to hide." His face was grim as he added, "And you know what will happen if you pull any chickenshit. You might be able to get away from us for a short time, but you know we'll find you."

He finished the call with an admonition to Wallace to have a good day. "Randy's not a quick learner," he said to the other two, "but he got the message. Now let's have dinner. I hate that food on the plane."

"Randy's still an asshole," Santucci muttered.

CHAPTER 9

Stone's connection with Colonel Benner in Bangkok was severed with a loud squeal. He quickly hung up the phone gritting his teeth at the sound, but somehow the obnoxious screech continued, not as loud across the room but still irritating. Stone thought better of saying anything as he studied Leila's face. She sat on the sofa across from him, her eyes fixed on an invisible spot above his head still trying to absorb what she'd overheard. She was oblivious to the howl issuing from the portable phone in her hand, which had gradually slipped down until the instrument rested on her chest.

She was totally unaware that her breasts stood out in relief as she unconsciously pressed the phone between them. She was a million miles away at the moment, and Matt Stone luxuriated in this opportunity to study a woman without being made self-conscious. This wasn't an ugly moment he was stealing. He was appreciating an attractive woman whom he wanted very much to help, though he was quite sure she would have been embarrassed if her soft brown eyes had come back into focus and she had seen him staring.

171

The softness of her natural blond hair fascinated him, and if she wasn't a real blond he was losing his touch. But it wasn't simply physical attraction that had drawn him to Leila, not at their age. It was much more, a combination of elegant features and the strong character and determination she had shown during the past couple of days.

While Leila sorted out what she had just overheard, Stone also mulled over the phone call. The girl interning at the American embassy had been questioned thoroughly. Colonel Benner had expressed confidence in the intern's identification of Edwin Kelley. His words had shocked Leila as she'd listened. It was almost as if Kelley, too, had made an appearance at the Wall with Jerry Santucci.

With a little help from the Thai authorities, they had also identified the man lunching with Kelley. During a computer search of the local police files, the girl from the embassy had recognized the photo of a Burmese active in smuggling gemstones into Thailand. He continued to operate without interference from Thai authorities because he was deemed an asset to the local jewelry industry.

This was the end of a tough day for Leila, and Stone had felt like an intruder as he watched the emotions parade across her lovely face during the call to Bangkok. He'd known her for only two days, yet at this moment he felt as if they'd been together for years. He had shared a series of wrenching experiences with her. Leila was somehow more deeply involved in this through her dead brother than any of them had realized originally. It was one more twist of fate for a woman who deserved better.

At first it had seemed strange to him that the simple act of holding her hand after they'd left the Corey farm relaxed her. But it also transformed his own feelings. As they drove across the rolling Maryland countryside that afternoon, he realized how long it had been since he'd held a girl's hand—and enjoyed it. Stone had been even more surprised to realize that he was still holding her hand fifteen minutes later.

Matt Stone's relationships with women had been perfunctory since his short marriage years before. That girl had been petite, bouncy, cute, and so sexually appealing that perhaps he'd married her so no one else could have her. But she was not cut out to be a navy wife, especially a SEAL's wife. She'd wanted a storybook marriage to a man who came home from work every evening at the same time and who was willing to go to nice parties with the right people, raise a typical suburban family, and go to church every Sunday dressed like it was Easter.

He still shuddered at the memory. They'd made such a mistake. The only positive thing that had come out of it was that they didn't have any children. Since then he'd avoided relationships. Women, on his terms, were fine, and many of them felt exactly the same way about him. But he had avoided any relationship without an escape clause.

As he'd driven through the countryside with Leila, he actually found it enjoyable to take his eyes from the road occasionally to glance over at her. It was an unknown pleasure of the purest sort, and she was with him! He was both relieved and excited to see her attractive face soften as the time passed. The crying was natural and had gone on long enough, he decided, to alleviate the shock of what she'd heard from Corey. Occasionally she squeezed his hand, probably unconsciously, and seemed to gain strength as she did so. It was a strange sensation for Stone, but he found himself enjoying it immensely as they drove in silence.

Eventually she removed her hand and dug into her purse. She found a handkerchief to dry her eyes, and then a compact with a mirror. After studying her face for a moment, she applied some lipstick. Then, dropping everything back in her purse, she said, "Damn good thing I don't wear makeup or I'd really look like hell." Leila turned to face him. "My eyes will lose their ugly redness after a while, and then you won't mind being seen with me if we stop for a burger somewhere." She was smiling. "See, no runny mascara, no muddy marks running across rouge. Just me, warts and all. How about it? Does a burger sound like as good a way as any to bring me back to the real world?"

"Absolutely." He was sure no wart, no blemish, would mar that face.

"Great. When you see a fast-food place or a diner—whatever's your pleasure—I'm game. But I'm also still a scared female," she added, grabbing his hand again, "and a little TLC still goes a long way."

When they settled into a booth in a diner, he studied her closely while she read the menu, when she walked away to the ladies' room, and when she was coming back looking at the other people in the diner. She was close to his own age, but somehow she seemed different from other women her age and he couldn't quite place what it was.

It had been a long, hard day, and he considered the play of emotions in her eyes as she'd listened over the portable phone. Now her eyes focused on him and she took a deep breath, nodding to indicate she was back in the real world again with him. The phone still squealed. "Hey, Leila, I think you ought to hang up the phone now," he said with a trace of a grin.

Her eyes dropped to the phone pressed tightly to her chest, and the raucous sound came to her. "Sorry." She pressed the button to cut off the squeal, stared at the instrument for a second, then put it back in its cradle.

"Come on," he said. "Let me take you back to the Marriott. You have to be exhausted."

"I am." She smiled wearily. It was time to go, but somehow Matt Stone represented stability, or was it comfort? Security? No. More than that. It was the male companionship that meant so much. "Okay. Let's go." *How long has it been since I knew I didn't want to leave a guy's place?*

Leila knew that many of her friends, men and women, considered her a hopeless spinster. That had begun after high school when a lot of girls her age decided anyone not engaged was an old maid. But none of them could come close to the same experiences she'd had. Education meant more to her than a "pimply guy and babies"—that was what she'd said when she struck back at them. The only man she'd slept with in college had been a professor, a nice guy but no one to share a life with. After that, she'd learned she could succeed in the working world as well as any man, but it wasn't easy to find a man there who wanted a working wife.

By her thirtieth birthday, she'd decided that marriage wasn't the answer to her dreams. She liked men. She liked to date, to dine out, to dance, to go to parties, to sleep with a man she honestly enjoyed occasionally, even to go on a weekend or short vacation. But she avoided long-term relationships. Her world was Leila Potter, and she was ensuring that she would never again be so hurt and so alone as she was when she lost Danny. Now she was experiencing something entirely different . . . and how long had she known Matt Stone?

And when Stone returned to the empty, borrowed apartment that night, he felt lonely for the first time in as long as he could remember. It was difficult to admit that to himself, and he wondered—no, he hoped that Leila was experiencing the same sensation. He hadn't known a woman like her—but then, he'd never looked for one either.

The Pentagon, comprising twenty-nine acres, is one of the world's most fascinating office buildings. It is composed of five wedged-shaped, separately designated but interlocked wings, each containing five levels intertwined with a maze of over seventeen miles of corridors leading to beehives of offices, many of them windowless, that enclose the twenty-three thousand people who work there each day. While it is intellectually challenging to navigate through the Pentagon, there is nothing especially attractive about the building inside or outside.

Yet in the middle of this labyrinth is a beautiful center court of almost five acres. Neat walkways are bordered by well-kept gardens, flowering shrubs, and trees. There are park benches everywhere. Here every individual from the lowest-level government employee to the chairman of the Joint Chiefs of Staff can find a few moments of relaxation. On a pleasant day one can enjoy the singing of birds and the aroma of fresh blossoms or munch quietly on a sandwich away from the clamor of military business. And no one can claim that the twenty-three thousand Pentagon employees lack a sense of humor because this lovely cloister bears an affectionate nickname—Ground Zero.

Some use the courtyard simply to relax while others seek it out to hide from the phones and the bustle of the interior. And some go there to avoid being overheard.

"Leila was with me when I called Colonel Benner last night," Matt Stone stated as soon as he and Leila and Penny Carson found a vacant bench shaded by a leafy tree. He'd explained in Penny's office a few moments before that there was more privacy in the Pentagon's park than inside. "Benner feels confident that the intern from our embassy saw Edwin Kelley having lunch at the Shangri-la Hotel in Bangkok. That's twice he's been sighted—first in Laos and then in Bangkok. And this is the guy who disappeared at the same time as Santucci," he said with enthusiasm.

"What makes Benner so positive?" Penny asked, frowning. People in her profession were automatically suspicious of any sighting claimed to be that of a missing American, especially when the man wasn't in a captive environment. Too often such reports came from someone who wanted to be paid off, some weak soul who wanted to attract attention, or just a crackpot who saw a POW in every white face. Matt had mentioned Benner's report before they came outside, but he hadn't gone into detail. But it still made no sense—first Santucci, then Kelley!

"For one thing," Stone answered, "I know that Nolan Benner was specifically selected for the Hanoi assignment because he has a thorough background in interviewing people and sorting reality from dreams. He's after clues that will lead him to remains. He offers a balance between overzealous civilians and the air force's needs in providing a final resolution on each of the missing pilots. He flew combat support missions out of Udorn in Thailand during the war, he speaks both Thai and Vietnamese, and his brother is still listed as missing in action. When he says he's confident in an ID, that's good enough for me."

Penny, still frowning, rose and walked across the pathway where she kicked a pebble back into the garden. The other day she'd been on to something special, a mystery, and perhaps an oddity from the past that needed to be revealed. Now it was no longer hers alone. And it was so much bigger.

When she turned back, her eyes darted to Stone before they settled again on Leila. "I've hardly slept in the last few days between the extra time on the computer and all the hours I've been awake trying to figure out what happened to Bravo Company. It's something I've been doing for you as much as myself." Now her special project was being broken up and parceled out to others.

Stone recognized the situation instantly, a combination of turf and bruised feelings, and maybe a dollop of exhaustion. "There's a lot more beneath the surface, Penny. According to this guy we talked to yesterday, Mr. Corey," he answered, "Kelley and Santucci were in business together back in 'sixty-nine."

"Drugs," Leila said. "The men in Bravo Company were out of their minds half the time. Apparently anyone who got in the dealers' way died, including my brother."

"That's why your digging is turning up all sorts of oddities," Stone said. "What you were coming up with didn't make sense because you and Leila were looking at it from an entirely different perspective twenty-five years later. You recognized unusual casualties. None of us had put Kelley and Santucci together before. Nobody'd ever said a word about drugs, not a word about a business. When it was all happening, the people who should have noticed something wrong either didn't have time to worry about it or they may have been killed, too. I don't know."

"What about Santucci? Why do you think he's in the Far East?"

Stone smiled. "The FBI's running a computer check on him now. That's what I'm waiting for. Santucci's is a special case. If I can get a lead on him, we'll chase him down wherever he flew to. If not, I'll head for Bangkok. I know Kelley's there. Colonel Benner's hired some locals to track him, at his home, his office, wherever. Maybe that's where Santucci went, too. Now there's a reason to investigate, a warm body to find. Benner's job is really to chase down remains. Now that he's gotten a live one, it becomes DIA's job."

"How about you?" Penny asked Leila. "What are your plans?" She hadn't looked at Leila because she was both hurt and embarrassed, but now she turned and her expression was almost accusing.

"More than anything else in the world I want to confront Jerry Santucci face to face again."

"And when you do . . . ?"

When I do . . . Leila closed her eyes and was chewing on her lower lip when she heard someone calling out to Penny in a loud voice. Looking up, she saw an army colonel striding purposefully toward them.

"Captain Carson," Randy Wallace called out from thirty feet away. "I've been looking everywhere for you." He barely acknowledged the existence of the other two with a glance. "Army business, I assume?"

Penny turned in surprise. "Good morning, Colonel." Christ, Randy looked like hell, as if he hadn't been sleeping. "I've been hoping you'd have an opportunity to meet these people," she said brightly. "This is Commander Stone, who's been assigned from DIA as an investigator, and this is Leila Potter, who was sent to us by Congressman Goodrich's office. She's the one who identified that man who was listed as an MIA."

Wallace nodded to them both. "It's likely that will eventually be classified as a case of mistaken identity. Captain, may I talk to you privately?"

"Certainly. Is this just going to take a minute or do you want me to come back to your office when I'm finished here?"

"I'd like you to come back to my office—now," he answered irritably. Randy Wallace was bouncing up and down on his toes, his red-lined eyes blinking impatiently. "It's important, Captain . . . and classified."

There was no room for argument. Randy Wallace was usually the picture of patience, but this time he was very definite. "Can you find your way back to my office?" Penny asked Stone. "I'd still like to understand . . . I'd still like to spend some more time with Leila."

"No problem. How's half an hour?"

"Will we be more than half an hour, Colonel?" Penny asked Wallace.

"Not if we leave here right now," Wallace snapped. He never turned around to acknowledge her presence as she followed him back to their section.

Randy Wallace shut his office door and gestured toward the guest chair in front of his desk. When she was seated, he dropped tiredly into his own chair expelling a great sigh. Then he leaned forward and folded his arms on the desk like a schoolmaster. His thin hair hung raggedly, and his round face seemed to have been carved with more deeply etched lines.

Sheer drama, she thought. This will go beyond his normal bullshit.

"Penny, this is advice from a close friend who cares for you a great deal. Drop this wild-goose chase . . . now." How the hell could he explain it? My God, he didn't want to see her killed. Laid, yes. That was a goal in life. Dead, no.

"You mean the Santucci case?" she burst out with a mix of shock and surprise.

"It's a bummer. Believe me, it's a bummer. I have that on good advice. I can't tell you the source at this moment, but believe me I know a lot more about it than I can tell you now."

"Colonel Wallace, my security clearance isn't much different from the army's chief of staff. If there's something influencing this sighting, I need to know. The Santucci sighting is my baby." Penny Carson, you have opened a can of worms, she thought to herself. Was someone higher up already lifting the rug to sweep this shit under?

"Captain . . . Penny . . ." Wallace's eyes were blinking rapidly. He wanted to plead with her, to tell her that her life was in danger, but that would be absolutely insane. He saw her back stiffen and her mouth narrow into a straight line at his use of her first name for the second time in the last minute. "I know, I know," he corrected himself, "I'm the one who insists on military correctness during working hours. Captain Carson, regardless of security clearances, there is also such a thing as the need to know."

First Matt Stone was taking over her witness. That hurt, but now there was an even better reason to fight back. Now Randy was attempting to take everything away from her. That stunk up the whole goddamn Pentagon! "I need to know. I've put my heart into this Santucci affair," she snapped angrily. "It's"—she searched for the right words— "it's ludicrous to sit there and tell me there's additional information and then go on to tell me to drop the whole thing. Colonel, I have a need to know."

"I want you to drop it as of this moment, Captain," he said abruptly. "If you refuse, you give me no choice. I'll have you relieved." He folded his arms across his chest authoritatively, hoping she'd back off, yet more sure that it was the wrong thing to say as he watched her expression change.

"I'll go higher. I mean it. I'll go as high as I have to." She rose to her feet and leaned across his desk. "Goddammit," she said shrilly, "you can't pull this shit on me." She knew before she spoke that she was taking a chance, one that she would most likely regret. "I'll go all the way up to SECDEF if I have to get the message across that I'm getting a raw deal and there're a couple of pricks out there who have pulled the scam of the century and . . ."

"Captain," he shouted. He jumped to his feet, towering over her. "You are entirely out of line."

"Bullshit, Colonel Wallace, sir," she bellowed back in his face. "I was just about to come into your office and report officially to you that we now have a positive ID on the Bravo Company platoon commander who was listed as MIA on the same day as Santucci. Colonel Benner confirmed that to DIA late last night. His name is Edwin Kelley, the same one who was in that photograph from Laos, the same one who poor Major Joslin was chasing down."

Penny Carson stopped in mid-sentence. It appeared for a second as if Randy Wallace might have a heart attack. His jowls seemed to lose muscular control, shaking as if they'd become separate entities from his face. The color drained from his face as he slowly lowered himself into his chair. Penny was relieved when his mouth dropped open and he took a deep breath.

"Sit down, Captain." He spoke softly as if just coming out of a deep sleep. Wallace looked at her closely. What in the world was happening? he wondered. After all these years, was it all coming apart? And so quickly? First Santucci and now Eddie? How could it have happened? Now, he thought grimly, there was no choice but to accede to Hugh Young's demands. That was preferable to exposure, better than giving up the financial comfort he'd grown used to. "We're both out of line. I apologize. Shouting accomplishes nothing. I should have approached this problem in an entirely different way."

Penny remained standing, resolute even though an olive branch was held out to her.

"Please, sit down." His voice was barely audible. "People can't work together like this."

She sat. Was she going to get away with what she'd just said? "I apologize, Colonel." She didn't feel in the least bit apologetic but perhaps this was the way to appease him, to cajole him into sharing the intelligence he'd mentioned. Her mother'd always said you get more with honey than vinegar.

His voice was expressionless as he continued. "I want to tell you everything concerning the Santucci case." He was trying to create a plausible story as he spoke. "I insisted that I should involve you, but was voted down. I promise I will get . . . no, I'm going to demand that you be allowed access to this new intelligence." He was thinking quickly. How the hell did one go about something like this? All he'd ever wanted to do was go to bed with her, and now this.

"Believe me, I appreciate that, Colonel."

"I have to attend a briefing at sixteen hundred hours. I should be available by seventeen-thirty, maybe eighteen hundred. By that time I will have insisted that you be totally immersed in this newly classified intelligence." He was grasping at straws, trying to think logically, but at the same time he was terrified by the realization that Penny Carson did, in fact, know too much. If Hugh and Eddie ever found out, he would fall too. All these years . . . I can't give them up now. "I expect to be able to brief you personally then. The only way I know to apologize for this outburst is to buy you a drink, maybe a light dinner, if you'll let me. I'd really like to do it. We'll cover everything then. Okay?" he asked more brightly.

Penny was dumbfounded. There was only one answer. "Sure."

"Great. You won't be sorry. I'll come by your office, just like the other evening." *Damn Hugh Young.*

There was a message in Penny's office for Matt Stone to call a number at the FBI.

"We double-checked everything, Commander," the special agent in charge announced. "I think we located your man."

"I want to put this on the speakerphone. I'm with the woman who recognized Santucci at the Wall and the Full Accounting officer in charge of the investigation. That okay with you?" Stone asked.

"Go ahead, Commander. I'll just keep talking and you can ask any questions after I finish reading what I have here." The FBI agent's voice seemed to be coming from a very old radio when they switched to the speakerphone. "Later today your witness can confirm the photo we have. Only thirteen people fit the profile established by our computer for the day she saw that MIA at the Wall.

"Ten of those were possible. However, eight were as legitimate as the day is long. The ninth was ducking out on an angry girlfriend, and we had a hell of time convincing him we didn't care as long as he hadn't broken any laws. The tenth—your man—flew United all the way. Dulles to San Francisco. San Francisco to Hong Kong. He was traveling with an American passport under the name of William George Harrison. Apparently he's an expatriate American. The passport was legal according to Immigration, but the address in Hong Kong he used on his departure papers was no good. We faxed it to our office there for confirmation, and they told us it was a phony. The place doesn't exist. Neither does William George Harrison.

"We haven't been able to figure out how this man obtained the passport, but we'll know in another day or so. That generally means the guy had good papers when he prepared the application. The photo on record for this guy named Harrison was decent enough for a couple of United employees to confirm this same guy was on those flights. We're interviewing a stewardess in San Francisco right now who apparently spent some time talking with him on the Hong Kong flight. And we need your Miss Potter to give us a final ID just to confirm that we're talking about the same guy. When can we do that?"

"How about as soon as we can get over to your office?" Stone asked.

"We can fax this photo if that'll help."

"Don't bother. I have some more items I want to cover directly with you," he said vaguely, preferring to wait until he was face to face and the FBI couldn't refuse to do him another favor. "Perhaps you'll have something more substantial from that stew while we're there. We'll do it on your turf." He was going to see if he could twist a few arms, hoping the Bureau's people in Bangkok could do much the same in tracing Kelley as they'd done with Santucci.

There was no doubt in Leila's mind, less than an hour later, when she saw the FBI's copy of William George Harrison's passport photo. The scar on the right cheekbone wasn't as pronounced, the hair not so curly, but his face had been familiar to her since she was fifteen—almost sixteen—years old. It was Jerry Santucci.

The transcript of the interview with the stewardess came through the fax machine while they were there. Maria Poon regularly flew the Hong Kong route. She was an American of Chinese extraction who spoke fluent Cantonese. Santucci had initiated contact with her on more than one occasion during the last few years, speaking Cantonese almost as well as a native.

As a come-on, he'd claimed that he'd been avoiding Caucasian women for twenty-five years because they lacked the sensitivity and emotion of the Oriental. She'd spoken with him because he apparently thought he was impressing her with his fluency in both languages. Ms. Poon was married and had turned down repeated dinner offers from him, although Santucci regularly dismissed marriage as a valid reason. He claimed to be an international businessman, exhibited a detailed knowledge of a number of Asian cities, and boasted of an acquaintance with political figures in many of the countries he mentioned.

But he was elusive even when attempting to initiate contact with a female. Ms. Poon had no address for him although he indicated that his company had built and was headquartered in their own skyscraper in the Central District, Hong Kong's financial center, near the Mandarin Hotel. He also boasted of a beautiful fountain in the lobby, but he never mentioned the name of his company.

When asked if she knew how to contact him, she at first shook her head. Then she remembered that he'd insisted on her taking a phone number in case she changed her mind. She fumbled through her purse and found the slip of paper that Santucci had given her. It wasn't a business card and there was no name on it. When they called the number from the FBI's San Francisco office, a neutral female voice on an answering machine acknowledged that number and requested that a message be left. There was no indication of the name of the party who would receive the message. Except for his efforts to impress Ms. Poon, the only trail Santucci had left was the mention of an office building with a beautiful fountain near the Mandarin.

"He's out there, Leila. Jerry's in Hong Kong." Matt Stone studied her face as the raw emotion was transposed into sheer determination. "I . . . we can find him . . . for Danny." He couldn't find the words to express what he knew was surging through her mind.

"You said that I could go with you if we found out where he'd gone." Each of her words were measured, confirming each of her purposes in her own mind—Jerry Santucci . . . once more . . . for Danny . . . even more so for Leila Potter's peace of mind. Leila looked up at him, aware that she'd made a decision she couldn't go back on.

"You've already been appointed to Chuck Goodrich's staff. He knew you had to go, as much for him as for every name on the Wall."

"And no one's going to question my going?"

"Sure they will, if they find out how it was arranged. But you'll already be out of the country."

T. T. "Tommy" Chang knew Hong Kong as if he had designed the city himself. Whether he was on the island in the Central District or in Wanchai or Causeway Bay, or across Victoria Harbor on the Kowloon Peninsula in the teeming streets of Tsimshatsui or Hung Hom, he knew each alley and each building, and he understood the people, many of whom lived their whole lives without ever leaving those districts.

One of nine children brought up in a single-room tenement apartment in the Hung Hom district, his earliest goal as a child was to become a policeman because he knew policemen could go wherever they wanted to—and he wanted to get out of the Hung Hom because he was sure it was a dead end. He also wanted to go into one of the beautiful homes he could see across the harbor on Victoria Peak, and he was sure a policeman would be able to do that, too. It never occurred to him that only Caucasians and very wealthy Chinese lived there.

Tommy was by far the brightest kid in his school, and he did achieve his dream to become a policeman. After a year on the force he was assigned to the detective division because he possessed one of the quickest young minds in the department. It didn't take him long to learn that the ability to speak perfect English was the guarantee to promotion, so he went to school at night until he spoke almost as well as the tourists. And that was what brought him to the attention of the FBI.

The FBI's strong interest in Hong Kong expanded with the number of American businesses there, the flow of money between the two countries, and the flow of illicit goods, including narcotics. Although the FBI did not have legal jurisdiction in foreign countries, it maintained close professional relationships with many law enforcement agencies and established programs to train local police officers who would work closely with them. The Bureau also wanted to have a secure but covert foothold on the island when the Beijing government assumed control in 1997. The FBI recruited T. T. Chang because he was more like an American than many of the Chinese living in the United States, and then they brought him to the States for training. When he returned to Hong Kong, he was called Tommy Chang.

It was no surprise to Tommy when his boss, another FBI-trained policeman, released him from regular duty and sent him over to the American embassy. When the FBI briefed him on the Santucci case, he knew immediately that he'd seen the office building near the Mandarin; he remembered the beauty of that lobby fountain illuminated by colored spotlights. Finding it would be simple.

After memorizing the details of Jerry Santucci's features, Tommy walked a spiral of streets from the Mandarin until he came upon the building Santucci had boasted about. Even in the daytime, the fountain was beautiful. A bronze plaque identified the structure as the International Charities Center, and it proved to be the headquarters of International Charities, Ltd. Perhaps locating the elusive Mr. Santucci would be equally easy.

Tommy Chang was a patient man. He was in the vicinity of the building that morning before the first employees pushed their way through the swinging glass doors, and he stayed there, a master of the fine art of remaining unobserved, throughout the day. When the night watchman secured the doors after dark, he was positive he hadn't missed a soul who came near those glass doors. And he was also sure Santucci had not ventured near the building.

After dark, when Hong Kong's finances were allowed to rest for a few hours and the Central District was at its quietest, Chang undertook a detailed investigation of alternate entrances to the building. He circled it slowly, working his way down the dark alleys, unsure of what he was looking for, yet certain now that the man described to him would likely avoid the public entrance.

He found an emergency exit at the rear that could be activated only from the inside. He also located an entrance where trucks could back in to pick up trash, but was sure from the smell that it wouldn't be used by anyone who dressed like this Santucci. And finally, as he eased his way out from behind the building through the shadows toward the front, he discovered an unmarked door illuminated by a single light. To one side he found a sophisticated, almost invisible entry mechanism with a series of numbered buttons. He knew that the proper code had to be punched in before entry could be achieved.

What Tommy overlooked at that hour of the night, and could not be blamed for missing, was a highly sophisticated sensing device capable of recording every movement of each roach and rat in the alley. As soon as the security man, who occupied an office not too far from Hugh Young's executive suite, was alerted, he activated cameras that followed Tommy Chang's movements, including his discovery of the coded entry device. It also recorded his shadowy features electronically, eventually converting them to a smooth photographic image.

When he returned to his apartment that night, Chang immediately called his FBI contact and indicated that he'd located the probable office headquarters Ms. Poon had mentioned, the International Charities building. There was, however, nothing to substantiate the suspicion that Santucci actually worked there or that he was affiliated with the company. The following morning, Tommy promised, before any employees arrived there, he would be back watching that alley where he expected Jerry Santucci would eventually appear.

But by that time, the likeness of Tommy Chang had been faxed from Inchar's security office to Jerry Santucci's apartment, along with a report that the individual was Lieutenant T. T. Chang, a detective with the Hong Kong police who also worked with the FBI.

Santucci phoned the security office and asked to be called before he left his own place the next morning for Inchar. He assumed that Detective Chang would be watching the alley and he wanted to make arrangements for his disposal. Representatives of the Chinese Petroleum Ministry from Beijing were expected to lunch with him and senior officers of Inchar's energy subsidiary the next day, and he intended to avoid anything awkward. There was no point in inconveniencing himself.

"Colonel Wallace here," Randy Wallace said officiously, after picking up his office phone before the second ring.

"Big fucking deal, Randy."

Oh, shit! Oh, shit, shit, shit. Why didn't his plane crash?

"Hugh, this phone is not the place to—"

"Shut up and listen, Randy. I'm at Dulles now. There is no indication that anyone is following me, but I can't be too careful after the problems Jerry and Eddie have experienced. I am going to take a cab into the District to Union Station. Then I am going to buy myself a fat Metro ticket and ride myself through a bunch of transfer stations before I finally get my ass out to your place. By the time I get to your door, I will know if anyone is wise." Hugh Young had insisted on a key to any place Randy Wallace had ever lived. He'd received the key to Wallace's apartment the moment Randy had moved out of the house he and his wife had shared.

"Christ, Hugh, if someone is on to you, that means they could implicate me." Wallace's voice ended on a high note.

"Randy, Randy, Randy," Young responded with an unpleasant laugh, "I wouldn't allow that because you're the type of person who probably wouldn't hold up under questioning. Don't sweat it. When can I expect you to show up?"

"I'm not coming home right away."

"Randy . . ."

"I'm having drinks with the investigating officer who's on to Jerry."

There was a nasty snicker on the phone. "Going to do the job, Randy?"

"I . . . I don't know. I don't think so. Not yet anyway. I want to find out how much more she's found out today." He hesitated before saying, "It's really getting out of hand, Hugh. It's scary. They've traced Jerry to Hong Kong and there's an ID on Eddie."

"What the fuck?" Young exploded. "What's going on in your office, Randy? Are you selling out to someone?"

"Christ, no. Of course not. Hugh, listen for just a minute. I can't talk about it now. I mean, someone could walk in here at any minute. That would really do it, wouldn't it?" he added, pouting at the phone, experiencing a moment's bravery. "Listen, just wait for me at my apartment. Have a drink. There's some fillets in the freezer. Take them out, and I'll cook us up something nice when I get back. I may have a lot more by the time I'm finished with this broad."

"Like I said, get rid of her, Randy. It's time to earn your keep. She's in too deep."

"Hugh, I'm going to hang up. Just take my word for it that I need to learn from her for the time being." And with that he hung up the phone, the first time he'd ever dared to cut off Hugh Young. He didn't want to kill Penny Carson. But, oh, how he wanted to screw her.

Hugh Young left Dulles by cab and was dropped at Union Station, where he studied the crowds. Then he went down the escalator to the Metro. He changed from one Metro line to another, even traveling to the end of different lines in Virginia and Maryland to see if anyone else would get back on the train again. When he was satisfied that he remained anonymous, he rode the Red Line to Wallace's apartment where he took a long shower, shaved, and put on fresh clothes.

Then he called an individual who'd done some ugly contract jobs for Inchar in Hong Kong before a witness identification forced him to return to the States. "I have a job for you, maybe more than one. You will be able to retire and live like a king afterward." Young said they would discuss everything at lunch the next day at noon at Washington's finest French restaurant. After completing that call, he reserved a table for two.

Then he removed two fillets from the freezer and poured himself a large glass of Randy Wallace's Jack Daniel's. *Probably your last supper, Randy,* he chuckled to himself, *but it's one I'd have chosen for myself if I knew it might be my last.*

CHAPTER 10

Ed Kelley stepped out of the air-conditioned Rolls in front of his office on Silom Road and was instantly aware of the droplets of perspiration forming on his skin. It wasn't quite eight-thirty, but the temperature had already climbed past ninety degrees. Not only was Bangkok the hottest city in the world, but its constant extreme humidity also made it the largest steam bath. Without air conditioning, it might also have been the world's largest, flattest oven.

And it was also the most beautiful, Kelley thought with a half smile, strolling across the sidewalk. As he lifted his right foot to climb the first step toward the front door, an individual he'd never seen before instantly attracted his attention. Like Young and Santucci, Ed Kelley was constantly aware of his surroundings. Anyone, anything out of the ordinary, was suspicious until proven otherwise. Hugh Young would say almost every time the three of them were together that such awareness, whether it was intuitive or acquired, was what had made them rich and comfortable.

It was this insight that had allowed them to weed out the rats as early as their distribution days in Vietnam—initially the greedy ones throughout the system who'd tried to make extra money for themselves by shortchanging the three of them, and later the Inchar employees who'd learned more about the business than they should have. How many times had their intuition saved their necks?

No one acted quite like that person in Bangkok in the morning. Everyone had a place to go. The man's back was propped casually against the cool stone facade of the building, which was still in shade. What was so . . . ? Kelley looked away momentarily and then allowed his eyes to snap back to the man. Second impression! He was a Thai and he was reading the *Bangkok Post,* and . . . that was it! The *Bangkok Post* was an English-language newspaper! Most Thais spoke some English. But most Thais read one of the local papers printed in their own language.

Kelley continued up the stairs without hesitation but veered off to his right instead of going directly into the building. The doorman, whose most important responsibility was to spot Mr. Kelley each morning, was forced to let the door swing shut as his man headed off to the side. Kelley stopped before a vendor who had claimed the same shaded location for years, and purchased a small bag of fresh, sweet pineapple. With his briefcase resting at his feet, Kelley carefully extracted a slender slice of the juicy fruit. Holding his handkerchief primly under his chin, he munched on the fruit slowly, apparently concentrating on the vendor, who was expertly dissecting another pineapple with a machete.

The man behind the *Bangkok Post* seemed to pay no attention to Kelley, casually folding the pages back and forth as if he was just perusing the headlines before he went on to work. He was tall for a Thai, but there was no doubting he was a native. He drew the paper closer as he seemed to sense that he was being studied. His shoulders were broad and his arms unusually muscular. A Thai like that was normally either in the military or on the police force and Kelley didn't care for either one at that moment.

Kelley dabbed at his lips with the handkerchief, dried his sticky fingers, picked up his briefcase in his free hand, and strolled slowly over to the front door, which was opened instantly.

"Sawasdee, sir," the doorman said. Holding the door open with his elbow, he raised his hands in a prayerlike gesture and touched the tip of his nose with a slight inclination of his head.

Kelley stepped into the small air-conditioned lobby. *"Sawasdee,* Shutat," he answered, inclining his head politely. He experienced instant pleasure as the droplets of sweat immediately begin to chill. "How long has that gentleman reading the paper been outside?"

Shutat had been suspicious also. "I saw him come an hour now, Mr. Kelley. Too much time to still read paper," he said thoughtfully. "Should I send him away?"

"No, don't do anything. I'm going to have Prosit follow him." Kelley moved over to the house telephone on the far side of the small lobby beyond the man's field of vision and called upstairs to the Inchar office.

In less than a minute the elevator door opened and a small Thai stepped into the lobby. Kelley nodded to him as he entered the elevator. The man outside had now folded his paper and sidled over to the vendor. He bought a bag of pineapple and attempted a conversation—a useless exercise, for the vendor was mute. Prosit had slipped out a side door, unseen by the stranger who glanced once more into the lobby as he ate a stick of pineapple.

Kelley, his finger still on the hold button, watched through the glass doors as the large Thai strode off down the street with Prosit, now an invisible member of the teeming masses, following. Then he let the door slide shut and rode the elevator up to the Inchar office.

"Sawasdee." Song's smile of greeting was always special to Kelley. He'd never been able to accept her unique charm as anything other than a gift for him and him alone.

He dropped the bag of pineapple on Song's desk and inclined his head slightly. *"Sawasdee."* Then he commented as always on how lovely she was, well aware that few women excited him as she did. He closed the office door behind him and sat down to peruse the *Bangkok Post,* left on his desk by Song, and to wait for Prosit to return with a report on the man he was trailing.

Fifty-five minutes later, a lightly perspiring Prosit was standing before Kelley's desk. "He walked down Silom to Rama 4 and crossed the street to the right. I know he was suspicious because he stopped at many storefronts and watched for a while to see if anyone is following him. Then he stopped after maybe one hundred meters down Rama 4. I know he's waiting for someone in a car because he keeps looking at his watch, then down the street toward oncoming traffic. So I stop a tuk-tuk and pay the driver just to argue price with me," he commented with a laugh. "He's very surprised, but tuk-tuk drivers do anything for money. When I see a black car pick up our man, I jump aboard and give tuk-tuk driver more money to make sure he don't disappear."

Kelley laughed out loud. He hadn't ridden one of those open three-wheeled vehicles in the smoggy Bangkok streets in years. "How much does it cost to get a tuk-tuk driver to pay attention, Prosit?"

"One hundred baht each time," he answered, "but I also promise big tip if he don't lose our man." Then his face became very serious. "We follow that man down Wireless Road, Mr. Kelley, to American embassy. He get out of car and talk to American in army uniform—colonel, I think—for a couple minutes. Then colonel hands him money, and we follow him back to close by. He go into small office building on Suriwong Road." That was the next major thoroughfare parallel to Silom Road.

"Could you find out where he went in there, or what he was doing?"

"Not as easy. But I pay tuk-tuk driver again to go into building so no one recognizes me." Again, Prosit's dark face broadened into a grin. "This time tuk-tuk driver have to pay old cleaning lady one hundred baht. Then she says our man used to be policeman, but now he works on his own. For that one, I give tuk-tuk driver three hundred baht because he say he more important than cleaning lady."

"You did very well, Prosit." Kelley pulled open a desk drawer and extracted a wad of bills. He counted out two thousand baht and handed it to Prosit. "That covers your expenses. And if you don't take your wife out for a good dinner with the extra, I'm going to get you in trouble with her."

"Thank you, Mr. Kelley." He was all smiles as he slid the money into his pocket. "But I think something has to be done with this man. Very big," Prosit said, spreading his arms. "He could be very dangerous to us."

"Prosit, you know exactly what I want done with him. And I trust you to make sure it is done as well as always." Kelley knew there would be no trace of the man within a few hours. Prosit's contacts in the Bangkok underworld were superb. Kelley removed an envelope from his top drawer, counted out another dozen bills, placed them in the envelope, and passed it across to Prosit. "You may keep the remainder as long as the job is done well. But I'm more concerned with this American colonel you saw. You have friends in their embassy. It doesn't matter what it takes to find out who he is. Knowing that is as important as the other matter."

"No problem, Mr. Kelley. Right away."

Kelley sat back in his chair. Prosit had been loyal for a number of years and there was never any question of a job not being completed efficiently, no matter how complex or unpleasant it might be. "I'll tell you what. Get these things done for me and then I'm going to send you and your wife down to Phuket for a holiday." Kelley didn't think it was a good idea for Prosit to become too involved in the problems Inchar was experiencing. Phuket was an exclusive resort island on Thailand's southwest coast. It would be a good place for Prosit and his wife to relax.

Tommy Chang had spent much of the night awake, thinking about Jerry Santucci and the door with the sophisticated security system in the alley alongside International Charities, Ltd. He was certain that was a key to the man he was searching for. In the morning he came from Wanchai on the tram as the sun rose, stepping off a couple of blocks behind the Mandarin. Tommy wandered down to Connaught Road Central to watch the Star Ferries bustle about the busy early morning harbor. Eventually he headed back up Ice House Street. He passed in front of the International Charities building a couple of times, strolling up and down Chater Road, and that was when he was first seen by one of Inchar's security personnel. He slowed to stare down the alley each time he passed. Once the Central District began to fill with people, he settled across the street, directly opposite the alley.

The chirp of the telephone awakened Jerry Santucci at exactly six-fifteen. It was the duty security officer at Inchar reporting that the Hong Kong detective had been sighted, exactly as Jerry had predicted.

After a shower and shave, Santucci made one phone call back to security and a second to a man who could handle a Hong Kong detective. He prepared a light breakfast of green tea and rice balls while watching the morning news in Cantonese. Then he dressed, choosing a new silk suit that had been delivered the previous day from his tailor. It was a light gray, and he'd selected it because the tailor's female assistant remarked that it was a perfect complement to the *exciting* gray hair that set off his handsome, dark features. *Exciting!* That's all it had taken, but he wished the tailor's assistant had been younger and prettier.

At exactly seven forty-five, he exited the front door of his house near the top of Victoria Peak and stepped into the waiting limousine.

Instead of being delivered to the front of the Inchar Building, he directed the chauffeur to drop him at the corner of Chater and Murray. From there he strolled down Chater, making sure Inchar's security man picked up on him as he passed. Santucci spotted Tommy Chang from fifty meters away on the opposite side of the street. When he came to the alley, he turned down it and took three or four steps before stopping to glance at his watch. Then he made a great show of taking a slip of paper from his pocket, looking again at his watch, then turning around and walking out of the alley. He moved quickly down the street, hoping it had been obvious that he'd almost forgotten an appointment.

He waited for the walk light at the intersection with Des Voeux Road Central and, when he crossed, strode purposefully west on Des Voeux—a man on a mission.

Tommy Chang had spotted Santucci moments earlier striding down the opposite side of Chater with the morning sun behind him. Not very tall for a round-eye. Then he noticed the silk suit. Wow! Big bucks. Not hard to keep an eye on someone who stands out like that.

He was overjoyed when Santucci turned down the alley, and waited expectantly, anticipating that he would punch in the appropriate code to enter the alley door. Once he did that, Tommy Chang would immediately call in the confirmation that Jerry Santucci was indeed a part of International Charities and that he wanted backup before moving in.

But then Tommy saw his man stop, glance first at his watch, then at a slip of paper that had been in his jacket pocket. Santucci did an about-face and exited the alley, turning left. He must have forgotten an appointment! Tommy had no choice. He couldn't let Santucci disappear. Tommy followed on the opposite side, crossing at the Des Voeux intersection, almost trotting to maintain a position parallel to his man.

Santucci continued down Des Voeux Central with a purposeful stride, past the trendy Landmark Complex and its fancy shops, past the vendors just opening their stalls on Li Yuen East and West, past the boutiques and banks and office buildings that defined the Central District. Certainly, Tommy reasoned, he planned to stop in one of the banks.

At Queen Victoria Street, the sidewalks were so crowded that Tommy Chang decided he'd better cross over to the same side. He dodged between cars and buses and barely leapt out of the way of one of the rumbling trams that stopped only when the operator concluded there was a reason. Just in time, too, for the crowds were bunching as they neared the Central Market and Cloth Alley. The overpowering aroma of the Central Market drifted down Des Voeux, assaulting his senses. Where the hell was Santucci going?

Tommy couldn't believe his eyes when he saw Jerry Santucci, custom-tailored silk suit and all, turn left and climb the front steps of the Central Market. That was indeed baffling. The Central Market was Hong Kong's largest public market, where everyone from housewives to world-renowned chefs appeared in the morning to purchase food. The first floor was entirely dedicated to seafood, the second to meat and poultry, the third to vegetables and fruit. Tommy followed, staying as close as possible.

Santucci confounded Chang as he wandered nonchalantly past the stalls, stopping occasionally to watch or to say a word or two to people he apparently knew. With the Chinese penchant for freshness, the fish were cleaned on the spot. Scales flew like snow. Men and women perched on low stools or squatted on their heels in the deepening carpet of scales and guts and blood, filleting gorgeously colored fish with razor-sharp cleavers. Tiny crawfish and six-inch tiger shrimp were being boiled in vats. The smell was overpowering. Fish juices and blood splattered everywhere and on everyone. Yet Chang was positive that these people saw Santucci coming and made an extra effort to ensure he passed without a spot appearing on his elegant new suit.

They circled the entire floor before Santucci climbed the stone steps to the second level. The clucking of chickens combined with the bleat of lambs and the squealing of piglets to assault the ears even before the immense slaughterhouse came into view. People in the fowl section were in the process of wringing chickens' and ducks' necks before they passed them on to others who eviscerated, boiled, and plucked them, and then cut them into parts. Nothing was wasted. Blood sluiced down the gutters carved in the stone floor as baby animals were bled to death. Pig and sheep carcasses were bought whole or cut into pieces for family use. Sides of beef hung from giant hooks, some curing, others in the process of being sawed and hacked apart as cooks selected what they needed for the family or the restaurant that day. The stench was overwhelming.

Once again, after circling the area and greeting vendors as if they were all part of his extended family, Santucci headed up the stairs to the third floor. The stink of cabbages clogged the nostrils before one reached the top of the steps. The only thing missing here was the cats who acted as both pets and floor cleaners on the first two levels. Santucci's act mesmerized Tommy Chang. He followed at a distance, watching his man stop at stalls to exchange a word or two, accepting a huge orange at one and strewing the skin on the floor as he peeled it expertly with a stilettolike knife. What is this? What is he doing here? The blade of Santucci's knife flashed as he wiped it on his handkerchief and folded the blade expertly into the handle with one hand.

Then Santucci moved unexpectedly, almost as if he knew someone was following him, to the stairway on his left and trotted quickly down the steps to the second floor. Tommy Chang, afraid of losing him, ran down the steps two at a time. Where did he go? The jostling crowd was still heavy, but he spotted the silk suit moving purposefully up the aisle toward the beef section.

Tommy moved faster, pushing people aside to keep up. This time, Santucci wasn't stopping to talk. Once again, he was a man on a mission. Chang slowed down when he was sure he was once again close enough. The stench of blood and intestines and sizzling fat seemed to combine with that of the fish guts and boiling tiger shrimp from the floor beneath and the cabbage from above. His senses were reeling. Why was Santucci here? Why?

Santucci seemed to disappear before his eyes. One moment he was there, the next he was slipping between two whole beef carcasses suspended above the floor on hooks. Tommy Chang raced ahead, darting to the right, brushing against the cool red meat, pushing one of the hefty bodies aside to peer ahead. It swung on its hook to one side, then came back to press him into the still bloody cavity of another carcass. He pushed away, frantically peering around the hanging bodies as he moved deeper into the slaughtering area. What the hell was this Santucci about? He's not one of us!

Suddenly, there was Jerry Santucci facing him, no more than five meters away, his arms folded across the chest of the beautiful silk suit, legs set slightly apart, a malevolent grin on his face. Tommy Chang's last cogent thought—*Yes, he is one of us*—was cut short by the razor-sharp cleaver that cut neatly through his neck, instantly severing his backbone. His corpse had hardly touched the bloody stone floor before two ancient, wizened women leapt out to remove his clothes.

Jerry Santucci slipped out between the beef carcasses and headed down the aisle, nodding to the vendors. Out on Des Voeux Central, he turned right and headed toward the International Charities Building, a man on a mission.

In less than a minute, as two interested, uncaring cats watched, Tommy Chang was chopped into the offal that would be disposed of later in the day. Tommy Chang no longer existed to threaten the secrets of the Inchar conglomerate.

Those who worked in the Central Market could not remember, nor were they particular concerned about, the number of people they had disposed of for Mr. Santucci. On the other hand, none of them ever forgot that they often realized more through his contributions than they did from their trade. They could also recite the names of the children who had been well educated over the years because of Mr. Santucci's generosity.

Randy Wallace and Penny Carson were both exhausted, he from fear, too much alcohol, and too little sleep the past week, she from long hours reconstructing a twenty-five-year-old crime. They sat facing each other in the fashionably dim lighting of an Italian restaurant in the Crystal City underground mall, sipping their first drinks and straining to make small talk. Wallace had suggested the Fort Myer officers' club again; Penny said she wanted to put distance between herself and the military. That was almost impossible around the District, especially in Arlington where the overflow from the Pentagon worked in the office buildings above. But they'd both been to this place and knew it was quiet during the week. It was only half full, and there were no uniforms but their own in evidence. Conversation had been limited at best.

Randy finally spoke up. "You know, it's very difficult to get into a conversation when we aren't looking at each other." That was true. As they struggled to keep the small talk going, their eyes studied their drinks, the cocktail napkins, the other diners, anything but each other. "I'm sorry about blowing up today. The tension's getting to me, too. Just so you don't forget, I apologize again. It won't happen anymore. Scout's honor."

Christ, won't he ever give up on that "scout's honor" bullshit? Penny thought. But he's trying, she reminded herself. He's your boss. He controls your future. "I was out of line. Captains don't talk to colonels like that. Thanks for the chance to say I'm sorry, too. I think my temper's in a little better shape now." She sipped her drink through the hollow swizzle stick. "I'm too emotionally involved in this sighting at the Wall. I love my job. You know that. We go for months without anything solid; then all of a sudden an MIA shows his face right in our own backyard. And then this guy, Kelley, and the possibility that he and Santucci might be connected, because they disappeared together . . ."

She shook her head wistfully. "And I got so tied up with Leila Potter. Hell, Randy," she said, looking him in the eye, "I've become her . . . or part of her. I understand what she's going through. What's happened to her in the past few days—one shock after another—doesn't happen to most people in a lifetime. I cried with her. My emotions went up and down with hers. Can you conceive of what it must feel like when someone tries to murder you?"

Wallace shook his head, appalled and frightened that the operation had finally resulted in a murder right here in the District. It didn't bother him that his associates killed people in Asian cities, but here? He finished his drink in one gulp. "Nope, it's beyond me," he answered softly.

Wallace caught their waitress's attention across the room and pointed at his drink for a refill. "You, too?" he asked.

"Not yet, thanks."

He held up his index finger to signal just his own.

"And then Matt Stone comes along and sticks his nose into the work I was doing with Leila. He can go way over my head, Randy. Our little group is an administrative arm of DOD trying to clean up a mess that America left more than twenty years ago, and we're doing it the military way. Stone has politicians behind him and seems to know everyone in the FBI and every other three-letter agency. So there I am with my computer—Captain Penny Carson, diligent as hell—digging up this sloppy crap perpetrated when I was still in elementary school, yet it's good solid stuff.

"I'm doing my job so well that all of a sudden I've got everyone's attention, but Stone's coming up with what really happened over there. He's the one who found this William Corey guy who's been keeping a secret for twenty-five years and who pours out his heart to them about a drug ring operating right in the front lines."

She sat back in the booth and folded her arms across her chest. "I mean, this is crazy." She took a deep swallow of her own drink and leaned forward on the table. "Yes, I'll have another when she comes with yours." Staring into the glass, unseeing, she failed to notice the shock on Wallace's face when she mentioned Billy Corey's tale.

"I'd better talk with Commander Stone and Miss Potter first thing in the morning," Wallace said. "Some of this stuff sounds a little farfetched." *Fucking Jerry!* Wallace could feel his stomach churning. If Santucci had just minded his own goddamn business instead of pulling that infantile stunt at the Wall. "You see, what I wanted to tell you earlier today, but couldn't"—he was searching for something that would satisfy Penny and slow down Commander Stone—"is that this has reached the highest levels in DOD . . . way beyond our group. Anyway, I've been told to take it easy on this investigation while the big guns get into the act."

"Wait a minute, Randy. What are you trying to tell me? You don't mean this case is being taken away from me completely?" Her eyes were narrowed now, and angry.

"Well, no, not exactly. You can still do what you're doing.

It's just that . . . well, they don't want Commander Stone and Leila Potter to step into areas they might not understand."

"Randy, you don't seem to get it. Don't you read the memos in your in-basket? You can't stop them. I can't stop them. Nobody can. They're already off to Hong Kong. Why do you think I'm so upset?" She glanced at her watch. "They're in the air. I sweated my heart out for Leila Potter and now, no matter what else I dig out of the files in the next few days, this investigation is heading out to Hong Kong . . . and Bangkok, too, I guess."

She waved her hand as if a pesky mosquito were buzzing her. "Hell, that's what had me so upset when I confronted you earlier today. I didn't know they'd be leaving so soon, but I knew I was going to be left riding a desk. You just sort of brought all my frustration to the surface." Then she peered more closely at Wallace. "What's the matter? You look sick."

Wallace felt sick. Hugh Young had come all the way to Washington, and Stone and Potter were heading toward Hong Kong. Wallace knew Hugh would blame him . . . for everything. "No, no problem," he said. But there was one hell of a problem. Hugh would want his head. "I don't suppose there's any way to stop them?" he asked weakly.

"Randy, I don't know who in the Pentagon told you the higher-ups were going to take care of this, but they didn't get the idea across to DIA or the FBI or Full Accounting in Hawaii, because Stone had complete authorization for this jaunt they're taking. For that matter, they even allowed Leila to go along, and she's a civilian without the appropriate security clearance."

Wallace lifted his glass to his lips and found it empty. "Damn it all. I asked her to bring me another drink."

"She did. That's your second."

"Well, it's time for a third," he said dejectedly, waving the glass in the air. "I don't suppose you've heard any more about that platoon commander—the one they thought might have been in Bangkok."

"Colonel Benner reported a positive ID on him." She repeated what Matt Stone had told her. "Edwin Kelley's his name. An intern from our embassy there was having lunch at a hotel along the river and overheard a conversation between Kelley and an Oriental man. She was amazed at how the American handled the discussion, as if he were a native, and she couldn't get it out of her mind how familiar he looked for some reason.

"She mentioned it when she got back to the embassy. Benner said that when she described him, he took her over to the bulletin board and pointed out the photo of the American sighted in Laos. He'd just pinned it there that morning, sort of a shot in the dark. She'd seen it before lunch and that's why this guy had caught her eye. They even identified the man Kelley was talking with, some smuggler from Rangoon."

"Amazing." *Fuck Kelley, too! The asshole. Letting someone take that picture . . . after all these years.* The last thing he wanted to do was see Hugh Young. "Amazing," he repeated. The alcohol in his stomach was sending a continuously unpleasant message. *The whole fucking world's coming apart.* He glanced across at Penny. She was too pretty to kill. He knew he couldn't do it himself. Murder wasn't in his job description. He'd been willing to take their money and be a rat, and he would have done it all again if the opportunity presented itself. But he couldn't bring himself to kill another person, especially one he wanted to screw so bad he could taste it. Let Hugh take care of that. Hell, he'd probably get a boot out of it.

"Amazing," he said once more, looking into Penny's pretty brown eyes. Somehow, as tired as she'd looked in the office, she'd managed to do wonders for her appearance in just a few minutes in the ladies' room before they left the Pentagon. *Christ, I'd give everything I had to spend just one night in the sack with her.*

"You said maybe we'd have a light dinner," she reminded him. "How about it? The food smells good here. Better than getting drunk."

"Sure. Let's eat. And I'll have another drink, too," he said obstinately. If he was going to face Hugh Young tonight, he was going to be fortified.

Hugh's reaction to Wallace's news was as close to a tantrum as Randy had ever seen in an adult. Nor had the Jack Daniel's improved his temper. He spouted more obscenities than Randy had heard since his Vietnam days, and he ended by ridiculing Wallace for every failure a man might be capable of. Then he placed calls to Santucci and Kelley in their offices, warning them of everything Wallace had related. His anger eased only when they told him they had removed potential problems that same day by eliminating observers who were the obvious result of such information. None of them—Young, Kelley, or Santucci—needed to be reminded of the necessity for caution until the remaining obstacles were removed.

"This broad in your office, the one who started it all," Young asked Randy when he'd finished the calls, poured another Jack Daniel's, and stretched out on the sofa, "may I at least assume you've taken care of her?"

Randy Wallace hung his head. He was drunk again, defenseless. Still, he'd poured himself a glass of bourbon the moment he walked through his front door. "Not really," he answered softly.

"Not really," Young mimicked. "Not really. What does that mean? Either you've solved that problem or she's in a position to make things even worse. Where's your backbone, Randy?"

"But, Hugh, the real problems are on their way to Hong Kong. Captain Carson is just a paper pusher. She—"

"She knows everything. Maybe she's already gone over your head to tell others. She can destroy us. You've told me what she's come up with. So don't give me that shit. If you weren't so drunk, I'd send you out to do the job right now. Tomorrow won't be soon enough, but you're in no shape to do it now."

"Hugh," Randy whined, "you can't do something like that in the Pentagon. That's suicide." To think he'd almost told Hugh about the cooperation the FBI had given Stone.

Thank God he hadn't asked how Jerry'd been traced so quickly.

"You don't do well at fielding messages, do you?" Hugh commented acidly. He rose quickly from the sofa and yanked the glass from Wallace's hand. Half of what remained in the glass spilled down Randy's shirt. Young poured the rest down the sink. "You don't need any more of that stuff, babykins. No way," he said, turning and pointing a finger at the other, "no way you're going to squirm out of this. You're going to make sure she never makes it to the Pentagon tomorrow morning."

"But, Hugh—"

"How does she get to work each day?"

"The Metro mostly. She's near a station."

"Okay," he said thoughtfully, "you're going to pick her up and take her for a ride."

"Hugh, please," he sniveled. "Let's get serious. You know me. I'm not cut out for that sort of thing. I can't go through with it."

Hugh Young was formulating a plan as he spoke. "Don't talk garbage like that, Randy. I'm going to make a man out of you if it's at all possible. You're going to call her now. You're going to say you just received a call about a special meeting tomorrow. I don't care where it is as long as you make it clear you'll meet her for breakfast somewhere to brief her beforehand. We don't want anyone to see you picking her up at her place. The rest will be easy."

Wallace's head was cradled in his hands, his elbows on his knees. Was this really happening to him? He was a rat who would lower himself for the right amount of money, but he wasn't a killer! "Hugh, this girl . . . this girl is like a daughter to me." There were tears in his eyes when he looked up at Young. He was pleading. "I can't go through with it . . . not Penny."

Young's lips broadened into a grin. "Whoops. Penny, you say. Not Captain, but Penny. Randy, I do believe you have the hots for this lady. Is that why you can't do it?"

"It's not that so much, Hugh. I'm just not capable of killing someone like that."

"I see." Young's grin remained even though his voice had assumed a serious note. "So it's okay for Randy Wallace to take our money, lots of it, to be a traitor to his country, but he can't remove someone who's a threat to his friends." Now he was taunting the other man. Hugh enjoyed seeing men like Wallace grovel. "And these are the same friends who have paid him all that money over the years in case that threat ever arose. Well, thank God—any god you care to choose, Randy, if you think that god would put up with someone like you—thank that god that I am here to help you."

"What are you saying, Hugh?" Tears rolled down his jowly cheeks.

"You are going to call your favorite captain right now and make that appointment to meet her for breakfast tomorrow morning. Now, where would a logical place for an outside briefing be?"

"The NIS—the Naval Investigative Service. They're over in the Navy Yard, on the Anacostia River. That sounds logical. Why not there?" Wallace answered softly. Christ, he'd say anything to end this. "NIS might help with an investigation like this."

"Where would you meet her?"

"I know a Denny's in McLean that's convenient."

"As long as she drives her car to meet you."

"Why is the car so important?"

Hugh glared at him. "What is wrong with you, Randy? Because we don't want you to be seen picking her up at her place. I already told you that. Do you want neighbors identifying you as the last person to see her alive? Because we don't want her to take the Metro. Because I'm telling you and you're going to do what I tell you."

With Hugh sitting next to him, Wallace finally made the call to Penny Carson. His explanation was logical, especially after their conversation that evening. He told her he'd already called his assistant to explain that they both would be in later in the morning. Penny was willing to do whatever he suggested. And it was late enough that she wouldn't call anyone, since he'd already said he'd covered them both.

"Perfect, Randy, perfect." Hugh commented when the call was finished. "You're redeeming yourself. You're going to be a pro."

"Hugh, a few other people have been involved in Penny's investigation. I don't see how doing this to her is going to—"

"Don't worry, Randy. I'll take care of everything from here on. You don't want to do your job, so someone else has to. What you're going to do for me before you go to bed is make a list of everyone involved in Penny Carson's research and how much each of them could possibly know." He was going to have to forget about the photos that still existed; it was much more important to remove anyone who'd actually been working closely with Randy's captain. Maybe Eddie would have to have a little cosmetic surgery.

"Just a few, maybe two, three people know about her research; it's been pretty closely contained. You know, we don't like any word to get out to the press because of the families. So Penny's work was pretty much independent."

"Just give me the list. I'll decide what to do. After that, all you have to do is meet her for breakfast. Head out just like you're going to a very important briefing. I'll take it from there. I'll show you how this sort of thing is done."

Just the way Hugh said it scared Wallace. But as long as he didn't have to do the killing, he decided he could at least be an accessory. The money was too good to resist. He decided that there were definitely three people who knew about the research: Penny's yeoman, a reserve captain doing a few weeks of active duty, and his own yeoman. After he'd prepared Young's list, he asked hopefully, "So what now?"

"Go to bed, Randy. You look like hell," he noted with satisfaction. "You've been drinking too much and not getting enough sleep. I want you to be healthy and look your best for your lady love."

"Hugh . . ." he whined.

"Come on, Randy. I can tell you're poking her. You can't fool a buddy."

"I wish I was," Wallace said sheepishly.

"Hey, there're lots of other women in the world. This one was in a position to ruin your retirement program. Now go." He pointed toward Wallace's bedroom. "Get in there and get some sleep. I've got some calls to make."

Hugh Young realized an era was nearing an end, even though he didn't fully want to admit it to himself. The system he'd created, the people he'd picked, the helter-skelter development of new profit centers, the never-ending search for the perfect woman—the whole sybaritic experience was never going to be the same again. But he was prepared for the change. If it all eventually ended up with Hugh Young as the sole survivor, then so be it. If he was forced to disappear tomorrow, he couldn't care less. He had the means. He'd made preparations. Hugh Young would survive.

The following morning Randy Wallace met Penny Carson at exactly six-thirty at the Denny's on Dolly Madison Boulevard in McLean. He answered her questions vaguely, explaining that NIS hadn't said much to him other than they'd taken over some project from the FBI. God, what a waste, he thought to himself. If only there'd been more time, I know I could have nailed her.

Within a couple of blocks after they left, Wallace was sure someone was following them. He squirmed to relieve the tension in his muscles. He answered Penny's questions with monosyllables. What were they going to do?

At the next stoplight, he glanced in his rearview mirror and saw someone get out of the passenger side of the car behind him. The man came up on them quickly, opened the back door, and jumped in. There was no avoiding the .38 he carried though he kept it hidden from other motorists.

He ordered them not to speak and indicated that Randy should make a U-turn at the next light and head west. Then he reached over the seat and took Penny's purse, rifling through it until he found her car keys. He ordered Wallace to pull into a gas station. There he passed the keys to another man who drove off in the opposite direction.

Back on the highway, Penny remained still. The man with the gun was in total control. As Randy Wallace eased the car through traffic, she turned slightly to look at him. He was staring straight ahead, both hands gripping the wheel. His mouth was set in a straight line, and she could see his jowls quivering. She was scared, terrified, but the only person she might depend on was even more frightened. Why didn't he say something? Ask the man what he wanted? Ask where they were going?

They continued west, passing under the Beltway, past the Tyson's Corner mall. Another glance as they moved into green countryside convinced her that Wallace was useless.

Randy was frightened. Yet he had already convinced himself that it was preferable that this happen to Penny rather than to him. But so many things were racing through his mind, especially when he saw the other car following so close behind. He wasn't going to pull anything funny. He'd promised Hugh that he'd go through with this, and he would.

He stole a quick look at Penny, hoping she wouldn't notice. Her eyes stared straight ahead and her fingers were locked together in her lap. So he murmured, "Hey, everything's going to be okay."

Penny looked over at him. The anger in her eyes shocked him.

She can't know. Really, she can't. How horrible it would be to know and have to experience each moment until your death. *Why is Hugh doing it this way? He knows I'm not cut out for this shit.* Penny seemed prettier than ever now, even with the fear in her eyes. "Really . . . it's going to be . . ." He was searching for the right words.

"It's going to be what, Randy? Do you want me to find out what this man intends to do?" Her voice was shrill and angry.

"Shut up!" the man in the back seat snarled.

Finally his own fear overcame Randy Wallace. Even though he knew he wasn't the target, the tension was just too much. He suggested that the man should just let them out and take the car. The only response was a warning to be quiet and keep going. This guy was playing it to the hilt, thought Wallace. But that was probably the way the pros worked.

Eventually Wallace was told to turn off the main highway near the Manassas battlefield, and they drove over country roads for another few minutes until the man ordered Randy to turn down a dirt road. The other car still followed.

The man told Wallace to pull off beneath a stand of trees beside a slow, muddy river. The other car stopped inches from their rear bumper. Wallace watched in the rearview mirror as two men stepped out of that vehicle. They came up on either side of his car and opened the front doors. *How awful to know . . . poor, poor Penny . . .*

"Get out," one of them barked.

"No!" It was Penny. She continued to sit very still. Her eyes remained tightly shut. Her fingers were still linked but now they shook uncontrollably along with the rest of her body. Only her lips moved. "No," she repeated in a cry of anguish.

She knows. Oh, God, oh, God, oh, God, she knows. The knot in Wallace's stomach, the one that had been growing for days, grew even heavier, and he was sure—no, he knew—he would vomit.

A pair of hands reached in, unsnapped Penny's safety belt, grabbed her arm roughly, and yanked her out. She crumpled to the ground. "No!" she cried once again.

Randy Wallace undid his own safety belt with shaking hands and climbed out. He was shocked at how unsteady his legs were and thankful that his life would not end in this manner. He didn't want to see it happen to anyone, especially not Penny, not that pretty creature. The small, hard eyes of the stranger bored into his own, and he had to look away as he said, "I don't want to see this. I don't think I could—" He gagged twice and then vomited down his front.

"Walk away over there." The man gestured toward the river.

"Thanks. I appreciate this." Randy's voice was a bare

whisper. "I'll put in a good word with Hugh." He was ashamed of himself for not showing more bravery, but he'd always liked Penny Carson.

"You asshole!" she screamed.

At least she was telling them off.

"Randy, you asshole! You asshole—" Her last words ended in deep sobs.

She knows . . . she understands about me . . . it wasn't supposed to be . . . oh God. Life couldn't ever be any worse than this. Randy Wallace experienced a sense of shame that he would have thought impossible moments before. He never should have been so greedy. This was definitely the worst moment of the commitment he'd made to Hugh Young so many years before. It was time to break it off.

He heard Penny repeating, "No, no, no . . ." as he kept walking thankfully away.

He closed his eyes instinctively at the sound of the shot, a mental image of Penny vivid in his mind. *How sad—*

The thought would never be completed. Wallace heard a second explosion at the same instant he felt a jarring crunch at the base of his skull. He was never aware of how many times his corpse rolled over with the impact.

Not only had Randy Wallace outlived his usefulness to International Charities, Ltd., but he had also made a pitiful display of himself the night before in front of the most important member of the corporation.

CHAPTER 11

I DON'T KNOW WHAT I'LL DO—OR SAY, FOR THAT MATTER—IF I see Jerry again." Leila spoke with conviction. "I've thought about it so often since the Wall, especially on the flight over here, and I still have no idea." Yet here she was in Hong Kong. The possibility of encountering him face to face, so remote a few days before, impossible a week ago, had become a reality. Hong Kong! Even that was hard to believe. She'd never been this far from home before. But her world had turned upside down in just one week.

Matt Stone sat across from her sipping a beer. "If you see him again, Leila, you can be damn sure you won't be alone this time."

"Believe me, Leila, there will always be someone around, whether it's our people or Mr. Chan's." The man who spoke was an acquaintance of Stone's, Danny Slade, another navy commander who'd met them as they came through Immigration at Kai Tak Airport.

"Thanks, Danny, you're kind to say so. But I'm so exhausted after the trip over here that I think I'd sleep like a baby tonight even if I knew he was going to break down my door." They were having a light dinner in the café of a hotel in Kowloon. It was an older hotel catering primarily to an Asian clientele and had been selected by W. P. Chan because few Americans stayed there.

The fourth individual at their table was Detective W. P. Chan of the Hong Kong police force. He was a diminutive individual, smaller even than Leila, with tiny black eyes, a full head of rich black hair, and a round, ageless, expressionless face. But Slade had explained as they drove in from the airport that Chan also had a reputation as one of the toughest men on the Hong Kong force. Slade had said with a grin, "He's known as the Mongoose because of his temperament and persistence. He's tenacious, as they say, and he's also a Hong Kong legend."

"Miss Potter," Chan said solemnly, "I will back up Commander Slade completely on your safety. But his tall white Americans can't enjoy the anonymity that my own people do. Caucasians, unfortunately, are recognized quite readily in Hong Kong, especially those who are obviously not tourists. My best men will be on duty twenty-four hours a day here in the hotel. And they will know every step you take while you're in Hong Kong." His English was as clear of any accent as their own, and he employed Americanisms like a native. W. P. Chan had been selected years before to take part in the FBI training program at Quantico because he'd already become one of the top special investigators in his own country.

"W.P. is correct. It would be foolish to use round-eyes," Slade agreed. "A dead giveaway to someone like Santucci." Danny Slade was hard to read. He had a full head of prematurely gray hair which went along with his rank, but clear blue eyes and smooth baby face made him appear much younger. His thin lips barely moved when he talked. "W.P.'s men are good—great, as a matter of fact."

"I am as eager to see Santucci as you are, Miss Potter," Chan continued. "The man I assigned to locate him, Tommy Chang, is a trusted friend of mine. I recommended him to your FBI. We have worked together for years. There is absolutely no reason that he should have made his presence known. But the simple fact that he didn't call in this morning tells me that he was discovered."

He paused for a moment and appeared thoughtful. Then his face brightened. "Such talk is unpleasant. I am very pleased that you came here to help us, though. I like Americans. I like your informal ways. Here, people sometimes fail to understand the most vital things because they are so concerned with formalities. I'm not a formal person, and I don't care to have formalities stand in our way. I, too, would like to call you Leila if you don't object. May I?"

"Certainly." She'd been watching W. P. Chan as he spoke. His face had remained expressionless even as he made an effort to eliminate what he considered a barrier. Why not carry that effort one step further? "That's very sweet of you. Danny called you W.P. a moment ago," she said. "That seems very American, but I think he told me earlier you've lived in Hong Kong all your life. Do you prefer the initials?"

"That depends on whom I'm with. My wife never uses them." He smiled for the first time. "Let me tell you a story," he said solemnly. "My father moved to San Francisco when he was very young. That's why my name is Westernized. He worked very hard and made a great deal of money by our standards. He was approaching middle age when he decided he finally had enough money to get married. And soon after he did, all these babies started to appear, one a year for a while—all daughters."

Chan beamed as he told the story. "When my father looked about him at the streets of Chinatown, he made the decision that life was too fast in San Francisco. He was afraid to bring up girls in a place like that. So he brought the entire family back to Hong Kong, where I was born—the first and only son.

"I think he was happy that I finally appeared because I made number seven—a very lucky number and a good place to stop making babies. I was supposed to go to America just like him. That's why I was taught English and brought up like an American boy. However, much to his disappointment, I loved Hong Kong. The poor man was dead before I ever went to the United States." He smiled wistfully. "So now, Miss Leila," he said, "you know why my name is Westernized. You and I, now we have no formality between us." His tiny black eyes seemed to disappear as he grinned with satisfaction.

"What does the W.P. stand for?" she asked.

"My father called me Walter. He thought that was a very fine American name. He said that was the name of an American who was very kind to him when he first arrived there. The *P* doesn't stand for anything. My father noticed that most Americans signed their names with a first name and a middle initial. I don't think he ever thought about a middle name, just the initial. I changed my first name to a Chinese name for my own satisfaction."

"What is it now?"

"Woo," he answered.

"Woo. Is that what you prefer?"

"That's what my wife prefers. It was an old family name. That's why I chose it, so I could be like all the other Chinese in Hong Kong."

"Is that what you want to be called?"

The little man smiled brightly. "That would be like me calling you Potter. Actually, with Americans, I suppose I prefer what Danny calls me—W.P. I like the sound of that. Don't you?"

"Definitely." After traveling for sixteen hours, Leila felt as if her world was completely upside down. Now she'd met a native of Hong Kong who was known as the Mongoose and who preferred to be addressed like an American. But he was also totally dedicated to finding Jerry Santucci because he desperately wanted to find out what had happened to Tommy Chang.

The name International Charities was purposely misleading. To an American it might indicate an organization similar to the United Way, a conglomeration of charities designed to minimize the effort and overhead in obtaining funds while reducing multiple appeals for financial contributions. To raise such a worthy effort to the international level was certainly a laudable objective.

Contrary to that assumption, the name had been selected by Hugh Young in a moment of hilarity. Hong Kong had been chosen as their home base for a number of reasons, not the least of which was the fact that the island was the financial capital of Asia. A company could also operate on the island without government interference. The business of Hong Kong was to make as much money as possible, and the community welcomed companies that generated cash without asking difficult questions. While it remained unwritten, there was a fundamental law in the colony that was cited with reverence: *economic gain*. And finally, Hong Kong was an international hub, attracting both the most respectable and the most disreputable members of the world's business community.

Most of those who entered the business when it was purely narcotics were divided into two groups—managers, like Ed Kelley, and operators, like Jerry Santucci. Very few operators remained with the company; they had either tired of the Southeast Asian life or just gradually drifted away. They were lucky because they understood so little about the business that they were allowed to leave. They were no threat.

Of those not absorbed into the hierarchy of the business, few managed to survive. That was especially true of the Caucasians. They knew too much about Hugh Young and his system, and unfortunately for them, Young had learned not to trust their type. He knew Asians were close-mouthed. He also learned at an early stage that he could trust some of them to go off on their own and later come back as friends and customers of Inchar. Hugh appreciated loyalty as well as he understood perfidy, and he rewarded one group while he disposed of the other. It would have been impossible for most American businessmen to understand this path to success, or the absolute loyalty required.

At the time the agreement was reached to make the island

their permanent home, they were renting office space, spilling over into other buildings as their business expanded faster than any of them had predicted. They grew so fast that they had no time to decide, nor did they care, what they were or what their company was called.

"The time has come," Hugh Young announced one evening as they celebrated their decision to build a corporate headquarters, "to create a permanent, respectable front for ourselves." They were dining in a private room at Gaddi's in the Peninsula Hotel, and corks from vintage champagne popped continuously that night. "We need a proper name because someday in the near future we're going to move into the finest skyscraper in Hong Kong and it's going to look right across Victoria Harbor."

Jerry Santucci rose unsteadily from his chair. "I'd like to make a toast." He raised his glass high, and champagne slopped across his silk suit jacket and down his silk tie. "Here's to Bravo Company, the source of our success." He remained standing after they all drank. "I suggest we call ourselves the Bravo Fund, since that was where we first started lining our pockets."

"I like the word 'fund,'" Kelley responded. "Sounds like a mutual fund, turning money into more money."

Norm Hersey, a Brit who'd been naturally attracted by Hugh Young's ambitious plans in Saigon and had fine-tuned their initial distribution system, disagreed. "Bravo is too military, too American," he commented drunkenly. "We don't want to attract unwanted attention from the United States. Make the name more international."

The other non-American members agreed. Though they were not founders, they had achieved status within the organization because of their own unique talents and significant contributions to profits. It didn't take long for them to convince the group of American expatriates that Hersey's suggestion made sense. They were, in fact, an international group.

"International!" Young piped up. "That's right. That has to be part of our name."

"Well, why not call it the International Fund?" said Kelley.

They argued back and forth about corporate names through the remainder of the dinner until Hugh Young spoke up when the room was blue with cigar smoke, "Charity!" he roared. "We are a charity unto ourselves." He jumped to his feet. "Full glasses, gentlemen." Champagne bottles were emptied into overflowing crystal glasses. Hugh climbed onto a chair and raised his glass. "Here's to every one of us and to our International Charities, Limited. May we benefit beyond our wildest dreams."

"Beyond our wildest dreams," Norm Hersey echoed, guzzling champagne from the bottle.

Few people in Hong Kong or on the Pacific Rim would ever question that name. That would have been ill-mannered. Most were more than willing to accept the shortened "Inchar" and never insisted that vague responses to their queries be expanded upon. And the reason was simple: the people of Inchar brought a golden touch to whomever they decided to work with. Their cash reserves were bottomless. Their vision was incomparable.

Inchar had somehow opened doors to government offices that promoted an automatic stamp of approval on every idea that was broached. No one cared to argue with success. Their contacts in palaces, parliament buildings, and city halls were superb, and business associates soon came to realize that Inchar was never turned down for a license, a charter, a sanction, or whatever was necessary to conduct business on an international basis in any country.

When W. P. Chan stepped through the tall glass doors of International Charities, Ltd., the morning after his meeting with the Americans, he never wondered about the corporate name. Such names meant nothing to him. But he was immediately taken by the beautiful fountain in the lobby. Too many of the new office buildings in Hong Kong had been designed with the brisk efficiency of Westerners. The architecture and workmanship here were obviously Oriental. An equally attractive garden, unusual in its subtlety, surrounded three sides of the fountain. W.P. instantly admired the people who had done this. They understood Hong Kong.

The tenants of the building were posted alphabetically in both English and Chinese on a directory near the security station. Inchar seemed to occupy at least a third of the total. A number of Inchar companies were listed under such broad headings as Energy, Finance, Construction, Hospitality, Communications, and Electronics. Those companies represented nations covering the entire Pacific Rim. However, there were no names of people, and there was no listing for a holding company called International Charities, Ltd., even though he was standing in the lobby of Inchar House. Chan thought that would be interesting to consider when his staff was researching the corporate names as they appeared on the photographs of the directory that he'd taken with the miniature camera in his large and garish tie clip.

"May I assist you, sir?" a uniformed guard inquired in Cantonese. Anyone unfamiliar enough with the companies in the building to stand before that board for so long was obviously someone to be questioned.

W.P. never looked at the guard, never changed his expression. "Santucci's not listed here," he snapped back in his perfect American English.

The guard gave no indication that the name was at all familiar. But his English was equally fluent. "Excuse me?"

"Jerry Santucci's name's not here. Where the hell is he?"

"I don't follow you, sir. I don't believe I know that name," he replied evenly. He studied the tiny man and saw only a gentleman with an expressionless face. "Who again?" He removed a small directory from beneath the counter at the same time he pressed a button that would ring in the outer office of the suite in the lower level of the building. The secretary down there, Connie, would alert Mr. Santucci.

Chan smiled inwardly. He'd anticipated there might be a warning buzzer and had barely noted the extra movement. Yet the guard had definitely touched a button or switch of some kind. *Score one*, he thought to himself. The man was familiar with Santucci's name. He stepped closer to the security desk and leaned forward with his arms resting on the counter. He looked up at the guard and squinted until his eyes were barely visible. "Jerry's an old friend of mine," he said confidentially. "Someone told me that he worked in this building. I just wanted to stop by and say hello." *And I want to find out what happened to Tommy Chang.* He had no doubt their conversation was being recorded.

"A lot of people work here, sir. Can you tell me what company your friend works for?"

Chan's eyes had scanned the lobby when he pushed through the glass doors. Unobtrusive security cameras recorded every movement, and most likely he was being observed somewhere in the building as the guard held his attention. "I don't really know." He pointed at the board with the names of all companies. "I didn't know there'd be so many here. Maybe it's one of the companies that belong to that Inchar. Do you know anything about that company?"

"Inchar owns this building, and as you can see, there are a lot of divisions. Can you describe this gentleman for me?" The guard was trained to hold someone's attention long enough for identification to be completed.

Chan described Santucci according to the photo he'd seen and Leila's detailed observation.

"There may be someone who answers that description here. Yes, it sounds familiar." The guard was playing his role well. He produced a pen and a sheet of paper. "If you'll be kind enough to leave your address and phone number, perhaps I can locate this Mr. Santucci."

Chan decided this man was much too smooth to aspire to the position of security guard as a career. "That wouldn't do much good I'm afraid. You see, I'll be heading back to San Francisco in a couple of days."

The guard's eyebrows rose slightly. "An American. I didn't realize . . ."

"Sure. That's where I got to know Jerry. We were in the army together." Chan appeared thoughtful before saying,

"Of course, if you can locate him in the next day or so, I guess I could give you my hotel address." *Set the hook ever so gently.*

"If you don't mind, sir." The guard could barely believe his good fortune. Mr. Santucci often gave employees bonuses for extra service.

In his luxurious office suite in the bowels of the Inchar building, the expression on Jerry Santucci's face was one of disbelief as he stared at the picture on the remote TV screen. At first he'd been amused by the prim little man he'd never seen before. But that quickly changed to anger when Chan described him much too perfectly to the guard—including the scar on his right cheekbone. The final remark about the army brought an obscenity to his lips.

"My Chinese friends are all female," he shouted at the top of his lungs. He pressed the intercom button and called to Connie in the outer office, "Get somebody on that little bastard's ass the minute he leaves this building . . . No, not just anybody. Put Chau on him." Chau was by far the best when it came to tracking someone, the original two-legged bloodhound.

Let the games begin, W. P. Chan mused as he gave the signal to bring in the man who'd followed him from Inchar back to the hotel in Kowloon. No one had ever tracked W.P. without somehow giving himself away, and his record remained intact. He derived a certain amount of sadistic pleasure from grabbing someone like that, turning the hunter into the target.

His instructions to his own men were always to give the target a chance to use the telephone. Let him make a report before grabbing him, or at least let him make contact. A few times they'd been able to trace such a call. W.P. had no idea if Jerry Santucci was in the Inchar building or if he was even in Hong Kong, and it really didn't matter at this stage. But the interception of the man sent after Chan would send a very simple, very obvious message: *We know you're out there somewhere!*

The photos of the directory in the Inchar lobby were analyzed thoroughly. Within two hours, men and women from Chan's staff in plain clothes were visiting various offices in Inchar House. Some surprised receptionists by claiming they were there to interview for jobs and were angered to learn they'd been misled.

They sometimes mentioned the names of individuals who had asked them to come in for an interview. When Chan's people were told that no one by that name worked for the company, they demanded the name of the person in that position. It was often easier to elicit real names and hard information when one was irate about such an inconvenience. The ploy worked everywhere else, but it did not work with the polite, well-trained, and cool employees at Inchar. The personnel in those offices were sympathetic to such claims, but they revealed nothing. Later that afternoon, W. P. Chan considered what he'd learned—everything and nothing. Nor was there ever a hint of charity.

During that same day, additional police officers posed as reporters preparing articles about international business prospects in the face of the pending change to Beijing rule in 1997. That appealed to managers in the offices unattached to Inchar, who readily offered what little they knew about Inchar when questioned. But the Inchar managers, to an individual, were unavailable. The structure of their organization was much too powerful to intimidate.

Researchers plowing through the records of companies chartered in Hong Kong would have no better luck in the following days. An absolute minimum of information was available. The island attracted business because it respected the concept of privacy. Like Swiss banks, your rights remained sacred as long as you generated capital. According to the records, International Charities, Ltd., was founded by the same officers who currently served in those positions. They were a mix of Caucasians and Orientals from throughout the Pacific Rim nations and they were squeaky clean. Not one of them had any sort of criminal record. No black mark existed against any Inchar company or any individual

associated with them. While they were respected professionally by the business community, they remained extremely
private people.

Even on that first day of dissecting Inchar, there was
absolutely no record of individuals named Geraldo
Vincente Santucci and Edwin Antonio Kelley ever being
associated with International Charities or any of its subsidiary operations.

Hugh Young arrived in Hong Kong on the evening flight
from San Francisco expecting the chauffeur to take him to
the office. Instead, he was surprised to learn that he was
going directly to his residence on Victoria Peak where Jerry
Santucci was waiting to brief him.

Santucci was pacing, tigerlike in his anger, as he explained
the events of the previous day. "Hugh, I don't know what's
going on, and I'm getting pissed. Really pissed." His face
seemed a prisoner of his dangerous black eyes and the scar
on his cheek that seemed to grow brighter. "I was a prisoner
in my own home, and now I got to use the office like I was
carrying some dangerous disease. For Christ's sake," Jerry
raged, "I had to use the security backup we devised for an
emergency when I left tonight—by the back exit." He
waved his arms expressively. In a little more than two days,
their roles had switched. Now it was Santucci raising his
voice against the other. Yet he could see that Hugh Young
wasn't overly concerned.

"But the system did work, didn't it, Jerry?"

Santucci was taken aback by Hugh's response. "Well . . .
sure. The limo was right there. I climbed in, and away we
went without ever seeing the sky. You know how I prefer to
walk, maybe have a beer, before I take the tram up here."

"Jerry, calm down." Hugh was tired. His body and mind
were rebelling together. It seemed as if he'd spent half his
life in the air this week. Actually it was more than half. He'd
been to Washington and back in less than three days. If it
hadn't been for that asshole Randy Wallace, he would never
have had to leave Hong Kong. But he knew there would be
no rest until he calmed Santucci down. Jerry'd done no

more than make use of the system that had been devised for them by security experts, and this was the only time he'd had to use it so far. "You've just proved that all that money was well spent. The system works. Right?"

There was an underground garage beneath Inchar House for the use of the company's executives. To one side, behind a false wall, was a separate garage designed expressly to service their secret offices. Their chauffeurs could actually fit two limos in there at the same time. Security cameras provided a picture of the garage and the streets outside. When the guard on duty was alerted, he would control the hidden doors, opening them only when it was safe to depart. With darkened windows in the limos, Jerry had been perfectly safe when he'd left that night. A trail vehicle in radio contact with his chauffeur would have spotted anyone following and eliminated that problem before they ever gave away their Victoria Peak destination.

"Right," Jerry echoed. "But I still feel like a prisoner. Who the hell do these people think they are, bothering me like that?" As he ended the sentence, he turned to Young curiously. "Yeah, who are they, Hugh? Christ, Chinese who speak English better than I speak Cantonese. Would someone try to muscle in on us?"

Young had hoped the whole sordid mess could wait until the following day, but there would be no getting around Jerry tonight. He strode over to a large, soft sofa set in front of a bay window that looked out across Victoria Harbor and flopped down on it. He ran his fingers through his blond hair, resolved to calm Jerry's anger. "I'll tell you as much as I know in a minute." When the limo had deposited Hugh at the front door, he'd told his chauffeur to have the butler bring two drinks. "Sit down. I already ordered toddies," he said to Santucci. "I don't say another word until I drink." He stretched his arms and legs, relieving tired muscles. He examined his hands, pleased as always with the sparkling diamonds that seemed to complement the harbor lights.

"Yeah, yeah, yeah." Jerry paid no attention to him, continuing to pace the room.

Young waited silently, staring out the floor-to-ceiling

window at Victoria Harbor, to him still one of the most captivating sights in the world, until the butler brought out a tray with two large glasses of Jack Daniel's over ice. "Thanks, Ming." Young took his first, sipping the brown liquid and holding it in his mouth for a moment as if it were wine, then taking a deep drink. "Ming," he called before the butler was out the door, "bring out the bottle and an ice bucket and leave it with us. And you can go through my suitcase and drag out that big chunk of cheddar I brought back. Whack off a hunk and bring that out, too."

Young looked over his shoulder at Jerry, who stopped pacing just long enough to take a drink. "Jerry, sit, damn it. Two days, just two days, and you're making an asshole out of yourself. Take it easy. We'll talk as soon as Ming has us set up for a while." When Santucci had settled on the sofa, he asked, "How about some dinner, too?"

"Gotta eat sometime, I suppose."

"Good. That's how to start being sensible. We'll both shut up for a few minutes, slug down a little bit, and enjoy the view. Then we'll talk like gentlemen." Hugh Young still worked out enough to stay in fairly decent shape. While the slight belly that he'd had even in Saigon was larger, he still looked like an athlete, his thick neck and broad shoulders imposing enough to intimidate others—except Santucci.

They sipped their drinks in silence, looking down at the fairyland that was Hong Kong. The night was clear, and twinkling lights on the Hong Kong and Kowloon shores defined Victoria Harbor. Ships of every size and nationality, from tiny family junks to giant cruise ships and tankers, plied their business across the shining water. When Ming came back with the bottle, the ice, and the cheese, Young asked him to tell the kitchen staff to serve dinner in one hour.

Jerry added more ice and bourbon to their glasses and cut off some cheese. He nibbled at a chunk of it and turned to Young. "Okay, Hugh? Do I looked relaxed enough now?" The black eyebrows and hairline still threatened to merge, and his eyes continued to flash a danger signal.

"You look like a new man, Jerry," Hugh lied. "Sort of like a test pilot. You were the first to check out the departure system under realistic conditions, and it worked. Congratulations." The bourbon and cheddar were a reviving combination. "Okay, let me regale you with the facts. *Numero uno,*" he began with a flourish, "after all these years, we no longer have a man in the Pentagon. Randy Wallace has always been an asshole, but he managed to turn that into an art form the past week or so."

Santucci's forehead wrinkled. "Gonzo?"

"Gonzo. Besides not being a great thinker, I believe our friend Randy was also a victim of too much booze and not enough puss. And he unfortunately wanted to put the boots to the chicky he should have eliminated."

"Is she out of the way now, too?"

"She certainly is. But those two were just the beginning. Jerry," he continued with a serious note in his voice. "That's only one problem solved. You see, that stunt you pulled at the Wall was like pissing on the White House steps." He looked at Santucci over the top of his glass. "You were noticed by the wrong person. That innocent little stunt was just the tip of the iceberg. You are an official sighting— an American listed as missing in Vietnam who has been identified by a reliable source—and, as such, you have become a hunted man. You're going to spend a lot of time testing the effectiveness of our security system."

"Shit."

"Shit is right. Before I left D.C., our late friend Randy had learned quite a bit. In addition to your being famous in all the wrong places, our Mr. Kelley has also become an official sighting."

Santucci frowned. "He took care of that matter."

"Yes, and he created another problem. He took out an army major who was in Laos on an official Pentagon mission, prompting another investigation, and he managed to get his photo distributed. He then took a curtain call by being seen and identified at the Bangkok Shangri-la by a State Department intern who thought he was cute. If Randy wasn't mistaken, the Pentagon has someone in Bangkok right now who would love to meet Eddie Kelley."

Jerry didn't care for the tone of Young's voice. He was quickly losing what he'd thought would be the upper hand in this discussion. "Hugh, there's no reason to get bent out of shape. Maybe these things will blow over if we keep a low profile for a while and—"

"You bet your ass a low profile," Young snapped back. "Because that broad who saw you at the Wall is in Hong Kong now, goddammit." The gold chains around his neck danced as he slammed a fist into his palm. "So is the investigating officer from DIA, and Randy managed to learn that he's got both FBI and CIA support on this thing. Think that explains some of your problems the past couple of days?"

Santucci glared but knew better than to respond.

"These are pros, Jerry. It's a new ball game, and the score is probably two to one. You took out one of their people. That's one for you. But they have apparently detained Chau, one of our best men. At least he hasn't reported back, and you know what that normally means. One against you. And then there's the matter of the little Chinese gentleman who visited our lobby this morning, the one whose English so impressed you. And the people you mentioned who flooded our building today. Not normal. That's two against you. Right?"

"So, Hugh, say what you're going to say and get it over with."

Young dropped fresh ice cubes into their glasses and added some more bourbon. Then he cut off some hunks of cheddar. "Do you think you need a vacation, Jerry?" He selected a piece of cheese and pushed the plate in Jerry's direction.

Santucci stared down at Victoria Harbor. He watched a distant spotlight in the bow of a freighter scanning the water for a mooring buoy. "No. I started this. I'll finish what I started." He looked back at Young, his eyes brittle nuggets of coal as they remained fixed on his partner. Never before had there been a strain in their relationship, and this wasn't going to be recorded as the first if he could help it. "I don't need anyone else to do my dirty work for me. That's the way we've worked for twenty-five years. That's the way it should continue."

"Of course, you're correct. But we should plan everything together. If you're sighted again, though, you'll have to disappear for a while. Okay with you?"

"It's a deal."

"Great." Young glanced at his watch. "Still time before dinner. I've got to bring Eddie up to date." *Damn straight I will, and after I finish, that son of a bitch is going to fall into line just like Jerry.*

Ed Kelley eyed the woman in his bed longingly. *Blossom, as beautiful and fragile as a freshly plucked flower.* This was only the second time she'd been with him. Her name in Thai was that of an exotic blossom, but it was too long—half a dozen syllables too long—to use when making love, so he'd explained on her first night that he would called her his Blossom from that moment on.

She was just twenty years old, and he was the first American she'd ever been with. The name Blossom sounded lovely and special to her, and she boasted about it to her friends. She also told them that the man was absolutely insatiable in bed, and then she bragged that he'd told her she was the first woman who had satisfied him in years. For his part, Kelley had said nothing to his acquaintances because this one was going to be his alone and he didn't want her spoiled. Young girls were too impressionable.

Now Blossom was delightfully naked, stretched out full length on orchid sheets in his bedroom, and his head should have been spinning in fascination. She was slightly taller than the average Thai woman, her figure decidedly fuller than most, and her complexion darker. Ed was convinced by the shade of her skin that her father must have been a mixed American GI.

Blossom had no idea who her father was. But she delighted in claiming she was part American because he was an American named Kirby. Her mother had told her that when she was a baby her father used to call her Pat. Then he disappeared and was never heard from again. After that, her mother hated all Americans and returned to calling her by her Thai name, and that was how she'd become Blossom. It didn't really matter to Kelley because the union had produced a beautiful child, a woman beyond comprehension, a treasure not to share with your friends.

Once, she'd asked Kelley teasingly, "Maybe you want an American girlfriend? You can call me Patkirby," she said with a proud smile, running the two names together.

"Blossom, you're not a Patkirby. You're a gorgeous Oriental blossom. You're just blooming."

As he stared at her now, Kelley was sure his Blossom was as appealing as she had been twenty minutes before when they were making love, but Hugh Young's call had ruined everything. It almost seemed the telephone had flashed just to pull his eyes from this beautiful creature. Fucking useless instrument! Blossom stretched; Eddie stared. Her hands locked above her head and her toes pointed at him. A light patina of perspiration still shone on her body, highlighting every detail that tantalized him. She spread her legs slightly and smiled at him, silently sending a message that he was the only man in her world and she needed him very much that very moment.

If only Hugh knew . . . if only that son of a bitch knew what he'd just ruined. Blossom, Ed Kelley knew, had been looking forward with anticipation to a long night of sensuality, a night she was sure would turn this into a long-term relationship, and she was doing what Blossom did best. *Damn Hugh! You son of a bitch!* The first time had been highly erotic for Kelley, and so quick. But that was to be expected with a new woman.

He knew that for her it had been an easily forgettable start to a night that he'd promised himself would be memorable. She'd whispered for him to forget about her this time; this one was to relax him. Then the phone had rung. *And I was relaxed, Hugh, really relaxed.* Now, because he simply stared at her as she teased him with her body, Blossom sat up on the edge of the bed and poured two glasses of very cold champagne, which had been chilling in the ice bucket.

Kelley took the proffered glass without noticing, sipped without tasting, and looked at Blossom without really seeing her as she posed spread-legged before him. *You son of a bitch, Hugh.*

"Eddie," she whispered softly, "your Blossom wants to make love with you." She tossed off the champagne with a flourish, then moved back to the bed, spreading herself in slow motion across the orchid-colored sheets. Her Eddie had told her that she was irresistible when she did that, but the expected reaction was missing. "Eddie?"

"That son of a bitch," he said out loud.

"Who?"

"Hugh," he answered without really knowing she'd asked or that he'd answered.

"Eddie, who is this Hugh? What is wrong with you?" His glass, barely touched, was still cradled in his hand. Whoever Hugh was, she decided, he was definitely a son of a bitch. "He is son of a bitch," she finally agreed crossly in a loud voice. She had contrived her introduction to Kelley because everyone who knew of him said he was very special and very wealthy. Now she was thinking that maybe he was too old . . . or maybe it was her? No, that was impossible after the things he'd told her that first night. "Eddie," she persisted, sitting up with her legs dangling over the edge of the bed, "is something wrong with your Blossom . . . or are you a queer boy?" Her lower lip stuck out in an exaggerated pout.

That he heard. He was beside the bed in an instant, his hand snaking out, his palm making a cracking sound against her cheek. The slap was as much for Hugh as for her. "Don't ever speak to me like that," he snapped.

Blossom fell back across the bed from the blow. Instant tears, as much from surprise as from the blow, flowed down her cheeks. She had no idea how to respond because he'd acted so strangely before he lashed out. All she could say was, "Eddie . . . what . . ." Other words failed to come. She would have to choose her words very carefully.

No matter what, she didn't want to ruin her relationship with this very wealthy Caucasian who acted so much like a Thai. She'd never been fully accepted as a Thai because of her mixed blood, and she saw Ed Kelley as somewhat like her, with his sharp blue eyes so stark against his dark hair. Both of them seemed to bridge two worlds.

"Just don't ever say that to me again," he said with a nasty snarl. He took a sip of the champagne without really noticing what was in the glass, then a second one. Blossom's tears glistened in the light, and he added more softly, "Can't you see I've got some big problems?"

That was obvious, even to Blossom. They were caused by that son of a bitch named Hugh. "I'm sorry, Eddie. I love you," she offered. "I really love you."

Kelley stared down at Blossom, enchanted once again by what he saw. He didn't intend to lose this one. When you were approaching your mid-forties, you didn't kick a woman like Blossom out of your bed. But Hugh Young had been pissed when he called, and Ed realized he had every right to be. There was a time for screwing and a time for working. If he disregarded Hugh and spent the rest of the night with Blossom, he might just be screwing himself forever. But if he started now to do what he had to do, there would be more than enough time later for screwing Blossom. She would be begging for mercy.

"Honey, I love you, too. But not tonight." He forced himself to walk away from the bed to the chair where Blossom had thrown his clothes. He pulled on his shorts. "If you really love me, you'll learn that sometimes my business is so important that I have to go back to work at the oddest times."

Blossom pouted again, but this time she knew better than to test his patience. She stood up and placed her hands on her hips provocatively. "Okay this time, Eddie." But when she saw the way he stared at her, Blossom knew she still possessed a great deal of control. She added, "But we were going to do some things tonight that . . ." Then she shrugged and walked over to her own clothes, assured that she had the upper hand even though he had hit her. "I hope this doesn't happen next time." She half turned so that her breasts were outlined against the bedside lamp. That should make him think.

Kelley turned away from her. He was thinking, all right, thinking in a good-humored way about how to get even with Hugh once this was all over. Right at that moment he longed to introduce Hugh to some young, tender thing with teeth in it. Serve the son of a bitch right.

He sent Blossom back to her own place in his limo. Then he went into his study and dialed Prosit's number. Kelley was relieved when he recognized the sleepy voice answering the phone. Thank God he hadn't sent Prosit and his wife to Phuket immediately.

Kelley didn't care to engage in niceties at that hour. "What have your contacts developed on this colonel at the American embassy?" He was sure it was the same man Randy Wallace had mentioned, a former Green Beret named Benner who'd spent a lot of time in Vietnam during the war and knew the country and the language. He wasn't sure why the man was in Bangkok, but he was sure that Benner had helped that girl in the embassy identify his picture.

Prosit patiently explained that he'd only been able to establish his contacts that afternoon. "Mr. Kelley, it was just this morning, after I followed that man to the embassy, that you asked—"

"You're right, Prosit. I know that, but all of a sudden he's become an even bigger problem than we thought. Mr. Young just called from Hong Kong and is very anxious to learn as much as he can about this colonel, who may be scheduled to leave Bangkok shortly. And I want you to find where one of the State Department interns is living. Mr. Young was able to identify her. Her name is Marclay Davis." That would be enough. Prosit would take care of everything and get back to him.

Hugh had left no doubts about what had to happen. There would be no witnesses! The U.S. government wouldn't be happy when the young lady disappeared. But they would be even madder when they lost a colonel.

CHAPTER 12

EXHAUSTION? EMOTION? PHYSICAL OR MENTAL? HOW DID ONE tell the difference? Leila Potter could sense it in her muscles. It had awakened her, but her eyes were still closed. She could feel the sheets touching her skin. Am I asleep? she wondered. She was drifting somewhere in between.

In that limbo between sleep and wakefulness, everything seemed to revolve around one question: How long had it been since that day at the Wall? A day? A week? A year? No, it was ten days . . . or was it nine after crossing the date line? *Was that the beginning of my life or the end?* There was no simple answer. *Why am I doing this to myself?* Again there was no answer. Answers are hard to come by when you're on the borders of consciousness.

Quite suddenly, as if reacting to an electric shock, Leila rolled onto her side and reached blindly across the bed, eyes still closed, fumbling for the security of Matt's warm body.

Nothing. No one. But he was here! Her eyes snapped open. There wasn't the slightest doubt in her mind. She nuzzled the spare pillow, saw the indentation where his head had rested, and closed her eyes, reveling in the male aroma of after-shave lotion and sweat. There was nothing imaginative about that. This was no self-induced trance.

Leila rolled back, and her eyes caught the morning sunlight peeking around the edges of the curtains. Reality was out there, and it was waiting for her. No, there was no need to avoid the realities of life that had brought them to Hong Kong. She could separate those things.

Chuck Goodrich had been at Dulles to see her off. "I came especially to see you, Leila, not Matt. I've seen him off in other times, tough times, and he always came back."

Leila smiled. "I'll be back, too."

Goodrich had a cigar, which he couldn't smoke in the airport, and he chewed it fiercely as he struggled for words. "I had to come here because I couldn't . . . I can't quite explain how I feel, and I can't tell anyone else until it's all over. But somehow . . . there's so much similarity to the day in 1973 when I stepped off that plane in Manila with the other POWs. Some of us just smiled, still unable to believe it all. Others cried. Some got down on their knees and kissed that American soil. The agony was supposed to be over . . . but it never has been for a lot of people."

He took the cigar from his mouth and stared at it. "You're doing this for them as much as for yourself. I know it's for Danny, but I don't know how to say it any other way, and I don't know how I'm going to explain why I set you up for this trip if anything goes wrong." He stopped speaking as he spoke the last word.

"Everything's going to be fine," Leila said, and she gave his hand a squeeze.

"Stick close to my buddy here." Goodrich gave her a hug, shook Stone's hand, and jammed the well-chewed cigar back in his mouth. He'd said enough.

Now she was in Hong Kong—she and Matt. And she had stuck closer to him than she would ever have imagined. The suddenness of needing each other was separate and, for the moment, absolutely delicious. She closed her eyes in an effort to remember how it had happened. What had the two of them found in each other at the same instant? At her age—Matt's, too, for that matter—such things weren't supposed to be so urgent. *But they were last night.*

Leila picked up the other pillow and fluffed it until the male aroma came to her again, then hugged it tightly. She was pleased with herself. There had been men in her life—one she had loved, one or two borderline cases that seemed less important in retrospect, one case of infatuation that had been over as quickly as it started, and a few relationships that had satisfied both parties. *Do I love Matt Stone?* she asked herself. The answer at that point was easy; no, she didn't. There hadn't been enough time . . . but he was someone she could love, if . . . *Don't be ridiculous!* It had been a mutual, urgent coupling—no, that wasn't the right word, but a more appropriate one eluded her—that they had both needed. Leila fervently hoped that Matt would be as pleased with himself as she felt at that moment.

She laughed out loud. *Damn, but you were terrific last night, and that's because there have never been two people who have needed each other so much before in the history of the world.* She laughed even louder, hoping he might hear her. He must be next door in his own room—the prude—taking a shower alone. He was probably afraid W.P. would find them together. Or maybe he was worried she wouldn't see it all in the same light in the morning. *Oh, but last night was glorious.* And she hoped it would happen again. It was nothing either of them had planned. Some things just happened. That made it so much more exciting. A little dash of sin was what made the world go around. *Imagine your thinking like that at the grand old age of forty-one! You could almost be someone's grandmother now . . . if you'd found someone.* But she hadn't. For some reason buried so deep that it rarely concerned her, she'd avoided risking the inner pain that real love might cause.

She remembered their discussion during the long flight across the Pacific. What would happen if Santucci had gone underground? Matt hadn't wanted to explain what might have to be done if the Hong Kong police couldn't unearth him. But Leila knew what might attract Jerry, and she made it easier on Matt when he stumbled around the words. "Matt," she said, "I may have to be the bait to get him out in the open. That may be the only way."

After the suggestion was on the table, they had stared at each other. Nothing more was said. Words would have been useless. She'd been tough enough to accept the possible danger. Matt had never known a woman who'd been through what Leila had and could still face up to more of the same. So they had simply held each other's eyes and gradually understood that they were more than two people brought together by strange events. That look was a silent acknowledgment of shared needs, shared danger. Neither one had planned or even expected these events. They were just two people swept into an untenable situation who understood that they could salvage something special in their own way. Perhaps their sense of closeness had started in Billy Corey's decrepit farmyard. Perhaps it had happened during the ride back through the Maryland countryside, or when Leila had insisted that they go across town to the FBI office together.

She wondered if that same dream—not really a dream, but a series of troubling, recurrent mental images—would have occurred if Matt had stayed all night—the Wall, Jerry, the gunman in the bathroom. Those images were like snapshots, but they always faded back to one picture, that of Jerry Santucci turning around at the Wall and looking into her eyes—that moment of recognition.

Leila had not been aware of Matt leaving her bed. This first night in Hong Kong had been the only time she'd slept well since that day at the Wall. But that agonizing process of awakening, those moments in limbo that had seemed like an eternity, continued to bring back that overwhelming image of Jerry, that telltale scar on his right cheekbone standing out as if etched by neon. Even Matt Stone could not erase that image from her consciousness.

Leila picked up the phone and pressed the buttons for Stone's room. She could hear the first ring through the adjoining door in concert with the sound in the receiver. There never was a second ring.

"Commander Stone," he answered formally.

"Leila Potter," she responded with a pleasant lilt. "This is your wakeup call, sir. I'd hoped I could just tap you on the shoulder instead."

There was an instant of silence, followed by, "Well, I wasn't sure that . . . Leila, I . . ."

"Shh," she hushed him. "Don't say anything. If last evening is an example of the way you help a friend celebrate tough decisions, then I have a lot to look forward to."

"You're right. I don't know why I left." But he had. He wasn't used to one-night stands with women like Leila. As a matter of fact, he wasn't accustomed to women like her at all. His former wife's vision of a man was the opposite of the life he led, and she'd told him in so many words that he wasn't fit to live with a normal woman. That one had stung him, but good, and a man who imagined himself as a warrior couldn't expose himself to hurt feelings. Not again.

There was no reason to get married and have a family in his business, because women wanted so much more in a relationship, and as he grew older he thought he understood why. They wanted something besides a warm body. So he'd divided women into two distinct types, and until the past few days he'd never gotten involved with Leila's type—the ones who required too much of a man. Now he wasn't sure if he could live by such a rigid rule. The lovemaking had been so different with her. He wished he were there, beside her, not speaking on a phone.

"No postmortems, my friend," Leila said. "There's nothing to analyze, not when you've reached our stage of adulthood," she added with a little-girl giggle. "How about breakfast in the coffee shop in half an hour? We'll be on our second cup of coffee by the time W.P. shows up." She'd been tempted to invite him in for a shower, but Stone seemed to need time to let everything fall into place.

"Want me to knock on your door when I'm ready?" he asked.

"I'll tell you what. Considering that we're such good friends, use the adjoining door. My side's not locked. Is yours?"

"No," he answered softly.

When she was younger, she might have been foolish enough to say she loved him. Now she said, "Let's keep it that way," and hung up the phone. No, she didn't love him, not in the traditional romantic way—at least not yet. Why should she? But Matt Stone was no one-night stand. Even during the urgency of the moment, they had been gentle and loving to each other . . . and they would be again.

As she showered and then dried her hair, Leila pondered how rapidly life was changing. Was it for better or worse? She remembered her friend Joan Thompson explaining the old Chinese curse: "May you live in interesting times." That didn't mean that the times would be good, just that your life would keep changing, and here she was in the perfect place for a Chinese curse—Hong Kong! Sometimes the times control you, Joan had said, and sometimes you control them. No one had been seduced last night. She and Matt had reacted like two people thrust pell-mell into interesting times, and they'd responded mutually. The fine line between pleasure and pain, physical or mental, could sometimes be all but invisible. There were times in life when you had to grasp reality tenaciously, even make love to it, in order to maintain your grip on sanity. Matt Stone had become her reality. As long as he was nearby, she could accept those dreams. Matt would be her pillar of strength. She was willing to be the bait for Jerry Santucci. She would do her part.

Stone did knock before he came into her room. "Habit," he said as an excuse. "Always an officer and a gentleman." He turned back toward the door as the telephone began to ring in his own room.

"Forget it, just this once," Leila said. "If they want you badly enough, they'll call back." She wrapped her arms around him, inhaling the wonderful scent of after-shave, and kissed him deeply. "Now, isn't that a nice way for a lady to greet a gentleman in the morning? Much better than running for a telephone."

"Can't beat it," he agreed. The ringing had stopped. "I'll

tell the front desk to chase me down in the coffee shop if they call back. It can only be W.P. or someone calling from the States. Now it's my turn to greet the lady properly." He returned her kiss with the same urgency. How had this ever happened to them? God, how he wanted to protect her from these people!

W. P. Chan, a round-faced, smiling elf in a dark suit, slipped into the coffee shop booth beside Leila and exchanged pleasantries with both of them. He noted their large English breakfasts with distaste and ordered a cup of coffee for himself, filling it to the brim with milk when it arrived. W.P.'s eyes had been canvassing the restaurant from the moment he came through the door. It was a habit he'd never been able to shake, but his scrutiny did not include the two people he'd joined.

He was about to fill them in on what the Hong Kong police had accomplished overnight when he noticed Stone's eyes for the first time. W.P. was an unabashed student of human expression. He could spot guilt, lies, feigned sorrow or happiness—the entire range of human emotions. Detection was his business and he was an expert. Yesterday Stone's facial muscles had been tight, mirroring much more than just the weariness of the trip from Washington. Today the expression in his eyes and his relaxed attitude reflected an entirely different attitude.

W.P. ignored the polite small talk, shifting his gaze to Leila. She had been the picture of anguish and indecision yesterday evening, and of course her distress had been compounded by the flight from Washington. Today she was at peace with herself. W.P. smiled inwardly. The two Americans had discovered each other. They were sharing a much different world than when he'd left them last night. That was pleasing. They would make his job much easier. He did not consider himself an incurable romantic, but he treasured the inner peace of his own home, and he was happy for these people.

"We had a long discussion about Jerry Santucci last night,

W.P.," Leila offered. "There's no doubt he knows someone is on his track. He's retaliated already, and he probably will again. He doesn't seem to care about anyone, and apparently he's not particular about who gets hurt as long as he protects himself. He's lashing out without exposing himself. But we're sure he has to know I'm involved. He doesn't know what you and Matt look like. But he'll come out if he sees me."

W.P. raised his eyebrows. "You haven't any doubts about that, have you?"

"Not now."

"Why?"

"You yourself said one of your best men had been assigned to trail him, and now he's missing. If Santucci has no qualms about killing one of your people, why should he hesitate to kill a civilian like me?"

W.P. sighed. "It's unfortunate, but you're right. Tommy Chang remains officially listed as missing, but I've already told his wife that he's dead. A man like Tommy would fail to report back to me only if he was dead. No one would ever take him alive anyway." He looked her square in the eye. "You're right about Santucci," he repeated. "No one is going to surprise him."

There was sadness in Leila's eyes. "I'm sorry," she said honestly. "You and Mr. Chang were friends, weren't you?"

W.P. nodded gravely. "Yes, we were. Tommy was also like a son to me." He held up an index finger and fixed her with a sad smile. "One more reason for me to find Santucci. But I can see you have started this conversation in order to make some suggestions."

Leila smiled and was about to answer when Danny Slade appeared and slid in beside Stone. W.P. recognized in an instant, again without a word spoken, that there was a great deal on Slade's mind.

Danny nodded to each of them with little more than a grunt for a greeting. "Sorry I'm late." He refused breakfast, asking only for coffee.

Leila was intent on explaining herself to the detective. "I don't know whether you'll like this suggestion or not, W.P., but Matt and I feel that if Jerry Santucci has gone underground, then I'm probably the one who can draw him out."

"It's an idea," Stone said, noting the odd expression that crossed Slade's face as she spoke. "We don't have to go ahead with it if—"

"You'd better rethink that," Slade blurted. "I got a call from your FBI friends when they couldn't raise you this morning," he said to Stone. "It must have been about the time you left your room to come down here. They told me that the captain working with Leila never came into work at the Pentagon yesterday morning."

"Penny Carson?" Leila asked. "Is that who you're talking about?"

Slade stared into his coffee without looking in her direction. "That's right. Neither did her boss, Lieutenant Colonel Wallace." His voice was so soft it was barely audible. "Some high school kids out necking discovered their two bodies by a river out in the Virginia countryside. They'd both been murdered." His eyes finally held Leila's as he said, "I'm sorry I have to be the one to tell you."

Leila gasped. "How could . . . ?" but she had no idea how to finish. Not Penny! That was ridiculous. She'd done nothing to hurt anybody.

Slade turned to Matt Stone. "Professional job, according to the FBI. The Bureau was brought in because Penny Carson was working on Leila's case and because of a possible link to Leila." He handed Matt a slip of paper. "This agent would like to talk with you. The FBI is trying to reconstruct the events leading to the murder. No idea why this guy Wallace was hit, too. According to Penny Carson's friends, she didn't much care for Wallace, so there was no reason for her to go for a joyride with the guy."

Leila was very still, her eyes tightly shut.

W. P. Chan reached out and took her hands and held them tight. "Last night," he said to her softly, "I cried with Tommy Chang's wife. She is much like you—lovely, sensitive, also very tough, but a lady who does not accept the baser elements of human nature. She would like to go after Santucci also. I know everything you have gone through during the last week, and I understand exactly what you are thinking. Now, as I did last night, I will share the sorrow with you."

He turned slightly to Stone and spoke softly. "Let me talk with Leila for a while. I understand exactly how she feels now. You can help us by making that call to Washington and obtaining as many details as possible about these two murders in Virginia. The situation has changed radically since your arrival here, and the killings in Washington have compounded the problem. We want to protect Leila from these people, and she could be in as much danger here as if she was back home. Why don't you and Danny go ahead and make that call. I will take her up to her room shortly." When Matt hesitated, Chan added, "It is in Leila's best interest." His voice remained soft, but there was a tone of command in the background. As soon as he stopped speaking, it was as if he'd dismissed them.

Then, still gripping Leila's hands in his much smaller one, W. P. Chan put his free arm around her, pulling her to him until her head was on his shoulder. Tears welled up in his own eyes. "Tommy Chang was like a son to me and his wife like a daughter. I know how sad you feel." The little man's voice was steady but soft, full of understanding. "Just as I promised Tommy's wife, I also promise you. We will work hard together now to find these evil people. I am deeply honored that you want to help me. But first we must grieve for those close to us who have brought us this far. It will make us stronger and more determined." W. P. Chan was also a master in the simplest forms of human therapy. He wept, too.

Leila cried softly on the tiny shoulder, comforted by the act of shared sorrow.

Colonel Nolan Benner had been ordered to report for duty at the U.S. Full Accounting office in Hanoi. He'd already sent a fax to Hong Kong updating Stone on the Bangkok situation. Since he had been requested to assist in completing the signed statement of Marclay Davis, the State

Department intern who had recognized Edwin Kelley at the Shangri-la, he was waiting in her boss's office by eight o'clock that morning.

The rumors linking Kelley with the murder of Major Joslin in Laos had frightened Marclay Davis, and she had no desire to remain in Bangkok. So, after her statement was complete, Benner made arrangements for her to return to Washington. He even promised her boss that he'd escort her to the airport and see that she got on the plane.

But before Benner could find Miss Davis, he was given a message to call the Full Accounting office in Washington. It was after eight in the evening at the Pentagon, and he was surprised to hear background noise in the office as if it were morning. Even more surprising, the commanding officer of Full Accounting was waiting to speak with him.

"Forget Hanoi, Nolan. We need you right where you are." Ben Miele was the kind of general who demanded people's attention whether in person or on the phone, and he always got right to the point. "And I'm telling you right now you better cover your ass. I think that Kelley guy's another Al Capone." Miele was broad-shouldered, built like a linebacker, and people who didn't know him were always unsure of his mood because he always smiled, even when he was serious. That affected those under him more than if he'd exhibited anger when he was disappointed with their performance.

Miele had succeeded as usual in getting Nolan Benner's full attention. "General, I'm supposed to be heading for the airport in a few hours. This Miss Davis, the one who ID'd Kelley, is scared to death, after everything she's heard about Kelley, and she'd be even more terrified if she could listen to you." Why the hell did Miele always start out that way? "Can you explain what's going on over the phone?"

"Simple, Nolan. We're supposed to be a noncombatant unit, and instead we seem to be in the middle of a war. Two of our people were murdered yesterday less than fifty miles from here. Not a prayer that those killings don't have everything to do with Kelley and Santucci. One of the victims was pretty Penny Carson, who was researching the sighting at the Wall last week. The other was that asshole, Randy Wallace, her boss." General Miele had never been accused of being diplomatic. He was blunt, and his language was descriptive.

Benner thought for a second. He knew Kelley had been in Bangkok for at least three consecutive days now. For that matter, he'd been told that Santucci had been in Hong Kong for the same amount of time. Nothing was falling into place. What was Miele driving at? "Those murders may be linked to the Kelley-Santucci affair, General, but both suspects are out here. Why do you think there's any danger for me?"

General Miele was ready to hammer home his point. "FBI says it was a professional job on Penny and the asshole. That's the second professional hit in a week. The woman who identified Santucci would have been the first to buy the farm if the hit man hadn't botched that job in the Crystal City Marriott. The information DIA has gotten the past twelve hours indicates someone's playing hardball in Hong Kong, too, even with the police. They took out a cop who was believed to have a lead on Santucci. That girl with you there in Bangkok, the one who sighted Kelley . . . what's her name?"

"Marclay Davis."

"That's right, the one with the strange name. You stay on her butt, Nolan, and when she hollers, I don't want to hear that you got off it. Make her like it," he added with something between a snicker and a growl. "That's how much the brass here are worried. She's a witness. She saw Kelley in that Shangri-la Hotel. If Kelley and Santucci know as much as they seem to, she could lose her ass before she knows it wasn't attached."

"How are Kelley and Santucci getting their information?" There was no point in explaining what he'd already done for Marclay Davis's security. It would never meet Ben Miele's perfectionist standards.

"Beats me. Beats everybody around here as far as I can tell. If you ask me, they got a contact, a mole of some kind, but it has to be someone really deep, because everyone here's baffled."

"I'm supposed to be meeting Marclay Davis right now in the embassy, sir. And I was intending to escort her to the airport when I went there myself on the way to Hanoi. Why not just get her out of town right now?"

"She's safer inside the embassy for the moment until we have a better feel for the situation. The best way—hell, the only way as far as I'm concerned—would be double-tight security, military aircraft, and then escorted from Andrews right into my office. That'll take some time to set up. My security type is already talking to his opposite with the Thai army. I'll coordinate arrangements myself and get back to you when I'm happy with the setup. Sound okay to you, Nolan?"

What could Benner say? Miele changed his orders with each phone call anyway. "Sounds fine to me."

"Well," Miele snorted, "how soon are you supposed to see her?"

"Wait one, sir. I'll check." Benner was told on the in-house phone that Marclay Davis had not yet arrived at the embassy. She'd received a call from an old friend who insisted on meeting her for breakfast, and her boss had given her permission. He'd forgotten to let Colonel Benner know she would be a little late.

"Jesus H. Christ, Nolan, that's exactly the type of thing I'm talking about. Apparently she's not as frightened as you thought. For all we know, that breakfast meeting is a setup and your girl—oh, shit, what's her name again?—could be dead meat already. I'm serious now, dead serious. After you find her, you're going to take her under your wing until we get her back here the right way. She's as valuable as the Potter woman. And she's pure poison to Kelley if she stays alive. You, Nolan, are going to stay with her until she's safely back here. You are her life. Eat with her. Shower with her. Tell you what. You'll like this. Sleep with her. Marry her for a couple of days if you have to."

Miele liked Benner and he also enjoyed teasing him at odd

times. Benner was tall and slender and looked elegant in uniform even after a day in the steam bath that was Bangkok. He was one of the few Green Berets who had ever been promoted into an essentially diplomatic billet, and he'd taken to the new situation comfortably. Miele loved to remind him of his earlier days, and Benner accepted the teasing good-naturedly.

Benner managed to say, "I'll take care of her, sir."

General Miele ended the call by stating the obvious: that an equally important goal was to track down Ed Kelley. Then he ordered Benner to contact Matt Stone in Hong Kong. "Now round up that woman's ass, Nolan."

Although she wasn't thrilled with the invitation, Marclay Davis had agreed to meet an old college friend of her mother's for breakfast at the coffee shop in the Oriental Hotel. What the hell, she decided, even though she'd never cared for this woman, maybe a visit with someone from home would get her mind off that day she'd recognized Kelley at the Shangri-la. So she called the embassy to tell them that she would be late and promised to take cabs from door to door. The Oriental was easily one of the world's finest hotels, and certainly as safe a place as one could find in Bangkok. Situated right on the Chao Phraya River, the grand old hotel was an institution in itself, and it seemed impossible that anyone like Kelley could come close to Marclay in such a gracious place.

Alice, her mother's friend, had come to Bangkok with her husband, an older gentleman who was president of a large Texas bank. Naturally, Alice explained when Marclay arrived, the only place for the two of them to stay was the Oriental. She boasted that the previous day she'd even taken afternoon tea in the Authors' Lounge, a room in the original section named in honor of the authors who'd made the Oriental famous in their books. Alice, in her inimitable fashion, was sure she had felt the presence of Joseph Conrad and Somerset Maugham. How wonderful, Marclay thought, to be able to concentrate on such inanities; no Edwin Kelley to concern you. As a matter of fact, Alice was going to insist that her husband reread one of Conrad's novels before they returned home.

It wasn't an exciting way to begin the day, but Marclay's night had been a restless one. As an added precaution, Colonel Benner had moved her to another hotel, the Narai on Silom Road, booking the room under his own name. The embassy continued to pay for the old room, and she left most of her clothes there for the benefit of overly curious hotel employees, but she was still frightened. After all, she'd learned from Benner that the man whom the colonel had sent to trail Kelley had disappeared.

There was no telling what could happen next, and Marclay was an admitted worrier. When she asked if the police were looking for Kelley, Benner explained that the embassy had already queried the Bangkok police. The police asked the embassy representative which Thai laws had been broken. So Kelley remained an American problem. It was apparent that Kelley had more friends within the police department than the embassy did.

Marclay, who'd barely slept the previous night, had decided it was best to keep busy. Now she listened to Alice drone on about her limousine tours around Bangkok and the dinners she and her husband had attended in the city and how they'd been able to find real American food. It was a very different experience from the life Marclay had enjoyed in Bangkok—until she unfortunately recognized Edwin Kelley.

She did look over the other diners as Alice rambled on. As always, it was primarily a Western group in the Oriental's coffee shop. They were either preoccupied with their English-language newspapers or studying other faces to see if there was anyone of importance present. It was so much like Washington that Marclay never noticed the man who'd followed her since she climbed into the taxi outside the Narai. Perhaps that was because Prosit fit in perfectly. He wore a coat and tie, sipped delicately partially fermented oolong while nibbling a croissant, and certainly appeared to belong at the Oriental as he leafed through the *Bangkok Post.*

Ed Kelley had long ago recognized Prosit's unique talents. He was a Thai who knew the Bangkok government and the professional underworld equally well, yet he could also look like the type of Thai that Westerners expected to see. Ed paid him exceedingly well over the years because Prosit could be as elegant or as dangerous as the moment required.

While Marclay was saying good-bye to Alice, Prosit dropped a thousand baht on the table, folded the *Post,* slipped it under his arm, and departed before her.

Having left the Oriental by a side door, Prosit, his tie and jacket gone, stopped to say a few words to the doorman, then moved quickly to the taxi he had driven to the hotel that morning. The doorman was another of his many old acquaintances. Prosit had bantered with him for a while after arriving, long enough to get his point across, and had excused himself when Marclay arrived, claiming he had to make some phone calls.

When she came out the front entrance and asked for a cab, the same doorman blew his whistle and gestured for Prosit to pull up. He held the door as Marclay stepped inside the vehicle, then tipped his hat politely. Watching the taxi disappear through the gates onto Oriental Avenue, he fingered the five thousand baht that Prosit had given him. A very profitable day already. There was no easier way to make money than to do a favor for an old friend. Wouldn't the young lady be surprised when her gentleman friend, the one Prosit claimed had hired him for this special occasion, unexpectedly proposed to her that morning?

While Marclay Davis breakfasted with her mother's friend under Prosit's watchful eye, Colonel Benner had parted with over a thousand baht before the doorman at the Narai Hotel remembered where the young lady had taken a cab that morning. Yes, she had asked him to bargain with the driver for the price to the Oriental. It had not been easy because the driver assumed anyone who wanted to go to the

Oriental could afford to pay well. She hadn't left that long ago, and for another thousand baht he remembered her mentioning something about convincing this friend of her mother's that eight o'clock was the latest she could meet for breakfast because she had to go to work.

Benner looked at his watch—eight-forty. No one ate breakfast that quickly at the Oriental. Breakfast, like everything else there, was intended to be an experience. The kitchen worked at the pace expected by the clientele. Benner climbed back in the embassy vehicle and told Sergeant Galacci, the marine driver he'd insisted upon, that time was in their favor—if Galacci could get their asses to the Oriental double quick.

Bangkok taxi drivers and tuk-tuk drivers and Frank Galacci, who'd extended his enlistment just to stay in Thailand, possessed a sixth sense for getting around the city in the shortest amount of time. Much of their success was based on understanding city traffic flow at various hours of the day, knowing which one-way streets could be negotiated in the wrong direction even if they met another vehicle, which parking lots allowed access to other streets, and what it took in sheer guts to make another equally aggressive driver give way. Those unique abilities, coupled with a dash of plain luck, quickly brought Benner to Oriental Avenue, the street outside the hotel between New Road and the Chao Phraya.

The Oriental's doorman studied the tall, rangy man approaching him. He carried himself like a policeman, maybe even a military man, but he was Caucasian and in civilian clothes. The doorman pulled open the lobby door for the man and enjoyed the brief rush of air-conditioned coolness.

"Khapkhun maak," Benner said, thanking him in Thai.

The doorman nodded politely. He was always wary when Caucasians spoke his language.

Benner knew the Oriental well and strode through the decorous Victorian-style lobby to the entrance of the coffee shop. He didn't want to be seen; his presence might upset

Marclay if she was still there. His eyes scanned the room until he spotted the frosted blond hair swept back on the sides. She was talking with an older American woman. That seemed safe enough.

The remainder of the people in the coffee shop appeared to be mostly tourists, older, well dressed, the type who always stayed in gracious, expensive hotels wherever they traveled. Only one individual warranted a second look; Benner's eyes settled on the only Thai in the coffee shop, and that was because the gentleman was flipping through a copy of the *Bangkok Post* like a European. Benner studied him, curious to see if he was actually reading the English-language paper. Apparently he was—whenever his eyes weren't drifting over to Marclay Davis. And that wasn't necessarily because he was interested in attractive blondes. He also kept checking his watch, clearly anticipating something.

Colonel Benner stepped back out of the doorway without being seen and went to the front entrance. He paused to survey the few cabs at that hour. Marclay Davis would certainly take one of them to the embassy. Most were unoccupied, their drivers gathered in the shade, talking. How the hell would the Thai in the coffee shop manage this—if he was the one? Benner didn't want to scare Marclay, nor did he want to give himself away if the Thai watching her was preparing to grab her. Who could say what would happen? He didn't want to leave anything to chance.

He mulled over his conversation with Ben Miele. The general had felt that it wasn't a matter of *if* but of *when*. Miele's orders brought a smile to his face. Hers was a rather attractive ass to cover, and he'd been ordered not to get off it until the general said so.

Benner moved back near the door of the coffee shop, just close enough to keep an eye on Marclay Davis. Sure enough, when the American lady was given the bill to sign, the Thai slipped some money under his coffee cup and left ahead of the women.

And that was why Colonel Nolan Benner was sitting in the

passenger seat of the embassy car when the Thai from the coffee shop appeared from the side of the hotel, minus jacket and tie, said something with a sly smile to the doorman, and moved over to the driver's door of one of the taxis. When Marclay appeared on the front step of the Oriental and asked for a taxi, the doorman blew his whistle and beckoned for a taxi—that same taxi—which eased up to the door.

"You want to take him now, Colonel?" Sergeant Galacci asked enthusiastically, removing a cigar from his mouth that Benner had forbidden him to light.

"Not yet. Two Americans in the military assaulting a Thai citizen without provocation? We want to follow, see where he takes us. We can grab him anytime."

The marine fondled the gun tucked in his belt. "I sure would like to use this," he said around the cigar, now gripped between his teeth. "I wouldn't want anything to happen to anyone as tasty as Miss Davis." His voice was gravelly and hoarse and he spoke as if he thought he was personally capable of protecting all womanhood.

"You know her?" The taxi was moving through the Oriental's gates.

"Not exactly, sir." He removed the big unlit cigar from his mouth once again and turned slightly to make his point. "But there aren't that many pretty round-eyes working for the embassy. Every guy in the embassy knows who she is." He pulled onto Oriental Avenue after giving the cab a slight lead.

"I don't figure that guy's really a cabbie," Benner said to Galacci as they turned right onto New Road. "But just make sure we don't lose him. She's our responsibility. General Miele would have my ass. Yours, too, Galacci."

General Miele would like a lot of ass, Galacci thought, grinning to himself. He'd driven for that crazy general before in Bangkok. Sergeant Galacci had also been warned by the general that his ass would be grass if any word of his all-night revels on Patpong Street ever got out. General Miele was a nice guy—lots of bluster, but a nice guy who just happened to like a good time. "Colonel, if he gets away and you get busted, you can have me busted, too."

The other car pulled into the center of the road and maneuvered in front of a double-decker bus to go left up Silom Road. The marine sat on his horn, scattering pedestrians and forcing a tuk-tuk to give way as he managed his own left turn. He glanced at Benner with his large, deep-set Italian eyes and sucked the big black cigar into the corner of his mouth. "And if I'm as good at the fine art of tailing someone in Bangkok as I say, how about seeing if I can stay here until I retire?"

"I'll do whatever I can, Sergeant, either way." He'd worried they were going to lose the cab at the first light, but somehow Galacci knew exactly what to do. "This place reminds me of a maze within a minefield."

Few people were awake when Bangkok traffic was light. For most, gridlock was a way of life in the city. To the outsider, it seemed that each of the eight million area residents commuted into the city every day, each in his own car. Actually, people also arrived and moved about by ferry, water taxi, bicycle, motorcycle, airport limo, bus, train, and minibus as well as on foot. But the traffic congestion remained overwhelming. The air remained heavy and blue with exhaust much of the day, and many people in open-air conveyances wore surgical masks. Vehicles and pedestrians were controlled by an elaborate traffic light system, and in many places there were also pedestrian subways under the streets or bridges over them just for walkers. But Bangkok's streets still remained a challenge to even the experts.

Frank Galacci had driven stock cars on dirt tracks in the Carolinas before enlisting. Maneuvering through Bangkok's streets had replaced that single lost love in his heart. Anyone who recognized the look on his face as he maneuvered ruthlessly through the intersections on Silom Road, big cigar poking out of the side of his face, recognized a man who was enjoying himself immensely. He was a large white devil in a large car and he loved it.

* * *

Prosit noticed the big vehicle on three separate occasions. The first two could have been coincidence but not the third, and he was a cautious man. He pushed his own luck by accelerating through a caution light. He could hear the horns blaring behind him as he watched the same large car in his rearview mirror also make it, weaving between vehicles already moving across Silom from Convent Road.

Prosit turned left down Thaniya. The other car did also. He took an alley near the end that led out to Rama 4 Road and turned right, quickly pulling over to the curb. There was no sight of the other.

"What are you doing?" Marclay Davis asked. There was a tinge of fear in her voice. She knew they'd been headed toward the American embassy until they turned down Thaniya. Then she saw the driver's eyes glued to the rearview mirror. "Why are you stopping here? I need to get to—"

Prosit slid a 9mm pistol just high enough above the top of the seat for her to see it. "You will please sit quietly," he said politely, "and shut up." The gun disappeared.

Marclay closed her eyes as ". . . the American embassy" slipped from her lips in a stunned whisper.

"I can put a bullet in your ear faster than you can pull the handle of that door and much faster than you could ever exit this car." As he spoke, his eyes were searching through the rear window for the other car. "And that is without watching you every minute, whether we are sitting here or this car is in motion. I see everything. I know by instinct, like a cobra, if you are going to try to escape. Please think about all of that before you do anything other than breathe. Another thing to think about is that you are of value to us alive only if we can interrogate you. Otherwise you would already be dead. Do you follow me?"

Marclay opened her eyes and her mouth but there was no sound. She nodded urgently and closed her eyes again.

Prosit's patience paid off. The driver of the vehicle that appeared to be following had been unable to see through the throng of pedestrians. There it was, no doubting that. The big car poked its nose cautiously into Rama 4. The driver attempted to remain hidden behind a bus waiting station, but Prosit had been involved in the same sort of game in the past. His pursuers knew he'd pulled over, but they weren't sure where.

"Who the fuck is following?" he snarled.

Marclay remained mute, terrified, shaking her head ever so slightly.

Prosit turned back to the wheel and put the car in gear. He was positive it had to be Americans. Such a big car. Who else? "Try anything," he snapped as he bulled his way into traffic, "pull one little bit of shit, and I'll splatter your brains all over this car." He accelerated, driving expertly, changing lanes to weave among drivers less anxious than he, knowing exactly where he wanted to go to shake the other car. No one should be able to follow for that long in such a mess. This was a test, a challenge.

They wheeled down alleys and side streets, twice crossing wide, canal-divided Sathorn Road before Prosit headed west down that boulevard toward the river.

Frank Galacci glanced over at Benner. One of the colonel's hands gripped the dashboard, the other was buried between the seats. "Relax, Colonel, this guy's good, but he ain't great. We got this knocked." The raising of his thick eyebrows over his large, expressive eyes was meant to put his passenger at ease.

"Any idea where he's going?" Benner managed.

"Probably across the river. Traffic's not so heavy over there." He reached down and extracted the pistol from his belt. "How about it, sir? If he gets away from the crowds, I don't know what's wrong with taking out one of his tires."

Benner stared at him with a querulous expression on his face. "Just like in the movies, Sergeant? You really think you could drive and shoot at the same time, like a cowboy?" He'd seen a lot of crazy things happen when he was a

Green Beret in Vietnam, but this was right up there with them.

The deep-set eyes surveyed Benner sadly before they returned to the road. "Well, sir, it might be easier if you held on to the wheel while I did the shooting. I was on the marine pistol team, you know. A crack shot, one of the best in the corps. I was marine recon, too, before I did in a knee. Just thought you ought to know."

They crossed the Sathorn Bridge over the Chao Phraya River. The taxi wove through traffic, turning north on Taksin Road.

"If I was him, I think I'd head back over the river again, sir. He's got to have figured out I'm just like stink on shit and he's not gonna shake me. And if I was still him," Galacci added, waving the cigar, "I'd probably try to lose us in Chinatown."

"Why there?"

"The streets go every which way, Colonel. I think a lot of that section was laid out two or three hundred years ago. No room for cars in a lot of those alleys, at least not big ones like this. It can just swallow you up."

The taxi sped north, weaving through thick traffic, until they once again crossed the Chao Phraya over the Memorial Bridge. Prosit had already realized that he wouldn't be able to shake the other car unless he did something desperate. He turned right down Maharat Road and headed for Chinatown. Kelley had explained that if anyone followed him he was definitely to stay away from the Inchar offices. That he'd done. But he couldn't shake them either. If Chinatown didn't work, he would eventually have to kill the American woman. Mr. Kelley had said that was equally important because she was a distinct hazard alive. Prosit knew that if he had to he could escape on foot in the old section.

"Colonel," Galacci said as they headed down increasingly narrow streets, "we're going to have a problem shortly.

You've never been in Chinatown. The way he's driving—the way I am—we're going to start hurting innocent folks." This time he kept his eyes on the narrow roads crowded with people.

The taxi careened down a side street, bouncing off a curb. As their own car followed, a tiny, ancient woman balancing baskets of dried fish on a pole across her shoulders, leapt backwards, spilling her load into the gutter.

"Okay, Galacci. You're right. We can't follow him any longer." They had to get Marclay Davis out of that car. Too many chances . . .

"Right. I'm going to slow him down right now." The unlit cigar disappeared into his shirt pocket. His gun appeared in his right hand in a single movement. "Take the wheel, sir." His other hand left the steering wheel.

There was no question in Galacci's mind about what had to be done. The sergeant arched his large body partially through the side window, the gun now grasped tightly in both hands. Benner grabbed the wheel, attempting to steady the vehicle as they careened down the alley. He heard one shot . . . a second . . .

Galacci dropped back onto the seat. "Got the son of a bitch," he reported gleefully, pushing Benner's hands away and grabbing the wheel. The car accelerated.

Benner saw the taxi swerve from side to side, then turn suddenly left down an alley, hanging precariously on two wheels before settling back down. The taxi was still fishtailing, but somehow it continued down the alley.

"Guy's good," Galacci shouted. "I took out his left rear tire. That crazy bastard's trying to pull it off on three wheels. What a guy!" The cigar was back in his mouth. "Another couple of seconds at best," he announced in his gravelly voice. "Just watch him. I never miss."

Galacci was right. The taxi was unable to hold the road. The vehicle fishtailed crazily until the tire peeled off the wheel. Then it began a sideways skid, a shower of sparks erupting from the metal rim.

"Hold on, sir. Got to do this."

The car shot forward as Galacci floored the gas pedal. Benner saw what the marine intended to do: he was aiming for the taxi's rear bumper.

Benner felt a rush of adrenaline, much like that sense of immortality that survivors remembered after a firefight. Thoughts came rapidly in those moments.

"I'll take the driver," Galacci shouted, bracing himself. "The broad's yours."

They hit the taxi on the left rear, at first pushing it sideways. Then Galacci whipped the wheel around, keeping his accelerator down as they pushed the cab, turning it farther sideways and toward the low buildings on the left. People on the crowded sidewalks scattered. The two cars remained locked together for an instant, metal grinding, tires squealing.

Then Galacci cried, "Now!" He jammed on his brakes.

The taxi, suddenly free, vaulted the curb, burst through a sidewalk stand, and slammed into a storefront.

Benner leapt out the passenger side, his own gun still on his hip. He dived low around the front of their own vehicle and lunged for the rear door of the taxi. Shots rang out as he yanked it open.

Marclay Davis was huddled on the floor of the taxi. Benner seized her ankles and yanked her out roughly. Then he grabbed her around the waist, rolling with her into the street and behind the taxi, and kept rolling through the filth and standing water in the alley until he was sure they were far enough from the taxi. Then, shielding her with his own body, he bounced to his knees, holding his pistol in front of him with both hands.

The first image that came to him was Frank Galacci, cigar clenched tightly between his teeth, advancing toward the taxi, pistol aimed at the driver's side of the cab. He peered through the shattered window. His hands dropped. "It's okay, Colonel," he called out with a casual wave and a grin. "I think I got him with the first shot. Stuck it right in his ear. I told you I was good," he said with a wide grin.

Benner lowered his own weapon and turned to look at the

young woman. Her eyes were tightly shut and she was shaking, but there was no sound. He reached out and laid a hand on her hip, patting her gently. "You're all right now. You're safe," he said softly.

When Benner looked up again, Frank Galacci had fired up his cigar and was puffing contentedly.

CHAPTER 13

Not too many hours before Leila was to learn that Penny Carson had been murdered, General Ben Miele held an unusual end-of-the-day press conference in Washington. He had a distinct reason for summoning the few energetic Pentagon reporters young enough and junior enough to be available for a late military briefing; the majority of the Pentagon's working press wouldn't be bothered at this hour, figuring that they would be subjected to more justification for the defense budget. After working the Pentagon for a while, a reporter learned there was no reason to show up in the press room for anyone less than the secretary of defense or one of his assistants, or perhaps members of the Joint Chiefs of Staff. Other than those few, the same news could be gleaned from the handouts that automatically appeared on their desks.

General Miele's wasn't an everyday name anyway. When he was mentioned, it was usually as an issuing authority confirming the dental identification of another missing serviceman. Nothing exciting for a journalist who was at most a pimply adolescent when the pilot in question was blown out of the skies.

Yet those few who shuffled into the briefing room were exactly the audience the general had hoped for.

"A couple of brave men, I see"—Ben Miele chuckled as he stepped up to the podium—"and an even braver lady." He smiled down at her and welcomed her by the name his press aide had provided. Miele was not outfitted in a freshly pressed uniform, even though his aide had indicated that was standard procedure. "It doesn't look to me like any of you ran home to change clothes before you came to hear me, and as you can note, neither did I." He spread his arms wide. "This is what Mrs. Miele approved before I walked out the door this morning."

General Miele looked like General Schwarzkopf—full, rosy cheeks, infectious smile, bull neck, broad shoulders, thick chest, arms that seemed about to pop the sleeves of his short-sleeved shirt, and a voice and demeanor that demanded attention. He also had a self-deprecating sense of humor. "And since you're probably the ones who had to turn down a drink to cover anything late-breaking, I'm buying up the hill at the fort after you finish the race for the phones." He laughed deeply at his own joke.

There was light applause.

"Let me see if I can make your time worthwhile," he continued. "You're about to be asked to do me a big favor now, and I'm going to promise that I will do the same for you later on, maybe make you rich and famous. And I've never welched on a promise in my life. My aide—that attractive lady's name is Lieutenant Pat Makin—is going to distribute two photographs to you right now."

Miele watched as his press aide handed each reporter two eight-by-ten glossies along with an envelope. "Now, that envelope's something special because it contains negatives of those photos, to make things easier for reproduction. The glossies are just so you'll be familiar with what we're going to discuss. And here's the kicker. There's also a press release in there which I'm going to have to ask you to quote verbatim rather than employ your reportorial talent. I know you're getting paid to write, and I'm getting paid to get you interested enough to want to write something. But this situation is different, as you'll learn shortly. Part of my promise is to make myself available to each of you, and that means I will not talk to anyone else first, when the time comes. At that time, I promise to answer absolutely every question I can within reasonable security limitations. But until then, I ask that you accept that noxious little blurb in the envelope."

The lone woman in the group laughed out loud.

"Thanks. With no television cameras to frighten me, I was beginning to wonder what might." He smiled pleasantly. "My own jokes, I suppose. Okay, you've had enough time to look at those photos. Anyone got any idea who those guys are?"

A few shook their heads. One of them held up a glossy and said, "This looks like a blowup of a passport photo."

"Young man, you may go to the head of the class. That's exactly what it is, and it is the only known recent photo of that gentleman. That has a number one printed on the back side. The man's name very likely could be Geraldo Vincente Santucci and I'll spell that just as soon as Lieutenant Makin finds me a grease pencil, or whatever it is they use on that," he said, pointing at a shiny white board. "The second photo, listed number two on the back side, was actually withheld over the past week from the press corps by no other important personage than me." General Miele's face was dead serious as he nodded at one of the reporters whose head had snapped up at the admission. "That's right. I readily admit I withheld it, and you already know how to spell my name to register a complaint if you don't like it after I tell why. The name of that second individual is pretty certain to be Edwin Antonio Kelley."

Lieutenant Makin handed him the writing instrument he was looking for.

Miele stepped off the podium and moved over to the white board. He very carefully printed out:

* * *

#1 GERALDO VINCENTE SANTUCCI
#2 EDWIN ANTONIO KELLEY

The female reporter raised her hand.

"Well, I was going to wait until I was finished to answer any questions, but perhaps what I say will have more impact if I don't leave gaps now. Go ahead."

"You're the first military spokesman I've encountered who admitted withholding something, General. Could you tell us why?"

"Sure." Miele, back on the podium, was grinning again. "It was none of your damn business at the time. Now, why? Because these men are believed to be authentic MIAs from Vietnam. Professionals like me, whose business it is to locate them, have been falling all over themselves trying to find them. Not only have both of these men been identified more than once in the past few days, one of them was actually seen at the Wall—and you got to believe me—taking a rubbing of his own name." Miele folded his arms and shook his head in disbelief. "By the way," he hastened to add, "that's not in your release and not for public consumption, if you'll bear with me. That was the one called Santucci, and I told you about the Wall to get your attention, if I haven't already got it. We think he's already back in Hong Kong where we have reason to believe he lives. The second one, Kelley, was last seen in Bangkok." He pointed to one of the men whose hand was in the air.

"General, usually your organization talks about former POWs. You haven't mentioned a word about prisoners today."

"What I said was MIA—missing in action. What that most often means, after all prisoners have been returned, is that there was nothing left of the individual to find. Both of these guys disappeared on the same day, from the same company, during what appeared to be the same firefight. The last time they were heard from, they reported they were surrounded by the enemy, their radioman was dead, and . . . poof, they disappeared." Miele waved his hands over his head like a magician. "MIA. Never to be seen again, but never forgotten in the memories of their grateful countrymen."

"I don't understand what you're driving at, General," one of the group piped up. "We never see any photos unless they're released from an independent source, and then you people usually get all bent out of shape denying information or countering leaks or—"

"Usually that's the name of the game. When we don't have the answers, we keep our mouths shut. I happen to think we've got some solid stuff here. But I'm going to keep my mouth shut officially and ask each of you to do the same thing. I've got to trust you, and you've got to trust me. I keep my promises. You each get the story when I can talk."

"Why are you telling us this at this hour? You'd get a larger audience tomorrow morning."

"Very perceptive again," Miele answered. "I'm telling you this now because it's early morning in Hong Kong and Bangkok, and I figure those photos are going to be faxed all over the world in a few minutes. They won't be printed for at least another day, if they're used at all, but they'll be passed around and the word will get out fast. And maybe that will help us find someone who doesn't want to be found. Plus I'm taking advantage of each one of you. We all know why you were on duty when I called this press conference. Those designated Pentagon reporters, the ones you folks call heavyweights, don't work past cocktail time unless they think we're going to war. Plus, I didn't want the big-name reporters because they wouldn't keep this story quiet for a couple of days. I wanted you people. I'm using you. I want to find these guys bad and I'm taking a chance. Take a chance on me."

The woman reporter was about to ask a question but thought better of it and chewed on her pen instead.

"Ma'am, you were going to ask why we can't find them or why we want to or any number of whys, weren't you?"

She nodded.

"That's what I can't tell you. Not yet anyway. But before you leave here this evening, Lieutenant Makin is going to take each of your names. That's so none of you get left out. When the time comes to release all the details—maybe tomorrow, maybe the next day, maybe next week—you're going to be the first ones to know. You'll get the shot at what could be one hell of a story. Again, I promise you that. So the only news that you can report is that I'm releasing the photos of two former servicemen listed as missing in action in Vietnam who have apparently come back to life.

"I'd like you to add that perhaps they're suffering from amnesia and that we want to help them. The reports have been so accurate, so damn dependable, that we're hoping anyone who sees either of these individuals will report the sighting to us. That's in the blurb I'm asking you to release." Miele stepped off the podium and went over to the board where he wrote down a phone number. "That's my office number. One of my people will be sitting on that phone twenty-four hours a day waiting for someone to call in with any information they might have."

"General, are you planning to go to Hong Kong or Bangkok to take part in the search for these men?"

"Not until I've had a drink or two with any of you who care to join me." He looked at his watch. "Give you all half an hour. Eighteen-thirty. Fort Meyer O Club. Lieutenant Makin will be at the door to make sure you get right to General Ben Miele, because he's the guy who's buying. That's six-thirty for any of you who are still on civilian time."

As he walked back to his office, Ben Miele thought about what he'd just done. It was absolutely counter to policy. Although he'd said that morning he was going to do something radical after hearing about Penny Carson, it hadn't been officially cleared. But neither had the possibility of going to Hong Kong.

Who gives a shit? It was for you, Penny.

W. P. Chan was accustomed to Americans and he enjoyed working with the law enforcement professionals, especially the highly skilled ones like the FBI. But in less than twenty-four hours he'd come to the conclusion that military investigators danced to a very different tune than policemen did. They were totally unpredictable. Perhaps it was this particular issue rather than the individuals. Even though the American involvement in Vietnam had ceased over twenty years earlier, the obsession with the event continued. They hadn't succeeded in their original objective, but while many would call the Vietnam War a loss, he knew there was also a strong belief that the little Asian country and its current government had been altered decidedly, and that could be considered positive. That was important to many people because when Americans died in a foreign war there had to be justification. It seemed to W.P. that it was the lack of that philosophical vindication that had created this American obsession.

He stared at the two pictures that had been passed on to him by a friend at the *South China Morning Post*. They were reasonably clear fax images of Santucci and Kelley. A short article accompanying the pictures suggested that these men could be suffering from amnesia and needed help. The photos and story would likely appear the next day.

What was it with these Americans? Would people really believe such a story after all these years? MIAs were still an obsession even though the generation that had gone to war was now middle-aged. W.P. had never quite understood why the Americans did things like this. Was Santucci supposed to know about this photo and react before the *Post* carried it?

And Leila Potter! In Hong Kong, women simply weren't allowed to become involved in something so dangerous. Yet she was as committed as the others, and she was firmly convinced, as were Stone and Slade, that her presence would draw Santucci out. Would these photos help them or hinder them?

W. P. Chan had done a great deal of thinking that morning before reaching his own decision. *There is also a certain moral authority in life and the weight of it belongs to Leila Potter today. I know because I have shared tears with*

*her—and my responsibility to her is that no tears ever be shed
for her because one of us made a mistake and one of these
people caught up with her.*

Chan was a man who considered the merits of each case in
much the same manner. This was the first time he had
subjugated his instincts to the desires of another individual.
What surprised him the most was that he was now sure that
Leila Potter was right, at least until a more suitable alternative existed. She was the one who could draw Santucci into
the open. To accede to the Americans' wishes—Leila's
wishes—was acceptable under these unusual circumstances. But he hoped that the Americans would eventually
be able to assuage their guilt over a war completed so long
ago. He was thankful that philosophically Asians possessed
a more realistic understanding of life and death.

Bait. I am human bait.

Leila Potter had considered what might happen to her and
the possibilities seemed infinite. What does it feel like?
Frightening? Challenging? Degrading? Is it dehumanizing
or do you rise to a new level of defiance and audacity in an
effort to face down your fears? And what does bait do in
Hong Kong that appears normal?

After the luxury of crying on W. P. Chan's shoulder that
morning, and after Matt Stone had learned of Ben Miele's
instinctive ploy with the press, Leila did what tourists do.
She shopped the elegant stores along Nathan Road in
Kowloon until just after noon. This wasn't something she
normally did, but it was her reward for becoming bait, her
few hours to relax before the dirty work began. When she
had the rare opportunity to visit city department stores in
the States, it was with the intention of purchasing something. Here she was browsing, searching for something that
might distract her, knowing that her mind was centered on
anything but shopping, and aware that one of W.P.'s men
was always near.

No matter what item she came upon, her mind remained
totally occupied with memories of Penny Carson. Penny
had been the ultimate innocent, drawn into this by sheer

fate. She was in the wrong place at the wrong time when the wrong people appeared. Leila would have had even more trouble dealing with her death if she were back in Washington. In Hong Kong, it was a distant tragedy blurred by the reality of Jerry Santucci.

Her day had been well planned by W.P. and Matt. A bit after noon, she took a cab to the ferry terminal and rode the Star Ferry across Victoria Harbor to the island of Hong Kong. It was an eerie sensation to realize that someone from W.P.'s Hong Kong police was nearby, keeping an eye on her, yet watching even more intently for anyone who showed the slightest interest in her.

Leila's mind wandered as she watched the tall buildings of the Central District grow closer. If someone made a move, would the police have time to protect her? But if they were going to kill her, why do it in public? Why not just a distant shot, one that no one would hear? She would simply be left sitting on the bench of the Star Ferry—very dead. Or death could come in the crowded streets. The sensation of being jostled and . . . and that would be the end.

She rose from the bench and walked, forcing herself not to run, to the bow railing. The air was clean, and it was good to see that the business of Hong Kong continued to skitter about Victoria Harbor. Worrying had yet to accomplish a single thing for a human being.

It was a short walk from the ferry pier up to the Bloom, a Cantonese restaurant located in the basement of the Pedder Building. W.P. had chosen the Bloom as a starting point because it was popular with the local business people at lunchtime. What better place if Jerry Santucci's business was nearby?

Matt Stone was waiting for her when she arrived at the door. He acknowledged the plainclothes policewoman who'd followed Leila from the pier, then waited at the foot of the stairs until she entered. His easy smile dispelled the little horrors that had tortured her as she moved from store to store on Nathan Road. Her self-incriminating guilt over Penny Carson was pushed into the back of her mind when they sat down at their table.

"Buy out any stores?" Matt asked pleasantly. What was it about blondes?

"Hardly. Shopping is a contact sport. You have to have your heart in it."

"Understood." Blondes with hair touching their shoulders, with soft brown eyes that made him tingle?

"You know," she began curiously, "I'm sure W.P. didn't go back on his word, but I never saw anyone following me. I wonder . . ."

"You're not supposed to notice them. If you did, then the bad guys would, too." Matt didn't know what it was about blondes. Maybe it was just this one who smiled even when she was scared and made him tingle because of it.

"I suppose you're right." She glanced at the menu briefly before looking up at Stone. "Are they here right now?"

Stone started to look around the restaurant, then frowned. "I'm sure they are. Hey." He clapped his hands lightly. "We're here to enjoy ourselves as well as be recognized. Think about something else." This wasn't the type of situation that appealed to Stone either. It was passive. He'd always lived in a world oriented to action. It wasn't until his assignment to DIA—to fill out his career, he'd been told kindly—that he began to feel the helplessness of passivity. But that was what intelligence work was, long periods of quiet investigation punctuated by occasional moments of success. "How about a drink? Will that help?"

She tilted her head to the side and smiled lazily at Stone, a very personal kind of smile. "Iced tea. A drink would put me to sleep. I traveled halfway around the world yesterday, or maybe it was the day before. I'm not sure which. Then I spent the night with a very close friend, and we found better things to do than sleep all night."

It was Stone's turn, and he tried to copy Leila's smile. "If that's what happens to you, you may never want a drink while you're in Hong Kong."

"Let's hope not. You know, when I went to Washington on business last week—I think it was last week but I'm not really positive about that anymore either—I really thought life was kind of dull. People were, too. Today, wandering through all those boutiques among those glitzy people who really looked as if they belonged in them, I decided I was dreaming. What do you think? Is this a dream?"

Stone looked pensive for a moment before he reached out and touched her hand lightly. "Feel that?"

She nodded.

"No dream. It's all real, Leila."

"Both the good and the bad? We really did spend last night together? And Penny really is dead?"

"I'm not sorry about last night, not at all. But I'm terribly sorry about Penny. I only knew her briefly, but I know how much she meant to you when you needed someone like her. But now we're in Hong Kong and we have a job to do. Let's concentrate on today." He looked up as the waiter came to the table. "What looks good to you?" he asked.

"I haven't even looked at the menu. I've been concentrating all my energy on you, and I think I'll continue to do more of the same."

"W.P. made some suggestions to me. That okay with you?"

"Go ahead. As you are now aware," she said with a suggestive wink, "I'm easy to please." After she'd said it, Leila wondered at her own boldness. Her life had never been filled with special relationships, and talking so freely about sexual experiences was foreign to her. Yet now she felt so comfortable. It was a good feeling.

Stone ordered.

"Do the Chinese have anything that'll make the bad dreams go away?" Leila asked softly.

"I wish they did. Believe me, if I knew of something, I'd get it for you. But right now you're going to have to let me do everything I can to make things better."

"Like I said, I'm easy . . . easier than I thought," she added wistfully. There it was again. She'd never even considered the words before they were out of her mouth.

After lunch Leila became a tourist again, but this time there was a definite plan. When she left Pedder Street, she turned right down Des Voeux Road Central, pausing to look in store windows, as she'd been told to do. She never searched the faces around her or looked behind her because W.P. had said that would be a giveaway to anyone intent on trailing her. The Caucasians who worked in the tall glass buildings had finished their lunches and were all back inside now. Instead, she saw a sea of Asian faces, people who were generally shorter with darker skin, black hair, and black eyes. That was when she realized that she was the one who was different. If someone was intent on finding Leila Potter, it wouldn't be difficult to pick her out.

She turned left at Ice House Street and headed toward the harbor. The Mandarin Hotel would be a couple of blocks down on her right, according to the small map W.P. had provided her. She found the hotel, took the escalator up to the second landing, and wandered through the elegant shops.

When Leila exited the front of the building, she could see the harbor directly in front of her where the taxis and buses were pulling up by the Star Terminal. For a second she thought she was lost and searched for a street sign. Then, there it was—Chater Road. She turned right and headed slowly down the street, staring up at the tall buildings. This was the right street, the place where Jerry was supposed to be. Somewhere around here. Somewhere . . .

She walked slowly, wary and self-conscious. She stopped to study a construction project, a new office building rising on a small patch of land. It soared more than twenty stories into the air and was surrounded completely by bamboo scaffolding strapped together with some kind of cloth or plastic strips. It looked so weak and tenuous, yet construction workers scampered about as they would in the steel structures back home. Green netting completely enclosed the work area to protect the people in the streets from falling objects.

Move on. You've a way to go.

Leila continued up Chater. She'd almost passed the building with the glass front before she looked up at the bronze nameplate: International Charities Center. Looking inside, she saw the name International Charities, Ltd., again in bronze, on the lobby wall. The waterfall, the directory,

the security desk, the . . . Easy . . . it was all exactly as
W. P. Chan had said. For a moment she was sure Jerry
Santucci, black eyes blazing beneath heavy dark eyebrows,
was rushing across the lobby floor to her.

And then she realized her eyes were closed. *Your imagination is your worst enemy, Leila.*

Shifting into automatic now, she continued down Chater.
W.P. had said quite forcefully that she shouldn't dawdle in
front of that building. She was supposed to be bait and she
was supposed to draw out Santucci, not make a presentation
of herself to him.

She turned left at the art museum and walked toward
Victoria Harbor, circling back to the ferry pier along the
quay. She waited patiently in line, purchased an upper-deck
ticket, and strolled up to the second level. Within a few
moments the next ferry had ground against the pilings,
unloaded its passengers, and she was aboard. Leila strolled
across the deck to the front where she could look across to
Kowloon. Matt would be waiting there.

Jerry Santucci eyed the pack of cigarettes on Connie's
desk. He'd never been a smoker, but the temptation was
there now. She'd said that they were a cure-all for the
nerves. He'd always assumed they were just a good excuse to
cover a short temper whenever she had her period. But now
he wondered.

Connie noticed his eyes fixed on the pack. "Forget it,
Jerry. All they'll do is make you miserable. Besides a
first-class case of nerves, you'll be coughing and choking and
making a general pain in the butt out of yourself. Hugh
would be very unhappy."

"Hugh is already unhappy. Hugh is unhappy about everything."

"More unhappy, then." Connie looked at her watch.
"Almost five-thirty. End of a rough day. Why don't you head
home? There's no reason to stay here."

"Hugh's still got the goddamn car," Santucci snapped
back. "Remember, Big Brother's orders state that I come
and go only in that vehicle and only through the security

area." He swiveled his head around in a circle as if he had a stiff neck. "Doesn't quite trust me, does he? Wants to escort me until he's sure I learn how to take care of myself. We've been partners for over twenty years, and now he's being my nursemaid." Jerry's mood was growing uglier as he considered his situation out loud.

Connie said nothing, waiting until he stopped swiveling his head. When he did, he was leaning over her desk to look down the front of her dress. "Sit, Jerry. Right there." She pointed at the plush guest sofa across the smallish front office. When he sat, she stood. "We know each other too well for you to be interested in me. The only reason I'm still here is because I promised Hugh I'd cover the phone in case that call came in from Singapore. If it doesn't ring before six o'clock, then they won't call until tomorrow. So can I mix you a drink?"

She'd come out from behind her desk and was standing with her hands on her hips, her legs slightly spread. Connie was as attractive as anyone they could have hired, a treat for the eyes who also happened to be capable. She'd known before she was hired that if she got the job she would be expected to dress to please visitors. Foreign officials and businessmen who were considered important enough to be allowed to visit Inchar's lower-level headquarters appreciated attractive women and were always in a better mood as a result. Connie'd never had a problem with that. In a society like Hong Kong's, male attention was good for a woman's ego. But Jerry Santucci's interest in her was a different matter. Her job description didn't include servicing management. His eyes continued to survey her full figure appreciatively. "Drink, Jerry?" she repeated.

"Join me?" Santucci asked, a slight smile at the corner of his lips.

"Of course." It was Connie's turn to smile now. "Jerry," she said, shaking her head as she moved toward the bar in the main office, "I'm almost old enough to be Suzie Wong's mother. As you've been told before, you're going to have to look elsewhere."

When she returned from the bar in Hugh's office, she

handed Santucci his Jack Daniel's and touched his glass with her own. "To better days for Jerry Santucci. I hope you find your next Suzie Wong soon."

Jerry sipped and watched while Connie drank down half her glass. "Coke?" he asked.

"As usual."

"I thought you were going to have a drink with me."

"I am."

"A real drink."

"You've never seen me drink anything alcoholic in this office, and you never will. That's not in my job description."

Santucci took a swallow of his drink, placed the glass on the teak table in front of him, and leaned forward, his elbows on his knees, chin in his hands.

Connie liked Jerry, even when he leered at her. His expression was neither mean nor ugly, just a suggestion if she ever decided to take advantage of it. She knew he'd climb into bed with her without hesitation because he looked at every woman as a challenge. He'd been that way since the day she came in for her first interview. Hugh Young had explained exactly how to handle Jerry, and he'd been right. Jerry accepted yes and no and was as generous and supportive as a boss could be. He simply believed that every woman who appealed to him deserved to spend some time in bed with him. They would be better people as a result. When he was rejected, he was like a child. This time he was experiencing male rejection of a kind that was difficult to accept. He'd made a grave mistake and felt he was being punished. Connie felt bad for him. "Feel better?"

He raised his head from his hands. "I guess so."

"That's the idea. Now, don't worry about Hugh. When he comes back, he'll have all the information on just what the Hong Kong police are snooping after."

"I don't give a shit about the police. It's that broad."

"We got half a dozen good pictures of her today, Jerry." Inchar's chief of security had been the only one to get near Leila Potter that day, and he had done so without the knowledge of a single one of W.P.'s people. "At the restaurant, in front of this building, on the ferry. With those photographs, we'll be able to find her hotel." Santucci had wanted to grab Leila Potter right away. Hugh had had to show him the photos of the Hong Kong police trailing her before he could convince Jerry that this was a trap.

Connie was right. She was always right. The only information they didn't have was where Leila Potter was staying. They'd been able to track her until she got off the Star Ferry on the Kowloon side, and then she disappeared in a car. Whoever was driving—and one of their people had reported that he was a Chinese, probably HK police—knew how to disappear into the afternoon traffic. That was the reason Hugh was out of the office now. He might have arranged to have Leila killed with a few calls, but there was an individual in Kowloon who owed them a big favor and Hugh wanted to remind him of that in person. No one could disappear forever, not even in Hong Kong, especially an attractive white woman.

"Another drink, Jerry?" Goddamn him, Connie thought. He looked so forlorn, like a little kid. But liquor wouldn't work either.

"Are you trying to get me drunk and seduce me?"

"Never, Jerry, not at the office, not at your place, not at mine, not anywhere, and not with a round-eye." She'd been through this with him many times before, and she'd answered in exactly the same manner. She knew he loved the part about round-eyes because he often teased that round-eyed women weren't in the same league as Asian women. There was something about Jerry Santucci that you had to love, but at the same time, you never quite trusted him.

"Me, too. But I just like to keep you on your toes."

That was the part she didn't trust. Connie was afraid that someday Jerry would lose his sense of humor. She'd mentioned this little game of Jerry's to Hugh a couple of times, and he always said Jerry played it with every woman, that it was just part of his ego problem. Connie'd promised herself years ago that she would never turn her back on Santucci when he'd had a couple of drinks. And she was about to get him that second drink when the warning lights above the door indicated someone was entering from the alley.

"That'll be Hugh," she said with relief. "The two of you can drink together."

Santucci watched carefully as she stood up and smoothed her skirt over her ample figure. Someday, he thought to himself, he'd have to try that out. Connie really didn't mean what she said. She couldn't. Besides, he was sure that Hugh had probably sampled some of it, so Jerry was going to make damn sure he did, too, before it was too late.

"Jerry," Hugh Young remarked as he came into the outer office. "Drinking with the employees? How nervous of you." His guttural laugh was forced. He knew their secretary would never drink, and that was why he'd also told her exactly what she should do if Jerry became too much of a problem: sit him down, get him a drink, let him stew, but don't let him con you with that little-boy charm. "Connie, you've done a good job of baby-sitting. Why don't you pack it up for the night?"

Jerry's eyes narrowed at the last comment. "Couldn't you think of something nicer to say, Hugh? That broad is out there somewhere, and she can fuck up everything. This isn't easy, you know."

"No, it's not. But it would be much easier for everyone if you'd relax. That Potter broad is having exactly the effect on you that they'd like it to."

"Where's she staying?"

"Give it time. At least we've got the possibilities narrowed down—I hope. Kowloon's a big place. It may take a day or so. Or they may give her location away by doing something stupid. But we'll find her, and we'll know when the time is right."

"It can't be soon enough for me."

"We're ahead of them, Jerry. Come on. The car's waiting."

Harry Jensen glanced in his rearview mirror again, aware of what he would see but somehow unable to stop himself. The sight was more chilling each time. The pickup truck, one of those redneck jobs where the springs lifted the body high above the frame, was still following him. Whenever he noticed one of those trucks, he automatically wondered at the IQ of anyone who would invest money in such a monstrosity. The tires were oversized, the chrome on a row of spotlights over the cab glistened in the wet reflection from the streetlights, and orange fog lights mounted in front of the grill glared like monster's eyes through the rear window of Harry's tiny red Miata.

Shit. All that truck needed was teeth and a little slobber dripping off the fenders. It was late and dark and wet, wind-driven rain fell in blinding gusts, and Harry was scared shitless.

When Chuck Goodrich got his dander up about something—in this case Penny Carson's murder, which had been discovered yesterday—time became nonexistent. On this rainy evening Goodrich's empty stomach had finally reminded the congressman that his staff was human. "Harry, why didn't you tell me how late it was?" he'd said. It was close to nine-thirty. "I should have sent out for sandwiches or pizza," he said apologetically. "Christ, tell them all I'm sorry and why don't they sleep in tomorrow. . . . No, scratch that. I want them over in the Pentagon the same time the inmates arrive there."

Goodrich had undertaken his own investigation of Bravo Company, building on everything Penny had dug up, and had pulled enough strings the day Penny's body was found so his people could do their own digging and pick up where Penny had been so viciously cut off. If an MIA like Santucci could come back from the dead, if he could escape the U.S. government so easily, then there could be one live soul who'd never intended to be missing. Goodrich wanted to find out how the Pentagon had blown it, and perhaps that would provide a means to learn if there could be other MIAs. He had only so much time before the military closed ranks.

So it was close to ten when an exhausted Harry Jensen had pulled onto Independence Avenue. There were few cars on the streets at that hour on a rainy night, and the big black pickup idling at the curb stood out like one more memorial to the futility of Washington life. Harry had noted it with disdain, unable as the headlights caught him full in the face to keep from treating the man at the wheel to a superior sneer when he turned the little red Miata west toward Route One and a beer and sandwich before he collapsed in bed. Perhaps the sneer had been noted, he thought, when the fog lights snapped on and the pickup closed in behind him. He was sure he would now have to undergo a couple of blocks of intimidation for something he should have known better than to do.

But the pickup had turned with him onto Route One South, followed him over the George Mason Bridge, and remained no more than twenty feet off his rear bumper no matter what his speed as he headed down the Shirley Highway. He took the Glebe Road exit and turned northwest at the foot of the ramp.

Oh, shit, I had to pull that asshole stunt for a goddamn weirdo. The pickup was now right on his bumper, headlights shining over the Miata, fogs so bright in his rear window that he had difficulty seeing the shiny black surface of the road. Glebe Road was a major thoroughfare, but it, too, was almost deserted on this foul night.

What the hell? Harry wondered. A queer-basher? Harry Jensen dismissed that immediately. They drove vehicles like this pickup, but they got liquored up first and then waited outside gay bars. People like that didn't hang around outside the Rayburn Office Building. And Jensen never frequented gay bars; that wasn't his style. This was definitely something else.

That was when Harry Jensen felt the first chilling sensation race through his body. *Is this how Penny bought it?*

The pickup's headlights suddenly flashed bright as they approached the first of the right turns into the Army Navy Country Club and the truck veered to the left and was instantly beside him. Harry's foot hit the gas pedal. The Miata skidded, and the steering wheel went light in his hands as the tires spun crazily on the wet pavement, and then he let up enough to regrip the pavement. The truck almost clipped the sports car's rear as it accelerated again and was once more beside him.

Harry found himself looking directly at the shiny front wheel hub of the pickup less than a foot away. He could see the giant bowed springs as he fought his wheel to steady the Miata. Harry hit the brakes to force the truck to speed past, but the other driver was thinking exactly as he was. Then Harry saw an arm extend from the open passenger's window and a hand swing around in his direction. In that hand was a long-barreled black revolver, pointing toward his head.

The Miata went into a slide as Harry whipped the wheel hard to the right and turned down Nineteenth Street toward the golf club. He could hear the roar of the pickup as the driver cramped his own wheel to the right and downshifted. The truck bounced off the curb and sideswiped a parked vehicle. Then the bright headlights steadied once again on the little sports car.

Adrenaline coursed through Harry Jensen's body. Sheer terror now controlled the tiny Miata. Why weren't there any people out here to help him? There'd been few cars on Route One, none to witness the scene on Glebe Road, and none on the side streets. He saw hardly any lights in the windows of the houses that lined Nineteenth. There wouldn't be a chance in hell if he pulled over and tried to run for a house.

Harry was sure his pants were wet, and he had no idea when that had happened. Had Penny felt this way? The pickup seemed to be gaining as he slewed the Miata around a bend into the golf club. Someone had to be at the club at this hour.

Harry's windshield spiderwebbed as a round hole appeared just below the rearview mirror. *Help me!* Was he screaming or was that cry purely in his mind? *Help me! Help me. . . .* He heard the roar of his own engine, the wind whistling through the hole in the windshield, and was sure there was an infernal growl coming from the pickup behind him as he raced into the darkness of the country club's grounds. He could see the warmth and safety of the lights of the clubhouse ahead.

Maybe . . . Oh, God, help me . . . please. Maybe . . .

The road turned to the left and a huge tree loomed up before him. As Harry turned the steering wheel, he felt the rear end slide away from him. The Miata was going sideways! *Why?*

Harry Jensen could see the shower of sparks and hear the screech of metal against a hard surface as his left rear tire disintegrated. *A bullet?* The Miata left the earth and catapulted toward the tree. There was a shattering crash of metal and glass and Harry's scream, which was cut off as his head met the dashboard.

The pickup came to a stop beside the wreckage. The passenger leapt out of the cab, gun in hand, and ran to the ball of junk that had been the Miata. There was no movement inside, only a soft groaning as if the person wanted to cry out but was unable to. The man carelessly tossed the revolver back in the cab to the driver. Then he climbed up on the running board and fumbled in the truck bed until he unhooked a bungee securing a five-gallon can. He then emptied the contents through the shattered window on the driver's side of the Miata, across the moaning form tangled in the wreckage, and on the outside of the vehicle. After securing the gas can in the back of the pickup, he struck a match in the lee of the truck's cab and lit a rolled up newspaper. Once it was blazing, he approached the wreck and tossed it at the Miata. There was a sharp popping sound, like a large balloon bursting, and the sports car was enveloped in a ball of flame.

The man jumped back into the passenger seat, and the pickup wheeled around and raced back out through the entrance of the golf club. The driver swung down streets they hadn't used before until he was again on Glebe Road. As they spend along the Shirley Highway past the Army Navy Country Club, the flames were clearly visible, reflected off the low clouds as the pickup headed back into Washington in the driving rain.

Harry Jensen was unfortunate enough to have been one of the key people targeted by Hugh Young before he left the District. At the time, it had seemed logical to Hugh that he could regain the cover they'd maintained for so many years, if certain key people were eliminated. That method had worked well over the years in the Far East, and it had seemed sensible when he was angry: eliminate the investigators and you eliminate the need for an investigation. Only after his return to Hong Kong did he acknowledge that a rash of killings would be met far differently in Washington than in the Far East. Unlike the cities where Inchar operated, Hugh did not own the police forces in and around D.C. It was bad judgment on his part, and he called off his hired killers as soon as he arrived in the Territory. But his change of mind had come too late for Harry Jensen.

CHAPTER 14

Ed Kelley CONTEMPLATED THE PHOTO WITH A MIXTURE OF humor and frustration. *Still a handsome devil, you old cocksman.* It was a copy of the picture that had been taken in Laos a couple of weeks before. "Tell me, my friend," he asked the image in a soft voice, "just how in hell do you blow away someone who is by now a virtual prisoner in the American embassy, scared absolutely shitless, guarded by U.S. marines, and quite capable of fingering you if you show your face for even a nanosecond?" He stared at the picture as if waiting for the lips to move. Would great words of wisdom be forthcoming?

The likeness was amazing, considering it had been blown up and transmitted by fax machines, certainly a testimonial to modern electronic technology. At least it wasn't full face. He had turned and was talking with Chu Li. Now the three Laotians had been cut out, and his face had been blown three or four times, but the photo was good. "How about coming up with a method of wasting that broad? Come on, genius. Spout forth."

His features had become slightly shaded through all the copying, giving him a somewhat darker complexion. Since he was turned slightly to the side, the cheekbones were now overemphasized and the vague pouches under his eyes, which had indeed concerned him the past few years, were more pronounced. "A handsome devil, old boy, but otherwise you're a deaf-mute. Your picture can't talk to them." But the man in the photo was also a dead ringer for him.

The photo had come from a contact at the Bangkok *Post* who'd simply faxed it to Kelley at his Inchar office shortly after it had been received at the *Post* from their Washington stringer. Kelley had been assured there was no story attached to the "for information only" photo, simply a tag indicating that this could be an American MIA suffering from amnesia who was assumed to be in the Bangkok area. Kelley's contact assured him that there would be no follow-up story, because the Americans had cried wolf once too often on this very subject. Even if a story came through, the *Post* would wait to see if there was a strong American reaction before printing anything. However, this was an unusual approach and could Mr. Kelley possibly comment? His contact had scrawled that note judiciously on the fax copy.

"You don't know how close you are to a final comment," Kelley murmured. "Right between the eyes."

The possibility of a story appeared remote for the time being. So what? Didn't some asshole say that a picture was worth a thousand words, or something like that? Ed Kelley was aware that his *Post* contact would eventually have to wonder how his expatriate friend happened to be associated with the MIA-POW situation. Inchar had always paid the newspaper man exceptionally well for providing reliable information and for keeping quiet. But what if one of the other curious souls at the Bangkok *Post* got wind of that photo? Kelley knew he couldn't take them all out.

"So concentrate on the broad." Kelley wasn't one to talk out loud to himself, not unless he'd done something stupid. At times like that he could get down on himself. Then he would remind his inner self, out loud and in so many words, not to be such an asshole in the future. But that's exactly what he'd been—stupid. "So now that you've admitted it, do something to make up for it."

Her name was Marclay Davis. The guy causing all the trouble was a Colonel Nolan Benner. Kelley wasn't even going to bother with the marine who'd blown away Prosit that morning because he knew from experience that those guys were a little too crazy to mess with. And while bribes had always worked in the past, this definitely was not the time to spread Inchar's unending supply of money in the proper places. What proper places, for Christ's sake? There weren't any at this point, and there was no time. After more than twenty years of unequaled success, this was the closest any of them had come to a challenge to their authority. As in the past, they would have to remove those individuals who presented the greatest danger to their survival. "Smoke 'em out and dust 'em off," he barked at the photo. "Why the hell couldn't you have come up with that? You dickless wonder," he added with a wicked grin.

Hell, the Davis broad was the only one who'd seen him and could provide a positive ID. If she was out of the picture, he'd get a crew cut, grow a mustache, and in five days no one could associate him with that side view—well maybe three-quarter.

Ed Kelley made a call to a colonel in Thai military intelligence who owed him a debt that could never really be repaid—unless Kelley asked him to assassinate King Bhumibol. The Thai army had access to everything in Bangkok, actually throughout the entire country. They also possessed one advantage that Kelley's own system never would—their prying was never questioned because their power was second to none. The military still basically ran the government, but they were behind the scenes now. Since the Davis woman probably would not be allowed out of the American embassy until they could move her back to the States, Kelley needed to find out exactly when she was to leave. And he was certain that Thai authorities would be asked to provide security.

The American embassy would arrange her transfer to

Don Muan Airport. She might be driven in a Thai or an American vehicle, but it would be under Thai guard. From sunrise until midnight, it would be slowed by traffic; that was a given in Bangkok. Late at night it would simply be a wonderful target. During the busy hours, innocents would be killed by the explosion, but that couldn't be helped. Kelley could lie low afterward, and the incident would eventually be forgotten. There were too many other problems in the world for the U.S. government to worry about one broad.

Ed Kelley hoped they would move her soon. Business was being interrupted. A few hours' delay could mean a few million dollars. A day? Two days? There was money to be made.

The police in Bangkok did not take kindly to high-speed chases in their city, and they became even more concerned when foreigners shot their citizens. Before Sergeant Galacci could get through to the American embassy on the two-way radio that morning, a number of city police had arrived by bicycle and patrol car. The fact that both Galacci and Benner were in civilian clothes made the situation even more difficult, and Marclay Davis was still so terrified that she could provide no help. Only the license plates assigned to the embassy protected the two men from going directly to jail.

It was therefore noon by the time the embassy staff had secured the release of Colonel Benner and Miss Davis from police questioning and had them back in U.S. custody. But to gain the colonel's release, it had been necessary to sacrifice Galacci for at least another twenty-four hours so that the Bangkok police could save face. However, those who knew the sergeant were certain the police would want to release him before the day was over. He had that effect on people when he was confined.

Marclay Davis was offered water, juice, iced tea—anything that might relax her—as soon as she and Benner were settled in the ambassador's outer office.

"Don't you people have anything stronger than that?" She

was still pale, and her eyes darted from face to face. "You don't seem to understand." She was seated next to Colonel Benner and turned to him. "Don't they know what happened out there? I really don't give a damn what time of day it is. They must have a basic American drink here. Vodka! Ice! You don't even have to know how to mix it. Just pour the vodka over the ice. Is that too difficult?"

"Give her whatever she wants," Benner said to one of the hesitant staffers.

"The ambassador will be available shortly, sir," she answered reluctantly.

"All right, then," Benner retorted angrily. "Bring two drinks. I'll join her. Better yet, bring three," he snapped. "Maybe the ambassador will join us when he sees how much fun we're having today. Bring the goddamn bottle," he roared as the staffer retreated from the room.

"Colonel, all I want to do is get out of here. I want to get home and hide under my bed and just forget everything." She'd managed to fluff her hair and put on fresh lipstick, but Marclay Davis still looked as if she'd jogged over to the embassy in the dressy outfit she'd put on that morning to meet her mother's friend.

"We'll get you out of here as soon as we can," Benner answered reassuringly. "After what happened this morning, we don't do anything without the proper security."

Marclay rolled her eyes. "I don't care how you do it, Colonel. Honestly, I'll take one of those little tuk-tuks to the airport if I have to."

"No tuk-tuks, no cabs, not even a crazy man like Sergeant Galacci. The ambassador wants to talk to us personally. You see, in most countries we have to let the locals provide security, and I'm sure he'll see that the arrangements are made properly."

A very uncertain embassy staffer returned with the vodka. It was borne on a silver tray. The ice was in a silver bucket. The glasses were a beautifully cut crystal that had to have come from among the embassy's formal tableware. The staffer dropped the cubes into the glasses one at a time with silver tongs.

Marclay gulped the first swallow as if it were water. "I've never been so terrified in my life." She rolled her eyes again and took another gulp.

Benner calculated that was at least the fifth time she'd made the same statement. "I was, too. I think Galacci was the only one who enjoyed himself." She'd been right: vodka was the answer. He was on duty, but really didn't give a damn. His job was supposed to be administrative; he was an investigator on his way to Hanoi when all of this had begun to happen. "Let's just relax and think things out until the ambassador's ready for us."

They sat at either end of a comfortable sofa in the ambassador's outer office and sipped their drinks. Within a few minutes the staffer who'd brought the tray announced that the ambassador would see them. "He will also join you for a drink to celebrate Miss Davis's return, of course."

Benner's report was short and very much to the point. In the presence of the ambassador, he was once again elegant in his demeanor even though he'd been rolling in the Chinatown alley in the same clothes. He was interrupted a few times with questions and twice Marclay Davis repeated how frightening the entire experience had been. The ambassador agreed that she should be transferred back to Washington on the next available military plane.

"Can it be as soon as today?" Marclay asked.

"Civilian flights generally leave here early in the morning, stop in Japan for refueling, and then go on from there so that they can arrive in daylight." The ambassador was totally sympathetic. "I understand and agree with General Miele's security requirements and we're doing what we can on this end right now. I've already been in touch with the prime minister's office, and he's guaranteed that the Thai army will provide security to escort you onto one of our military planes. I think that's by far the safest approach. They know their own people better than we do. There won't be any problems when they're running things."

"I'm having a wonderful time, really I am. I love this. Maybe it's because I'm dining in a man's room," Leila exclaimed. "Believe me, it's not something I've been making a habit of lately. I guess maybe I was afraid I might never enjoy anything so intimate again. . . ." Her voice trailed off. They were finishing a room service dinner in his room. She was so tired by the time the Star Ferry touched the pier in Kowloon—Matt said it was the twelve-hour jet lag—that he insisted they stay in that evening. She'd been studying her fingernails self-consciously, and now she looked up at Matt and found him grinning wickedly at her. When he smiled, she decided he really wasn't so hard looking, even though that trait also had its appeal. When he smiled, his eyes smiled, too, and they no longer radiated that brittle, challenging look. "And I'm looking forward to dessert, Commander Stone," she added huskily.

Other women he remembered who'd made a remark like that to him were generally satisfying but not especially memorable. But when Leila spoke, the lilt in her voice made him want to listen to her . . . forever? *No, you're kidding yourself, Stone.* "We didn't order dessert." He suddenly wanted her to challenge him.

"I'm aware of that." The corners of her mouth turned up ever so slightly.

"That wasn't the reason I suggested . . ." Was he backing off?

"Oh, I don't know about that." It was her turn to tease. "I suppose you're going to tell me you don't make a habit of doing this with other women."

Stone's eyebrows rose for a moment; then he wrinkled his forehead in embarrassment. "Well, no, to be honest. The opportunity just hasn't presented itself. It's sort of . . . Well, in my line of work we're just not in this situation." Why was it this woman could tease and embarrass him and make him enjoy it?

Leila experienced a sensation of power. No, it wasn't really power. It was more a sense of satisfaction because neither of them was a master of this sort of situation. She could see that she was able to embarrass him with the teasing, but she didn't want to do that. Strange that she should spend a lonely lifetime mostly turning down men who were trying to achieve exactly what she and Matt had found in a few days. Maybe it wouldn't be permanent, but this was something she would be able to treasure forever.

Actually, if she counted the time, she and Matt had spent only a few hours entirely alone—driving back and forth through the Maryland countryside to see Billy Corey, a flight halfway around the world—and then something just happened that first night in Hong Kong that she couldn't explain. Even if nothing ever came of it, she would be pleased with herself for having found Matt Stone.

"I'm teasing you. I've got a mean streak." She reached across the table and squeezed his hand. "I don't think something like we've found happens often, and I'm sorry I made you uncomfortable. I don't remember when I've enjoyed myself, or someone else, so much. I don't make a habit of living like this." She smiled engagingly. "You see, I'm pretty much a prude, so I really don't understand what's happening myself. It must be you, Matt. That's the only reason I can think of for bringing out a part of me I'd sort of forgotten . . . if I ever really knew it was there."

Stone poured some more wine in her glass. "I'm not familiar with these emotions either," he mused, amazed at how pleasant it was when someone just held your hand.

Leila caught his eye and smiled slightly. "People our age don't have the opportunity to discover another person often." She stretched her arms out in front of her. "But we all keep changing. I used to be such a tease when I was a kid. Oh, what a reputation I had. Wouldn't lay off the other kids. Then one day Danny came to me and told me that I wouldn't have any friends anymore if I didn't treat them better. Even then I thought he was kidding me, until he told me a couple of stories about how I'd made other kids cry. And they were all true. Danny was just trying to help out his kid sister. He was like that."

Stone sipped his wine but could think of nothing to say. Her eyes had grown shiny when she mentioned her brother's name and he realized she'd say more if she wanted to.

W. P. Chan had been right when he said that the kitchen

in their hotel was a good one. He'd explained that this hotel was where the Chinese like him dined when they were looking for a good American-style steak. "You wouldn't believe how many Chinese living in Hong Kong have spent years in the United States," he said. "They go out for American food just like you look for Chinese food back home. Order room service tonight." To Leila, he had added, "Sleep well. Maybe tomorrow you can apply for a job at Inchar." Without further explanation, W.P. had excused himself.

"Did W.P. talk with you about my applying for a job at Inchar tomorrow?" Leila asked, changing the subject.

"He told me that the idea of parading you around the Central District left something to be desired. After he thought about it, he said that he wouldn't show his face outside if he were Jerry Santucci. He's decided that the way these people have been operating, the fact that didn't do anything after their earlier reactions means they're trying to lie low. Our effort didn't bring Santucci into the open and we'll likely never know if you were recognized. We're still going to use you for bait, I'm afraid, but we're going to send you where the fish are supposed to be."

"And what do you think?"

"I think your safety is more important than anything else. I guess I'm not looking at this from the DIA's point of view anymore. I'm supposed to get my man regardless of what it takes. But I'm more worried about you." He stroked his cheek thoughtfully. "You know, at this point I should call back to DIA and tell them to replace me, tell them I've developed a strong personal interest in you to the detriment of my job. We're supposed to be very impersonal, you see."

"And I'm making things difficult for you."

"Not for me. You're doing wonders for me. But in my job I'm supposed to do whatever's necessary to complete the mission, and I really wondered about myself when W.P. said he wanted you to apply for a job at Inchar. My first reaction was to tell him no way."

"But you didn't."

"He's going to have his people around you all the time—taxi drivers, doormen, janitors, repair people, even others interviewing for a job while you're there. There's always going to be somebody."

Leila picked up her glass and tried to find her image as she stared down into the plum-colored wine. *How long has it been since anyone cared about me like this?* Harry Jensen had been wonderful. She knew Harry—understood what he was and in what way he cared for her—and loved him for his caring and honesty. But that was so different from this. She looked up and found Matt Stone studying her.

"Matt, you don't have to worry. I'd be here looking for Jerry Santucci without you if I had to," she replied softly, "though I can't imagine your not being here. I'm not doing this for me or you, or even for the good old U.S.A. I'm doing it for a kid named Danny Potter who died in the wrong place for all the wrong reasons." She could feel her eyes threatening to fill with tears again. Maybe it was a combination of the tiredness and the wine, maybe just remembering the big brother who was always looking out for his sister. "I want to do this more for Danny now than when this all started."

Stone smiled and nodded his understanding and touched his wineglass to hers. "For Danny." He looked at his watch for the fifth or sixth time since they'd sat down for dinner. "Now I really do have to make a phone call." He'd apologized each of the other times he glanced at his watch, explaining that he had a message to return a call to General Miele at exactly nine that night. "My apologies again. I promise I'm not bored. How could I be?" The phone was on the night table, and he sat on the edge of the bed as he placed the call.

Leila was drinking her wine when she heard the phone ringing in her own room next door. It was a different sound than at home, like the phones in European films. For a moment it hadn't registered. Then she was surprised, since no one knew where she was staying. Stone was preoccupied, waiting for Miele to come on the line, and obviously didn't notice it. She whispered about her own phone just as he began talking, then pointed to her room when she was certain he didn't hear her, and got up from the table to answer it. She'd forgotten W.P.'s insistence that she speak to no one.

"Yes," she said.

Leila heard a torrent of what she assumed was Chinese from a man on the other end.

"I'm sorry, I only speak English."

There was a slight pause. "Wait, peez," or at least that's what Leila thought she heard. Then she could hear someone speaking Chinese in the background.

Another voice, a woman's, came on and spoke in slow, broken English. "Sorry, lady. Is this English lady?"

"No, I'm not English."

"Lady, you speak English."

"But I'm American. Are you looking for someone from England or the United States?"

"Oh. I sorry. Wrong person. No bother." And the connection was broken.

Stone was just hanging up the phone when she came back in and sat down at the table. There was still an ounce or two of wine in her glass, and she sipped it thoughtfully. It seemed a strange call, yet perhaps it wasn't so strange in Hong Kong. W.P. said almost every educated person in the Territory spoke English. That was when she remembered his advice about the telephone.

"Something's bothering you," Matt stated when he sat down opposite her.

"Wrong number."

He tilted his head slightly. "Pardon?"

"My phone was ringing. I answered it. Wrong number."

"You're not supposed to answer," he admonished. "Besides, there's another name registered for your room." W.P. knew the hotel manager and had insisted that their rooms be registered under Chinese names.

"Someone said they were looking for an English lady."

"You didn't give your name!" Stone said more sharply than he'd intended.

"No. I had to explain that even though I spoke English I was an American." She related exactly what had been said.

A frown spread across his face. "Shouldn't happen," he murmured to himself.

"It sounded like a mistake."

"Correct, my American lady. Sounded like. Odd that someone looking for an English lady should start off in Chinese after you'd answered in English."

"All I said was yes."

He held up a hand. "It's still not right. Shouldn't have happened. I can't explain why. It's just a feeling."

"A feeling . . ." she repeated uneasily.

"It goes back a long way. Believe me. Every Navy SEAL I know who's been in combat and is still alive knows what that means. Don't go against your best instincts."

Leila nodded. "I'll buy that. I think my instincts may have saved my life last week. I guess I know what you mean."

"Let me change the subject." He licked his lips. "Like I said, I'm not too used to situations like ours, or maybe it's talking about them. But I believe you feel the same way about sleeping together last night that I do."

"You are a bit bashful, aren't you?" she said, grinning.

"No." It was embarrassing to have a woman say that to you. "I'm not shy or anything like that. We're too old for that. What I'm trying to say is that I don't want you—us, I mean—sleeping in your room." There should have been— and there had been—perfect cover at this hotel. W.P. had selected the hotel himself, coordinated the security arrangements, and expressed confidence in his own setup. Someone had penetrated it. "You're going to have to sleep here, starting right now. Get yourself settled while I check this out with W.P."

Then he called Chan and woke him up to explain Leila's call. "I decided the logical thing to do was stay put until I spoke to you."

W. P. Chan agreed. "Don't leave the hotel. That would make it that much harder for the system I've set up. I'm on my way." He knew he didn't have to explain to Stone that some of his security people had probably been removed already.

No one had been searching for Hugh Young that day. He remained an unknown who could come and go as he pleased. Jerry Santucci had been kept on the phone as much as possible cleaning up the finer points of the Batam Island project between Singapore and Jakarta. Hugh had assigned the trailing of Leila while she was on the island to the head of Inchar's security department, and the job had been done perfectly.

Part of Hugh's time that day was involved with politics—making a number of phone calls, almost all of them local. His first was to the civilian head of the Hong Kong police, a gentleman who shared the Inchar box with him each year on the opening day of racing at Happy Valley and who generally had the box to himself thereafter. The next call was to the local precinct chief who owed his position to Hugh Young's influence and whose luxurious motorized junk had been a gift from Inchar. That was followed by calls to the governor's executive secretary and to certain influential members of the Legislative Council and the Executive Council.

There was practically no one in a vital position who didn't appreciate Hugh Young's largess. His generosity was well known, and sometimes the subject of jokes among Hong Kong's in-group, that Inchar did not exist for the sole purpose of benefiting charities. Rather, knowing individuals often snickered that if Young did have a favorite charity, it was indeed them. Yet they never felt that they'd been bought; they were simply sharing Inchar's good fortune.

The only time any of them ever acknowledged to themselves the true relationship that had been established over the years was when Inchar requested their cooperation. While such a request was always polite and seemingly voluntary, there was never any doubt that it was also an order. And when they had met their obligation, they never spoke of it to another soul. On those rare occasions when an unpleasant rumor about such a situation did arise, the individual involved was assumed to have left Hong Kong. It would have been foolish and improper to inquire after them. Doing business in Hong Kong was a matter of adapting to the culture.

What little most people did know about Inchar's business was that it was a highly profitable conglomerate functioning on an international scale with exquisite contacts in each country where it did business. Inchar's privacy was firmly respected, just as they expected their own would be regarded in the same manner. That was what made Hong Kong function so efficiently. Good business was decidedly no one else's business.

Hugh Young also spent some time that day in the executive offices of those companies occupying space in Inchar House. Each of them had a special relationship with International Charities, Ltd. They either provided a service or product to Inchar that was the main source of their own income, or else Inchar controlled the foreign companies that were their principal source. Dependency had become a comfortable habit, and no one bit the hand that fed him, because to do so would have been economic suicide.

Young suggested to each company that if any other people appeared to inquire after jobs, as they had the previous day, they should be accommodated. Inchar would cover any of the costs involved. But Inchar's security department would coordinate interviews and manage any of the other incidentals involved. Their cooperation would be appreciated.

His busy day had ended when he returned from Kowloon after securing the final favor he needed in his search for Leila Potter, and relieved Connie of the responsibility of baby-sitting Jerry Santucci. Before he and Jerry headed to Victoria Peak for the night, Hugh sipped a drink and reviewed the Batam Island project, listening patiently to Santucci's complaints. Regardless of his bitching, Jerry had coordinated all the necessary details. Contracts had been signed by the finance ministers of Singapore and Indonesia and returned by fax, and the State Department official Jerry had visited on his trip to Washington had initialed an agreement that would limit tariff restrictions on products emanating from the deal.

It was a rewarding day and a tiring one, and once they were back on Victoria Peak Hugh felt he'd successfully countered most of the surprises of the past few days. But the best was yet to come. Jerry was boring him about being a prisoner in his own home when the butler informed Hugh just before nine-thirty that he had an important telephone call.

"Perhaps this is it, Jerry." He pressed the button for the speakerphone so they could both listen.

It was the man he'd visited in Kowloon that afternoon, the one who owed him a serious debt. The American woman, Leila Potter, had been located in a Chinese hotel. She was registered under a Chinese name. However, she fit the description Young had provided that afternoon, and she was in her room at that moment. She would be followed if she left. What did Mr. Young desire?

"You're absolutely sure you have the correct woman? One mistake could be the last one for both of us."

"Every source of information indicates that I am correct. The only option left would be to knock on her door and ask her name directly."

"Never mind. You've done enough. Remember, the authorities are"—how had one of them put it?—"very touchy about anything that would make the death of any American appear to have been intentional." An accident, the odd chance of being in the wrong place at the wrong time, sexual involvement with a citizen of the Territory—any of those were acceptable reasons to U.S. authorities for the death of an American. The State Department investigated similar circumstances worldwide on a daily basis. But just let it appear that an American's death in a foreign country had been planned, and investigating authorities swarmed like flies.

"The contract is expensive, Mr. Young, more than either of us anticipated." There was a pause. "I've been forced to engage a specialist from the Wanchai District."

Young frowned. Traditionally such jobs were parceled out to local gangs in a district. "Is there a problem?"

"It's been solved. The local leaders approve. You see, there is a detective involved whom the locals call the Mongoose. None of them would accept the money."

Young had heard the name. This Mongoose was respected by both the Caucasian and Oriental communities. "Why is he in this?"

"Rumors spread quickly. Apparently your Mr. Santucci killed a Hong Kong police detective named T. T. Chang. His body has disappeared. He and the Mongoose often worked together. They were very close. There are ugly rumors circulating in the district about the killing—that murdering that detective is going to bring back police harassment of the local gangs. And you know yourself that there is a certain amount of cooperation among the local gangs when they're unhappy. Now there's not enough money to convince them to participate."

"Your man from Wanchai isn't concerned?"

"Word about such things spreads quickly through the districts, Mr. Young, but he will do anything for the right amount of money."

"Is he as good as the ones you would have hired?"

"Better, I think. But it would have been impossible for me to hire anyone outside my district unless this situation occurred. This man's people are the finest in Hong Kong. He promised me that it will look exactly like a gang has gone from room to room on that floor. I trust him. But it will be more expensive than you anticipated."

"Then we'll make it worth your while."

Ed Kelley was stretched out on his back on his king-size bed, propped up by half a dozen pillows against the headboard. He was watching Blossom do what she always did best, which was to act just like Blossom. She was an absolute delight.

Blossom was a born exhibitionist, and she knew that her American loved to watch her every move. If there was one thing she enjoyed more than removing her clothes, it was parading about without them for wealthy Mr. Kelley. Watching his expression change gave her a feeling of power. On the big bed, she liked to roll, kneel, crawl, stretch, whatever it took to please her man. Then, just when he was reaching for her, she would jump off the bed and do more of the same as she moved about his huge bedroom. She especially liked to play the part of a cat, moving languidly about until she suddenly sprang onto a chair or table and assumed an erotic position while she studied him as a cat would.

Yet, as much as she adored this American who would make her the richest woman in Bangkok if she played her cards right, she also found him very strange. She had played similar games with others before Kelley, and to a man they could take only so much of her posturing before they came after her. Ed Kelley never did. He enjoyed her act. She could see that in his bright blue eyes. They were almost like a cat's eyes. And those eyes also told her that she was probably closer to that fortune than she'd ever be to one in her life. All she had to do was perform. But he always waited for her to come to him. Such patience, even when he was excited. Except for the appreciation in those eyes, he was the coolest, most withdrawn man she'd ever met. And when she described Kelley to her friends, they each indicated that they'd never encountered such a person. To think such an extraordinary man was also wealthy!

Blossom was playing cat. She had just leapt onto his dresser before an immense wall mirror. As she began posturing, moving in slow motion like a cat that knew it was being watched, she heard the phone ring. That was indeed strange. He never plugged the phone in when they were in the bedroom. Only once had he ever used the telephone when they were together, and then a soft buzzer on his bedside table had alerted him to the call. She was surprised by the phone's ring and pirouetted, barely keeping her balance.

In an instant, even before she'd turned, Kelley had rolled

onto his stomach and retrieved the phone from the floor beside the bed. As Blossom reached out to grab the mirror to keep from falling, Ed Kelley had already answered. She watched his eyes, and when it was evident that he wouldn't be paying any attention to her, she jumped down to the floor and stood with her arms folded across her chest, pouting like a spoiled child.

"What time?" Kelley looked across the bed at the clock. It was almost nine-thirty in the evening in Bangkok. "That's a little over three hours from now," he shouted. "Why the hell did you wait so long to call me?"

He rolled over on his back as he listened to the person on the other end. His eyes seemed to look right through Blossom. She headed for the bathroom in a huff.

"I don't care how heavy the security is, I pay you enough so that I'd expect you to call me and report exactly when Buddha himself was going to make a personal appearance. You get your men in position and I want someone to pick me up here in exactly twenty minutes." He slammed the phone down in anger.

Blossom was standing in front of the bathroom mirror toying with her eye makeup when Kelley pushed through the door. "Eddie," she began excitedly, "are you ready . . ."

He continued past her and reached in to turn on the shower. "You can get your clothes on, and I'll have you driven home or you can stay here. I don't really care."

"Eddie . . ." What a strange man!

Kelley rarely took hot showers because it was always so hot in Bangkok. Now he stepped under the cool water and pulled the shower door shut.

Blossom pouted to herself, then decided it was time to be assertive if she was going to be the richest girl in Bangkok. She pulled open the shower door and stepped inside. "Blossom is going to give you a good washing—"

Before she could finish the sentence, Kelley pushed her roughly back outside. "If you want to spend any more time with me, you're going to learn what business is about. Now get out of here." He pulled the door shut.

Blossom looked into the mirror to see if she could work up some tears, but she was too mad. She was also imagining that fortune disappearing. No, she wouldn't go home. She'd wait right there in his bed and welcome him back. After all, her friends often claimed a good woman was willing to wait for her man.

CHAPTER 15

THE HOTEL WHERE LEILA POTTER AND MATT STONE WERE staying was well up Nathan Road toward the Yaumatei District, away from the harbor. It was cheaper and favored mostly by Asians because it was farther away from elegant Salisbury Road and the glitzy hotels and boutiques that attracted wealthy Western tourists. While the quiet and the clientele appealed to W.P. from the vantage point of security, he did hope the recent renovation and the bright Art Deco lobby would make it pleasant for the Americans. Another advantage for the detective, and something neither Matt nor Leila had complained about, was the fact that many of the cheaper single rooms had no windows. He'd explained to them that it was necessary to sacrifice atmosphere for safety, and after all, their purpose in Hong Kong was definitely business.

Liu Fu had been engaged by Hugh Young's contact man in Kowloon to resolve the problem of the American woman. Mr. Liu had lived in the Wanchai District all his life and had risen to a respected position among the many gang leaders on the island. Over the years he'd become a successful exporter, gaining control of the cultured pearl and ivory industries. He also had taken over the indigenous gaming business on the Kowloon side, a feat never before attempted by even the most powerful gang lords. Control of this industry, which was as much a part of Hong Kong culture as the Star Ferry, was the end result of a ruthless plan. It might have ended with the loss of his own life if he hadn't prudently removed each of his potential enemies before the opportunity to dispose of him presented itself to them.

Liu's potential was so great that he probably could have become the most influential individual in the vast Hong Kong underworld, if he'd cared for such power. But instead, since he'd already amassed a vast fortune and truly believed that no single individual could control the vast Hong Kong crime empire, he preferred to lord over his own territory with the knowledge that everything he surveyed was under his control.

While Hugh Young was unaware of who had been hired to work for him, Liu made sure that he knew exactly who was paying the bills. He wouldn't work without knowing that. Liu Fu took great pride in the fact that he had actually been hired by the head of Inchar, even though a middleman had made the arrangements. Although he'd never met Hugh Young, he maintained a deep regard for any Caucasian who could accomplish what he and Inchar had in such a short time. Young seemed to Liu to be Chinese at heart, for his ruthlessness was already legend in the Territory. That *gweilo* would have been a gang lord if he'd had the good fortune to be born a Hong Kong Chinese instead of a foreign devil.

To the British and American business community, Hugh Young was a very lucky *gweilo*. He seemed to always be in the right place at the right time, and his ability to anticipate markets was phenomenal. And he'd been able to accomplish all of this without being either a part of the old boy network or British. Those two factors had always appeared to Westerners to be entry requirements for a successful business person in the Asian marketplace. That amused Liu. If only those naive *gweilos* knew how it was really done!

Liu even speculated that successfully carrying off this assignment just might mean an opportunity for some type of liaison between their two organizations. A connection between their two businesses was a natural. A dream, yes . . . but stranger unions had evolved in Hong Kong. It was indeed an honor to have been selected for this assignment.

Mr. Liu undertook the details of planning himself. It would later be important that Hugh Young be made aware of how this was carried off. The middleman had said nothing about how the problem was to be solved, only that it shouldn't appear that the Americans were singled out. The solution seemed almost too easy. Ransack a series of rooms on that floor of the hotel. Make it appear a gang effort. But don't leave bodies. Hong Kong gangs had a reputation for leaving the scene of the crime looking like a slaughterhouse. Death was the objective, but the presence of a corpse was unacceptable. This must reek of sophistication, something that would really confuse the police and impress the head of Inchar. Liu was certain the combination of important contacts he and Hugh Young had cultivated would eventually bring an end to any investigation.

Gaining access to the hotel and to the floor where the Americans were staying without attracting unwanted attention was Liu's initial goal. There would certainly be security —after all, he'd been warned that the Mongoose was personally involved—and that would have to be neutralized by gaining control of hotel management. In this case, that would be relatively simple because Liu controlled the local gaming industry.

Gambling was a disease in the Territory for rich and poor alike. Almost everyone contracted it, and for some it could prove fatal. While most addicted gamblers would acknowledge that continuous winning was primarily luck, it was more difficult for them to accept that losing also involved luck—bad luck. Liu's organization had shrewdly parlayed that weakness into a system that put no limits on the control they held over other people. Serious gamblers whose luck was down were allowed to play on credit, a policy that had not been part of Hong Kong's gaming heritage. The policy of allowing gambling on credit was the most powerful weapon in Liu's arsenal. As a result, an individual who owed money to a man like Liu Fu also owed his honor, his life, and sometimes even his youngest daughter until the debt was paid off.

That was how Liu so quickly isolated the hotel Leila and Matt occupied. It was almost as if the hotel had been transferred to another dimension. A segment of the general manager's debt was quickly dismissed. Detailed information concerning security brought him close to zero. A master key actually put him ahead of the game. While the general manager's loyalty was with his old acquaintance, W. P. Chan, he also knew that to refuse Liu directly would likely end his life. His future had long ago been purchased by Liu Fu.

The night manager, also a gambler, was required only to provide the room numbers and put through Liu's initial call that established Leila's presence in her room. That wasn't enough to fully erase his debt to Liu's organization, but he assumed that his participation was enough to guarantee his safe existence for a while. What the poor man didn't appreciate was that to a man like Liu his debts were minimal and his survival unimportant. In actuality, Liu anticipated that the man would be an excellent scapegoat for the general manager, who was a heavy gambler and could be expected to be in debt again in the near future. Dead men always had been excellent scapegoats in Hong Kong's underworld.

Liu Fu never involved himself directly in his own dirty work. That would have been foolish for a man of his stature. In almost every case, he distanced himself from the scene. This time, however, was very different. He wanted to impress Inchar, and that could only be done by ensuring a perfect job. It was a difficult decision to make—risking identification, even his own life—but he finally decided to accept the risk because of the importance of the client. He insisted that the hotel's general manager join him in an American whiskey in the manager's office. If a problem occurred, his lieutenant, who sat in the far corner of the room monitoring a hand-held radio, would have Liu involved instantly.

For a few minutes Leila's floor was actually sealed off by Liu's men. Anyone who intended to use the elevator or the stairs would be informed that a suspected gas leak was being investigated. Four rooms whose occupants were known to be out of the hotel were quickly and efficiently ransacked, evidence to anyone investigating later that a professional gang was at work. Liu had also promised that the trail he left would establish robbery as a motive if American officials pushed too hard.

W. P. Chan had seated himself in the far corner of the hotel lobby looking very much like a tired businessman reading a dog-eared copy of the *Asian Wall Street Journal.* As he was settling himself, he'd seen Liu Fu enter the general manager's office. That was a danger signal if ever there was one.

Matt Stone was stretched out on Leila's bed fully clothed. It had been twenty-five minutes since the call to Leila's room, less than twenty since W.P. said he was coming. Matt had doused the lights to accustom his eyes to the dark. The only light was leaking around the door frame from his adjoining room. He pressed the light button on his watch and strained to see the time—close to ten-thirty. Where the hell was W.P.?

Stone noticed the light disappear from around Leila's door frame. "Good night," he whispered to himself, knowing she couldn't hear him, hoping she would get some sleep in his room. God, how she needed sleep. Nothing had been normal in her life since Jerry Santucci had turned to meet her eyes at the Wall.

"Matt!" It was Leila's voice. He couldn't see, but he knew she was standing in the doorway.

How many minutes had it been? Less than a minute? Hell, less than thirty seconds. "What's the matter?" There was something in the way she'd said his name.

"I didn't touch the lights. I was still reading. All of a sudden, everything was dark."

Stone reached for the bedside light and snapped the

306

switch. Nothing. "No power." Why? There was no window to see if there were lights in the streets.

A light knock on the door seemed to echo through the room. Stone heard Leila suck in her breath sharply.

"Get back in the other room," he whispered. "Lock yourself in the bathroom. Quietly. Don't slam the door." He hadn't expected them to knock out the power. "Don't come out for anybody but me."

"Matt—"

"Go on, damn it," he hissed sharply. "The bathroom. Lock it. Put your hands over your ears. Run the water. Whatever it takes. You'll know when it's me."

"Matt?" It was almost a question, more a crutch. "All right." He could hear the rustle of her clothes in the black silence as she moved away.

Stone's eyes were accustomed to the dark. The position of every piece of furniture was fixed in his mind. He moved to the door connecting the two rooms and shut it silently. Another knock came, much louder this time. He moved toward the outer door, hugging the wall to cut down the angle of a shot. Be careful, Stone, he warned himself. This is not the type of work you're supposed to be doing. Your wars are over. He took a deep breath. A DIA investigator was not a James Bond. He was an intelligence specialist now, not a SEAL, not a hired gun. He positioned himself to one side of the door. "Yes," he called out. "Who is it?"

There was no answer. Then he heard muffled voices outside.

"Who is it?" he asked in a louder voice.

"Sorry, sir . . . so sorry." It was a female voice. The accent was Chinese. "Wrong room."

Someone was thinking ahead. They'd sent a woman. Leila would be more apt to open a door to another woman. He turned the lock and opened the door as far as the chain would allow to see if there were others outside. The hall was almost as black as the room but he could see the glow of a covered flashlight to the right. At least one other besides the woman. Or were there two others? He thought he heard whispering. More than two! Three? Four? Five? "What is it?" he asked sternly. "What's happened to the lights?" How the hell did this many people get up here? Where were W.P.'s security men? Where was W.P.? Maybe he had no choice. Maybe he was going to be forced to revert to the methods of the past.

"So sorry, sir." The woman's voice was apologetic and also came from the right. "I must have knocked on the wrong door."

"What happened to the lights?" he asked again with an added note of urgency in his voice. Buy a little time. Sound frightened. Did they know he was registered in the room next to Leila's? He felt the cool metal of the revolver in his hand.

"Sorry, sir. Just a problem with the circuit breakers." Same woman. But the Chinese accent wasn't so strong now. What did that mean? "We'll have it fixed in a minute. Please go back to bed." Her voice seemed to be farther down the hall to the right now, near . . . his own room. She knocked at that door.

Excellent English. Very little accent. Pros at work! He hoped Leila had done exactly what he ordered and locked herself in the bathroom.

"I have a message for you, Miss Potter," the woman's voice called out insistently. "The hotel phones aren't working."

"I'm sorry," Stone said, "but I know there's no one in that room." Distract them . . . anything. So much for giving up the warrior's game.

The SIG Sauer revolver Danny Slade had given him was cool against his cheek. He was reaching toward the chain of the partially open door when a flashlight snapped on directly in front of him. At the same instant he caught the flash of metal plunging down at him. He fell back instinctively as a fire ax smashed down through the chain, tearing it from the wall. The flashlight beam swung around, blinding him as a form hurtled through the door. Before Stone could bring the gun to bear, a head barreled into his middle and drove him backwards. A second hit him from the side. His head smashed against the near wall. The gun was ripped from his grasp. He was aware of other people—two, maybe three—pummeling him. A sharp pain arched through his left shoulder as he was pressed down into the corner of the bureau. Then his body was crashing downward. Quickly, even before he landed, another individual was on him, smothering him, slamming his head down violently as he hit the floor. Stone was struggling for air when he lost consciousness.

A flashlight swept the room, settling on the partially open bathroom door. "Try that." The speaker held the light in one hand. A short-barreled pistol was in the other. A second man pushed the door wide open. The flashlight swept the interior. "Nothing."

Then the flashlight turned toward the door to the adjoining room. Another turned the lock and yanked, jumping to the side as he pulled the door toward him. A third dived through the doorway, landing on his belly, revolver in one hand, flashlight in the other sweeping the room. They were methodical, perfectly trained. In seconds, always in motion, they'd covered that room while never allowing themselves to be stable targets.

The bed was rumpled. An open book lay on the covers. Someone had been there. The flashlight came around to the closed bathroom door. One of them slipped to the side and gently turned the knob. It was locked.

"Let her in," the one with the flashlight said, jerking his head toward the hall door.

The door to the hallway was opened, and a woman came in.

"She's in there." The flashlight targeted the bathroom door. "It's locked."

"Miss Potter," the woman called out as she moved over beside the bathroom door, "I'd like to talk with you, if you please."

Her eyes shone in the glow of the flashlight as she looked back at the man in charge when there was no answer. He simply nodded to her.

"Miss Potter, we don't mean to scare you, and we most

certainly don't want to harm you. If these gentlemen are forced to break down the door, you could be injured. I'd like to avoid that, but I have no control over them."

When there was still no answer, she said, "Miss Potter, to show good faith, I ask you to move away from the door. Perhaps you should get into the shower for your own protection." Then she stepped back. "I am going to count to five. You should be out of the way before I finish."

One of the men grasped his revolver with both hands and aimed at the doorknob, illuminated by the flashlight's beam.

"One . . . two . . . three . . . Please follow my instructions, Miss Potter. Four . . . five."

There was an explosion of wood and metal as two blunt-nosed slugs blew apart the lock mechanism.

A second man pushed the door in, directing his light into the bathroom. The beam reflected off the mirror over the sink, casting an eerie light back into the bedroom. There was no movement.

"Miss Potter, are you all right?"

No response.

One of the men stepped to the side of the door and listened intently. Then he turned slightly and nodded, pointing with his free hand toward the shower curtain.

"Miss Potter, we know you followed my advice and are behind the shower curtain. Please step out here with us and you will see that everything will be okay."

The man farthest away from the door raised his revolver in both hands until it was aimed at the middle of the pink shower curtain. Then he inclined his head once.

The closest one dived into the bathroom, yanking the shower curtain with him as he rolled.

Leila's back was to them, her shoulders hunched. She still wore the clothes she'd had on for dinner.

"Miss Potter," the woman said in the same even tone of voice, as she stepped into the bathroom and placed a hand on Leila's shoulder, "we'd like you to come with us. You won't be hurt."

Leila turned slowly looking right through the smaller

310

Chinese woman outlined in the flashlight's beam. "Where are we going?"

"Don't worry. You'll be safe." She held her hand out to Leila. "Let me help you."

Very slowly Leila stepped out onto the bathroom floor and let herself be led into the bedroom.

Leila was forced face first down on the bed. Her head was pushed into the covers, her feet were tied, and her hands were bound behind her back. Then strong hands flipped her over and a wide strip of tape was pressed roughly over her mouth, covering part of her nose. Leila shook her head. She was struggling frantically for breath when a bag was slipped over her head and fastened tightly around her neck. Then she was hoisted into the air like a doll and draped over someone's shoulder.

"Get the power back on," one of the men said to the other. "And make sure that elevator's still available." Then he spoke into a small hand-held radio. "We've got the woman. The man's unconscious. Is it clear to bring them both down?"

In the hotel's lobby, W.P. had been watching the front entrance over the top of his newspaper for the past few minutes, analyzing the scene, trying to figure out Liu's plan. His intelligence chief had reported that Liu had people outside. There was no indication that anyone had entered the building. It wasn't clear what their purpose would be. It was puzzling. Given the time since Matt's call to him, W.P. was sure they had to be moving.

As W.P. carefully turned a page of his paper, he caught a reflection as the revolving door turned. One of his men stepped into the lobby, halted for a moment to glance at his watch, and abruptly turned and went back outside. That meant Liu's people outside had been alerted for their part of the operation.

The next series of events took no more than twenty seconds. W.P. folded the paper and tossed it into a potted plant. That was the signal to another of his men, thumbing through magazines in the lobby news kiosk, to head toward the door. His appearance outside would be W.P.'s signal to move on Liu's men. A second officer, who had been nodding sleepily in an easy chair, rose quickly to his feet and moved to the elevators. He glanced at the floor indicators above the doors before punching the call button. Then he moved over to the elevator control panel and inserted a key into the control panel.

A single shot outside the front entrance shattered the silence. That was followed within seconds by a flurry of gunfire.

A lone bellboy had been lounging at the service desk, seemingly more asleep than awake. At the sound of that first shot, his hand darted under the counter and came up with a shotgun. W.P.'s man was pushing through the revolving door as the blast from both barrels caught him between the shoulder blades. He was hurled head first through the glass. The man by the elevator panel ducked out of sight, his key still inserted in the controls.

W.P. whirled and caught the bellboy with a single shot in the chest. His second entered just above the ear.

As the echo of the shotgun blasts was dying, the door to the general manager's office flew open. In less than a second Liu's lieutenant saw the bellboy reel backwards and slide down the wall, assessed the situation, realized their intelligence had been faulty, and ducked back inside.

In less than twenty seconds W.P. and his men had lost their cover and two men were already dead.

In Leila's room the voice coming back over the radio was urgent. "We've got trouble down here." It was Liu's lieutenant. "Use the elevator. On the double. Weapons ready."

"Where are the hall lights?" Except for flashlights, everything remained absolutely black.

"I can't locate the switch."

"Never mind. We've got trouble in the lobby . . . the elevator . . . step on it!" The speaker's flashlight swung about nervously. "Where's the elevator door?"

A second light turned back, illuminating the elevator

bank down the hall. One of the doors had been jammed open. A sharp shoulder ground into Leila's belly with each step as they sprinted down the hall. Her head cracked into the side wall as they darted into the elevator.

"What about the guy?"

"Oh, shit!"

"Liu said . . . Chu, you go back . . . finish him off."

"But we're not supposed to leave bodies."

"No time to argue. Do it! Take the stairs afterward."

Chu rushed back down the darkened hallway, the beam of his flashlight dancing off the walls.

The elevator light had been smashed. A beam of light settled on the panel. "Hit the button for the second floor," the one carrying Leila snapped.

"Second?"

"Just do as I say." The doors closed. The elevator descended. Then he shouted into his radio, "Status?"

"Uncertain. Gunfire in the lobby." It was Liu's voice this time. "Hold."

"Stopping at second floor. I'll report when we're there."

Matt Stone opened his eyes to blackness. He was lying on his back. For a moment he had no recollection of where he was. Then . . . *Leila!* He rolled onto his side, propping himself up on his elbow. Intense pain flooded his head.

Shouts echoed from somewhere. He was in their hotel— his room? her room? More voices . . . outside, down the hallway. *Leila!*

Where was Leila?

He heard feet pounding down the hallway. The beam of a flashlight grew brighter on the wall outside. Now it was outlining the door to the room he lay in. Someone was coming back. For what? Him?

His gun . . . It had been in his hand when . . . He couldn't remember what had happened, but he'd had his gun drawn.

His hand swept across the rug, frantically searching for the SIG Sauer. Had they taken it? The flashlight beam hit the ceiling, illuminating the room in a pale glow. Someone was coming in!

Stone pushed up onto his knees. There was another rush of pain in his head. What . . . what was that? A reflection . . . something bright. Something metal by the bed. *His gun!* He lunged for it as the flashlight came through the door.

His hand wrapped around the cool metal of the SIG Sauer.

He wheeled about on his knees. The beam swung toward him. For some reason—instinct, maybe—he rolled to one side.

There was a flash and explosion.

Stone kept rolling.

Another flash, another explosion.

Stone had the SIG Sauer up now. He fired toward the beam of the light one, two, three times.

A scream filled the room as the echo from Stone's last shot died. The flashlight spun through the air, smashed into something, dimmed, flickered . . . died.

Once again Stone was enveloped in total blackness. The pain in his head was overwhelming as he slumped to the floor.

Silence.

An explosion of automatic gunfire to the right of the front entrance disintegrated the lobby windows in a shower of plate glass. Slugs ricocheted through the marble lobby. W.P. dived head first, then scampered on his hands and knees to the partial cover of a thick marble column. The shooting ceased for a moment, and he rose to one knee. One of Liu's men carrying an AK-47 leapt through the hole where the windows had been. As he landed, he was swinging his weapon toward the policeman crouching near the elevator panel when W.P. put a slug through his forehead.

The elevator had stopped its descent. Each person in the general manager's office heard the radio report: "We're at the second floor."

W.P.'s man by the elevators had seen the red light stop at the second floor. He rose to his feet and turned the control-panel key to Off, then flattened himself in the recess of the elevator doors.

The general manager's door flew open against the outer wall with a crash.

W.P. whirled and was leveling his sights on the doorway when an object rolled into the lobby from the office. He ducked back just as the smoke grenade burst, spewing out an acrid green cloud. The smoke billowed outward as it was drawn toward the smashed window.

A hazy form staggered from the doorway. As W.P. squinted through the smoke and began to squeeze the trigger, it screamed, "No! W.P., please! No!" Two shots echoed from the office. The general manager stumbled forward and fell to the floor, his debt paid in full.

Liu's lieutenant was sprawled on his belly in the office doorway, revolver pointing across the lobby. He fired two wild shots through the smoke in W.P.'s direction. He saw a vague form fall back behind the column. Then he shouted into his radio, "Come down." Then, "Mr. Liu's on his way."

As Liu Fu dashed from the protection of the office, his lieutenant held W.P. behind the column with a series of evenly paced shots. Another of his men sprayed the remainder of the lobby with automatic fire from outside as Liu raced through the shattered glass on the lobby floor. He leapt through the window, dodging behind the cover of the automatic weapon. His lieutenant followed him.

Liu Fu was not about to die for a *gweilo*.

"Turn it on," W.P. shouted.

His man leapt upright in a hail of bullets from Liu's automatic weapons. The key to the elevator panel was returned to the On position.

W.P. rolled to his right, coming to his knees. He fired two quick shots through the smoke at Liu's lieutenant, sure that he'd hit him. But as W.P. squeezed the trigger for a third shot, he felt something strike his left shoulder. He was knocked backwards and fell hard. The left side of his body became numb instantly, and a coldness radiated outward from his shoulder. Beneath the thick green cover of smoke, he could see the other man fumbling another clip of ammunition into the base of his gun. W.P. rolled painfully onto his stomach, centered his sights on the man, and squeezed the trigger twice. He saw the other jerk sharply as the weapon dropped from his hands.

W.P. rose painfully to his feet, choking on the smoke. His left arm hung useless at his side. His remaining man was to one side of the elevator door with an automatic rifle held firmly in both hands. "When that door opens, you take the target separated from the American woman," W.P. said evenly. He was sure, as he looked down at the gun in his hand, that he had only one or two shots remaining in his clip. He tossed the weapon away and drew a second from the holster under his left arm. A bell sounded as the elevator stopped at the lobby floor.

W.P. dropped to his knees less than a dozen feet from the elevator with the revolver held out in front of him in his good hand. As the doors began to slide open, he saw a man with a body slung over his shoulder, his eyes wide with surprise. Smoke billowed toward the open door. Two others, a man and a woman, both carrying revolvers, were in a crouch as they inched forward uncertainly, their weapons extended toward the indistinct forms that seemed to waver in the thick smoke.

W.P. fell forward on his stomach, his gun up. His first shot was aimed at the knees of the man carrying Leila. The second bored into his stomach. The roar of his man's automatic weapon, so close to where W.P. lay, became a nightmare of sound as the other two were hurled sideways by the impact of the bullets. W.P.'s target was already pitching forward as his third shot tore into the man's chest.

W.P.'s last image was of Leila's body hurtling through the air in his direction. Knowing he was unable to move, he watched, helpless, until she crashed down on top of him. He felt pain. Then all was silence and darkness.

The automatic stopped firing only when the clip was empty. W.P.'s terrified policeman stared through the smoke at the carnage. Two torn bodies, scarcely resembling a man and a woman, lay to one side. A third person was sprawled half out of the elevator. The policeman turned slowly and peered through the thinning green smoke wafting through the shattered lobby windows.

Then he heard an unusual sound, a soft mewing, almost like a kitten, that seemed a welcome contrast to the sudden terrible violence of a moment ago. He looked down at W.P., aware as he stared at the crumpled form that the sound wasn't coming from the detective. It issued from the bound and hooded figure lying half across W.P. It was the sound of someone whimpering softly.

The policeman was certain his world moved in a dreamy slow motion as he bent down and lifted Leila from W.P.'s inert body. Then he knelt down and gently propped her back upright against his knee. Very carefully he untied the hood and lifted it over her head. Frightened brown eyes stared up at him. He removed the tape from her mouth as gently as possible.

"You are Miss Potter?" he asked, realizing as he spoke how foolish he must sound.

Her eyes held his own, but she said nothing.

"You are still frightened," he continued softly. "I am also." He eased her forward and cut through the bonds on her wrist with a penknife. "You are safe, Miss Potter," he said as he also cut through the rope around her ankles. "You aren't hurt, are you? I mean you haven't been shot, have you?"

Leila shook her head. Then she stared at the carnage by the elevator and closed her eyes.

"They're dead, Miss Potter. They can't hurt you anymore." He continued to talk softly to her, saying whatever came to his mind, until other policemen appeared, climbing gingerly through the open front of the hotel. When an ambulance attendant dropped to his knees beside them, he let the man take her. Then he reached over and ran his fingers over W.P.'s neck until he found a pulse. It was a strong one.

Don Muang, Thailand's major airport, is situated about twenty-two kilometers north of Bangkok. Beyond the crowded downtown area, the main highway from the city is generally straight. The land, a vast alluvial plain, is flat as far as the eye can see. The older factories close to the city change to more modern light industry about halfway to the airport. Yet the highway remains almost always congested with all manner of vehicles, and the businesses along the way are never still. As a result, even if the Thai army were ordered to protect one of its own, it would be almost impossible to maintain absolute security between the city and airport. However, a call had been received that afternoon at army headquarters. It originated from the Pentagon. The request for security assistance could come from an even higher level if necessary. The Thai chief of staff said that wouldn't be necessary. However, he dismissed the request for helicopters because of the danger to people on the ground if one was brought down.

Nolan Benner and the embassy security staff had studied alternative routes to the airport and had concluded that the only route that could possibly allow reasonable safety was the main one. The Thai colonel in charge of security had explained patiently that it was the only choice, and Benner reluctantly agreed. But he felt that creating alternative target choices might improve their chances.

At eleven o'clock that night, just as promised, six Thai army vehicles arrived in front of the American embassy. Two of them were jeeps to cover the front and the back of the convoy. Two others were light armored personnel carriers, each containing a squad of soldiers. Their purpose was obvious. There was no reason to disguise them. They projected firepower. Between them were two military passenger vehicles, both with darkened windows, both armored to protect VIPs. The soldiers climbed out and milled about, smoking and talking, until the embassy people had been seated in the cars. Then the Thai army remounted, and the caravan proceeded out the gates and set a course for the airport, sirens screaming and lights flashing in both jeeps. Their orders were to set a speed record to Don Muang.

Ed Kelley was perched on the roof of the empty Thonburi Machine Works, a dated factory that had operated with cheap labor and ancient machinery until the modern world closed in on it. The two-story building was long and low, set back from the west side service road that ran parallel to the main highway. A high cornice, decorated with worn dragons perhaps once intended to ward off evil spirits, provided excellent cover. Fifty yards behind the structure, a narrow canal wound its way back into Bangkok. A two-way radio was clipped to Kelley's shirt pocket, but it was purely to listen to the progress of the column of military vehicles racing out of the city. He'd been monitoring it since the small convoy's arrival at the embassy had been reported.

Kelley had been paying a very generous retainer to Swan, a retired lieutenant colonel in the Thai army, who maintained and kept highly trained a small paramilitary group of former enlisted men. Swan, who enjoyed being referred to as the general, was allowed by Inchar to hire himself out to anyone who required armed support in the region, but he remained indebted to Ed Kelley and Inchar's bottomless bank account. His clients were generally as far beyond the law as he was, but none of them could amass the firepower and the skill that he possessed. At times Swan had even helicoptered across borders to enforce whatever his clients felt needed enforcing. His small mercenary group was fearless, expensive, and highly effective.

On this evening Swan was crouched on the roof of Thonburi Machine Works beside Kelley, sometimes monitoring the same reports over his radio, but he was also communicating with his own people. The general had brought along two men armed with shoulder-launched missile tubes. Each of them carried three short-range missiles with impact warheads. Two others on the roof held sniper rifles. Across the main highway, on a warehouse roof, were two more snipers. None of them would shoot unless those on the roof of the Thonburi Machine Works were taken under fire. Swan's mercenaries had arrived in two oversized black Mercedes, now parked in concealed locations. There was also a high-speed boat idling on the canal behind the machine works.

A voice came over the radio. "Just entered the Rangsit. Going like hell."

"Traffic?" Swan inquired.

"Average for this time of night. So far the sirens and flashing lights on those jeeps seem to be doing their job perfectly. Traffic's scattering when they see a military convoy."

"Estimated distance from my position?"

"Maybe eight kilometers. Say four minutes plus at current speed."

Kelley looked to the south and saw masses of vehicle lights, even at that hour of the night. The sound of ancient trucks and buses and assorted vehicles, combined with the roar of jet engines at Don Muang, masked the convoy's sirens at that distance.

"Any change in order in their column?" Swan asked solemnly.

"Negative. Jeeps at front and rear of the column. Two personnel carriers and two generals' cars in the middle." To a Thai enlisted man, VIPs were always generals.

Swan looked inquiringly at Kelley. That had been the problem from the start. No one had been able to see which of the two passenger vehicles the girl had gotten into. There was no need to provoke a battle. But they wanted to make sure that Marclay Davis would be finished once and for all after this.

"All right," Swan said at last into the transmitter, "have Senita take a shot at it."

Senita was half Swan's age and a pure rebel. She was young and very beautiful and had come to Bangkok seeking adventure. Senita had heard of Patpong Street, and one look at the peasant girls prostituting themselves to foreigners made even more of a rebel of her. It didn't take long for her to learn of Swan's organization, and even less time to enchant the self-appointed general, who quickly fell under her spell. Swan desired her purely as his mistress—he claimed he would even marry her if she'd agree—and he would have preferred to keep her exclusively for himself. But Senita made it clear that he could have her only if she could participate in what she considered his wild and romantic operations. The fact that she reveled in guns and danger made her even more alluring to Swan.

Motorcycles were Senita's passion. The bigger and more powerful they were, the better. Swan had given her three of them, a new one each time she found a model that surpassed the previous one. Her way of showing Swan her devotion was to give him nude photos of herself posing provocatively on her machines. Senita grew to mean almost as much to Swan as Ed Kelley's money.

Senita had been trailing the convoy less than half a kilometer behind. When she was given Swan's signal, she gunned her bike. Within half a minute, she was beside the rear jeep waving and grinning at the four men in the vehicle. Senita's long black hair flew out behind her and she was dressed only in a skimpy, luminescent halter top and a bikini bottom. Since she was statuesque—built on Western proportions, thanks to a French father—little of her body was covered.

The jeep driver and an officer in the other seat up front grinned back approvingly, making halfhearted gestures for her to move back. Her only reaction to that was to raise an open can of beer and take a deep swallow. The men in the jeep shrugged—another drunk.

Senita pulled alongside the other units in the convoy, slowing to match their speed, laughing, waving her beer can, trying to peer inside, then moving on to the next. When she came to the lead jeep, she leaned forward and spoke into a transmitter buried in her instrument panel. "Nothing . . . nothing at all."

"We have you in sight, no more than three kilometers away now." Swan looked again at Kelley. "We still don't know which vehicle she's in."

"Tell her to keep trying and to do something to distract them."

"Keep trying," Swan repeated over the radio. "If they haven't bothered with you by now, they're not going to. Keep them watching you."

Senita knew exactly what would work, and it would be fun, too. With a simple twist of her fingers, she unsnapped the halter in the front and shook her arms one at a time. The halter disappeared into the night. She had the instant and undivided attention of the men in the front jeep, and she could tell her effort had the desired effect—their interest was slowing down the vehicles behind them."

She let the motorcycle slow a bit more, gradually dropping back until she was even with the first VIP car. She spotted two men in uniform in the front seat, but it was impossible to see in the back. She swerved closer, almost ticking the car's front bumper in an effort to peer into the rear of the vehicle. The driver angled toward the side of the road to avoid her and sat on his horn. She raised the beer can in salute and veered away.

"Still can't see occupants in first car. I'll try for number two." They were less than a minute from the Thonburi Machine Works.

The second car was so close to the rear bumper of the first that Senita decided it must be the one. She eased the motorcycle closer until she was even with the front wheel before turning to look at the driver. His eyes were moving from her to the car ahead, then back to her again. She blew him a kiss and, when she saw his broad smile, made an obscene gesture with her tongue. When he responded in kind, she rubbed her breasts with her free hand. The space between the two cars began to increase.

Senita slipped the bike between the two vehicles and made another gesture with her tongue for the wide-eyed driver as she turned on her seat to peer inside. The leering faces of two men in the back seat were almost even with those in the front seat. The American woman definitely wasn't in that one! The driver sat on his horn frantically.

With a light pressure on the handlebars, she slid out from between the cars. The driver waved enthusiastically as she drifted back past the window and blew him another kiss. Then she leaned forward and spoke into the transmitter, "There are definitely no women in the second automobile. Target has to be in the first one."

Senita was in heaven. This was what she had been born for—the huge machine between her legs, the speed, the wind over her naked body, the pure excitement of challenging the world! The driver of the rear jeep gave her the thumbs-up sign and a big grin as she slipped toward the back of the convoy. She made the same sign to him with her tongue and raised both arms in the air, turning halfway on the seat to expose herself. This was heaven! "What do you think, boys?" she shouted into the night. It didn't matter that they couldn't hear her. They knew what she felt. This was what made life fun.

Senita's little diversion had taken less than a minute, long enough for her to study the occupants of the little convoy, and short enough that the officer in charge dismissed her antics as drunken foolishness.

"Stand by," Swan's voice barked over the radio. "They're in range. First two missiles targeted on number one VIP car. Personnel carriers are likely armed and secondary targets if necessary. Stand by." A second later he saw that Senita was too close. "Senita, drop back, drop back!"

Senita wasn't listening. She and the jeep's driver were playing tongue games again as the convoy raced into the ambush.

The range was perfect, and Kelley barked, "Don't waste time. It's perfect now."

"Senita, get back! Get back before—"

"Fire, damn it, fire!" Kelley shouted.

Both launchers fired within a split second of each other. When Senita caught the flash from the corner of her eye, she knew it was already too late to save herself. Her speed was too fast. She did hear Swan's voice screaming over the speaker, "Senita! Senita!"

The first VIP car exploded in a blinding flash. For just a moment it seemed to have disappeared in the fireball that enveloped it. Then it slewed to the left. The driver of the second car jammed his wheel to the right, and the car slid off the road, leaping the ditch onto the service road, where it spun about crazily. The second personnel carrier bored on straight ahead, grazing the flaming car's rear bumper. That gave the burning car the impetus to flip over, and as it took that first lazy roll in the air, Senita's motorcycle appeared to slip right underneath it. But there was no room. She and the flaming wreck became one, as it rolled down the highway spewing burning gasoline.

"Senita . . . Senita . . . Senita . . ."

Kelley barely heard Swan's wails of anguish as he gazed at the scene below. The rear personnel carrier had veered off to the right, sliding crazily on the soft shoulder before it came to rest on its side in the ditch. The second VIP car, also burning, was tangled in a chain-link fence on the right-hand service road.

The whoosh of another missile caught him by surprise. It was all so close. The leading personnel carrier had slowed, and the rear door was already open, its troops ready to deploy. Kelley followed the flaming tail until the warhead exploded into its fuel tank. The carrier turned on its side and slid in flames into the ditch.

How many seconds had it all taken? Five? Ten? Fifteen? No more than that. Only the jeeps remained, and they were speeding away from the scene as fast as they could. No one in an open jeep would be crazy enough to wait around when heavy weapons were employed.

"That's it!" Kelley shouted. "That's it. Time to get out of here."

Tears were streaming down the general's face as he gave orders over the radio. He and Kelley would escape in the boat idling behind them on the darkened canal. His men would slip away in the Mercedes.

Ed Kelley continued to marvel at the exhibition of firepower he'd just witnessed as they raced down the canal into Bangkok. He hadn't seen anything like that since those horrible days in Vietnam. And those explosions had been incoming.

He hardly gave Swan a thought as the man sat in the bottom of the boat, legs drawn up to his chest, head buried in his knees, calling out his Senita's name for the entire return trip. But nothing else mattered to Ed Kelley. That embassy girl was dead now. It would be impossible for anyone else to recognize him. He had a passport with a photo that showed him with a mustache and a crew cut, and in just a few days his new mustache would be perfect. Young wanted him back at Inchar. Maybe he would have to stay for a week or two in Hong Kong with Hugh and Jerry before he could come back to his office . . . and to Blossom.

The two Thai jeeps, lights still flashing, sirens still blaring, raced through the gate on the south side of Don Muang Airport. They followed a line of waving red lights until they came to a stop beneath the wing of a U.S. Air Force C-130.

An air force major in tropical fatigues was waiting at the foot of the stairway leading up into the fuselage. "Colonel Benner?" he called out tentatively.

"Right here." Nolan Benner, dressed in a Thai Army uniform, climbed out of the rear of the lead jeep. He handed the helmet he'd been wearing and the M-16 he'd been cradling to the officer in the front seat. He walked back to the second jeep and peered into the back. "How you doing?"

Marclay Davis stared at him from underneath her helmet, an M-16 clutched tightly to her chest. Her camouflaged uniform was much too large. "Scared absolutely shitless, Colonel," she answered breathlessly.

Benner reached into the jeep and took the rifle. The soldier beside her undid the strap under her chin and lifted the helmet off her head. Marclay peered out at the U.S. markings on the aircraft. "Thank God."

She took Benner's hand and leaned on him as she climbed out of the jeep. There were no tears until the plane was in the air and thoughts of what had happened overcame her. When she stopped crying and finished with Benner's handkerchief, she accepted what she thought was a glass of water from the leading NCO and took a large gulp. It was pure vodka, and she smiled her thanks. After her second drink, she slept right through the refueling in Hong Kong.

Matt Stone was still unsteady the following morning when he was allowed to visit W. P. Chan in the hospital. Stone's head ached and his shoulder reacted painfully to every motion. His first words to the tiny detective were, "I was cursing you last night because you weren't with us, but you saved Leila's life—your way."

"It was the only way we could keep them from taking her. There were too many of them, and I had no time to bring in more people. They would have overpowered us if we'd done it any other way."

The bullet had passed just under W.P.'s collarbone, and he was still experiencing a great deal of pain. But he'd already refused a second round of painkillers. "We are fortunate, all of us, that she is alive," the detective said calmly. "But after everything that happened last night, we are no closer to Santucci." W.P. shook a finger at Stone as if he were about to scold him. "He must be a very powerful person indeed. Otherwise Liu Fu would not have become involved like that for a round-eye. Very powerful," he repeated more to himself than to Stone. "We misjudged these people. . . . Actually I was the one who misjudged them. I didn't believe that an American could have so much power in Hong Kong. This time I need your help to understand this man you want. Sometimes Santucci is Chinese, and sometimes he is an American gangster."

"There are people in Washington who believe he's much worse than that.

W.P.'s tiny, black eyes turned sadly on Stone. "I will walk out of here tonight if you will help me."

CHAPTER 16

Sleep had not come easily to Hugh Young that night, and he refused to waste time tossing and turning in his bed. At three A.M., he'd thrown back the orchid-colored silk sheets and sat up on the edge of his bed. He was unhappy with himself. Lying in the darkness waiting for sleep to overtake you was an exercise for fools. His options had included waking Cricket and inviting himself to her apartment for sex, or starting the working day early. Actually, if he chose the first she should come to the Peak, because the orchid sheets were her idea. Work, the second alternative, had seemed the more logical solution; he didn't have the energy at that hour to keep the energetic Cricket happy.

Once he'd decided to go to Inchar House, he turned on the coffee pot in his bathroom and headed down one flight to the indoor pool beneath his bedroom. The view of Victoria Harbor, busy no matter the time, was so breathtaking that he turned on only a single underwater light, just enough to keep him from cracking his head on the edge of the pool. After twenty fast laps and fifteen minutes bouncing between the steam bath and the shower, he stood naked before the floor-to-ceiling windows and reveled in the sight of Hong Kong at work. Never stop hustling. Never stop making money!

The coffee complemented the swim as he shaved. There was no longer any sensation of sleeplessness. He'd intended to wake his chauffeur before shaving but thought better of it. He hadn't the slightest interest in acting pleasant toward another human being, and besides, the drive would do him good.

Young took the Porsche, which he normally drove only on weekends, and that helped. Speed seemed just the medicine that he needed, and the hour was perfect for putting the car through its paces. He raced down the mountain road from Victoria Peak taking the turnoff to the coastal road on the southwestern side of the island. Hong Kong was an island of sharp coastline and small, steep hills, and the roads had surely been designed by a sports car lover. Young accelerated into curves, downshifted instead of braking, and was sure that he set a new personal record as he circumnavigated the island. He slowed only for Aberdeen, Repulse Bay, and Stanley before he came back into the city from the east through Causeway Bay and Wanchai.

And now, at five o'clock on a still dark morning, he sat before his desk and stared bleakly around his beautifully appointed office. The swim, the steam bath, and the carefree drive across the island's challenging roads were now past, neutralized by the reality of today. His solid teak desk was clean, except for the papers that he'd placed exactly in the middle for his attention that morning. The knickknacks and odds and ends that he had collected from around the world were arranged on the two Oriental coffee tables and on the shelves of the wall-to-wall, floor-to-ceiling bookcase. The surface of a man's desk was indicative of his personality, and Hugh Young meant to show those few who were allowed in this office that he was the picture of efficiency and organization. He didn't *do*—he had *done*. So . . . so what!

An untouched Jack Daniel's sat on one of the coffee tables where he'd first sat down to think. He'd poured that drink ten minutes before, thinking it might be the thing that would brighten his day. But just a sniff of the dark brown liquid convinced him that Old Mr. Jack wasn't the answer. Now he waited for the coffee to finish brewing in the outer office. The door to Connie's office was open and the aroma inviting, but he had no idea how it would taste. This was the first time he'd attempted to make it himself. Connie always had it ready whenever he wanted a cup. Even when he shaved, all he did was turn the switch on the coffee maker, which the maid set up each day when she cleaned his bedroom. He'd come to expect such service.

Hugh Young's current dilemma was something that he'd never had to consider in the years that it had taken Inchar to become what it was today. He was facing a people problem, and the people involved were closer to him than anyone else ever had been or ever would be—Jerry Santucci and Eddie Kelley. What had created this situation was nothing more than carelessness, and perhaps there was a problem with inflated egos, too. Jerry and Eddie had allowed the investigations to be expanded well out of proportion because of their wreckless efforts to dispose of the sources of their problems. True, they'd insist he'd been a party to the efforts getting beyond control—and he had to admit he might have been initially too casual in his approach—but then, no one was looking for him. Jerry and Eddie had blown their cover at almost the same time, almost as if they'd rehearsed.

Young looked down at his hands on the dark, polished wood of the desk and felt a surge of anger directed wholly at himself. *You asshole! Look at that.* His fingers seemed to be executing a dance all of their own. Starting with the little fingers of each hand, they were drumming methodically— little fingers, fourth fingers, middle fingers, index fingers. Then the little fingers would start over again on cue from the index fingers. His thumbs were hooked under the edge of the desk as if they were already aware of the absurdity of the exhibition the other digits had begun. *You asshole! Only assholes display nervous tics.*

But scolding himself wasn't going to solve the problem. He decided to try something he hadn't done for three years because it had seemed like a childish game, and men like

Hugh Young shouldn't involve themselves in such childishness. He removed a key from his middle desk drawer and crossed the room to unlock a five-foot-wide door at the right of the bookcase. There was nothing behind the door but a blank wall, but when the door was opened as far as it would go, it was a floor-to-ceiling dartboard. The reverse side of the door was cork, and the game was poker. A complete deck of fifty-two cards was painted on the upper half of the door. Any game could be played—five-card stud, seven-card, any of the wild games that came to mind, whatever the players selected.

A number of holes could be seen in the cards, the result of numerous games before Hugh had decided it wasn't appropriate. He and Jerry used to play it a lot at the end of the day when they first moved into Inchar House. But after a while it had seemed so childish for two adults controlling so many millions to be playing a dumb game. Jerry had been reluctant to stop playing, but Hugh had always been the boss and it was his office. The door stayed locked.

Hugh picked up both sets of darts from the rack at the bottom and began playing a game against himself, a green dart, then a red dart, back and forth until all ten had been thrown. *Sloppy!* He was out of practice. Not one ace. He decided that green had won—two eights and a one-eyed jack were three of a kind, and that beat a pair of tens.

A few games later, when red picked up the first ace and had a king and a ten, he aimed for a jack and queen to fill in the straight. No dice. Green caught jack and queen, then a second queen to win with a high pair. He forgot about the coffee and hurled one game after another trying to clear his mind of the onerous decision he was afraid he might have to make.

The carnage last night at the hotel in Kowloon potentially could destroy them all. No one could engineer something like that, especially the killing of four Hong Kong police officers, and simply walk away. It wouldn't take investigators long to track down Liu Fu. Young had already been told by one of his plants in the police department that Liu had been in charge and that the Mongoose had already implicated the Wanchai gang lord. It would take some time for the police to track Liu down, but Young knew that once they had him it would only be a matter of time until they extracted everything they wanted from him. He'd already arranged for the best assassin in Macao to take care of his own middleman and that crazy Liu Fu. Young had specifically warned his contact against anything like the shootout in the hotel. But the death of Liu Fu and the middleman wouldn't solve the entire problem.

The American woman who'd identified Jerry was still very much alive, and it would be almost impossible to track her down now. Young decided to play a game with all ten darts and concluded after the tenth one that he was getting his eye back again. Three aces when deuces were wild, three tens, and a pair of sevens. Only two wasted darts that time. Jerry, he thought, *you* are the problem, not that poor broad. Hugh Young had prepared himself for this situation years ago. Anyone could screw up, even those closest to him. He had to be ready to accept the situation and do what was necessary.

Eddie Kelley had phoned Young at two that morning, and that probably was the final blow as far as getting any sleep that night. It was hard to conceive of blowing up part of a Thai army convoy in order to take out one individual, probably one as scared as the broad right here in Hong Kong. Kelley certainly had chosen a unique way to remove a witness. Who in his right mind would fail to realize that the Thai government might be upset about the men who'd died in that mess? *Eddie—where did your common sense disappear to?* What had possessed him? Hugh Young could not comprehend how a man of Eddie's intelligence, a man with the ability to control worldwide markets and amass millions of dollars, could back himself into such a corner. And now Kelley would be arriving in Hong Kong late that day to confer with him and Jerry . . . while things cooled down in Bangkok? What made him think that—

The phone rang in the outer office, a reminder that his coffee should be ready. He had no intention of answering at this hour, and he never would have even during the day without knowing who wanted to talk with him. He poured his coffee and turned up the speaker to listen as the machine picked up the call.

"Mr. Young, this is Sam Mun. I called your home and was told by your butler that he'd heard you leave early this morning. I hope I have located you." Sam Mun was a chief inspector in Immigration at Kai Tak Airport who'd been loyal to Hugh Young for years. He was by far the most financially comfortable inspector in the Territory.

Young was tempted to pick up the phone, but he didn't care to have anyone know where he was right now. He sipped his coffee and listened.

"You asked me the other day to inform you of any unusual arrivals of Americans. I think you'll want to know that an American Air Force C-130 landed at Kai Tak about half an hour ago. It came directly from Bangkok. There were two passengers, neither of whom deplaned—U.S. Army Colonel Nolan Benner and Miss Marclay Davis. One of my men, who went aboard with the cleanup crew, heard the woman say that the aircraft couldn't be airborne again soon enough for her. The army officer is apparently accompanying her to Hawaii. He said someone else would escort her from there to Washington. I do hope this might be of some value to you. Please call me if you require additional information. Good morning, sir." Sam Mun had never failed to be excruciatingly polite when he was sure there would be something extra for him.

Hugh Young shook his head in disbelief. What the fuck was happening? At the time Eddie had called a couple of hours before to explain how he'd eliminated the only person who'd been able to identify him, she was actually in the air on her way to Hong Kong. The entire operation had been bungled. Both of them—Eddie and Jerry—their cover had been blown in less time than . . . *Shit! I think I'm going mad . . . fucking insane!*

In such moments of anger and frustration, Young sometimes overlooked a number of important elements in his favor. His sudden uncontrolled bursts of anger sometimes frightened him. The reaction was like a sneeze, uncontrollable, but once he recognized it he was able to calm himself. *They have the problems, not you.* He had never deserted from the military in time of war. His name wasn't on the Vietnam Memorial. And there was no reason for anyone to be looking for him. He could walk into any police headquarters in the world, look stupid, and ask if they were looking for Hugh Young. They would check their computer banks, respectfully say he was an unknown, and shake their heads sadly when he walked out the door. It would be no different walking into the CIA, the FBI, even the Pentagon. He could even introduce himself to the people who were looking for Jerry and Eddie, and not a soul would blink an eye. He was on no one's hit list, most wanted, top ten . . . no one's . . .

So, if I'm clean and they're poison, then why am I . . . ?

Young studied Ed Kelley as he lounged in a comfortable chair staring down from the Victoria Peak house at the lights of Victoria Harbor. He would look different shortly, a little more each day. Yet even with this effort to change his appearance, he would still be recognizable for another week by anyone who'd seen him before. The long face with the high cheekbones and the wide jaw would still be identifiable, even with the black mustache that was quickly filling in. Yet there was a difference. Any man with thick, curly hair who had it shorn into a brush cut had to look different. Perhaps a better term was "odd," Young mused. Kelley's hairline was receding, enough to place him in his forties. Was that it? No, it was those stark blue eyes, so light and piercing that they seemed to flash in his otherwise Italian face. Maybe it was years of familiarity, but Eddie looked just plain odd as far as Young was concerned.

"What's bugging you, Hugh?" Ed asked irritably. The staring made him uncomfortable.

"I'm trying to analyze your new persona, Eddie, trying to make up my mind what you really look like. And I think I know."

Kelley looked up warily. "Oh?"

"With that haircut and the half-ass mustache, you look retarded," Young answered with a snicker.

Kelley's mouth fell open.

Jerry Santucci snorted with delight.

"But in another couple of days," Kelley retorted, "I'm not going to look like a retarded Ed Kelley. Nobody's going to know who I am unless they're female friends and I take off my clothes. Now, Jerry, he sticks out like the old sore thumb."

"He's right, you know," Young agreed, glancing at Jerry. "You are what's known as persona non grata in the Territory."

"So? I haven't shown my face since you put the wraps on me."

"No, you haven't, and that's to our benefit. But I think we have to do better than that for a while. You ought to take an extended vacation somewhere until you are once again a forgotten man."

Santucci looked hurt. "Who's going to work with you?"

"I'll get by. I'd much rather get by than have the U.S. military come down on my head. That's what's going to happen, you know. They're going to be all over the place, Jerry, like stink on shit."

"So take them out," Santucci commented nastily. "It's not like we haven't done it before. I like it here."

"Have you noticed, Jerry, that removing people doesn't seem to be working? There appear to be more of them, and they're getting persistent. I think it would be better if they didn't keep searching around Hong Kong until they found you." Early that morning, as he sat alone in his office, Hugh Young had come to believe that Jerry Santucci's dead body would get these people off Inchar's back. He'd rationalized that a dead Santucci would satisfy them.

It was a tough decision to come to after working together for so many years, but he couldn't get Randy Wallace's comments out of his mind. Randy had said that the Pentagon's Full Accounting people wouldn't stop until they had proof of death for every individual listed as missing. Jerry's body would make excellent proof.

Hugh Young's decision had been that much harder because he'd almost regarded Jerry as a son, even though he was less than ten years older. However, Jerry would never be able to manage Inchar's vast empire. He was an operator, the kind who envisioned a business, set it up, made it show a profit, and then tired of it when it became too complicated and went on to the next. He was an entrepreneur, but he wasn't a corporate administrator. Though he was an exciting person to be with, whether it was on Inchar's yacht or chasing women through the exotic cities of Asia, Inchar and Hugh Young could do just fine without Jerry. The more he rationalized the decision as the day passed, the more Jerry Santucci became a fifth wheel. By sunset his continued existence appeared to threaten the stability of Inchar's vast operations.

"What about the retarded one here?" Jerry reached over and ran his hand across the top of Kelley's brush cut. "That broad who recognized him is free as a bird now. He wouldn't fool her even with that silly womb broom under his nose."

Kelley looked up at Hugh Young warily. In close to twenty-five years, Hugh had never shown the slightest antipathy toward either of them. But his attitude the last couple of hours had been anything but pleasant. "So?"

"A point well taken," Young responded. "I could clothe the two of you and feed you and keep you as dependents or prisoners or whatever you want to call it up here on the Peak until everything blows over. But I'm not so sure it would." He looked at Kelley curiously. "Do you really think that the Thai army is going to overlook your little party near the airport? Since that convoy was supposed to be so hush-hush, they have to figure out that there's a rat in their intelligence operation, and they'll dig until they—"

Kelley interrupted angrily. "There's more than one rat in that operation, Hugh. A lot of those guys are on the take. That's how they live so well on military pay."

"Granted. But name a situation where some asshole's used hot information to slaughter a couple dozen innocent Thai soldiers. And you yourself said that the convoy was arranged by the American embassy. For Christ's sake, Eddie, what do you think the United States is going to do?

Your photograph is going to be plastered everywhere in Southeast Asia. I'm going to have to start explaining to any of our customers who've met you that you have a double."

Young had become more certain as he worked Jerry's situation out in his mind that day that perhaps Eddie Kelley's corpse couldn't be discovered too quickly either. Perhaps the U.S. Army would be satisfied if they also found Eddie. Why not? Why would they bother to go into a drawn-out investigation on his background? If killing Eddie was the answer, it was also critical that they should find him in Bangkok, not in Hong Kong. But right now the heat was concentrated on Jerry. Get that problem out of the way first. Then a final decision could be made about Eddie.

"Okay. So I have a double. I'll go along with that. That's not too hard to explain. Maybe we can work up something about the bad side of my family, maybe a twin brother . . ."

"We can do that, too. But first we're going to make plans to get you back home to avoid any doubts. And I want you to cover your tracks in Bangkok. You have to silence your people in the Thai army."

"That's not so easy . . ." Kelley began.

"We've got all night to work it out, Eddie. I'm sure we'll come up with a plan. The three of us won't be able to function well without getting all of this behind us."

Stone was leafing through a two-day-old *Washington Post* without really paying attention to what he was reading when he heard the door open and shut in the adjoining room. He felt an unfamiliar but not unpleasant chill run down his spine as he jumped up and leaned through the connecting door. "I was going to send out a search party. I missed you." They had been moved to another hotel, a more comfortable one with enhanced security.

Leila Potter smiled. When was the last time someone had actually said that he missed her? It was a good feeling. "When you're with the famous W. P. Chan, the Mongoose himself, you feel secure." Leila tossed her coat over a chair and smiled at Stone. "And, my sailor friend, he's such a charming gentleman that you should even feel a little jealous."

Matt crossed over to her. "Considering how short a time we've known each other, I shouldn't be. But I'm insanely jealous about any man who even dares to look at you." He kissed her on the tip of the nose, brushed her lips with his own, then wrapped his arms around her and kissed her deeply. That same chill returned, this time more so.

Somewhere deep inside, she was positive that she was purring softly in response.

Her eyes were open and shiny when he finally pulled back. "You don't have to be jealous, Matt. All I want is you. If you'd been killed or badly hurt last night, I don't know what I would have done. I thought the world had come to an end . . . all that shooting. I was terrified of the man who was holding me. I'd never seen him before. I just knew he was Chinese, and I didn't know whose side he was on. And when I saw W.P. lying there in the lobby, his eyes shut, that bright blood beneath him, I was sure it was the end." A tear coursed down her cheek. "If that policeman hadn't started reassuring me before I could even speak . . ." She took a deep breath. *Get it out of your system. Exorcise all that vileness.*

Stone led her over to the sofa. "Come on, you don't have to talk about it."

Leila wiped her eyes with the back of her hand. "Like hell I don't."

She'd done so much thinking, wrestling with the Leila who lay so deep inside that she hardly knew her. The repressed Leila was alone, independent, a maverick who preferred to face problems on her own, to avoid relationships that meant the visible Leila would share herself with another. Since the day of her sixteenth birthday, the day an army officer and a priest had come to her door, that inner Leila had succeeded in meeting every challenge from that outside world. Love would hurt too much. Sharing would open her up to pain. Happiness could only bring more sadness. No man had ever been able to find and explore the inner Leila. But now Matt Stone had accomplished the impossible. He had found that other Leila, exposed her to his own inner fears and shown her how happiness could overcome pain, how love could become strength . . . and it had happened so quickly.

"That policeman of W.P.'s was so nice. And it wasn't long after he told me that W.P. had a strong pulse that his eyes opened. He looked at me without moving his head and asked, 'Who won?' He looked so serious I couldn't tell if he was kidding, and then he smiled. All of a sudden I was laughing and crying. And then I thought about you." She was holding Stone's hand, and she brought it up to her face and kissed it. Then, holding it in both hands, she rubbed her cheek against the back of it. "The next thing W.P. did was say your name. 'Matt,' he said, 'where's Matt? Is he all right?' And that's when I knew the reason my heart was beating so hard—because I loved you so much that I didn't want to ask that question myself. I was afraid of the answer."

When one of W.P.'s men came into the bedroom, Stone had been in the process of regaining consciousness. Over the years he'd knocked his head more times than he cared to remember, and as sound and light began to come back to him, he knew enough to just lie there and let the rest of his body send reports to his brain. His head ached, as it should have. There was sharp pain in the back of his shoulder, but he could move his arm. The policeman had called out his name twice, tentatively, as he inched cautiously into the room, afraid that Stone would be one more corpse. But Stone had answered him.

When the tingling sensation was gone and Stone could focus his eyes, the policeman helped him to his feet. Stone insisted on sticking his head under the shower, another habit he'd clung to in these situations. As he dried off, the policeman explained exactly what had taken place below. When they stepped off the elevator into the carnage of the lobby, a paramedic was treating W.P. and Leila was kneeling beside him holding his hand.

"He held my hand the other night in the restaurant," Leila

continued. "Remember? When Dan Slade told us about Penny? You and Dan had to leave the table, but W.P. held me and cried with me and told me about Tommy Chang, and then he listened while I told him about my brother and about Penny. That's why I couldn't just leave him lying there in the lobby by himself. And I thought maybe you'd still be alive if I didn't go up to the room." She kissed his hand again.

"You were right to stay." Matt gently raised her chin with the fingertips of his free hand and saw that her eyes were dry. "Feel better now?"

"As long as I'm with you. I trust you and feel safe with you, although . . ." She looked up at Matt and paused, glancing at him with a provocative grin.

"Go on."

"Although W.P. has been wonderful too," she finished. "But he can't hold me and kiss me and make love to me and make me forget everything, like Matt Stone can." She pushed him backwards until he sat down on the sofa.

Stone lay back with his hands folded across his chest, unable to remember the last time a woman had made him feel so good. For a moment he felt as excited as a teenage boy making out in the back seat of an old car, exploring the thrill of unknown territory.

"And W.P. would be shocked if I did this to him." She eased herself on top of him, slowly, rubbing languorously against him, never taking her eyes from his, until she sat on his chest, straddling him, her skirt up to her waist. "I guess he's more a father figure, because I'd never do this to him." She bent over and kissed him, forcing his mouth open with her tongue.

"I suppose I can't be considered a father figure," Matt whispered when she pulled back and rested her chin on her folded hands just inches from his face.

"No," Leila replied huskily. "Impossible." She stretched her legs out until she was lying directly on top of him and nestled her cheek against his. "Am I too heavy?"

"Never." He stroked her back with one hand and ran his fingers through her hair with the other.

"Matt?"

"What."

"I think I have a problem that I have to tell you about, 'cause there's no one else I can tell."

"Talk to me."

"I think . . . No, I don't think. I'm damn sure. I'm falling in love with you." Before he could respond, she pushed up until she was just above his face. "Don't say anything if you don't want to. And don't say anything yet, please. I suppose most people would say it's because of everything that's happened to me. Some people would probably say you've been so nice and understanding because you feel sorry for me. And a lot of people would make comments about my being a desperate middle-aged woman. But it isn't that. It isn't. It's you. No matter what happens, it's you. You're special." She held his face in her hands. "You know that, Stone? You're special. Oh, God, you're special." She kissed him quickly and rested her head on his chest.

"Well, let me tell you something, Potter. Those same crazy ideas have been running through my mind. But being a man, especially a middle-aged one wise enough to lean toward middle-aged women, I don't think I've ever taken love that seriously. Plus, I'm the kind who'd hesitate to say anything like this to a woman, because I'm paranoid about being laughed at." Now, how was he going to say it?

The words came out in a jumble each time he silently rehearsed them. It was so important for Leila to understand that what he was saying really came from the heart. He'd employed the word "love" a few times since his marriage had broken up, although he had known even as he said it that he didn't mean forever, just for a night, or a weekend, or a week. Not for a lifetime. So it had to be different if he was going to express exactly what he'd come to terms with in his own mind.

It had been so difficult to understand that he no longer wanted to be alone, that he wanted to share with someone, with Leila. He was no longer the lone warrior on a perpetual mission to make the world right. Those years were gone now, and he'd somehow survived them. It was a younger man's turn to save the world. It was Matt Stone's turn to find the love that had eluded him—no, he'd been the one to run from it—and to finally share with another person.

"You're making this so easy for me," he continued softly, "because you really opened yourself up with that little speech you just made. And you gave me the guts to say what I've been thinking. I'm in love with you, Leila. Now, what are you going to do about that?" And now that he'd said it, he was at peace with himself.

She popped her head up long enough to give him a quick kiss before nuzzling back into his chest. She squeezed him as tightly as she could.

"That's all the answer I needed." He was quiet for a few moments. "I know it happened to me that day out in the Maryland hills," he continued. "That was almost a week ago, and now it seems like a lifetime. I've been scared about it ever since because I was afraid you wouldn't have anything to do with me." There was another short pause. "I don't think I'll ever be scared again."

Leila propped herself up on her elbows and looked around the room. "You know what we have to do, Mr. Stone? We have to make this into a honeymoon cottage and celebrate. Let's call room service for a bottle of champagne. Then we're going to turn off most of the lights—but not all of them, because we want to be able to see the show we're going to put on."

"Show?" Stone inquired.

"We're going to make love, my love, like we were on a honeymoon. As the old saying goes, we're going to make love like there's no tomorrow."

"Stick with me, kid, for a lot of tomorrows."

I hope so, sailor. I hope so.

Leila couldn't tell Matt Stone what she and W.P. had agreed they had to do when they'd spent a few minutes alone in his hospital room. It was for her brother, Danny, and for Penny, and for Tommy Chang. It was a gamble. *Sometimes you have to do so much before you're totally free to love.*

W.P. had said, "My department may be able to do this

without your putting your neck on the line." But Leila knew he didn't really mean that.

"There are a lot of reasons not to. But there're more reasons for doing it."

W.P. nodded. He'd employed essentially the same words when the police commissioner told him to enjoy a paid leave until he was fully recovered. But he couldn't. There was someone missing in the puzzle, and he couldn't put his finger on who it was. Strangely enough, if any of the gang lords knew who was behind Santucci, they had nothing to say. W.P.'s men reported that someone exerted more power than anyone they'd ever encountered. That individual, he was sure, could eventually be forced to surface. But for now, Santucci would have to be their primary target.

The shoot-out at the hotel had ignited a controversy at Government House. Hong Kong authorities had always cooperated with U.S. and other international efforts to track down the criminal elements that too often selected the free-wheeling atmosphere of the Territory as a base for their criminal operations. But they insisted on becoming involved as soon as native blood was spilled. That made it definitely more than an American problem. Stone and Slade had been ordered by General Ben Miele to establish a plan with local authorities before further violence erupted. It would delay their search for Santucci, but a plan had been necessary. W.P. had explained that there really was no choice. His own people would expand their efforts, and he would continue his own search. He had to.

"Why do you want to do this yourself?" the detective asked Leila. "You came to Hong Kong with Matt for the sole purpose of confronting Jerry Santucci, not going after him by yourself. If I am correct, Matt Stone was the one who brought you here. He is the one assigned by your government."

Leila remembered the apologetic tone in W.P.'s voice. He desperately wanted this one chance with her to ferret out Santucci, to avenge the death of Tommy Chang and the other Hong Kong police who had been killed. He, too, was allowing something personal to influence his judgment. But he was also hesitant to interfere in something private. He was curious why her decision was so similar to his own.

"It's all right to ask. I want to do this mostly because Matt and I have found something together and, when that happens, men like Matt tend to be overly protective. I want to find Jerry once and for all, and I don't want to create a situation that will hurt what Matt and I have found. If this doesn't work, Matt will be fully involved with us by tomorrow noon."

Accepting her decision had been as easy as that. No, it wasn't easy. Love was supposed to be based on trust, and she was already violating that trust. She would find an excuse to leave the room early in the morning. W.P. would set it up with a phone call before sunup.

"A lot of tomorrows," Stone had said.

I really hope so, sailor. I want those tomorrows more than you'll ever know.

CHAPTER 17

W. P. CHAN'S EYES SNAPPED OPEN INSTINCTIVELY AT 3:59 A.M. He rolled automatically to his left, as he had done for so many years, to turn off the alarm before it wakened his wife. But intense pain shot so rapidly through his shoulder that it literally knocked him down on his back. He bit his lip and concentrated on the point beneath his collarbone close to his armpit, where the bullet had passed through his body.

When he was younger, he'd been certain that such an effort was akin to faith healing and, if so, that his injuries should be gone in the morning. But the damage was always still there the following day. Eventually maturity had forced him to acknowledge that accepting pain was simply a matter of mind control. Pain was enhanced or diminished by the brain, and he'd learned early on to manage it. That method was more realistic and effective than faith healing, and it was something he could believe in. But he would never heal himself, and he had to admit, the physical healing took longer as he grew older.

As he allowed the breath he'd been holding to escape, he turned his head toward the clock radio. Too late. Three fifty-nine was gone forever, as was the intensity of the ache in his shoulder. His eyes settled on the dial as the bright green numbers silently flicked to the hour of four and the radio came on. The high-pitched voice of a Hong Kong talk show host railing at a caller filled the tiny bedroom.

Gun-shy about rolling over again, W.P. sat up, swinging his feet onto the floor at the same time, and reached for the button.

"You don't need to turn the radio off. It doesn't bother me, Woo. I've been awake." His wife always called him by that name, a sign of affection. Although she'd never been to the United States, she'd accepted the American method of naming people, but she refused to call him Walter—the name his father had chosen. Her husband had adopted the name Woo to affirm his Chinese heritage, and she would honor it.

"Did I awaken you?"

"Not really. Oh, maybe, but I slipped in and out of sleep. I couldn't help listening to you."

He'd never before talked in his sleep, and she was troubled by its starting now. She'd lived with this man for thirty-five years, from the days of a tiny one-room apartment in a stinking slum where there was no running water to the relative comfort of their current home. Because her father-in-law called his son Walter and had enjoyed an American life-style, she had been ostracized by her own family.

She had fed her own expanding brood well on the pathetic income of a policeman, and she'd loved almost every moment of those difficult years because she loved her husband more than life itself. It wasn't even a matter of sharing because she was willing to give herself totally to this wonderful man. She worshiped him for his courage and honesty and decency, and she would gladly have sacrificed her own life to save his. But now she feared she might not have that opportunity. The bullet that had hit him the previous night was only scant inches from his heart. The next one . . .

"Was I talking in my sleep?"

"If you were, I couldn't understand what you were

saying." She reached up and turned on her bedside light. "Turn toward me."

He pivoted slowly from the waist until she had a three-quarter view of the bandages that went around his chest and over his shoulder. "It's still bleeding." She pointed accusingly at the spot where blood had oozed through to color the outside of the gauze. "You should at least stay in bed until the wound closes."

"You're right, of course. I should." He smiled wanly. "As in the past, there doesn't seem to be time to do the right thing. I'm feeling fine."

"You cried out a moment ago."

"A mistake. I rolled over on my left arm. The pain surprised me. It's all right now."

"What is . . ." She struggled to pronounce Leila's name.

W.P.'s face broke into a grin. "That's the name of the American woman I told you about."

"Is she attractive?"

"Extremely . . . for a Caucasian," he added, correcting himself. "You must meet her sometime. She is a wonderful person. You would like her man, too," he added casually.

"Oh, I'm sure I would." She smiled broadly. His wife was not a jealous woman, but she was competitive. "Why are you so concerned about this American woman?"

W.P. grasped his wife's hand. "If I could choose, I would like her for a daughter. She is very strong and very determined, and she has suffered more than she deserves. She is very Chinese." He searched for the proper word to explain Leila. "She is stoic."

"You can have another daughter if you need one," his wife answered, getting out of bed, "as long as she's out of diapers."

He marveled at his wife's sense of humor sometimes and decided he would have to relate that comment to Leila as soon as they met.

"I'll get you something to eat," she said.

"You don't have to. Get some sleep."

"I won't be able to sleep if I let you go out without something to eat." She threw a wrap over her narrow shoulders and shuffled through the bead curtain that separated the living area from the sleeping area. "And don't you try to change that bandage without my helping you. You can't do it properly."

W.P. rinsed the sleep from his face and began some stretching exercises to ease the tight muscles in his shoulder and chest. There was pain, but it was a steady throbbing rather than the sharp spasms of the previous day. He could live with that. The bottle of painkillers from the hospital was inviting, but he turned quickly away from them. Yes, they would ease the pain, but they could also inhibit his reactions and dull his thinking. Today he could not afford to be anything less than totally alert, not when Leila had agreed to help him.

As confident as Leila was in herself, as sure as she'd become that Jerry Santucci was her own personal burden, W.P. knew that she would not succeed alone. That was why the detective couldn't let her become involved at Inchar House with only a wounded Chinese to help her. He had quietly decided to involve Stone, but both W.P. and Matt had agreed that Leila would do much better if she was convinced she was totally on her own.

W.P. pondered the situation. He was playing off two people, Leila and Matt, against each other. Did they have any idea of what he was doing? Was this why Asians often seemed devious to those in the Western world? W.P. found himself in an unpleasant position with two people he'd grown to respect in a very short time. But there was no other way he could find Santucci or the person behind him. Inchar was an Asian operation, no matter how many round-eyes were involved in it, and no Westerners could penetrate such an organization on their own.

Leila was somewhere between sleep and consciousness when the telephone chirped. Before that sound, she'd been vaguely aware of smiling inwardly at the sheer joy of taking and giving pleasure. But she was also alert enough to be tentative about the coming day. *That's W.P. calling!* She must have been dozing for the last hour. She rolled over and answered her room phone before it rang again, hoping Stone had not heard it. She told W.P. she would be ready at exactly six-thirty when a police driver came by to pick her up, just as she'd agreed the previous evening.

For no more than a split second, she considered slipping out of bed and into the shower. There'd been no sound from Matt when the phone rang. Today she was inviting herself into the lion's den. She inched across the bed until their bodies touched, then rose on her elbow. The bathroom door was ajar and the light had been left on. She studied the outline of his face before bending down. She was about to kiss him when his eyes snapped open.

Stone slipped a hand around the back of her neck. "I would have been pissed if you'd tried to slip away." He pulled her down on top of him and kissed her hard.

"I'm sorry about the phone . . ." she began when he let go.

"Don't be. I've been awake the last half hour wondering how I was going to assault you—whether I'd wake you softly, maybe with a nice kiss, like you were about to do for me, or just leap aboard and shock you awake." He planted tiny kisses around her neck and ears as he spoke.

"Well, we must both share the same dirty mind, because I'd considered just hopping aboard, too. But for a woman that requires a little more cooperation from the man." How long had it been since she'd been at ease talking with a man like this? Had she ever?

Stone gave her a playful slap on the rump. "You'd be absolutely amazed, maybe even thrilled, at how fast you'd get that cooperation."

"I've got to get out early. I promised W.P. I'd meet him for breakfast. He says the commissioner's office wants to interview me about what happened at the hotel the other night." It seemed odd to her that, although she and Matt could reveal themselves to each other so readily, she could also lie to him like that. It was a white lie, of course, because she couldn't bring herself to the point of telling Matt that . . . No, now she was lying to herself.

Was there such a thing as a white lie between lovers? She

still couldn't fully admit, at least not to her own satisfaction, that Jerry Santucci had grown from the apparition that had materialized before her at the Wall to an obsession that totally possessed her. He had become a part of her, a cancer that had to be dissolved. It made no difference that tracking Santucci was part of Matt's job. Leila was certain that she would never be able to live with herself if Matt was hurt in the process of hunting down her personal devil. Was that a convincing reason to lie to him? Weren't close relationships like this supposed to be based on mutual trust . . . if this was what she hoped it was?

"And what are you doing afterward, my lady?" he inquired with a dirty cackle, wiggling his eyebrows like a clown. "If you're free, I have one or two original, sure-to-be-enjoyed ideas."

"If . . . if there's nothing else W.P. needs me for, the rest of the day is yours, if your original, sure-to-be-enjoyed imagination can fill the day." *Will there be a rest of the day?* There was no sense to the way anyone had died in the last ten days. They were simply dead. Dead is dead, no longer interested in the outcome. They were victims of violent death, and . . . and none of those deaths needed to happen, she thought. *Please let there be a rest of the day . . . and countless days thereafter.*

"My imagination is endless," Matt said. "But right now, there's something very important we have to do."

Leila ran her tongue around his lips. "That's what I'm up here for, sailor." She nipped the tip of his nose. "Ready or not."

When she rolled out of bed and looked at her watch, she said, "My God, it's ten after six. And I thought that was so quick."

"I guess this means we'd better not share the shower," he said with an evil grin. "W. P. Chan waits for no one."

The police guard who'd been outside her door all night escorted her to the lobby at exactly six-thirty, and as she climbed into the waiting police car, the driver was reporting over the radio, "Yes, sir. Right on time."

* * *

For the second morning in a row, Hugh Young was unable to sleep, but this time he was absolutely certain about what he must do. He had risen early even though the three men had been up until after midnight discussing the progress of Inchar's business. Much of it had been contentious since it was based on Santucci and Kelley keeping a low profile. Eddie and Jerry had finished a bottle of Jack Daniel's between them while Hugh sipped judiciously. When one was about to assume total control of a large corporation, alcohol became secondary. Hugh was confident about how he wanted things run while Jerry and Eddie sensed, and at the same time dismissed, the fact that they were balanced on a razor's edge.

There was no early swim this morning, not even coffee as he shaved. It would be a full day. As the sun rose, Young rousted Connie on the phone. "No rest for the wicked, my dear," he announced to the sleepy voice on the other end. "The good news for ruining your sleep is that I've decided to give you a bonus for absolute loyalty, but," he chortled, "the bad news is the only way to collect it is to meet me in the office within an hour." In a way he was correct. Connie's loyalty to Hugh Young was unquestioned, and she deserved whatever he might pay her.

Before leaving the Victoria Peak house, he left instructions for Santucci and Kelley to be delivered to Inchar's suboffice no later than eight forty-five that morning, then drove himself to the Central District. Connie was already making coffee when he came through the second-stage security door.

She turned to say something cute, but thought better of it as she saw the determined, almost ugly, expression on Young's face. "Good morning again, Hugh. I was about to say something about how radiant you are at this hour, but I don't think that's what you want to hear."

"I don't feel radiant and I don't feel nice." He knew what he had to do to protect Inchar and himself, and he would see it through no matter how unpleasant it might be. He managed a slight smile. "But you look lovely no matter the hour." She really did, and it struck him that if there was ever a reason to break his rules about personal office relationships, Connie was the best reason to do so. "You have just made my day a little more bearable with that smile."

Connie glanced at him warily. "I didn't know we had problems that were that bad."

"I do. You don't. But believe me, that promise I made on the phone an hour ago is as good as gold."

Matt Stone did nothing from the moment Leila left the room that might indicate he was anything other than a tourist. By the time he was finished shaving, the English breakfast he'd ordered was delivered to the room by a bellboy. When he dressed, it was in plain-colored slacks, a short-sleeved shirt, and penny loafers without socks. When he left the room near eight in the morning, he wore a Dodgers baseball cap and zipped up a beige windbreaker to cover the 9mm Beretta in the holster fitted at the small of his back.

The hearing aid barely visible behind his right ear was actually a receiver and the camera slung from his neck was the transmitter for his radio communications system. Anyone who happened to notice tourists would naturally assume that the fanny pack slung across his middle contained wallet, extra film, candy bars, and whatever else Americans considered necessary for a day in the city. A guidebook with detailed maps of the districts was in his hip pocket, and he had tucked a small spiral-bound notebook and a ballpoint pen in his breast pocket.

He walked through the Kowloon District that day, turning right down Chatham Road South to Salisbury Road. After noting the time, he wandered out on the Tsimshatsui Promenade and took pictures of the harbor as he ambled down to the Star Ferry. Stone snapped more pictures from the ferry's bow as it crossed to the island. He meandered through the lower streets of the Central District, stopping occasionally to scribble something in his notebook after snapping a photo, sometimes stopping a passerby to ask a question about the sights. At eight fifty-five, he was on Chater Road, not too far from Inchar House. According to his hearing aid, Dan Slade and W. P. Chan were also nearby, as were a number of plainclothes Hong Kong policemen who welcomed hearing Stone's slightly muffled voice through his camera.

At ten minutes after nine, aware only that W.P. was close by and that the lobby was under police surveillance, Leila strode purposefully through the glass doors of Inchar House. She paused to contemplate the dancing waters of the indoor waterfall, then walked directly to the reception desk and waited patiently while the security guard finished speaking on the phone. A camera rotated silently above the booth, surveying the area.

"May I help you?" The guard offered her a friendly smile and waited expectantly.

"Could you please direct me to Jerry Santucci's office." It wasn't phrased as a question. She didn't ask if she was in the correct building. It was a statement that Jerry was there. W.P. had said that this was the place. It could be no other. It didn't matter that Santucci hadn't been seen there by any of W.P.'s people; after all, he'd managed to disappear for almost twenty-five years.

The security guard pressed the buzzer beneath the counter. "Do you know which company?" He pointed at the lobby directory.

"International Charities. I know I'm in the correct building. This is Inchar House, I believe."

"Yes, it is. But I've never heard that name before." He took out a directory and opened it to a particular page. "Could you spell that for me . . . slowly, please." He appeared totally sincere as he looked up at Leila expectantly.

She spelled Santucci's name carefully, watching the guard's finger run down the page to *S.*

"International Charities is an international company, a fairly big one, but there aren't too many Inchar employees in Hong Kong. I know most of these people because they say hello on the way to the elevators every day, but I don't know that name." He appeared perplexed. "Why don't you look at the list of people who work here and see if there're any names you recognize?"

Leila ran her finger down the list. "This is very strange. Jerry's name isn't here." She looked squarely at the guard. "Considering everything, he's probably using a phony name." She emphasized the word "phony" and then continued, "You see, I got a call when he left his place to come here this morning, and then I was informed he was seen arriving here, so he must be in his office."

The guard's brows were knit with concern.

"Let me describe him."

Jerry Santucci stared at the television screen with his mouth open as Leila described him perfectly for the guard. "What the fuck is this?" he shouted at the clear image of Leila Potter. He knocked over his mug of coffee when he jumped to his feet to stare accusingly at the screen. "Who called her? Who saw me?" he asked accusingly. A hangover contributed to his anger. His eyes were bloodshot, and his features were contorted with displeasure.

"I'd say it was a very accurate description, considering how shoddy you look this morning," Young replied acidly. "She could certainly pick you out of a crowd."

Jerry whirled. "What's this about someone calling her, for Christ's sake? About when I left . . . and when I got here." He leaned forward on Young's desk. "What is that shit, Hugh?"

"I was about to ask you the same thing, Jerry. Are you trying to draw her in here to do the job yourself instead of leaving it up to the pros? I'd say that was—"

"What do you mean?" Jerry waved his arms. "I thought we worked out everything last night, and now I hear this shit." He glanced toward Ed Kelley, who was listening to the exchange curiously.

"We all thought so, Jerry," Young replied evenly. "When you so rudely interrupted me, I was about to say that this is a dangerous way to solve a personal problem. We've always agreed not to bring our personal problems to Inchar House."

Santucci's eyes darted from Young to Kelley and back again. Nothing seemed to pass between them. Instead they were looking back at the television screen with interest.

Leila had reached into her purse and extracted a wad of cash. She counted out four bills. "I know Jerry's here because my informant knows he'd be in serious trouble if he lied."

"Informant!" Santucci bellowed.

"Here's two thousand dollars if you'll help me." She held the money out to the guard.

"She said it was a guy who told her," Jerry exploded, again studying the other two. "A guy!" He licked his lips. "No one else knows what's going on but the three of us," he said accusingly. "What is this shit?" he repeated.

"I'm sorry," the security guard said politely. "We're not allowed to accept money from visitors. Perhaps someone else with the company might help you." He pointed at the directory on the countertop. He was growing uneasy as this woman seemed increasingly intent on remaining there until she got some satisfaction.

"What is this shit?" Santucci repeated in a louder voice. "Hugh? Eddie?"

"Okay, Jerry, you're convincing enough so I believe you," Young finally answered. "Perhaps this is some sort of setup. Time to find out who's stuck their nose in too far." He reached for the phone and punched some buttons. "Get something from Connie to clean up that coffee," he said to Santucci. "Then take a load off your feet until we get to the bottom of this."

The security guard's phone rang. "Excuse me," he said politely to Leila. He listened as Hugh Young explained what he should do. Then he replied, "Thank you very much for calling, sir." He replaced the phone and looked again at Leila. "Any names you recognize?"

"No," she answered. "But I know Jerry Santucci is in this building right now."

"Maybe someone else can help you," he said convincingly. "I hate to see you stuck like this." The guard dialed a number and when it was answered on the other end, he said calmly, "I have a lady trying to contact someone in the company that I don't know. Would you be kind enough to assist her?" After again hanging up, he said, "A lady will be with you in a moment."

Santucci, Kelley, and Young silently watched the screen as Leila thumbed through the security directory. She looked up when a young Chinese woman appeared.

"I was asked to help you." She was attractive, well dressed in an expensive yellow dress, and professionally sincere. "Would you be kind enough to come with me? We'll see if we can solve your problem."

Leila turned to the guard. "Is she the one you talked to on the phone?"

"Yes. I'm sure Connie will be happy to assist you." He smiled pleasantly and nodded. "I hope you have some success. Good morning."

The voices of Hong Kong detectives came clearly over the radio.

"Her escort is Chinese, good-looking, dressed in yellow. She's taking Miss Potter to the elevator bank," a voice noted calmly. "I can read the floor indicator with my binocs." A pause. "They're going up." Another momentary pause. "Let's see . . ." He ticked off the floors. "Passing fifteen . . . sixteen . . . seventeen . . . eighteen . . . nineteen . . . twenty . . . That's it. They stopped at twenty."

"I have the elevator bank in sight on twenty," another voice piped up from a building across from Inchar House. "I'm on twenty-one here, almost on the same level. Nothing yet . . . Wait, there's . . . there they are, yellow dress first, then Miss Potter. Don't know where they're headed yet. Wait a minute . . . they've stopped maybe twenty feet down the corridor, and yellow dress appears to be pushing another button. They're waiting for another elevator, I think. . . . Yes, they just stepped in. They're out of my sight. How about the top floors?"

Other voices on higher floors of the skyscraper across from Inchar House watched the elevator banks on the succeeding floors above twenty. But each one reported nothing apparent within seconds after an elevator should have arrived at the higher floors.

"W.P., something's wrong." It was Stone. "They've fooled us. She must have gone down somewhere."

"Top floors, report," W.P. ordered.

"Nothing in the penthouse. No one's done anything out of the ordinary. Floor beneath appears vacant. No movement."

"Then it must be one of the lower floors," W.P. responded evenly, "Cover the elevators on every floor down to the lobby."

But no one reported seeing Leila or the woman in the yellow dress getting off the elevators on any other floor.

Matt Stone could sense every muscle in his body shaking as he brought the camera to his eye and pointed it in the direction of the Museum of Art. "They've pulled a switch, W.P." It was a struggle to keep from shouting. *Leila, I'm so sorry I ever agreed to this.* "There's got to be some private office space or a private garage somewhere with a separate elevator, probably an elevator that doesn't go to the lobby or the floors they lease out. Maybe it goes to a rear exit."

The garage entrance, the emergency exits, and the refuse station in the rear of the building were all covered. "All rear exits are covered, Matt. But Tommy Chang mentioned something about following up on another entrance. Nothing ever came of that . . . at least I don't think so." W.P. considered what he'd just said. "What's your current location, Matt?"

"Between the museum and the Furama Hotel."

"Walk uphill. I'll be at the corner of Chater Garden."

The woman the guard had referred to as Connie remained politely quiet. As they waited in the lobby for the elevator, Leila asked her outright, "Connie, do you know Jerry Santucci?" This was the moment she had dreaded. Until now she knew that W.P.'s men could see her. But the minute she stepped into that elevator and the door slid shut, she was on her own. Fear, forced into the back of her mind until now, clutched her.

The other woman frowned as if searching her memory for the name. "No, I'm sorry. I don't," she said and offered nothing else.

"But you do work for International Charities?" Leila asked after they stepped into the elevator.

Connie stood with her arms folded, watching the light on the floor indicator bounce from left to right as they passed each level. "Yes, I do."

The elevator stopped at twenty, and the woman stepped out, covering the electric eye with her hand while she waited for Leila to step into the hall. "Is this the main office for International Charities?" Leila asked, looking at the flat teak display with that corporate name burned into the wood and outlined with gold trim.

"That is correct. Follow me, please." Leila saw broad floor-to-ceiling windows at either end of the hall that looked out on other tall office buildings. They walked about twenty feet to another elevator, and Connie pushed the button. The doors opened almost immediately. She stepped back and motioned for Leila to go inside.

"Where are we going?"

"Personnel department. I think that is what you call human relations in America."

Leila stepped in, and the doors shut as Connie pressed a button. "How do you know I'm an American?"

"I think Chu, the security guard, said so, didn't he?"

"No, I didn't tell him that." The elevator was going down. Leila looked up at the floor indicator. There were only three designations. *P*, which she assumed was penthouse; 20 for the floor they'd just left; and *B*, probably basement. "Why are we going to the basement?" Now the fear was real. W.P. hadn't anticipated something like this. They were descending into the unknown. . . .

The woman called Connie never turned around. "As I

said, we're going to the personnel office. Perhaps we can help you find Jerry . . . Santucci," she added hesitantly.

Was it the tone of her voice? The hesitation after Jerry's name? The fact that the woman wouldn't look her in the eye? Whatever it was, Leila felt the tic that was almost an electrical shock before the adrenaline surge began. "We're going to see Jerry, aren't we?" she asked quietly.

Her question was met with silence.

"Really, now." She had to act calm as she spoke to the woman in the yellow dress. "You don't have to be so mysterious. I can't go anywhere. This elevator only stops at three floors. There's nothing I can do, is there? We're stuck on this elevator until the door opens, and I imagine I have no choice. So it won't hurt to answer me, will it? Are we going to see Jerry?"

"Yes." Connie never turned, never moved, just stood before the door with her arms folded waiting for the elevator to stop.

After everything that had happened since that day at the Wall, Leila had never expected to see Jerry Santucci face to face again. He had seemed a ghost then, an apparition returned from the dead. As long as she was with Matt, Jerry had remained just that, a ghost. But now there was no Matt, and Jerry Santucci was about to become a terrifying reality. The elevator stopped, and the door slid silently open.

Connie turned slightly to look at Leila. Her expression was neither friendly nor hostile. She turned a key in the operating panel, removed it, and dropped it in her pocket, then stepped into the corridor and turned right, looking back once to make sure Leila was following. There was the outline of a door at the end of the corridor, but there was no doorknob. Connie punched a code into a wall panel, and the door slid open silently. As soon as Leila passed through, Connie touched another button and the door slid shut. They were in a pleasant, well-lit office with no windows and, when Leila turned back to look at the door they'd just come through, it blended so perfectly with the wall that it was impossible to see.

"Where are we now?"

"My office."

"Do you work for Jerry?"

"Only when I have to." The look of distaste on Connie's face was evident.

"But he does work for Inchar?"

"He helped found the company."

Leila indicated a door to one side of a large desk. "Is Jerry in there?"

Connie nodded. "Yes."

Leila's throat contracted. She had to struggle for her next breath.

Connie pushed a button on the intercom.

"Yes, Connie."

It didn't sound like Jerry's voice.

"She's here, Hugh."

"Bring her in."

Leila looked curiously at Connie. She had to swallow before she could speak. "Who is Hugh?" she inquired evenly.

There was no answer forthcoming. Connie held the door open until Leila stepped inside, then pulled it shut without following her.

Leila had taken two steps into the large, ornate office when she stopped dead. She sensed that her mouth had dropped open of its own accord and she thought she said "Jerry!" But if she did, she never heard the sound.

Jerry Santucci stood to one side of the room staring at her with unconcealed hatred. His face was flushed with anger. "Bitch!" The word came out in an ugly snarl.

A reasonably tall, stocky blond man in an elegant suit was standing behind the desk. "Jerry," he said very firmly, "sit down, please."

Santucci hesitated, clenched fists slapping against his sides, continuing to stare at Leila. "Bitch," he repeated under his breath, but he dropped reluctantly into a chair.

When she'd seen Jerry at the Wall, the shock of recognition and the brief moments they'd stared at each other had left Leila with a totally different image of Jerry Santucci. That day he'd seemed simply an older version of the boy who'd come to dinner with Danny before they shipped out to Vietnam. Now she saw a middle-aged man who'd stolen the face she once thought cute.

The eyes, the eyebrows, the olive skin—each seemed darker now, almost sinister, although they once had made him handsome and alluring to a young girl. What had seemed a sensuous mouth now appeared cruel. The scar on his cheek from his first stolen car was now exaggerated by the natural lines in his face, a deformity that enhanced his malevolence. Fear suffused her body, but it was not the instant fear that came as a reaction to the attempts on her life, or the fear of anticipation before she came into this room. This fear crept over her like a mist. *He is evil.*

"You," the man by the desk said to her, "sit there." He indicated one of two chairs before the desk.

"Why did you bring me here?" To Leila, her voice sounded tiny and insignificant. She wondered if she'd been heard when there was no response from the man by the desk. Perhaps her fear had struck her mute and she was only imagining that she could speak.

"I said sit down." There was nothing pleasant about the blond man's tone of voice.

She sat.

"You know, Jerry, she is kind of cute." It was an unexpected voice and it frightened her. She looked to her left and saw a man with a brush cut and a mustache that had yet to fill in, balanced on the arm of a chair. There was a grin on his face but it was an unpleasant one, the smirk of a neighborhood bully. Ed Kelley's voice was taunting. "I must say you've got great taste in older women." He was enjoying himself at Santucci's expense.

"Did you come here alone?" the man by the desk asked.

"Hugh, let's get on with it. Screw the small talk." Santucci's mind was still fixed on Leila's comment to the lobby security guard about someone calling her to explain where he was.

"Answer my question," Hugh said to her.

"I'm alone." The voice was her own, but it sounded so tiny.

"What about your detective friend, Mr. Chan?"

"I don't—"

"Don't tell me you don't know him. My people have seen you with him a couple of times."

Santucci stood up abruptly. "Hugh, let's get rid of her and hustle our asses out of here. This is ridiculous."

Young was about to respond when Connie's voice came over the intercom. "Hugh, pick up on five."

He snatched up the telephone. "Yes." The fifth line was used only by his security force. He listened without comment, staring straight ahead, his eyes falling on Leila just once. His only response before hanging up was "I want the helicopter on the penthouse pad forty-five minutes from now. No later. And tell Bing that he should be sitting behind the wheel of the limo like a goddamn jockey." He slammed the receiver down.

"For Christ's sake, Hugh. What's all this bullshit? Let's just get the job done." Jerry Santucci rose from his chair and took a step toward Leila. "Do you want me to—"

"Son of a bitch," Young shouted angrily, turning on Santucci, "will you sit your ass down in that chair and shut up?" When Jerry hesitated, Hugh rose to his feet. "You have nothing more to say until I tell you to speak." He whirled and glared at Kelley. "And the same goes for you. Don't say another goddamn thing to Jerry. You were just trying to piss him off. Don't say anything else to any of us. I've had it with the games both of you are playing." It was the first time either man had ever seen Hugh Young lose his temper completely. They both sat down, more out of surprise than submissiveness.

Leila gripped the arms of her chair as she witnessed the exchange. Nothing this day had gone the way W.P. said it should.

"Now I'll tell you both something else," Young said. "She didn't come here on her own. That was the call I've been expecting from Security since she showed in the lobby. One of our men is sure he saw Chan somewhere out there. Just a glimpse before he disappeared in the crowd. That means there has to be a shitload of other cops, after that screwup of Liu Fu's the other night."

"Bitch," Santucci muttered, glancing at Leila. Then, to Hugh, he said, "You know, if she never comes out of here, they'll never have another thing on us."

Leila closed her eyes. Killing her would make no difference to someone like Jerry Santucci. Why did it have to end this way?

Hugh Young knew about W. P. Chan, the Mongoose, and he was sure that if Leila did not come out of Inchar House, sooner or later the police would come in. "Jerry, if she doesn't leave here, eventually they will come in. We are all going to leave separately. Eddie is going back to Bangkok as fast as we can get him there, and you are . . . I'm not sure where we're going to send you. But you are going to be out of sight for a good long time."

"What about business, Hugh?" Ed Kelley wasn't about to challenge Young's mood, but he leaned forward in his chair with his elbows on his knees. "We can't just run away."

"Don't give me that shit, Eddie. Remember how you've boasted that you can run Bangkok over the telephone while that Blossom broad bounces up and down on you? Believe me, you'll do just fine." He raised his eyebrows and gestured with his index finger. "If you want a better excuse than Blossom, tell people you broke your leg playing polo. People will think you're in the same league as Jim Thompson, maybe even bigger."

Kelley sat back in the chair and folded his arms to show there would be no further argument. "You win, Hugh," he said with a grin. "I like your style."

After a sideways glance at a still fuming Santucci, who glanced at him quickly before shifting his menacing gaze back to Leila, Young pressed the button for the outer office.

Connie appeared in the door. "Yes, Hugh."

"Come on in here. Stand over next to her." He pointed at Leila and said, "Get up."

Leila stood, and Connie moved over to stand beside her.

Young pursed his lips. "Quite a difference. No way she could wear anything of yours," he said to Connie.

Connie was almost half a foot shorter than Leila. She looked up at the woman standing next to her and shook her head with a slight smile. "Nope."

"Could you outfit her in a yellow dress like yours? I mean could you run down the street and get her some clothes that would fit well enough to get her out of here looking like you?"

Connie looked Leila up and down. "Your American dress must be about size eight or nine. Is that right?"

Leila frowned, but she said nothing. At first, fear had numbed her. But the next reaction was a surprising rebellion. Whatever they were driving at, she was past cooperating.

"She'll answer if you want," Young said.

"That's all right, Hugh. That makes her about a British twelve or a Continental forty. I'll be close enough."

"How about that lovely blond hair? Can you get a long black wig to cover that well enough?"

"Right now?" Connie asked.

Young took out his wallet and extracted a wad of cash. "Get a blond wig, too, something that'll come close to matching her hair." He counted out ten thousand dollars and handed it to Connie. "And get a red dress for yourself. I don't want you looking the same. Will that cover it?"

"She's going to be very well dressed, for this amount of money, Hugh."

Young shrugged. "That's not a bad investment if it works. Get going, Connie. Be back in forty-five minutes." Then he turned to Santucci. "Jerry, it's time. You'll be leaving for Singapore shortly. Since you're the great lover of Hong Kong, I'm waiting with anticipation to see which broad you're going to choose as a traveling companion. Get your ass up to the twentieth floor and pick one out. And make sure she's about the same size as this one. She has to fit into her clothes."

* * *

Matt Stone left W.P. at the corner of Murray and Chater and concentrated on how a tourist would act as he headed down the hill and turned left. A Navy SEAL would storm the place. . . . No, think again. The SEALs frowned on anything as dumb as that. That would be the last resort. You take advantage of all your intelligence, you formulate a plan, you outline your attack in detail—and then you storm the place. He stopped to snap a picture of a statue in a nicely flowering garden.

W.P. had explained as quickly as possible his last telephone conversation with Tommy Chang before he disappeared. As always with Tommy, the conversation was short with a promise of details to follow. But he had mentioned another entrance to Inchar House, which Tommy never had a chance to explain. That must have been the secret that had killed Tommy.

Stone was angry with himself for allowing Leila to go off on her own. No such thing as a SEAL allowing a buddy to go charging off like that. Now he was going to play bumbling tourist and stumble down alleys looking for entrances with unusual security devices. Then would he be dumb enough to storm the place?

Inchar House was beautiful and modern with its soaring glass front and the unique waterfall as a centerpiece in the lobby. *Where would you charge, Stone? Maybe into a secret door behind the waterfall?* He managed a trace of a smile as he imagined the looks on the faces of the people in that fancy lobby as he emerged from behind that waterfall, dripping wet, Beretta in hand, looking just like the SEALs in the posters, and explained to those people in suits and ties and expensive dresses that he'd been searching for a secret door.

He stopped to take a picture of the Cenotaph near the alley that ran back along one side of Inchar House when a woman in yellow caught his eye. She was just emerging from the alley and appeared to be in a hurry as she turned left and threaded her way through the sidewalk crowd. That had to be the one they'd been talking about who took Leila into the elevator. Where the hell was she going in such a hurry?

"W.P., I've got the yellow dress in sight and she's in a hell of a hurry. I'm following her. It's a hunch." Matt Stone's hunches had paid off more than once; a couple of times they had saved his life. He dropped the camera and let it bang against his chest as he set off after her. He followed her up Ice House Street, then right onto Des Voeux Road Central.

She turned abruptly into a store. Stone slowed, stopping to gaze in the window. It was a women's store, and there were customers actually trying on clothes on the floor. *Don't most male tourists window shop like this, Stone? Oh, don't you feel like an asshole standing here while people wonder if you're trying to see some chick running around in her underwear?*

The woman in yellow was talking animatedly to a salesgirl in a green sheath dress slit well up her thighs. He considered going inside, then thought better of it. He felt awkward speaking to W.P. while trying not to look like he was taking a picture of the inside of the shop. "I have her inside a woman's clothing store on Des Voeux. Hold on." He paced. He watched other tourists. He marveled at the complex bamboo scaffolding rising thirty stories around a new high-rise. He appreciated the young, exquisitely tiny Chinese women window shopping. And deep inside, he continued to wonder at his poor judgment in letting Leila go off alone.

The woman in the yellow dress exited in less than fifteen minutes, her arms full of packages. Should he follow her? No, he knew where she was going. He had to find out what she'd bought. "She's heading back toward Inchar House, W.P. I'm checking in this store to see what she bought."

Inside, he saw the salesgirl in the green sheath moving toward the rear of the store and called out to her. She turned, stared at him curiously, and continued. Stone caught her by the arm just before she went through a door in the back. "Please, that girl in the yellow dress, the one who just left here . . ."

The salesgirl tried to back away from him.

"I'm sorry . . . I'm sorry. I just want to ask a question." He could see he was attracting attention. Why didn't he have a badge he could whip out? He pulled out his wallet and waved it in her face. "I'm with the American police, working with the Hong Kong police," he added breathlessly. "We've been following that woman in the yellow dress." He could see he wasn't gaining any sympathy. "Did she pay you in cash?"

The girl nodded.

"I have to warn you. She's a criminal." He was desperate. What to say? "She works for a forger. The money's no good. The money she gave you . . . phony money." That got her attention. "I need to know what she bought here."

"Some dresses." The girl looked confused.

"She couldn't have had time to try any on. Did she?"

"No."

"Were they her size?"

"No . . . no, one much bigger, one maybe her size."

"What color?"

"Yellow . . . red."

"Which one was her size?"

She shrugged. "I . . . red, I think . . . but maybe . . . I can't be sure." Large eyes close to tears mirrored fear and confusion.

"Anything else?"

"Wigs. She—"

"Shh." Stone put his finger to her lips to hush her because he had heard W.P.'s voice on his radio receiver. "Say again," he shouted into his camera.

The salesgirl's eyes grew larger as she watched him speaking into a camera.

"We have an unidentified helicopter landing on the roof of Inchar House." W.P.'s voice was muffled.

"Can you keep it from taking off?"

"We're bringing in the helo we had over at Happy Valley, but we can't take any chances of an accident in the Central District."

"I'm on the way," Stone shouted into the camera. "The yellow dress has left the store. She bought two dresses and wigs." He turned back to the salesgirl. "Was there a blond wig?"

Her hands were drawn into tiny fists, held up against her chin. She nodded. "Yes . . . blond . . . black."

"Sounds like she bought a dress and wig for Leila . . . could be a switch." Stone turned and bolted from the store. *Oh, sweet Jesus, a helicopter!* He ran as fast as he could, weaving through the sidewalk crowds. His eyes swept the crowds, but there was no way he could pick out the yellow dress.

CHAPTER 18

A BLACK CADILLAC LIMO WITH DARKENED WINDOWS HAS JUST entered the garage in the rear of Inchar House." The excitement in the policeman's voice was evident even as it came through the hearing aid in Stone's ear.

"Can you see inside?" W.P. asked. "ID anybody?"

"Negative. Couldn't see any passengers. It was just doors up, doors down. No idea."

"On the way."

W.P. had considered remaining near the rear of Inchar House until the helicopter swooped down to land on the penthouse pad. Then he'd moved up the hill by the new Hong Kong Bank Building to get a better view. He borrowed binoculars from his man at that station and saw exactly what had been reported—an empty helicopter perched on a reinforced rooftop pad. When his man asked if he thought that would be the method of taking away the woman, W.P. was ready to answer affirmatively, until he pondered the situation more seriously. That limo had changed his thinking. His answer, as he raced down the hill toward the rear of Inchar House, coupled with Stone's report from the dress shop, was a shout over his shoulder that he had no idea.

W.P. was running as best he could, and it hurt. The impact of each step sent new pains surging from his wound to the aching muscles in his back and chest. The bullet hole itself burned as if a white-hot brand had been forced through the opening until it emerged on the other side.

There was much to imagine, nothing to see, when W.P., his complexion ashen, arrived at the stakeout point behind Inchar House. The entrance from the street was wide enough for cars to make the turn from either direction. The driveway sloped down to the automatic doors, which could be activated by a card or most likely by an operator inside who recognized an approaching vehicle.

"What else did you see?" W.P. inquired breathlessly. He was dizzy from the pain and the running.

"Nothing else, sir. The Cadillac is a black stretch limo. All the windows are darkened."

If you are half the man you believe you are, you will be able to survive this until Leila is safe, W.P. told himself. "Did he use a card to activate the garage door?" *Or was it controlled only from the inside?*

"No, sir. He must have been expected. It opened for him. I don't think he even came to a stop."

The receiver in his ear radiated sound that jarred every corner of his brain. "W.P., this is Stone. I can't catch up with the girl. The sidewalks are mobbed with people. Is someone watching the alley at the front of the building?"

W.P. detected the urgency in Stone's voice. "Everything's covered. Whatever happens, you'll hear it over this circuit." After a short pause for breath, he added, "Matt, come up here with me. I think I need you here." The pain was persistent. Though W.P. had no fear for himself, he was afraid it would cloud his judgment. Things were becoming too confusing to sort into their proper order, yet he sensed that the people who had Leila were aware of their presence. Right now, those people had the upper hand. He sat down heavily on the bumper of a car and breathed deeply, hoping to clear his head. *They know you're here and they're setting you up.* These people were deadly, and W.P. wasn't sure he could cope alone. Who was that someone behind Santucci?

Whoever, it was someone much smarter and certainly more dangerous and he had no idea who it was.

A policeman beside him touched his shoulder gently and silently pointed at his shirt. W.P. looked down. He saw the red stain seeping through the bandages onto the front of his short-sleeved white shirt and hoped the people inside weren't watching him.

Connie held up the dress so that Young could compare the color to her own.

"Not a bad match," Young commented. "Very good, Connie. And you bought a dress for yourself, and the wigs?" Of course she did. Connie was so efficient that it would be a pity to lose her. But no one was irreplaceable. Hugh Young knew in his heart that he had been absolutely right all these years, that eventually he would have to go it alone. Now he knew it was time to take care of Hugh Young.

Connie placed the wigs and dresses on his desk for inspection.

Hugh winked at Kelley and Santucci. "Look okay to you?" It was equally important for them to take part, to feel that everything was a mutual decision.

Kelley nodded without comment.

"So is the rest of this scheme of yours going to remain a secret, Hugh? Are we all going to become cross-dressers, or are you going to let us in on it?" After selecting the girl on the twentieth floor who appeared closest in size to Leila, Jerry Santucci had spent the remainder of the time Connie was gone outlining the status of each of his continuing projects. Hugh Young had made it clear that Jerry would simply disappear from Inchar until Young determined that he could return. He wanted to make a point of reassuring Santucci that none of his efforts would be dropped. That reassurance had kept him quiet, until now.

"No secret, Jerry. The lady's going to put on the yellow dress." He gestured to Connie. "Give it to her."

Leila was still sitting in the chair in front of Young's desk and had no choice but to accept the yellow dress that was dropped in her lap.

"Go ahead," Young said to Leila, "put it on."

"Where?" she asked softly. She understood exactly what was in his mind. She would look like Connie when she left here.

"Right here. Where else do you think?"

An idea came to Leila: *If you know in your heart the end is near and there's no way out, take someone with you. And don't make it easy for this asshole.* "No . . . if you please, no." She clenched the yellow dress in her fists and stared back at Young with a determined look on her face. She knew she had little choice, but time was so important at this stage. To attempt a show of force, to see just how far she could push him any effort at all . . .

"Bullshit. You're going to strip down right now and put that dress on, or Jerry's going to do it for you."

There was no response from Leila. She held his gaze.

Jerry Santucci jumped to his feet. "Enough of this crap. After all the trouble she's made, I'll show her . . ."

Connie stepped in front of Leila as she spoke to Young. "Hugh, let me take her out to my office. Not here. And especially not with Jerry's help. We can't afford the time and I don't think you want her going out of here looking like damaged goods. I'll make sure she's ready." She smiled slightly. "You want me to change, too, and there's not a chance I'd put on a show in here any more than she wants to. Don't worry, there's no place she can go." She stepped back and placed a reassuring hand on Leila's shoulder. "You don't want to waste time playing games you're going to lose, not with them."

Young waved his hand, dismissing them both. "Fine, Connie, fine. Just leave the door open in case you have a problem."

Leila hesitated. Was this woman helping her? Was there a chance to . . . A chance to what? What would she do? How would she know when to make her move?

Connie's hand was still on Leila's shoulder and she bent down and said softly, "Believe me, this is the best thing you can do for yourself at the moment. Come on with me. I'll give you a hand."

Leila rose silently to her feet and walked out to the outer office with Connie. Leila had concluded it was better to say nothing at all, even to the Chinese woman. Somehow, sooner or later, there would have to be a chance. She had no idea whether Connie sympathized with her or just wanted to stay close to Hugh, but she was right about cooperating for now.

Young turned to Santucci. "Sit down, Jerry . . . again." Then he remembered the woman Santucci had brought down from the twentieth floor. He pressed the speaker button to the outer office. "And the girl in your office, Connie, she puts on her stuff," he added. The one Santucci had picked was British, younger than Leila but close to her size, and that was all that mattered. "And there's one more thing, Jerry. Let's give you a little mustache, like Eddie's." Hugh had kept a compact disguise kit, bought years ago on a business trip to the States, in his desk for years. He'd picked it up on a whim, just on the off chance that he might one day have to make a quick exit. Many times he'd considered disposing of it. Thank God he hadn't bothered to do so.

"Why?" Santucci didn't bother to mask his belligerence.

"Because we don't want you to look so much like Jerry Santucci. These people are watching us. When you're at the top of the building on the landing pad, I don't want you to be easy to ID with binoculars. It'll be that much more difficult if they see someone with a mustache. I want you alive, Jerry. Just listen for a change and shut up."

The voice snapped like a whip over the radio. "Rooftop door's opening. I can make out three people . . . still in the shadows." It came from the policeman perched on the roof of a building looking down on Inchar House. "Let's see . . . two men, one woman. One's probably the pilot."

"Chinese or Caucasian?" W.P. interrupted. An invisible demon was moving that hot poker back and forth inside the bullet hole.

"One Chinese male going into the helicopter. Has to be the pilot. Other two still standing just inside the door."

Stone had appeared moments before beside W.P.

"Danny," he called into his transmitter, "position now?" Dan Slade was riding in the police helicopter.

"Airborne, holding near some high-rises to the east, using them for cover. We can see that bird, but I don't think they can see us."

"Engine started, rotor engaged on the pad," the police spotter reported.

"Any ID on subjects?" W.P. called in frustration.

"Just stepped through the door. Caucasian male, Caucasian female about the same size as the man. Could be the subject described to us. Wearing a blue skirt, white blouse, blond hair, and really stacked."

W.P. snapped his fingers. "That's what Leila was wearing this morning. These people don't do anything this dumb. What do you think?" He studied Stone. "Trick?"

Matt closed his eyes. Christ, Leila was with these people. Just one slip and . . . There was no time for mental gymnastics. "This is the most obvious, right? It's too easy. They have to know we're here or they wouldn't try this." He opened his eyes and looked to W.P. for help. But the detective remained silent. "And Leila's slender, not what anyone would call 'stacked.' What can you give us on the Caucasian male?" he asked the spotter.

"Wait . . . he's just turning toward me. White male, average height, short hair, mustache, carrying a briefcase. They just climbed into the bird. Out of sight now, getting ready to lift off." The description didn't really sound like Santucci. It didn't sound like Kelley either. But they were sending off a woman who could be Leila, or who could be dressed in Leila's clothes.

"Danny, did you copy?" Stone called out on the radio.

"Roger, we have them in sight and are closing. Will stay to the rear and follow . . ."

There was nothing Stone could do. He was earthbound. If it was Leila, only Dan Slade could stop them now.

Neither Stone nor W.P. heard Slade's final words. Their attention was riveted to the garage door at the rear of Inchar House as it rolled up. The Cadillac limo was half in the light, half in shadow. But they could see that it was facing out, and people could be seen in the background behind it, one of them pointing angrily at the open door. An Oriental man in a chauffeur's hat pulled open the driver's door and waited as three others moved toward the rear door on the opposite side. The door closed.

"That's Santucci, the one on the left. It has to be." W.P. was peering through binoculars, whispering as if they could be heard inside the garage.

Stone wasn't so sure. It was difficult to make a positive identification at that distance. This one had a mustache, too. "Looks something like the guy Leila described," Stone muttered, "but with a mustache? The female is in a red outfit. She's an Oriental, I think . . . could be the one from the store." He shifted the focus ever so slightly to see if he could get a clearer image of the woman's face. "I can't tell if she's the one . . ."

W.P. called over the radio for a trail car. Then he reached out and touched Stone's arm. "I'm sure that's Santucci. He's about the right size." He wanted it to be. He was so tired now, and he didn't care if this Santucci had a mustache. It had to be him, and W.P. had to stop him for Tommy Chang's sake . . . for Leila's sake. "Do you want him for yourself, Matt?"

Oh, shit. I want him so badly, but . . . Stone turned his binoculars skyward and studied the helicopter turning toward the harbor.

W.P. knew what Stone wanted.

But I want Leila more. "Leila's still in that building, W.P. I know it. That helicopter's got to be a decoy. I don't know who these people are, but it's not her. She wouldn't have gone off like that. She would have put up a struggle or done something . . . anything . . . to attract attention." His eyes mirrored self-doubt. "I'm sure," he said emphatically. His gaze traveled from W.P. to the garage and then to the hill where the police car was waiting. *I want Santucci. I want to kill the bastard myself, but Leila . . .* "She's here. I'm staying until she comes out . . . or maybe I'll have to go in."

W.P. wanted Jerry Santucci more than anyone would ever understand. He knew he should stay. He was in charge. But pain had surpassed reason; pain had supplanted everything, with vengeance. "Santucci is mine, Matt, more mine than yours." W.P. walked slowly up the hill to the police car. It was an unmarked vehicle. He winced at the pain in his shoulder as he pulled open the front door and climbed in beside the driver.

The black limo pulled out and turned left toward Wanchai and Causeway Bay. W.P. instructed the driver to stay back until they were in an area where civilians wouldn't be hurt. He lifted the mike that lay on the seat and said, "Stay close, Matt. Keep talking to me."

It was the end of one lifetime, the start of another. Hugh Young had even experienced a brief moment of emptiness as the time came for Eddie Kelley and Jerry Santucci to leave, bear-hugging both of them, demanding they report back to him in no less than twenty-four hours. "Hey, it won't be long before we're emptying another jug of Mr. Jack." And then they were gone.

Young heaved a sigh of relief as he looked about the empty office. He waved his Beretta in Leila's direction before placing it on the desk. "I'm sure you have no doubt that I'll use this if you give me a reason. It would be better for you just to go along with me rather than try to fight it all. I want to leave this island. At the right time, if I'm able to get away, you'll get out of this mess alive. So you have a choice. Right?" He'd told the others they'd get out alive. Because they always had, Jerry and Eddie believed they would and that it was better to do as they were ordered than to take chances with the police. Inchar would survive. They would survive.

Leila had said nothing since she left the room with Connie to change her clothes, and she had no intention of talking now. If her silence was disturbing to this person, then it was worthwhile. Never for a second did she believe he would allow her to live. But she had bought time by going along with Connie. Now she would go along with this man until an opportunity, anything at all, appeared.

Young never intended that Leila would survive the end of

the day, but right now he needed her long enough to make sure of his own disappearance. It would take weeks, more likely months, before the authorities could sort out the Inchar system. But it was definitely time for Hugh Young to go. Jerry hadn't a prayer, and Eddie, he knew, wouldn't be taken alive. They would both be corpses shortly, and that would remove the last vestige of pressure from him. Hugh Young remained an unknown to the outside world. There was no trail someone could follow from Santucci or Kelley back to him. Inchar was a Hong Kong entity. It had little to do with the United States, and once the Americans were able to confirm that Santucci and Kelley were dead, there was no reason to chase after him. He fully intended to disappear this day and remain invisible. Even if they eventually turned up information on him, his trail would be very cold. The country home he'd purchased in Singapore a few years before would provide an elegant life-style, and there would be more money than he could ever spend. He'd worked hard—very, very hard. It was time to take full advantage of the rewards.

As far as International Charities, Ltd., was concerned, he had instructed Connie early that morning to transfer a small fortune into numbered accounts in three separate banks. He'd also insisted she include a healthy sum for herself. Her eyes had widened when he wrote down the sum. Young trusted that her loyalty over the years combined with that numbered account for herself was a guarantee that she would follow his instructions to the letter. Inchar might even be able to survive on its own, although that was no longer a matter of concern to him. Connie's misfortune was to be in Eddie's company.

While Leila fidgeted in her chair, Young made some final telephone calls, checked his watch half a dozen times, and finally announced, "It's time to go. There's a car waiting for us out front." He slipped the Beretta into his pocket. "The gun is in my hand. I'm an expert with it. You'll be dead if you cause a problem for me. The odds are that I'll be out of the country before anyone would believe I was the one who killed you." He came out from behind the desk. "Enough said? You'll cooperate for the time being, won't you? Better alive than dead."

Leila stood up and nodded her assent. She was sure Young would do exactly what he claimed. So she would pretend to cooperate a little longer. The yellow dress that Connie had bought was tight, and the black wig was uncomfortable. But when Connie allowed her to use the bathroom, Leila had barely recognized herself.

They took the elevator beside the outer office to the twentieth floor, took another one down to the lobby, and strolled past the waterfall and out through the massive glass doors of Inchar House. A black Jaguar sedan waited at the curb.

As he looked down from the helicopter at the panorama of Hong Kong below, Jerry Santucci was beginning to like the idea of getting away on his own for a while. Why not be a free spirit? Hugh would take care of the details, dot the *i*'s, cross the *t*'s, make sure the cash supply held up. *Leave it to Hugh to come up with the right idea.* When Hugh had slid two one-way tickets across the desk shortly after he'd arrived at the office that morning, he'd explained that Singapore would be a perfect place to lie low for a while. Then he showed Jerry the passports that required only photos. "I want a picture of you with that mustache, Jerry." And he'd told Jerry to make sure that the girl he picked out on the twentieth floor was good-looking because she was going to be traveling with him. *What a guy, that Hugh.*

That was all the encouragement Jerry had required when he got off the elevator on the twentieth floor. It was a great idea—Singapore, tall drinks at Raffles, the good life. A fabulous idea. He needed a change of scenery. As he studied the girls on the twentieth floor that morning, looking for someone about Leila's size, the thought struck him that it had been years since he'd had a round-eye, and then he saw the perfect one smiling at him. *Little does she realize her good fortune,* he said to himself when he brought her down to the suboffice. *What the hell, Hugh? Why not live life to the hilt? For tomorrow we die.* He laughed at the idea. There would be many tomorrows before he got to that one.

The helicopter banked slightly as it turned toward Victoria Harbor. Jerry slipped his arm around the shoulders of the British girl and pulled her close. No time like the present. She was reasonably attractive, but he'd selected her as much for a magnificent chest as anything else. Chinese girls were mostly flat. The boobs on this one would be a welcome change of scenery.

She looked strangely at him, wondering why she'd ever agreed to this charade. Singapore? One minute she was sitting behind a boring desk on the twentieth floor, the next she'd been escorted to an office no one knew about in the subbasement. It was the first time she'd ever met the head of Inchar, and in no time she realized that she'd agreed to this crazy idea. Mr. Young said he'd take care of everything—a new wardrobe, the works. What would her boyfriend say when she came back? There were all those rumors about how wealthy Mr. Santucci was, but was that reason enough to go off like this, even if Mr. Young did assure her that she'd never have to work for the rest of her life? All she had to do was wear this American woman's clothes when they left.

At the time, the proposition seemed like winning the sweepstakes. Now she looked more closely at Jerry Santucci and saw that he was staring down at her chest. The American girl's blouse was much too small, and she looked as if she was about to burst out of it. Then Mr. Santucci's hand moved down inside her blouse. The expression on his face gave her a sick feeling in the pit of her stomach. Those eyes . . . they were evil. Was it worth this?

The police were watching. Leila knew that. It was all part of W.P.'s plan. Maybe he or Matt were nearby. If they weren't, she had to do something to draw attention to herself.

"Oh . . ." Leila gave a little cry as she slipped and reached out for Young's free arm.

He half turned, eyes narrowing as he backed away from her. "What the hell?" He had swung around just enough so that the Beretta, still in his pocket, was pointed in her direction.

"No . . . no, it's alright," she reassured him. "My heel. I caught it on the step."

He looked down. Her shoe was half off. His eyes relaxed as he looked quickly to either side. "Put it back on."

"Thanks. Just stand there for a second so I can balance." She held on to his arm as she slipped the shoe back on her foot, brushing her head against his shoulder. The black wig slipped back on her head slightly and she reached up and pulled it down, exaggerating the bangs over her eyes.

Young led her across the sidewalk and held open the back door of the black Jaguar as he scanned the area. He saw nothing unusual before he slid in beside her.

"Hey, remember that yellow dress we were watching for on the upper floors? Did anyone else just see that?" The tinny voice seemed to echo in Stone's ear.

"You mean the one that was just on the front steps?" one of W.P.'s spotters answered.

"Yeah, that's the one. Dress looks the same, but I don't think it's the same woman. It can't be," another responded. "That one was Chinese, tiny, well packed. I saw her on twenty for a second waiting for the elevator. The one on the steps was bigger . . . English or American, I'd say."

"No, that's not what I mean," the first voice said. "Did you see what happened when she slipped on the steps and grabbed the blond guy? I think she was wearing a wig. It looked like it slipped."

"Quiet on the circuit," Stone bellowed. "Who can tell me where she went?"

The first voice answered. "Got into a black Jaguar with the blond guy."

"Which way are they going?"

The first voice came back. "Let me get my glasses on them again. Christ, where'd they go? Every car down there's black. I'm on the third floor across from Inchar looking down on them. Anyone down the street see that black Jag?"

Stone pressed the camera into his chest to avoid interrupting. It took all his willpower to keep quiet. *Leila* . . .

"Car got a chauffeur?"

"Had to be one. They got in the back seat."

"Got a Jag here," a new voice piped up, "turning up Murray Road. Black, four doors, no chauffeur's hat on the driver. Tinted windows, can't see the passengers."

There couldn't be another car like that at this moment in that place! "That's got to be it," Stone shouted. "Do we have a tail car nearby?"

There was a sergeant standing next to Stone. "Closest one is tagging along with Mr. Chan now, sir. Others are down on Connaught, Chater near Des Voeux, and over on Ice House."

Stone saw the locations on the map. The Murray Road tail car was the one they needed, and that one was with W.P. "Motorcycles?" he asked.

The sergeant punched a button on his radio and spoke a couple of words of Chinese into the mike. "There's one on Jackson. He'll try to follow if he can get to Murray in time."

"Get one for me!" Stone barked. "I'll ride behind."

Once again the sergeant spoke into his mike. "On the way, Mr. Stone."

W. P. Chan was relaxed now. He wasn't sure why because he was still dizzy, but it wasn't as bad as when he stopped running. He was also positive he wouldn't lose consciousness. But he knew he was still bleeding because the stain on the front of his shirt now spread across the left side of his chest and almost down to his waist. It was cold, too. He thought about how careful his wife had been that morning when she wrapped him with new bandages. How mad she would be if she could see him now. He resolved to have a medic rebandage the wound at the station before he returned home that evening.

He was daydreaming and, when he looked up, he was confused. Had he slept for a second? "Where are we?"

"Gloucester Road." The driver pointed at a large structure. "That's the Arts Center over there." He glanced at the bloodstain and asked, "Are you all right, sir?"

Time was disjointed. How had they gotten into Wanchai already from the Central District? "Thank you for asking. I'll make it." W.P.'s Beretta had been resting in his lap since they started out. He forgot that he'd already checked the clip, and extracted it once again, reinserted it, then placed a second clip in his breast pocket. Habits like that were second nature and he was pleased with himself for remembering. *You're doing okay. You're going to be fine.* "I expect they're heading for the Cross-Harbor Tunnel," he muttered.

"I'd say just about everyone on Gloucester Road is," the driver commented.

W.P. picked up the microphone. "Matt, I think the black limousine is headed for the airport. I can't let them get to the tunnel or they might lose us. I'm going to try to force them off the road before then." He switched to another circuit and requested backup before the tunnel, then went back to the original frequency. "I've been listening to you. Luck, my friend." But he wasn't sure why he'd said that. Had they located Leila? Actually, he felt much better now, almost as if he was floating. The pain had all but disappeared, or maybe it had just become numbness. That had happened to him with other injuries. Someone had once told him that was how the body dealt with pain. He tested the area with his hand and felt nothing. Numb . . . That was good.

Slade watched the other helicopter level as it came out of the turn. "Helo has settled on a northeast course," he said into the mike. "Looks to my pilot like they're heading right up the harbor for Kai Tak."

"Get him when he lands," W.P. responded. "You can't do anything over the harbor. Too dangerous."

Slade looked down. Victoria Harbor glistened like a polished diamond.

* * *

The British girl looked down on the harbor from the window of the helicopter. She saw junks of every size and shape, tankers, ferries, freighters, huge yachts, barges, tugs, ocean liners, sailboats, everything that floated. It was a beautiful sight, but she had difficulty concentrating because Jerry Santucci's hand was inside her brassiere. She tried to make believe that the glory of flying off to Singapore on a whim with a wealthy man was a crazy, wonderful dream come true.

Santucci nuzzled her ear. "I can hardly wait until we get there. You're not going to need any clothes for days. You can't imagine the fun." Hugh had been farsighted. A lark like this was just what he needed.

But this wasn't fun, she decided. His hand was rough, and he was acting like some kind of animal. There was nothing exciting about this. *If some guy tried this on a first date, my knee would be buried in his crotch.* Maybe this was the dumbest thing she'd ever done. She wished she was in one of those yachts down below. Yachtsmen were supposed to be gentlemen and wouldn't be acting like this.

An individual on one of the yachts was actually concentrating on the helicopter. He had been watching it through binoculars since it lifted off from the Inchar penthouse. He followed it as it passed over the Star Ferry pier and turned northeast over the harbor. The helicopter that seemed to be following wasn't expected, but it was of no interest to him. This one was his only concern. If the other was too close, that was their tough shit.

He waited until the first helo passed overhead and was just about centered between North Point on the Hong Kong side and Hung Hom on the mainland side before he pressed the button on the transmitter in his hand. The reaction was instant.

The British girl had finally made a decision. *Enough of this shit. I'll call for someone to pick me up at Kai Tak.* She took hold of Jerry Santucci's wrist, yanked his hand out of her brassiere, and was sinking her teeth into his still groping hand when the inside of the helicopter turned a brilliant white. There was a sensation of heat and then—nothing.

"Matt!" Slade shouted. Then he was hanging from his seat belt. The helicopter carrying Jerry Santucci erupted into a ball of flame. Chunks of metal and rotors and engine burst outward from the fireball. Slade's pilot had instinctively banked hard to the left. The shock wave from the blast forced their own helicopter into a steeper turn, and the pilot fought the controls struggling to bring them back on the level.

Dan Slade watched flaming debris tumble down toward the crowded harbor. "There's nothing left, Matt. Santucci or whoever was aboard just got blown apart. Nothing's left."

Stone had switched to a throat mike while he was waiting for the motorcycle. What if Leila had been in the Inchar helicopter? He forced himself to ask calmly, "You okay, Danny?" He was so sure she was in the car, but what if . . . ?

"Roger. If we'd been any closer, we'd be swimming now."

Stone studied the map the police sergeant held for him. "Have your pilot take you to the Royal Hong Kong Yacht Club. W.P.'s got to stop the limo before it gets into the tunnel. He sounds like he could use a hand."

A motorcycle piloted by a helmeted police officer came to a stop beside them. The driver raced the deep-throated engine, waiting for Stone to climb on the back.

Stone grasped the back of the seat as he perched on a metal supply box bolted to the rear fender. How long had it been since the black Jaguar turned up Murray? Thirty seconds? A minute? More? Less? Someone had reported the car halted in traffic at the Queensway traffic light just before the motorcycle pulled up for him. "Location on the Jaguar?" he called out as they headed east on Des Voeux.

There was an officer with binoculars on the Des Voeux Road corner of Chater Garden. He reported his position and said excitedly, "The Jag just turned up the hill on Garden Road in the direction of the Peak Tram."

Stone's driver wore a throat mike also. "I copied," he said. As they approached the Queens Road intersection, he snapped on his flashing lights. They squirmed their way through heavy oncoming traffic until it seemed to close in on them, no longer enough room for even a motorcycle to squeeze through. "Hold on," he shouted, and they mounted a sidewalk to avoid an oncoming tour bus. When they bounced down over the curb, they were headed up Garden Road.

Stone's rear ached where the edges of the steel box ground in harder with each bump. His eyes watered as he peered over the man's shoulder searching for the black Jaguar. The traffic was thick—cars, taxis, tourists on foot—and all of it seemed to be heading toward the terminal station for the Victoria Peak Tram. There was no Jag to be seen. Stone was on his own. W.P.'s remaining spotters were still below.

"There!" The driver pointed up the hill toward the tram station. A black Jaguar sedan with a tinted rear window, signal light still blinking, was pulled over to the side near the corner of Garden and Lower Albert Road. He flipped off the flashing lights.

Stone felt the cool metal of the 9mm revolver as he slipped it from the holster. The driver was hugging the other parked cars on Garden as they approached the Jaguar. "Instructions."

"Stay on the pavement, just as you're doing now. Stop two cars behind. You approach on foot from the driver's side. I'll do the same on the passenger side."

The engine was cut before they'd come to a complete stop. Stone slid off backwards and stayed close to the parked cars as he moved cautiously up the sidewalk. In an instant, the officer slid off on the other side. The motorcycle fell to the street. Gun in hand, he approached in the same manner as Stone.

They were both crouched at the rear of the Jaguar on either side. Its engine was still running. "I'll take the rear door on my side on the count of three," Stone said. "You get that driver out of the car at the same time."

"One . . ." Stone could feel his heart pounding madly as he inched his way forward. "Two . . ." *Leila.* "Three!" He lunged for the door handle. The door swung outward.

Stone's finger was increasing the pressure on the trigger of the 9mm.

Empty!

Angry Chinese voices erupted on the other side and Stone caught a glimpse of a body flying out the driver's door. He dashed around to the street side. A man in a white shirt was sprawled on his back in the street, with the helmeted officer on top of him. His revolver was pressed hard under the man's chin, forcing his head back. Incomprehensible Chinese words flew back and forth until the gun came away from the man's chin and was pressed into one of his eye sockets. Two more sharp words issued from the man on the bottom before the policeman relieved the pressure of the barrel in the man's eye.

"The man and woman went into the tram station." The officer pointed over his shoulder at the Lower Peak Tram Terminal. Tourists were crowding inside the glass and metal terminal to climb aboard the funicular train. Shiny tracks rose out of the station house at a forty-five-degree angle. The modern cars were hauled along tracks by cables attached to electric motors to the top of 1,800-foot Victoria Peak.

Stone jammed the 9mm back into the holster as he ran up the hill, dodging through an uncaring, milling crowd more interested in taking photographs. An obedient line was in place to purchase tickets. He bulled into the line, pushing people aside and entered through the glass exit doors. A train was just preparing to pull out as he ran back alongside the cars. Every seat seemed to be filled and there were people holding on to overhead straps.

Leila . . . Leila . . . Was she aboard this one? *Wait, is that . . .* It wasn't Leila. That one was Caucasian and blond. *Leila was wearing a yellow dress with a black wig. Yellow dress, Black wig . . .* And that's when he saw her. She was sitting on an inner seat against the side in the second section from the rear. A stocky blond man was seated beside her, his head turned in her direction as he spoke to her. Stone headed for the rear entrance.

The doors began to slide shut. Stone lunged, pushing with his shoulder and his hands, and dived through the entrance in the section behind theirs as the surprised passengers closest to him backed away. The doors clicked shut, and the wheels began to rumble against the metal tracks as the tram exited the station into the sunlight.

"W.P., do you read me?" Slade called.

"Yes." W. P. Chan's voice was soft.

"We're in a hover over the yacht club. What's your position?"

W.P. really didn't want to talk now. It was so hard to concentrate, but he was beginning to think he might need help. "Passing Wanchai Stadium, getting close to the approaches to the tunnel." The driver was making his move, racing to get alongside the Cadillac before the road began to descend into the black hole of the tunnel.

Slade thought he could identify the black limo. "Can you force him off the road?"

"About to . . ." W.P. had his gun in his hand, and he wanted to shoot. But he couldn't see through the tinted windows, and it was increasingly difficult to steady the automatic.

W.P. was keying the mike as the police car came alongside the limo. His driver turned into the Cadillac without another word. The limo seemed to rise momentarily onto two wheels, then settled back down, swerving against the curbing, then back into the police vehicle.

W.P.'s driver yanked his wheel over hard again, and jammed the gas pedal to the floor. Slade could hear the clash of metal against metal and the screech of tires through his earpiece as he watched the two cars joust, locked momentarily in combat. Then the limo mounted the curb, spun in a complete circle, and went into an uncontrolled slide sideways across the grassy area that led to the Causeway Bay Typhoon Shelter. The police car hit the curb at a sharp angle, vaulting into the air.

Slade's pilot directed the helicopter across the highway area and was bringing it down on the skids no more than thirty yards away when the police car came down nose first, burying its grill in the grass. Then it began to tumble end over end—roof, trunk, rear fender—turning a cartwheel before it spun again, sending pieces of metal and glass flying off each time it hit.

The frame on the passenger side of the limo bent inward as it careened sideways into a huge cement water fountain. Its own momentum forced the car to roll over on its side. Slade watched in dismay as the police car's final slow-motion tumble slammed its front end down into the underside of the Cadillac.

Dan Slade never heard the popping sound of the limo's gas tank igniting over the sound of the helo's rotors as he jumped to the ground. But he did see the bright yellow flash as the gasoline burst into flame. Then he was racing toward the wreckage.

The black Cadillac was engulfed in fire. Flames snaked over the front end of the police car and were licking hungrily through its broken windshield as Slade approached. The driver's head lolled at an impossible angle. Through shimmering waves of heat Slade caught a slight movement as W.P., his face covered with blood, pawed feebly at his safety belt.

Slade gave a yank at the door, but it was jammed into the frame. He could feel the hair on his arm crackle as he reached through the shattered window and unsnapped the safety belt. Heat seemed to envelope him as he grabbed W.P.'s shirt. Blisters bubbled on his skin. He turned the small body enough to get his hands under W.P.'s armpits. As he struggled, flames licked out and encircled his arms.

W.P.'s face was blistering from the intense heat as Slade heaved back. A jagged piece of broken glass tore deep into his arm. Blood spurted from his torn flesh. But W.P.'s head and shoulders were through the window. It was impossible to draw a breath as the smoke and heat gagged him. W.P.'s shirt turned brown, then wrinkled into a dirty yellow flame. Slade, eyes blinded by tears, fell backwards with one final heave and W.P.'s body popped through the window and landed on top of him. Danny felt hands under his own arms and then he was being dragged away, still holding on to W.P.

When they were far enough from the flames, Slade heard a

voice calling his name. It seemed distant, directionless. What about the people in the other car? he wondered. Could they be alive? Instinct made him roll over onto his stomach to face the wreckage. Pain suffused his body as he pulled his SIG Sauer from the holster. He lay there, blackened arms extended, his blood pulsing into the grass, pointing it into the burning vehicles, waiting for someone to emerge through the flames.

But no one ever appeared.

Hugh Young sensed victory. Jerry and Eddie had allowed him a clean and easy departure. The only individual who could place him with either Santucci or Kelley sat beside him. He hadn't wanted her to go with either Jerry or Eddie. They'd made enough mistakes already. One more and they might just survive, and he wanted none of the three alive. When they got to the top of Victoria Peak, they would walk down to his place, and he would eliminate Leila Potter. Then he would put together what few things he needed for Singapore, and take a taxi to Kai Tak. In a couple of hours he would be in Singapore ready to start a new life of leisure.

The idea of Singapore was more appealing as he contemplated a future filled with comfort and luxury. Mental lists raced through his mind as the tram rattled toward Victoria Peak . . . and the future.

There was the usual mix of passengers on the tram—Chinese, Caucasian, tourists, commuters, schoolchildren. They were a happy, talkative group, except for those in the rear who stared nervously at Matt Stone as the car began its ascent up the steep tracks.

Stone struggled mentally to adjust to his surrounding. *Get hold of yourself. Analyze the situation before you make a move.*

The tram was built so that the angle of the floor remained level as it climbed the steeply angled track. It seemed incongruous to Stone that they were moving by houses and apartment buildings that appeared to be sliding down past them.

He eased back into a corner to catch his breath and think, oblivious to the many eyes watching him. It was important that neither Leila nor the blond man had seen him. How the hell could he do this without getting Leila hurt? He looked up at the chart over the door. It showed five intermediate stops before the top of Victoria Peak during an eight-minute trip. It had to be over in eight minutes. No, seven. Maybe even less.

The conductor had not seen Stone's headlong dash through the waiting line. He was still at the head of the car when they approached the first stop. There were only four more stops now, and probably six minutes left at best. *How the hell do I . . . ?* Using the 9mm would be crazy. There were so many people. He saw that no one left when the doors slid open at the first station. But he could tell out of the corner of his eye that the passengers in his section were still watching him warily as a few more stepped in. The doors closed, and the tram continued its impossible climb.

Less than six minutes. Tree limbs and brush reached out for the sun from the edge of the cut in the mountain, scraping against the passing windows. More people began to relax as the tram stopped at the second and third stations. *Maybe the crazy man was coming to his senses.* But he could still sense their eyes occasionally returning to him, just to be sure this crazy man didn't do anything dangerous.

Four minutes at the most. People should be settled down.

After the fourth stop, Stone was sure he could make his move. The conductor was working his way through to the rear. Stone moved toward the section where Leila sat with the blond man. They were both staring straight ahead now. Maybe he could get close enough to grab the son of a bitch, just long enough for Leila to get out of danger. Then it would just be the two of them. *Maybe I can hold him until we get to the top. Then I don't care as long as Leila . . .* But he sensed it wasn't going to happen that way. Nothing good was every easy.

Those people who'd witnessed his charge onto the tram hadn't forgotten him, and now the crazed man was on the move again. They stepped quickly aside as he approached.

A few, noting his movement, abruptly left during the few seconds the tram was at the fifth stop.

There was a certain telltale cast to the eyes of people in uncertain situations who didn't know how to remove themselves. It radiated from those passengers who now studied Stone's movements judiciously. They hadn't wanted to get off before they arrived at the top, yet they were wondering if they'd made a bad decision. Their faces reflected wonder, danger, and a definite urge to survive. Now they seemed to be searching for a safe hiding place in case this stranger attempted something even crazier—a place to duck with the hope that it would be another person rather than they who suffered. Their uncertainty was telegraphed by their eyes and actions. First one, then a second, then a few others, turned to look back from the seats. The curiosity spread.

Leila turned a split second before Hugh Young, and her sharp intake of breath had Young reaching for his own weapon, a Beretta 9mm. He was already turning as the gray metal weapon appeared in his hand, and some of the observers were already moving to protect themselves.

Stone saw Leila's mouth open. "Matt!" Then he saw her reach for Young's gun. They were no more than fifteen feet away. But the distance was too great, the time too short now that guns were involved.

Young lashed out with his elbow, slamming Leila's head back against the window. The Beretta was coming around in Stone's direction as Young began to rise from his seat. Passengers reacted instinctively, searching desperately for any kind of cover. Panicked screams alerted those unaware that something terrifying was taking place.

The SIG-Sauer appeared in Stone's hand in a catlike, automatic reaction. The other weapon had now swung completely around in his direction and the grayish metal shape had been transformed into the black hole at the end of the barrel that was no longer wavering. It was aimed toward Matt's body.

Stone lunged to one side as the automatic in Young's hand exploded. He felt nothing. Had the shot really missed him? His SIG-Sauer centered on the blond man. He squeezed the trigger just as Young launched himself across the car. Glass shattered. Passengers howled in terror. Both men were in motion. Neither one could aim at the other, but they each fired two more shots. Hysterical screaming rose in a wailing crescendo as the tram rolled into the terminal house at the top of Victoria Peak.

Hugh Young was crouched near an exit when the doors slid back. He fired one more shot as he rolled out onto the platform. Stone lunged for the nearest door, leapt straight out on the platform, and landed with bent knees, steadying his SIG-Sauer as a shot rang out.

Hugh Young, twenty feet away, had anticipated him. He was kneeling, holding his automatic in both hands.

Stone felt a sharp pain in his left thigh as the impact of Young's bullet spun him around. He landed on his shoulder and rolled, bringing the SIG-Sauer up in Young's direction. He squeezed the trigger as the muzzle of Young's gun flashed in his direction again. Both shots were off. Stone rolled again, fired once, then a second time before the other gun could catch up with him.

Hugh Young was knocked backwards by one of the slugs. He crashed into a gift stall scattering tiny glass tram cars across the floor. Stone rose to his knees, brought up the SIG-Sauer to shoot again, but all he could see was running people behind his target. There was no clear shot.

Young stumbled to his feet. The front of his shirt was covered with blood. He turned and staggered off toward the exit. Stone pushed himself to his feet to find there was no feeling in his left leg. He moved toward the exit in a crablike hop, the SIG-Sauer waving wildly in his hand.

He came out into the sunlight on a path that meandered along the edge of the peak. Metal fencing with a wide top railing separated them from a chasm to the left that seemed to fall all the way to the harbor's edge. Startled tourists turned and ran in horror as Hugh Young, his shirt blood-soaked, stumbled along the railing, pulling himself along hand over hand to keep upright. Stone, his pants red with blood, hobbled after him.

Young half turned, raised his automatic, and took a wild

shot. For a moment he seemed to lose his footing, twisting down onto one knee. Then he stopped and turned completely, raising himself on the railing, his arm draped over the edge for support, and attempted to level the gun barrel on Stone.

Stone stopped in his tracks. There was nowhere to hide, nothing between him and the muzzle of Young's gun but sunlight and air. He whipped the SIG-Sauer up with both hands and fired directly into Young's chest. The man stumbled backwards, struggled to bring the gun back in Stone's direction again, then seemed to wrestle with his own wavering arm. But his body was swaying, and his next shot went into the air.

Stone, balancing on one leg, knew as he squeezed the trigger that his final shot was perfect. The blood gushed from Young's throat as his body arched and seemed to hang, suspended momentarily on the railing, before the impact of Stone's last bullet and Young's own weight gave in to gravity and he slipped backwards, disappearing over the edge of Victoria Peak.

Matt Stone slumped down, his back against the railing. Pain and shock clouded his senses. The only sensation he understood came as Leila knelt down beside him and cradled his head against her shoulder.

EPILOGUE

THE HEARING ROOM WAS SMALL. CONFERENCE TABLES AND chairs had been hastily assembled and were less ornate than those used for the televised public displays that politicians loved so well. There were no observers, no media representatives, and no microphones. Seven senators sat side by side at two long tables that had been pushed together. Two men sat facing them at a smaller table.

The committee chairman, half-glasses perched on the end of his nose, stretched his neck and turned slightly, his gaze settling on the recorder at one end of the table. "Strike the witness's last comment from the record. I believe he misinterpreted Senator Power's question." The chairman's eyes, expressing no interest in dissent, swept over the other senators on either side, taking a quick silent vote of agreement. Even Senator Power, the banty rooster of the committee, who'd asked why Congress hadn't been consulted before the Pentagon conducted an illegal military operation in a foreign country, remained mute. The chairman looked back at the witness. "Is that acceptable to you, Commander Stone?"

Matt Stone leaned over to Chuck Goodrich and remarked

softly, "I really don't give a shit whether it's included in the record or not. Such an asshole question deserves an answer like that."

"Commander Stone concurs with your assessment, Senator." Then Goodrich whispered back in response, "You know, I could be one of those assholes someday. Would you want someone to say something like that to me?"

Stone studied Senator Power contemptuously before glancing back at the man beside him. "Are you kidding?" Then he saw Goodrich's mustache quiver as the corners of his mouth turned up in an almost invisible grin.

"They have ways of getting even, Matt. Leave well enough alone."

"Commander, do you have any other comments you believe would be appropriate to these proceedings?" The chairman studied Stone over the top of his glasses. "As I said at the beginning of this session, these are closed-door hearings, and I, or we—this committee—are open to anything you may feel is relevant to reopening POW-MIA hearings."

Stone knew the chairman had been in-country at approximately the same time he had. But could he understand? "All I can say, Senator, is that the hearings shouldn't be reopened, not if you want the healing in this country to go on. That war has been over for more than twenty years. There is no reason for the governments of Vietnam or Laos to still be holding prisoners. Nor does it make any sense to believe that they could remain unaware of some demented individuals or village still imprisoning someone. No, sir, any Americans sighted are there by choice. It's time to forget the mistakes made by well-intentioned people in this country. Let it go."

"Even though you and Miss Potter could have been killed by men listed as MIA?" one of the other committee members inquired.

Stone considered what he could say. About the war. About bureaucratic, even military, efforts to suppress evidence. About those who made money from others' misfortune. About men like Young and Santucci and Kelley. About . . . No, there was no reason to say those things. "We encountered deserters—common criminals—not MIAs. I have nothing else to say. If I may, I'd like to be excused."

"Thank you, Commander," the committee chairman said. "I'm sure I don't need to remind you that this closed hearing is classified and you shouldn't discuss your testimony with anyone." He removed the glasses and gestured toward Stone with them. "If you will excuse me, Commander, there is one more comment I'd like to make. You don't remember me out of uniform, do you?" He smiled warmly. "But I remember you. You were on your second tour then, and my boat took you and four other SEALs to a drop-off point up the Vam Co Dong, not too far from the Parrot's Beak.

"Twenty-four hours later we picked up you and your men, along with some prisoners you were sent after. None of you had a scratch. Later on, we learned that you'd destroyed a special conclave of senior VC cadre, and your prisoners were the intelligence coup of the year. When my boat group moved south into the Ca Mau, we found that your name was already a legend down there. I've got to tell you I was proud to tell people that I knew you . . . and I still am. I believe we should accept your counsel—and let the POW-MIA issue go. My personal thanks, Commander Stone, for visiting with us today."

Stone's response was a slight smile and a nod.

"Are there any additional remarks before we adjourn?"

Senator Power's eyes fell on Goodrich. "Does the honorable congressman have any comments to add? Perhaps you would recommend that a committee be established to investigate how an organization like International Charities could fool so many people."

Chuck Goodrich glanced down at his folded hands before he answered. "With all due respect to the committee, Senator, companies like Inchar are not all that common, but they're not a complete oddity either. It is a Hong Kong–chartered corporation, and there are very few questions asked of such companies as long as they make money and don't cause trouble—and Inchar scored on both counts. There are any number of cases of similar companies incorporated in the United States, many of whom manage to issue stock, float bond issues, and hoodwink some of our best and brightest. I would hesitate to guess how many of such outfits exist at this moment. Let the Hong Kong authorities worry about Inchar if they want to. It's their concern, not ours. Once again, let it go." Goodrich looked down at his watch. "Gentlemen, if there's nothing else and you'll excuse us, we have a very important appointment to keep."

"Thank you both for appearing."

The committee chairman watched as the two men moved slowly down the aisle, the congressman walking with a hitch in his gait from untreated injuries he'd suffered as a POW, and the naval officer bearing much of his weight on a cane from an injury received confronting what they all hoped had been the last missing American.

Late afternoon sun reflected orange-red off the Wall's polished luster like a beacon glowing from within. Members of tour groups hung back self-consciously from individuals intent on locating a specific name. National Park Rangers circulated among the visitors, helping to look up names in the register, providing directions to the correct panel, mounting ladders to take rubbings of names near the top, offering understanding to those still unable to understand or accept. Some visitors studied mementos left by the silent, dark monolith; others watched the people who stopped and stared. Most whispered as though each name on the Wall were listening.

"Make a hole, make a hole . . ."

Leila cocked her head at the deep, foghorn voice of the man in the wheelchair who'd taken it upon himself to clear a path for them. Was he the same one . . . the one from her first visit?

"Make a hole!" He was a veteran on a mission, clearing a path for another wheelchair occupant, this one a tiny, badly scarred Chinese gentleman.

Leila was amazed, as she had been on previous visits, how people moved aside, as if responding to the orders of a drill sergeant. No, this veteran probably wasn't the same one she'd met on her first visit. They all looked so much alike—almost always with straggly, shoulder-length hair, camouflage fatigues, some with medals, and most of them with that gaunt, faraway look, as if they'd never come home.

"Make a hole . . ."

No, probably not the same one, but weren't they all brothers?

"That's it, make a hole. Thank you, thank you. Make a hole."

"Forty-two East," Goodrich whispered, his eyes running from top to bottom.

"That's right," Leila responded softly.

Stone stopped W.P.'s wheelchair and turned it to face the panel.

"Danny," W.P. asked, "where is he?"

"Line forty-four."

Stone pointed to the name: Daniel Jeffrey Potter. It was at eye level for him.

W.P. tilted his head back to make it out. "Oh, yes. Yes. I see him now."

"Relative?" the veteran in the wheelchair inquired solemnly.

"My brother." Leila reached into her purse and extracted a silver ID bracelet. She studied the name inscribed on it for a second—Geraldo Vincente Santucci—then allowed it to slip from her grasp.

"You don't want to leave that there long, ma'am," the veteran said. "The rangers pick up everything once or twice a day."

"It's okay. He's not coming back."

"You can never tell," the man in the wheelchair persisted, waving his hand toward the POW-MIA booths behind them. "Look at those. There's a lot still believe there's Americans over there," he said hopefully.

"Believe me, that one's never coming back."

W.P. had been studying the mementos left that day. He reached out and touched Stone's sleeve. "Matt, I'd like to leave something, too." He took out his wallet and thumbed through it until he found a small passport-size picture. "If I could."

Stone accepted the photograph W.P. handed him and looked curiously at it for a moment. "Who's this, W.P.?"

"Tommy Chang. He was like a son to me . . . as close as one could be."

Stone bent down and placed the photo at the base of Forty-two East.

The other wheelchair inched closer. The shaggy veteran bent forward to examine the miniature picture. "Is he up here?"

"No," W.P. answered, "but he's another casualty of that war."

Chuck Goodrich opened the manila envelope he'd been carrying under his arm and extracted two more photos. He handed one to Leila, then placed the other at the base of the Wall. "Harry'd be pleased."

"Penny, too." Leila set Penny Carson's photo beside Harry Jensen's. "They were buddies."

The man in the wheelchair studied the photos before looking back up curiously at the four people beside him. "They casualties, too?"

Goodrich nodded. "You don't have to have your name on the Wall to be a casualty."

"Boy, don't I know that. They come here every day."

Stone leaned over slightly and showed the veteran the photo he was carrying. "We've got one more."

"Man, let me tell you. Some days are flower days. Some days are flag days. I guess this is a photograph day." He looked at the picture briefly, then held it up toward them. "What do you know!" he exclaimed. "That's you and the lady. Not everybody's a casualty." He handed the photo back. "Handsome couple."

Stone bent over and placed the picture of Leila and himself beside the others.

"I don't get it. You're alive."

It was Leila who spoke after a pause. "I just wanted to let Danny know that one of his brothers finally brought his little sister home and everything's okay now." She turned up

W.P.'s coat collar and placed a hand affectionately on his shoulder. "It's getting cold out. We ought to be getting back."

"Make a hole . . . make a hole . . ." The veteran in the wheelchair led them through a group of people who'd stopped to observe the latest mementos beneath Forty-two East.